The War Of The Earthen Empire
Awakening of the Souls

By
Eli Keogh
Co created by
Travis Burgin

Edited by:
Eli Keogh
Bridget Sugars
Travis Burgin
Bryce Sloan

Copyright © 2025 by Eli Keogh

First Paper edition

ISBN 978-1-7644522-0-5

Published by Odyssey Realms
odysseyrealms.com

Content warning

The following story contains content and arcs people might find distressing and or disturbing.

Proceed with caution

Implications of harm to children
Graphic Violence
Supernatural Themes
Religious Themes
Nudity
Thoughts of mental health
Family abuse
Work related abuse
Themes of PTSD
Thoughts of suicide
Implications of Rape

Acknowledgements

I thank and acknowledge Travis, Bridget and Bryce for helping me bring this to life. Helping with lore and ideation whenever I got stuck and helping me with the editing process which took far longer when I was on my own if it weren't for Bryce's help. It went from years to months instead.
I thank Bridget for being the first proof reader and giving story feedback which was highly encouraging and I thank Travis for helping to create this chaotic world as well as the character Kaji and being the initial decider on the gods. Who will not be mentioned for reasons of spoilers.

Introduction

The year was 2030, the year that Earth was almost destroyed. Many ancient cultures predicted the end of days but none got it right. It wasn't predictable, it was sudden. For almost a decade before this day: the day the earth collapsed, the world was at a stand still, chaos and unrest ruled the world and discord and disaster followed. Humans fought pointless conflicts, diseases spread far and wide, wars waged for no real rhyme nor reason. It was a decade of hell, and when the world held their breath, praying that it was over. It happened.

A cataclysmic event that no one could ever see coming. The ground broke and waves as high as the sky befell the earth. As it is now no one would recognise this planet.

Have you ever wondered what the future would look like? I did once but now I wish I never knew.

Over a thousand years have passed since the cataclysm, now the Earth only holds two distinct continents for humanity to call home, if you could call it home.

Hondon: the larger of the two continents, a supercontinent, Eurasia, Africa and the Americas joined into one, sinking Japan and many other island nations in the process. A landmass so large it covers half the world. It holds many huge land locked micro oceans, some filled with salt water and the rest filled with fresh water. This place is an ecological nightmare, any biome you can think of from the uninhabited frozen north to the scorching desert at the centre, this place was not kind to those who made it home.

Mir the smaller of the two is a place that should not exist geologically, yet nonetheless it does. A ring of mountains surrounds a huge archipelago of islands. The continents of Australia, Antarctica and South Eastern Asia collapsed in together. The ring of mountains miraculously manages to keep this ordain collection of islands separate from the rest of the world. The last true paradise for human kind.

Now why would I say paradise? Oh wait, I forgot to mention the demonic entities that roam the land of Hondon.

Once believed to be nothing more than a nightmarish tale: these demonic entities with their deathly red eyes are all too real. They came with a wave of corruption that mutated the land and all fauna and flora, including humans. Humanity struggles to survive, as these twisted monsters become more and more prevalent, perverting into the dominant force of Hondon. This was the turning point. It was time for us to step back in to help.

My brothers, sisters and all the friends I had made along the way decided to lock the darkness away. However, to do so would require great loss. We shifted the very continents themselves to separate the source of the darkness from its army.

What was once some of the largest continents on earth, shifted and we created Hondon. A land that bears the scars of darkness and still feels its sting to this

4

day. We made it as large and as vast as we could to stretch the darkness as thin as possible but it has only done so much.

But to help as well we also saved many human lives and created the last true safe place on earth, Mir. Using what was left of the planet's resources we found a place for them to live and recover but unknown to them they are our last hope. For you see a great secret lies beneath Mir and if it is ever found, it would be unknown if the world will survive.

We knew this was only a temporary solution but that is why my friend and I never stopped looking forward to a true future, a future away from the darkness. We held out hope as my nephew with his final breath birthed a prophecy. I still remember it to this day.

What once was whole, now torn as foretold,
Set upon a quest, with a purpose bold.
To unite as one, and reclaim the hold,
Through grief and strife, their hearts grow cold.
Betrayed like iron, sharp and dire,
Two stand as one, to ignite the fire.
Darkness weeps as one sleeps evermore,
To allow humanity's light to be reborn.

This prophecy, it's time is near, I can feel it. I have seen who will embrace my domain, I will ignite the flames deep within his soul to give him the power he needs to stand up to the coming darkness. I too sense my friend has found someone even though he has always been hard to please. He has found someone quite like himself, a calm facade hiding a raging storm, stalwart and blunt but caring and capable of great emotional strength. Destiny is calling, so I do hope that they are ready. With luck, they won't falter under the pressure.

Chapter 1

The cloudless sky gives audience to the wide and colourful cluster of stars that still twinkle as the sun still has not yet graced the land with its presence. The city below still illuminated by the lit street lamps which gives a warm inviting glow to the bare sleeping streets.

The city stands testament to all those that came before it, seeing the rise and fall of many leaders while situated at its centre, a large palace stood stalwart unchanged for over one thousand years. It could be seen as a paradise on earth. Far beyond the tranquility of the sleeping city are sprawling mountains with a flat plateau, unnatural against the jagged peaks of the plethora of other mountains.

The sound of footsteps on rock and gravel break the silence of the clear morning. The walking noise echoed as they made their way towards the start of the sprawling mountains. As they began the ascend the glow of the sun reaching the horizon greets them with the new day.

As the morning sun began to illuminate the sky, land and sea, the stars began to disappear. But the footsteps he followed are easier to see as he keeps up with his faster friend. A gentle breeze blew past them, making it as if to be welcomed to this special place and as they continued the sun reached past and illuminated the path in which they hike.

But as they walked a man donned in clothing that's seen better days and a falcon feathered cloak gazed back at the path they had trekked, trying to see all the footprints below him. He clutches a deep dark wooden ornate chest as he sees the rising sun now above the horizon.

'It's taken a long time for the sun to rise on such a peaceful day.'

†

The room is small and clammy with cracks in the walls likely made by the moisture in the thick air, there are no windows and the only light to the room is a flame lit torch by the doorway. The single piece of furniture in the room is a bed that is far too small for Ookonan's large frame as he crouches over it with his belongings laid out on the bed.

Ookonan is a tall man with a thick chiselled jaw, strong toned facial features and high cheekbones, a brutish look despite his elvan heritage. He has deep dark purple eyes like a cosmos, blond hair that sits messily on his head, short enough to show his pointed ears, yet his skin is well tanned from living the life of a nomad.

Kneeling by the bed, he is packing away his belongings, making sure to put things away in the most efficient way possible, for his own comfort and the durability of the bag. The last thing he has left are a couple leather sacks, which he puts away in the side of the backpack before closing it and fastening it shut. He slowly stands up while re-adjusting his jacket as he notices someone is in the doorway.

'Hey, you alright in there?' Jan calls out as he stands in the doorway.

'Yeah… What did you need?' He asks grudgingly, as he continues to organise his belongings without glancing at the man.

'Are you still coming? To the-'

'To the hunt? The Defence?' He asks abruptly, cutting Jan off as he places his sheathed sword next to his backpack.

'Yes… aaar you still-'

'Just give me a moment.' He says again firmly, turning his back pack to the side and takes out three leather sacks which he opens to check their contents.

Ookonan peers in the side of his bag to double check it. On each sack the contents are written in an Hondonian dialect each containing a thick red powder. He opens the other side seeing 12 smaller leather pouches, all filled with dried plants or other powders. Some are tea and some are herbs. Seeing they are fine and the twine is holding he places his pack aside.

Turning around, Ookonan sits on the bed. As he sits down, sparks of electricity come from his fingertips. The sparks are a bright blue as though he is a power conductor or that his hands are being electrocuted. He looks at his hand, confused, not knowing what just happened. Scratching the back of his head, hoping he just needs a little more sleep, yet as he blinks he sees electrical sparks from the corner of his eye, tickling him in the process.

'Huh.' He grunts, looking around feeling more confused. 'Did… Did you see that?' He asks Jan, who is unmoved at the doorway.

'See what?' he asked, annoyed at him, making him wait this long even though this newbie volunteered to head out with them. Jan watches Ookonan, confused and more annoyed as this rough hewn character sits on the bed, still barefoot, without any form of urgency.

'Must have been my imagination.' He says with a relaxed tone as he leans forward and grabs his thick leather boots. He glances at Jan who seems to be getting more agitated as he fidgets with his jacket sleeves.

'Yeah anyway, if you are done making excuses.' Jan replies, trying to hurry Ookonan along. All he can think about is the men waiting in the building entrance, waiting for the giant to be ready to tag along as promised.

'Just a minute.' Ookonan says, rolling his eyes at him. He undoes the laces on his boots and slips them onto each foot. He leans forward and does the laces up tightly before tucking his pants into the boot tops, being sure not to let any of the outside debris touch too much skin.

He takes a deep breath and stands up, he stretches and grabs his sword which has seen better days, covered in scuff marks, dents and scratches. He walks over to Jan who seems small next to him as he stands above the doorframe of the old building. Everything makes Ookonan feel like a giant as he stands over two metres in height.

'He is coming! We will be there soon, do not leave just yet.' Jan shouted down the long hallway. His voice echoing through the rusted ancient building.

'Aaahh, what a bunch of clafarging idiots.' Ookonan muttered under his breath as he followed Jan out the room. 'Season your homes.'

†

Ookonan is escorted by Jan down the hallway and past the rooms of the ancient rusted structure. The hall is full of moisture, cracks and holes that have likely been there and getting worse for centuries. The walls are covered in old fungal-like vines as no sunlight seems to ever reach through the building. Old thick rusted metal beams are seen through the walls, so old Ookonan is surprised they are still there and standing.

The beams creak as Ookonan and Jan walk past them and out into an open concealed space still within the ancient building structure. The room. if you could call it that is very open, with beams of metal holding the place up. Walls are cracked displaced concrete, with panels of wood covering the outside world.

As they step through the small room where the rest of the men had gathered, they fall in line behind Scott, the commander. As Scott walked towards the side door, he opened it to reveal what could only be a small indoor village. There are firepits all around the settlement, both on the ground and hanging, lighting the place up. Along the walls are small wooden houses more like little huts. There are also huts further up the walls, which are built in units and attached to these walls. Ookonan noticed some connected by rope bridges, but he never got to see these closely, as when he wandered in, night had already fallen. Women stand out on the verandahs of the small houses, cooking in large pots and watching children as they run and play. A few even waved to the new face, to his face, as he was part of their city guard, even though it's not much of a city. Seeing this place gave Ookonan a powerful feeling - he wanted to protect it.

As they head to the exit Ookonan begins analysing each member of the hunting party. Not including himself there are seven men. Most looked nervous and anxious as if the fear of the outside was weighing heavily on their minds. He could see it, the unbridled fear of what they would see and the fact that they may never return. However, in his observations one man stood out. He was calm, and controlled the level of fear in his eyes. He was scared but it wasn't going to rule him. Jan introduced this man as Scott. As they walked towards the exit Scott mentioned for Ookonan to walk with him.

Scott is a tall Human, but like everyone else, he is small next to Ookonan. He is large around the midsection with thin limbs, he is an unfit looking man with a shaved face, he is balding and what remains is blond. He has blue eyes and a round face. He has a keen look of entitlement smudged across his face that suggests he has lived a fairly privileged life.

'What took you so long?' Scott said sternly and angrily. He is a man who wishes to be a dictator.

'Ask him not me.' Jan says, gesturing to Ookonan, trying to deflect the blame as they reached the exit of the settlement.

Scott looks up at the tall Ookonan. He is a smug and angry man, puffing up his chest in an attempt to show dominance towards Ookonan, who is more than a head length taller than him. 'Hmm' He almost huffed at Ookonan, trying not to be intimidated by him.

'You have a strange way of showing appreciation' Ookonan muttered to him, almost expressionless, as they wait at the gate and the men huddled around Scott and Jan.

Scott ignores Ookonan's remark and proceeds to talk to the group again 'So we have learned that these things are fast very. Fast.' He says, speaking with egotistical assertion. 'What else have we learned?'

'You either die or become one or both, there is no winning with these things' Jan exclaims anxiously, having never faced one himself.

'Anything else?' Scott asks the men loudly. He looks around at the men, all but Ookonan look terrified, each believing they are not coming home after they leave the settlement.

'If you bothered to listen to me you might learn something.' Ookonan says, rolling his eyes at the men, feeling disappointed in them.

'Do we have weapons ready?' Scott asks the men loudly, while continuing to ignore Ookonan. 'Are we all ready?' He calls out again.

'Okay I guess no one is listening.' Ookonan mutters to himself.

Scott remains in the middle of the men as the gate finally begins to open.The men hold their weapons to their sides. They look at each other buzzing with anxiety as they march out of the makeshift iron and wood gate.

'They proved themselves to be a bunch of clafarging idiots…. Again.' Ookonan says, lagging behind the group, recalling this was not the first nor the last time he would deal with a group of people who thought themselves more important than the ones in the settlement.

'HEY!!' A woman calls out stopping Ookonan before he could fully exit the gate.

He stops walking to look around in search of the woman's voice. He sees the children playing, and others going about their business until he spots her. A woman cutting vegetables.

'Huh?' he hums, feeling slightly confused about where the voice comes from and who would care.

The woman points a cleaver at him, she has a stern, sharp look to her. 'WATCH YOUR LANGUAGE.' She shouts as she goes back to cutting up the food.

As Ookonan turned and looked out after the hunting party he spoke. 'I stand corrected, everyone in this settlement is a Clafarging Idiot.'

He walks over to the woman and looks at the cut up vegetables on the cutting board as she scoops it all up and puts it all into a pot filled with saucy spicy looking liquid. Seemingly filled with herbs and now vegetables.

'Are there herbs and spices in that?' He asks her calmly.

'WHAT'S IT TO YOU?' The woman shouts back at him.

'Hang them around the place, the demonics hate it'

The woman looks at Ookonan, she calms down now realising his intention. She watches him walk away, now catching up to the group of men.

As the gate closed behind him he saw not one sack being used as a ward. He sighed to himself and removed one of his sacks filled with red powder, quickly using a hanging vine to tie it over the gate. 'At least that will give a little protection for them.' he says as he turned and jogged after the hunting party.

Chapter 2

It's quiet, calm and peaceful in the continent of Mir, the sun is high in the sky, the air is clean with a soft breeze, along with the sounds of rustling leaves in the large tree which stands in the centre of the courtyard. The tree has thick roots spreading across the courtyard with thick green grass around its roots. Around the courtyard are stone columns holding up undercover walkways, which have stone paths that lead into other buildings surrounding the imperial palace.

The grass is cut neatly around the columns, walkways and structure, surrounding and in the courtyard yet around the tree roots and trunk the grass is tufted and wild.

Kaji Tohroshatan, a human with Japanese heritage, is sitting in one of the thick branches. He is a fairly large person, with thick strong limbs, dark brown skin. He has curly hair and dark brown eyes that are almost black in colour, soft gentle facial features, a top lip thicker than his bottom, chubby cheeks yet a sharp jawline and a wide nose.

He sits on a branch of the old tree reading a book on the ancient origins of Mir, which is written in the Mirish language that talks of old worldly things, and shows a diagram of a Jet Pack FJ-17 on the right page of the book with the text reading.

Asi majucha ila na nakish hija ila kunai kanji zaluh kalidap mo yenan
ulaji jaku
(*It is believed that ancient people could fly in machines like these*)

He looks at the diagram and its description, mesmerised by its design and function. Were the ancients advanced? How did it work? How could it work?

Kaji looks at it intrigued. 'Huh?.. So is that what existed in ancient times?'

He leans back on the tree trunk letting his left leg swing off the edge of the branch. He lets the air out of his lungs as he looks at the jet engine diagram trying to understand how something made of metal could lift off the ground, let alone fly. Only birds can do that, it's just not possible, he thought.

He turns the page revealing an old photo of a Kangaroo, with a description of what it is believed to be and where it is from; and it states:

Kangaroo: Na pakarigala ila Miron ilana hallamo ko Australia, ilana ila lemb
yareheanomohop nakish ramijish tigirinam mo ila nakish.
(Kangaroo: *On the outskirts of Mir on the Australian ridge consists of*
animals that potentially looked like this)

He brushes his hand over the text intrigued by the animal and words, and he tries to pronounce the word aloud. "Kan. Ga. Roo?" He sighs, looking up and thinks. What kind of animal could this have been? Animals like this just do not exist. The ancient world is a strange one, he thought to himself.

Kaji stops looking at the pages, contemplating, realising that he has never been off the central island, the capital, he glances back down at the old picture of the Kangaroo staring at it, studying it and wondering to himself how such a creature would move.

'Interesting... I wonder if they still exist on the edges.' He says slowly to himself.

From the top of the tree a yellow leaf breaks off and falls slowly to the ground. It twirls and twists through the air, leading through the branches down towards Kaji.

As the leaf sways and brushes past him he turns and notices the leaf, he reaches out to touch it as it falls. It brushes through his fingertips, but as his fingers touch the leaf, it starts to turn red with bright crimson embers in the exact areas his fingertips touch. The embers quickly yet slowly burn around the leaf as it continues to fall.

He pulls his hand back, shocked. He looks at his hand from back to front, confused. Leaning over he watches the leaf as it falls to the roots of the tree burning up with embers on the way down. Jumping down from the tree to have a closer look at the burned leaf covered with embers, and sitting on a root of the tree, he gazes at his fingertips then back at the embers, confused.

'Did... that... really happen?' He asked himself. He touches part of the leaf which lights up the embers again, he pulls back his hand to look at his fingers. 'How is this happening?'

He takes a moment to consider. This must be a dream or just imagination, he thinks as he watches the leaf burn up and turn to ash.

'It's really not like anyone is going to believe that happened.' He says quietly to himself. 'Ha, let's. Just... Ignore it.... Maybe.'

An unintelligible yell came from the distance shouting for Kaji. He remained still, trying to understand how he set a leaf aflame with his fingers.

'Tohro!' A girl's voice called. 'Are you finished studying?'
'Yah... I think.' He shouted back.

'You are either done or you ain't' she shouts. The girl louder as she comes closer to the courtyard.

He remains crouched and still, and turning his head he looks at the courtyard exit, where his sister Hono is jogging towards the arched walkway. Beyond the courtyard, hills, lush with trees and emerald grass sloped to cliffs, and beyond these cliffs the sea shone and nearby islands shimmered.

'Hono... can you come here quickly?' Kaji asked his sister before looking back at the roots of the tree.

Hono's footsteps become louder as she slows down at the entrance of the courtyard. As she reached the entrance she slowed down but did not enter. 'Why' she asked, standing on the edge of the courtyard.

Kaji remains unmoved trying not to be stunned by what happened earlier. He hopes that his sister might have an answer to why the leaf started burning up as he touched it. He wonders if there is any form of explanation. He remains still as he looks at the tree roots, attempting to understand what happened to the leaf.

'Can you come and look at something?'
'Fine!' She said with an annoyed tone, she sagged herself as she walked over to him. 'But you are going swimming right after I look.'
'Yes I know.'

She approaches Kaji from behind, he crouches by the tree. He stares at the roots while still holding a book, she leans over him and looks at the

Kangaroo on the page believing Kaji is looking at the book, which is wide open and sitting on a tree root.

'What is it?' She asks him, questioning why he called her over. She looks down at the book again now noticing the picture of the kangaroo. 'Those don't exist anymore.'

He looks up at Hono dumbfounded 'Uh.Huh…………' he hums not sure why she told him that. He looks around himself, realising the book is open. He quickly closes it. 'Anyway…… Do you think magic exists?'

'Why do you ask?' She asks him, unsure of the question.Hono looks at him puzzled.

'Well, do you see this on the ground?' He asks, pointing to the ash on the roots of the tree where the leaf burned up. He notices she is looking at him like he is an idiot. 'The little ash?'.He asks, trying to reassure her there was a burned up leaf on the root

She sighs and squats down next to him to see what he is looking at, she looks around the roots of the tree, she sees nothing but thick tree roots and thick grass in between each root.

'Tohro there is nothing there but grass… You don't seriously think you are one of the dreamers do you? That would be ridiculous.' She stands up and looks down at Kaji. 'Stop overthinking and let's go and have some fun!'

Hono takes a breath and squats back down and looks into Kaji's eyes. She softens her voice while speaking to him. 'It's like you have forgotten how to, as you will be taking over father someday' She grabs Kajis' shoulders and speaks a little more sternly to him. 'Forget. About. It.'

He looks away from his sister and relaxes his shoulders. 'Okay… I mean…' He says under his breath as he looks back at her. 'My mind is probably playing tricks.'

'Exactly!' She says. She stands up and helps him to his feet. 'Now let's go!'

She keeps hold of his arm dragging him away from the tree and out of the courtyard and into the grassy hills towards the sea.

†

The sound of the ocean waves is loud and noticeable as it hits against the rocks on the cliffs. They both are running towards the cliff by the beach, Kaji takes off his shirt as they run, while Hono doesn't remove a thing.

The two run towards the cliff edge and they both jump. The world goes silent for a moment while Kaji is in the air, he is thinking about the last time he stopped studying and had fun with his friends. It has been a while. He looks at the water, he sees his feet still in the air and he sees his friends, Alefosio, Koloa and Toakase.

He lands in the water and falls through into the depths of the deep mysterious blue. He can see the bubbles around him as the light touches the water creating beams of light, disappearing into the deeper darker blue of the refreshing water.

Swimming back up to the surface he shakes his head and is immediately greeted by his friends who splash water at his face.

'FINALLY TOHRO JOINS US!' Toakase shouts loudly and happily as she splashes Kaji in the face with more water.

Alefosio launches himself at Kaji, grabbing him with his massive thick arms. 'What took you so long? Busy burning out your brain?' He asks while rubbing Kaji's head with his knuckles.

'Yeah hahaha. About time I went for a swim.' He laughs leaning forward, smiling brightly and laughing loudly, while also trying to avoid Alefosio's grand head rub.

Koloa splashes Hono with water as she swims closer to the group, she growls at him, he laughs while swimming away, leading her to swim fast after him. Toakase jumps onto Alefosio's shoulders, only for him to flip her off backwards. The group continues to play and laugh in the deep water, something Kaji has not done in more than a year.

Chapter 3

Ookonan and the men have ventured far from the settlement building
and deep into the black forest. The humidity is so high, and the air is just as
thick, causing Ookonan to feel uncomfortably sweaty in his large leather
jacket. The air is cold and thick as a thick deep mist rolls through the forest,
making it difficult for any light to penetrate through the trees.

The forest is thick and black with numerous trees that have bark as
dark as the night sky. The forest floor is covered with large tree roots,
seemingly going on forever. Up within the tree branches hangs slime, a deadly
toxic residue that comes from the living death. It can turn anyone or anything
into a demonic. If there is no change into a demonic it slowly kills and
consumes the infected and everything in its path. The slime covers the trees,
the roots and it oozes from any crevices. If life is sensed, the slime would often
follow.

Ookonan is careful where to step, ensuring he doesn't step in any of
the slime covering the forest floor and tree roots. He observes the other men,
who are only slightly aware of the slim, but unaware of its dangers. Several of
the men are more cautious of the tall roots of the trees than what else is around
them watching their step.

Ookonan peers at the last member of the group: Scott or something
was how he introduced himself. He seemed like the narcissistic type. He was

the only person walking carelessly without a weapon; his steps are loud, he is tripping over roots, he is stepping on the slime, and he is not listening to any subtle sounds in the forest. This man was a danger to everyone who was here.

'I do not understand how they keep finding us.' Scott's voice echoed carelessly, giving zero care for the hungry monsters in the still black forest.

'What do you mean?' Ookonan quietly asks, not giving Scott the dignity of a glance as he continues to observe the surrounding forest. His elvish ears twitch as he listens for any subtle but almost silent sounds.

Scott comes to an abrupt stop, he turns to Ookonan, as he puffs up his chest in an attempt to assert dominance. 'Shut up… Keep quiet and speak when spoken to.' He snaps loudly.

Ookonan rolls his eyes at him and continues to walk forward, refusing to give the little man a glance. He looks over at the trees ahead noticing large scratch marks all over them. He walks slower, giving himself more time to scan for more evidence of anything in the forest. He sees tracks in the mud a few metres ahead.

Scott turns to Ookonan tense with rage, 'Shut Up!' He commands at Ookonan, his mind full of ego, and his chest puffed high. 'You need to listen to me you-'

'What?' Ookonan interrupts as he towers over Scott.

Scott steps onto a tree root making a miserable attempt at getting to Ookonan's eye level. To get into Ookonan's face, he puffs up his chest but still only reaches Ookonan's chest. His fists are clenched, his face and neck are red and veiny as he fills with unjustifiable rage. 'You need to listen to me, I know about these things. Ever since I was kicked out of Ques I have dealt with these things-'

Ookonan pushes him off the tree root, cutting him off mid sentence again. He bends over him while keeping his hands off him. He speaks very sternly and softly with Scott attempting not get too angry with him

'I know more than anyone what "These things are". I have never lived in a city and I have never stayed in a place longer than a week. These things as you call them are demonics, they used to be living like you or I and I do not see you lasting very long with them. Now let me ask you this.'

'What then?' Scott stutters, shallowing away from the giant man. His cowardness started to show through.

'Have you actually fought one? Are you a vatpik who tries to be the boss?' He asks through gritted teeth, his frustration building with each word uttered.

Scott trembles, his knees shaking as his hands quiver uncontrollably. He tries to hide his undeniable cowardice. His face no longer red, instead, almost pale, as if the world he knew had been ripped out from under him. But his chest was still high, as he couldn't deny it, he did think of himself as the boss.

'No-' He lied, 'You have no right.' He said finally finding his voice albeit barely before it was drowned out by an unholy screech. He quivered away from Ookonan, the last thing he wanted to do was fight any of those things.

The screams are followed by sounds of gurgling and scurries in the bushes, frightening the men who are getting tense as they prepare themselves. Scott cowers more with his knees shaking uncontrollably as fear starts to consume him, yet he does not want the people back at the settlement to think of him as a coward. Suddenly, all sound from the forest eerily came to a stopstill. The men slowly moved together, their movements making more sound than intended. As they moved, Ookonan stood vigilant as they moved, his hand poised on the hilt of his blade. His instincts were screaming at him.

'Did anyone hear that?' Cephelo asked anxiously.

Scott scuffles to straighten back up, the last thing he wants is to show his weakness. He feels the need to assert dominance over the other men as he puffs his chest up. He approached the member angrily, still shaking from fear and hurt over his broken ego.

'Sshhush. Be quiet and only speak when spoken to.' He shrieks.

'I heard nothing.' Jan says, looking around, his heart is racing as fear builds in him as he looks back at the other men and Scott.

Another mangled, distorted screech, from what could only be a demonic echo screech loudly echoes from the distance. It sounds deeper, more brutal, and far more powerful. It's brutal, deeper and more powerful than the last.

'There!' Cephelo quietly shrieked. 'Did you hear that?'

Ookonan remained calm, he's done this many times before throughout his life. He knows how to remain calm while the other men tense more. Scott stops and looks around before taking a few steps backwards and away from the group.

'Get your weapons ready…' Ookonan exhales apprehensively. 'They are closer than you think.'

Scott's heart is racing wildly as he attempts to start walking back down the trail they had come from. Ookonan's ears twitch, he turns his head to the sound of Scott trying to get away as he scowls at him and approaches him angrily.

'Where do you think you are going?' Ookonan asks sternly.

Scott stops moving and looks up at Ookonan shaking uncontrollably.
'N-no w-w-where. I am going nowhere.'
'You always do this. You leave us here to die and you head back.'
Gäff says furiously. He grips his axe and goes to approach Scott, but is stopped
by Jan.
'You are a coward who tries to be the boss. I do not think that will be
happening again tonight with this stranger helping us.' Jan sneers through
gritted teeth.
'Today is not your day...' Ookonan says calmly. He manages a tight
and firm grasp onto his shoulder. Scott starts to throw a series of
uncoordinated punches at Ookonan in retaliation, however very few land. The
punches that do land feel as if they are padded with cotton: soft, weak, and
ultimately pathetic.'Hmm... It also looks like you did not even bring a
weapon.'
The growling, gurgling sounds of the demonics get louder as they all
move through the forest. Occasionally a demonic would scream, which sounds
scratchy but often human like.
Scott tenses with every sound he hears, but is shoved forward by
Ookonan and jabbed in the back by Jan who puts, forcing him to continue
walking with the group.
'Is this why you would always return unharmed and often without
anyone else?' A member asks angrily.
Scott turns his head to look at the member who last spoke, he feels
embarrassed and has a clear look of dread in his eyes. 'Lemicölään.'
'Maybe you should not say that to other people.' Ookonan says
directly to Scott, looking down at him. 'Yes?'
Scott looks back up at Ookonan feeling shameful in his cowardness.
He tilts his head back down and looks at his feet walking through the mud and
stepping over and onto the roots of the trees.
The anxiety of the men grows as the screams and gurgles of the
demonics get louder and nearer, as the men can now hear footsteps other than
their own. The men stop walking, they look around and see glowing red eyes
within the black fog, between the trees, the shapes of demonics can be seen.
'Do we all have our weapons out?' Ookonan asks, scanning around
them, looking for the demonics. 'They are getting closer.'
The men all grip their weapons, two men draw swords, while the
others just tighten their grip, all except Scott who remains armless. Jan looks
over at him and hands him his spare axe, he reluctantly grabs it, shaking,
fearful that he will be forced to fight.

Ookonan steps away from the men and crouches down below the bushes as he slowly and silently walks to an open space. He watches for the glowing red eyes as he continues silently towards a large boulder covered in roots in the centre of the open space amongst the thick black forest. He places his back to the root covered boulder, catching his breath as the anxiety starts to hit him, he looks back over at the men. Jan has followed him in the same fashion, somehow not as quiet, surprising as the man is almost half his size.

Ookonan surveys the forest, noticing that a few of the men are walking out into the open searching for a place to hide, while one of the men jumps into a bush and crouches down. While he did that, another blood curdling scream became audible and vibrated through the opening.

'How close do you think they are?' Jan asks.

Ookonan quickly turns his head to look at Jan. 'Very' He mutters.

Scott, still standing in the thicker part of the forest, looks around at all the other men who are attempting to hide or are standing by a tree waiting for the attack to happen. He walks backwards towards some thick roots and bushes and trees in a miserable attempt to hide. He notices a couple roots between two large and thick trees, still shaking uncontrollably; he walks over to the roots and crouches down between them, clutching his weapon while listening to the sounds of the demonics.

Cephelo quickly scurries off to one of the trees, placing his back against the trunk. He crouches between the large roots with his eyes peeled on Jan and Ookonan. He waits patiently for Ookonan's signal before doing anything himself. He grips his axe tighter, focusing on anything other than the dread of the demonics.

Gäff looks around, noticing that two men are standing in the open unsure what to do with themselves. He quickly gets into one of the bushes and crouches down, peering through as he watches Ookonan.

'Just try and listen and hold on.' Ookonan whispers to Jan.

'Do you-'

'SHH. Quiet.' Ookonan whispers, covering Jan's mouth.

The demonic screams and chainsaw-like growls get painfully loud as they echo through the forest. The screams, now deafeningly close as their smashing wet footsteps become audible to all the men, sounding like sledgehammers on the mud and slime. Ookonan closes his eyes as he breathes out, in order to take a moment to collect his thoughts and relax his body and mind.

'They are here.' He says grimly.

He opens his eyes, his head now clear, he swiftly looks ahead. He gets off the ground, scanning his surroundings as he quickly moves. He thrusts himself forward, as he launches his sword through a demonic. The demonic's skin is black, slimy, and almost metallic like. Its eyes glow bright red and their teeth are as sharp as a knife. It's almost skeletal in appearance: bony and lacking any flesh on its face. It has long pointed claw-like fingers that could pass off like spiders with fangs for legs, its feet are bony and skeletal with talons for toes, and its teeth are long, sharp, jagged and rock-like. It even has flesh hanging off it in places from the death like rot.

Ookonan removes the sword from the demonic and takes a step back, placing distance between himself and the demonic. The demonic remains standing, seemingly unharmed, it bares its rock-like teeth ready to attack. It screams at Ookonan who swings his battered sword, hitting it in the head before moving backwards into a longer stance ready to move towards the demonic again. He slices his sword upwards from the crotch towards its jaw, cutting its torso into two.

Jan holds his axe with a tight grip, as he launches himself into the air, with his axe above his head, towards a demonic slightly shorter than himself. He slams the axe down through the demonics head, smashing it through the ground, killing it slowly.

Ookonan has moved to another demonic. He is low in his stance, aiming his battered sword at its knees. He swings the sword at the demonics lower legs, obliterating them almost with ease. As the demonic starts to fall he swings up at the head smashing through its skull.

Cephelo draws out a dagger from his belt as he walks up behind a demonic and stabs it through the back of the head, his blade penetrating through to the monster's mouth. The demonic struggles, cutting him with its long claw-like fingers in the process. He fails to notice he has been injured as he repeatedly stabs and beats it to death.

'AAAAHHHHH DIE DIE' He screams. Once the demonic is pulverised beyond recognition he quickly gets to his feet, he looks to his right and runs at another demonic holding both his weapons.

The demonic looks towards Cephelo, screaming while it twitches and runs at him, reaching out with its long finger claws. He attempts to dodge them while aiming his daggers towards the skull of the creature, stabbing it through its eyes while getting impaled in the stomach by its long sharp nails; he successfully kills the demonic but falls to his death in the process.

Ookonan is moving swiftly through the demonic hordes, cutting through them as he moves. He launches himself at a demonic impaling it with his sword, as he slams it to the ground, getting into a long low stance and preparing his leg to stomp on its head. He removes his sword and stomps on the beast's head, crushing it, effortlessly. He takes a quick moment to catch his breath as he turns his head, noticing another demonic running towards him, both twitching and screaming. He runs towards it and slides against the ground, swinging his sword at the demonic, smashing it in half with brute force.

'HAYAAAA' Ookonan shouts loudly, as his sword swings through the air. Another monster is cleaved in two by his own hands.

He breathes heavily as he raises to his feet, observing his surrounding area and the rest of his party as he does so. Fresh inky crimson blood slowly seeps out of the grotesque wounds of a motionless Cephelo. He is dead. Scott is nowhere to be seen. The remaining living men are clearly strained and on the verge of forfeit, with the only true fight left being with Jan. His axe was chipped but defence shone in his eyes. He has a demonic affixed on top of him trying to devour him with its long sharp rock like teeth. Jan screams as he fights to hold it off of himself.

'VEHHHK. HOLD ON I WILL BE RIGHT THERE!' Ookonan shouts loudly as he notices Jan's struggle.

He sprints over to Jan, now seeing him defend himself against a puss filled demonic. Absolutely covered in pulsating boils, it has him pinned against the ground. He battles to keep it off him as it snaps its jaw in an attempt to get a good bite out of him.

Ookonan launches his sword through its back before ripping the blade through its side, giving Jan a chance to get off the ground and away from any flying demonic substances. The demonic squirms on the ground screaming as it wails its arms wildly. Ookonan examines it briefly before stomping on its face, crushing it into a splattering mess through the mud; killing it instantly.

'Thanks.' Jan said, catching his breath.

'Keep moving.' Ookonan ordered. He turns his focus away from Jan, and back to the surrounding area, quickly noticing a demonic launching itself at him. Without thinking, he hits it in the centre of the face with the pommel of his sword, knocking it to the ground. Pitch black blood splutters mercilessly as Ookonan stomps on its head and smashes it through the mud.
He quickly fixes his stance, and twists around, spinning as he does so, severing a charging monster in two seconds flat. The mangled body falls to the ground, splashing into the mud as its head rolls off into the roots of the trees. Its eyes which were once glowing a bright red are now a dull and lifeless grey, as if they were extinguished like a dying flame.

Another loud scream vibrates through the branches of the trees as Ookonan races across the open space towards the other men. A few of the men are looking up at the demonic struggling to get down from the tree branches, praying it never does. It hangs from one hand only letting go when Ookonan is below it. Ookonan puts his blunt sword above his back as the demonic falls, landing on the metallic blade of the sword, partially disembowelling itself before flopping onto the forest floor. Ookonan purposefully strides towards the monster, slicing its neck clean off. As the demonic's head rolls forward, its lava red eyes slowly dim before going completely blank.

He turns back around, taking some deep breaths as he observes the area. Jan is smashing demonics with his axe while shouting at them to die. Three of the men are dead on the ground with horrific injuries, pools of crimson blood expanding below them. While two of the men are smashing already dead demonics with their weapons and stomping on them with their feet. The only person Ookonan could not locate is Scott.

Ookonan surveyed the surrounding area, but all he could see was blackish and white fog, some dim light from the sky, trees, mud, roots, and a lot of dead and decapitated demonics. Scott was ultimately nowhere to be seen.

'Ah, there are a lot more than I imagined around here.' Ookonan exclaimed while catching his breath. 'These people are lucky to still be existing with this many demonics... Full blood demonics of all things.'

Echoing through the forest, in the near distance is a blood-curdling roar. Ookonan examines his surrounding area in terror as dread surges through his body. He could feel it in his bones.   'Oooohh no, no, no not tonight!! That sounds like a clafarging brood mother!' He exclaims, knowing it will be a tedious fight with no guarantee anyone will be surviving the night.

†

Scott is crouched alone between the two large tree roots approximately fifty metres away from the heart of the fight as he pathetically cowers with pitiful fear. He can hear the demonic screams and the shouting of the men as they fight. He didn't want to be seen as a coward, but even more he didn't want to die. Nevertheless, he has proven himself to be worse than a coward and his prospects of surviving are slimming by the second.

'Do not find me... Do not find me... Please...' He begs under his breath.

A blood curdling roar is heard from a short distance away, leaving the forest completely silent in an unsettling and disheartening aftermath. Scott, who is still in his crouched position, looks up as he shakes with fear, plaintively battling the tears which are threatening to run down his rough face. 'Why would he not just let me leave? Why?' He shrieks as moisture escapes his tear ducts, dampening his pathetic face.

He pushes his back onto the tree trunk, squatting lower between the roots. His eyes squint in fearful disbelief as he scans his surroundings. He can see in the distance a large monster with glowing blackish red eyes. This monster has long sharp fingers on one arm while the other arm looks like a long thick sharp weapon. It looks nine months pregnant, with an enlarged stomach that appears to be moving in different directions as though something is inside. Worst of all, it appears to have a third leg sticking out of its knee, bent and deformed.

The monster runs behind a tree showing only its sharp elongated fingers, looking almost like a large spider. Scott's breathing fastens as it becomes almost uncontrollable. He hopes the Brood mother has not seen him, and he wishes that she never does, yet she moves between the trees as though she is tormenting him.

The monster moves rapidly, running behind another tree. All that Scott can see of the beast is the deformed leg that sticks out of its knee. The leg moves slowly, twitching lightly as though it's waving at him.

He drops his axe and watches the broodmother with his full attention as she moves from tree to tree showing off her natural weapons. He no longer remembers where he is as he keeps his eyes locked on the monster in the shadows, lost in a trance as the beast moves between the trees. . She gives off another bone chilling scream before changing her trajectory, heading directly towards Scott with great speed.

Its bulging tumour covered belly shifts with its quick strides, while its sagging breasts bounce side to side and its extra leg swings back and forth. He looks from side to side, searching for a potential way out of his dire and hapless situation. He notices that the monster has its eyes on him, but before he could conjure a reaction he is met face to face with the broodmother.

She is tall, large and mostly solid, ignoring the slimy liquid that covers her body. She makes him feel tiny, stripping Scott of the ability to think, move and even breathe. She grabs him with her sharp-edged fingers and lifts him to her eye level as she breathes on him with her cold clammy breath. Her teeth are razor-sharp, her eyes are ignited a blackish red, glowing like magma, and her face is covered in black boils. He only notices the tentacles protruding from her back as they brush past his face.

She screams at him before thrusting her sword-esc arm through his abdomen and lifting him higher into the air. She looks into his eyes, staring deep into his soul as she watches him bleed and suffer.'AAAAAAAAAAHHHHHHHHHHHHHHHHH ghhgghg.' Scott screams as deep viscid maroon blood gushes from his dry lips and his fresh wounds as he meets his end.

The broodmother lowers her arm as she directs her attention towards the other men; leaving Scott to slide off of her arm and land on the thick roots of the trees below, breaking his fragile bones and splattering his syrupy blood against the mud, mixing brown with red. He lays there motionless as his eyes glass over. She steps on him and strides towards the others.

†

Ookonan feels the third tremor of the broodmothers roar pulsing through his body. He barely manages to hold back his own scream. His eyes widen and his breathing slows as he looks into the direction of the deafening sound vibrating through the trees.

'Vekk… Vekk. Why today? I just can not be bothered… Vvvvekkkkkk.' He grips his sword tighter, he readies his stance and takes another deep breath. He knows that he must fight her, because if he doesn't, all the people he and the other men are trying to help will perish.

The broodmother pushes through the trees, with her extra leg brushing past the trunks and tall roots. Her bulbous, boil covered belly somehow manages to push through the tight spaces. As she steps out into the open, her glowing reddish black eyes fixate on Ookonan.

He can finally see what the monster truly is. His stomach sinks as he realises how colossally large this broodmother is, standing over a metre taller than him. She, like the other demonics, has long sharp rock-like pointed teeth and slimy skin that's almost metallic. Her arms are longer than her legs, with one ending in a hand with sharp stretched spider-like fingers, while the other ends in what looks like a thick sword. The final thing he notices, which he finds gravely disturbing about her, is that her extra leg isn't actually an extra leg but rather is her six long wet and slimy tentacles that stick out either side of her pus filled spine.

She launches herself at him with her organic weapon ready to strike. She thrusts it at him to which he quickly evades and cuts off that extra grotesque leg attached to her knee.

The broodmother falls onto her knees in a temporarily stunned state, as she shrieks with unbridled rage and potentially pain. She stands back up, towering over him as she grunts and growls while watching his stance and sword closely. Suddenly and somehow her belly seems to reach for him, with a claw-like hand pushing against the thick boil covered skin followed by a screaming skeletal face. There is another demonic inside her.

Ookonan jumps out of the way as hastily as he can, recalculating his steps and movements. He quickly examines where to move and strike next on this large monster. So he takes a step to his left and changes his stance with his sword, watching what the broodmother does next.

'WAAAAAHHHHHHRRRRREGGGGR!' She screams. Loud enough to drown out all other noises in the black forest.

He watches her patiently and closely as the broodmothers arm is raised and poised, ready to strike him down at any second. It comes down at full relentless force. A loud whoosh sound was heard as the blade sliced through the air almost too fast to track. She swings it in all directions, banging and thrashing it around. As she moves towards Ookonan, her surroundings fill with debris and shrapnel from the wild strikes. As Ookonan dances around the strikes, he makes a hapless attempt to parry them but instead ends up damaging his blade as the cracks and chips along the metal get noticeably larger.

As she readies an overhead strike, he takes a moment to catch his breath.

As she swings her arm down with all her might, he masterfully blocks the broodmothers weapon and rolls away. A large explosion of dirt and debris shoots through the air as the broodmothers weapon strikes the ground.

She turned and lunged at him. It didn't matter what was in the way, stone, root or body; all was sliced by this thing, charged with power and speed straight at Ookonan. As he moved to dodge the strike, her other arm lashed out faster than he could move.

With her long spider-like fingers, she grabs him and pulls him in close. She screeches with a twisted sense of delight as she flings him through the air into a tree on the other side of the clearing.

Ookonan lands with a sickening crack. He grimaces in pain as he manages to stand back up with shaky legs. Wind begins to spin and twirl around him; it moves around him and only him in this dank stagnant forest.

He shoots off running as fast as he can as the brood mother stalks him, charging at him and trying to strike him. But he is faster, with undying determination. He jumps at a tree, planting himself on it. For a moment, the world stood still. He pushed himself off the tree with all of his might, cracking and denting it as he launched himself at her.

The wind around him propels him forward, as if fighting alongside him, allowing him to move faster than he ever thought was possible.

'AAAAAAHHHHHHHHRRRRR.' He roars as he nears the broodmother with his blade raised. Time feels as if it's slowing as he repositions himself, ready to strike.With the sound of thunder and a sudden ripple of electricity, the broodmother was launched away from Ookonan. It was as though she was hit by the missile of a trebuchet, leaving her to roll along the mud. Ookonan lands with a flourished twirl, the storm still strong around him as it appears to grow in intensity, the forest atmosphere changing and the fog thickening anew.

The Broodmother stands, slowly getting back to her feet. Thick black blood oozes from bursted boils on her face. She bares her long sharp teeth as her five remaining tentacles grow from her back. She steadies herself, now ready for him.

He rushes towards her and as he does he feels the hairs stand on the back of his neck. His vision goes fuzzy as he starts to see visions. He can see a calm, clean living room with a cool atmospheric feel. The vision morphs from looking down at a book to upwards at the room as he sees three separate people. He sees an older woman, a much younger woman, and a man. They all look very unusual, bearing features he has never seen before.

He pushes the vision aside as best as he can as the wind grows stronger around him, water vapour from the ground joins the storm and sparks of electricity flicker in the wind. He rushes, as fast as he possibly can to the back of the monster as he cuts off three of her tentacles.

'EEEEAAAAAAHHHHHHHHHh.' She screams in agony as inky black blood oozes from her fresh wounds.

'I am not done yet, you little derkusi.' Ookonan exclaims loudly.

Small sparks of electricity flicker through the wind around him as he anticipates the broodmothers next move. Tentacles grow from her back as she poises herself, ready to attack Ookonan from all directions. She lifts her hefty arm into the air, ready to strike downwards towards him.

He manages to dodge and roll away from the large swinging appendage. He strikes and slashes at every tentacle that nears him, slicing every one of them off her back. She screams in agonising pain as Ookonan ducks between her legs, ignoring her cry.

He thrusts his sword deep into her enormous belly as a large surge of electricity bursts through him and his blade. He could feel a rush of adrenaline and a burst of dopamine pump through his veins. He truly felt alive. The electricity fries the broodmother and the demonics residing within her as the gloomy unlit forest surrounding them is invigorated with vibrant blue light. Ookonan's attention is pulled towards the other men, who are either dead or on the precipice of death. Ookonan is blasted back from the impact he created, leaving lingering swirls of wind and specks of electricity in the air and around the broodmother. He slides along the muddy ground, keeping his eyes on the monster as she stands, almost motionless. Her lower body is scorched and glowing red from the electric blast as a thick black tar like substance oozes from her wounds.

'How are you not dead?' He mutters, both confused and frustrated.

The broodmother falls backwards as mud, blood and fluids spray around her in a three metre radius. The broodmother is dead. Ookonan feels a surge of relief flooding through him, relaxing as the wind and electricity slows down right up until it disperses.

'Woah.' Jan expressed, amazed by what he had just witnessed.

Jan strikes a demonic with his axe as he looks at the dead brood mother. His eyes wander towards Ookonan, as they express monumental shock. He couldn't believe what he had witnessed. He makes an effort to gather his thoughts as he walks towards Ookonan. 'H-how did you do that?' Jan asks wide eyed as he stumbles over his own words.

Ookonan looks at him, also unsure of what to say. He is just as confused as everyone else. He had never seen anyone do that before let alone himself. 'I-I-I do not know.' He stutters, catching his breath.

The three remaining men walk over, staring at the cooked broodmother, wide eyed in disbelief but relieved that the fight is finally over. Each of them are sideswept in awe as no one has ever seen someone conduct electricity let alone take down a monster like that before.

'That was insane... Impossible. H-how did you do that?' Gäff asked.

'Yes. Give us your secret.' Jan implores eagerly.

Ookonan takes a step back from the men, unsure if the wind and electricity was a fluke or if there is something unusual about the forest. 'Look, I am just as confused as you are right now.' He examines the exhausted men, who are all covered in fresh yet drying viscous crimson blood before looking over at Jan. 'This must make you the new leader, I can not see that vatpik anywhere.'

Jan stares at Ookonan, stunned as he points at himself. He couldn't believe he was being called a leader, all he was ever called, especially by Scott, was a loser.

'Yes I mean you, if he has died or run back like a coward, then he is no leader. But you stayed and that is a leader.' Ookonan expresses with sincerity.

'Well anyway if you are going to ignore what you did, we should all be heading back.' Jan states.

'Ahh, I best be going.' Ookonan tells Jan.

'You left your belongings back at our place.' Gäff says as he steps in front of Ookonan looking up at him. 'Why not you come back, get cleaned up, grab your stuff then be going?'

Ookonan looks down at Gäff and nods in agreement. He scans the area, noticing one man trying to shake some of the demonic blood off himself and another standing, tapping a demonic's head with his boot. He agreed with Gäff to bring him back to at least get cleaned up.

'Okay, I will head back with you, but I am not staying.' Ookonan exclaims. 'Also do you lot have herbs and spices?'

'Yes…. why?' Jan asks, feeling a little confused with the question.

'You need to season your home. It keeps the demonics and infections they carry. Out.' Ookonan explains to the men. 'How many have you lost?'

'We have lost a lot of people.' Gäff declares somberly.

'Demonics hate paprika the most, but each herb and spice has a function of its own. Demonics particularly hate spices, paprika is an overall winner. Start seasoning your town.' Ookonan says to the men sternly.

The men look at each other, collecting themselves and their weapons. They leave the dead behind and start to walk back through the forest towards the settlement building.

'How effective is it though?' Jan inquires.

'Enough to not hunt every night.'

'Okay I will let them know when we get back, we must start seasoning our town.' Jan says to Ookonan and the other men as they all step over the soon to be decayed corpses and the thick tree roots.

Chapter 4

The waves of the ocean can be heard clearly and easily from Kaji's room, with the sounds of the waves hitting the beaches and cliffs of the island, sounding soft and calming yet fierce. His room is a curious design with his bed, desk and shelves built into the walls. Plants lazily drape their vines around the room with their tendrils exploring the entrance of his shelves which are filled with books and trinkets.

Kaji sits at his desk with the soft moonlight and the amber lamp dimly illuminating his space. In front of him lay an assortment of books, a notebook and a collection of pens. He grabs an open book and brings it closer to himself, it's an ancient language which was once prevalent across the globe, a flexible language now long gone. He sighs and closes the book, putting it away on a shelf next to his desk, before reaching for another, an heirloom he inherited containing his family's ancient language.

TITLED
(*Tokyo Japanese*)
(東京都　日本語)

'Uhhg I forgot this kanji...' He grunts, staring at the cover of the book. 'What does it mean?' He takes a deep breath and decides to ignore the cover as he opens the book. All he saw was kanji followed by more kanji. He held his head in frustration, only remembering a third of what was on the page. Kaji decided that his only viable option was to read between the kanji and figure out the contextual meanings, but as he started to read, someone knocked on his door, ruining his focus.

'Yes? Come in.' He said while keeping his eyes transfixed on the pages. The door slowly creaked open, the sound so annoying, Kaji's hands tensed as he begrudgingly glanced at the door, seeing his sister Hono peering through the small opening. 'Oh… Hey Hono.'

'Mum says it's lights out soon.' She states bluntly as she lets herself into his room.

'Okay…' He says, returning his focus back onto the book. Still bewildered by the symbols on the page. 'I do need to learn this so the language doesn't die.' He says as he turns the page over to find himself bombarded with more kanji. Defeat washes over Kaji as he thinks to himself that he cannot keep the imperial language alive.

'I know…' Hono states. 'Uuhh.'

'What is it?' He asks, throwing down his pen and turning his attention to Hono.

'Remember that Father wants you to be up early taking care of the stone right?'

'I know Hono.' He sighs, while leaning back in his chair. 'When am I ever late? Honestly.'

She looks at him and raises an eyebrow. 'There is a first time for everything, Tohro.' She scoffs.

He looks back at her, surprised. Kaji is used to her jokes and never taking him seriously, but this statement felt serious. 'True… Anyway… Uhh.' He vocalises unsure on how to combat her statement with his own. 'Have you been studying your nihongo?' He asks, quickly changing the subject.

'No… Why?'

He looks at her and frowns, disappointed in her lack of commitment to their ancient family language. The language that goes back thousands of years and allegedly had more than thousands of speakers. Now only a small handful of people can understand it.

'Hey! It's not my fault I dont care.' She states, full of sass.

'No!' He reacted suddenly, hitting his hands on his desk. 'I just needed some help with my Kanji. I'm stuck with a few words and sorts.' He explains, while feeling embarrassed with his short tempered outburst and lack of ability to read the ancient words.

Hono drops her shoulders and relaxes her body, she sympathises with her brother. She knows he has a lot of pressure on him from their father, being the sole heir to the imperial family and forced to look after a dumb rock at the top of the mountain the family home resides on.

'Oh… Do yoou… Mind if I have a look?' She asks awkwardly.

He gestures for her to sit next to him as he changes his stance in order to sit sideways on his chair, looking at both her and the book. 'I have forgotten what these kanjis are.' He explains, gesturing towards the book.

'Ahhhgh that means doctor!' She says, slapping her head while trying not to laugh. 'How do you not know that?! That one means nose and that one is rice field.' She says, pointing to the kanji on the pages.

'How do you not know this? It's basic stuff. Stop learning Hondonian languages, you will never go there anyway and start remembering our family language. It's really not that hard.' She says to him, half jokingly and half judgmentally. Hono knows Kaji has a tendency for the unknown, reading and exploring mysteries rather than focusing on family stuff, but sometimes it's hard not to be annoyed with him for his foolishness.

Kaji starts to feel restless, he loves languages but some languages are harder than others. He has a hard time with Nihongo, there is too much to memorise. It's not like he does not understand the spoken language, his parents speak it all the time, he just feels frustrated not knowing how to read the language.

'Well I have to be up early tomorrow to mend the sacred rock.' He says as he stands, feeling more frustrated. He stretches his legs then puts out the light before walking over to his bed. Hono makes her way back to the entrance of the room.

'I better be off to bed. Goodnight.' He mutters.

'Oh… Okay. Goodnight.' She says while stepping out of the room and closing the door behind herself.

†

Kaji lays in his bed facing the ceiling, his blankets pulled up high above his shoulders exposing only his head, which is sunk deep into his pillow. The moonlight comes through his window illuminating his face and his room a cool blue.

His eyes twitch restlessly as he sleeps, with beads of sweat forming on his skin. Discomfort rises in his body with concerning haste: his legs kicking and his arms tensing as he is trapped in some disturbing and inescapable nightmare.

He can see the black forest and feel thick humid air crawling against his skin. It tastes stale. He can see strange looking people but also a filthy hand holding a battered sword. Kaji also discerns the outlines of the unearthly demonics, the men, the slime, the thick mud, and the blood, so much blood. Wet, sticky, and crimson red in colour. His temperature begins to rise, rapidly causing him to sweat profusely as he watches Ookonan fight the demonic horde.

His lungs start to burn, causing his breathing to become staggered and painful as though he was stuck in his demented dream, his soul lingering in the black forest. He can hear heavy footsteps and see an inky black skeletal Monster approach him. This particular monster was large, fat, and swollen with tentacles protruding from its back, and boils covering each of their slimy surfaces, an odd combination Kaji has never seen before. It terrified him.

He is somehow fighting this monster, blocking her strikes and hacking at her body with a pathetic excuse for a sword. Before Kaji could fully process the situation, Ookonan's body starts to spark, the air twists around him with enough strength to move him faster and as this happens Kaji starts to feel an intense burn in his chest, slowly expanding through the rest of his body.

Kaji awakens with his sheets on fire. He can see flames running down his arms and his shirt, it isn't just his sheets that were ignited but he himself was too.

'Ahh… ahh.' He panics without screaming, noticing the flames that surround him are clinging to his skin rather than spreading.

He watches Ookonan, the unusual looking man fight the almost humanoid monster. As soon as Ookonan blasts the monster with lighting, he feels a surge of intense pain pump through his body, like fire pumping through his veins.

'Ahhhhh…. Ooh shh. Oh no no no.' He panics, as he launches himself out of bed. He quickly takes off his shirt, throws it to the ground and stomps on it in an attempt to extinguish the white-hot flames. He looks back at his bed where he was laying, the fire had disappeared leaving scorch marks all over the blankets and mattress.

He looks at himself realising the fire is coming from within. 'No no no… Ahh it burns.' He cries, as he starts to panic, unsure of what to do in a situation such as this. He looks around the room, feeling the pain transcend within himself.

He rushes to the door and lets himself out of the room before running down the hall, leaving a scorching trail behind himself.

'Shi shi shi no no no.' He panics while breathing heavily. 'Why?'

He reaches the bathroom and briskly opens the door, leaving a large scorch mark on it. He rushes to the bathtub, turning on the tap as he takes off his pants now noticing that they had almost burnt off.

'Okay okay okay, I must be dreaming. This isn't real.' He says to himself as he waits for the water to fill the bottom of the bathtub before getting in as to try not to burn the tub itself.

He steps into the cold water and it immediately starts to sizzle and boil, filling the room with steam.

'Eehh oohh that's cold.' He shivers feeling the cold water on his skin while simultaneously feeling the burning sensation pumping through his veins. It is a strange sensation that he isn't used to.

He makes an attempt to relax, collecting his thoughts and calming his breathing as the bath fills with water. Finally the fire inside of himself slowly begins to extinguish taking the pain with it. 'Deep breaths Tohro, deep breaths. Let's think about this…. No, I'm dreaming.'

He starts to calm down as he looks around the room, realising that he has left the bathroom door wide open. The door and floor are both covered in scorch marks and the carpet outside the bathroom is now charred black by the blaze he caused.

'Too late for that now… Anyway, that leaf today… Maybe that was me. If I wake up here in the morning then this is real, if I wake up in bed it's not real… The morning will tell if I don't drown.' He says to himself. He leans back into the water as the tap continues to run and the visions fade away. He closes his eyes and thinks to himself, this can't be real, none of this is real, it's just a dream and I will soon wake up in the comfort of my own bed.

†

Morning has now arrived. The room is bright as Kaji lays naked and dazed in a bathtub halfway filled with water. There are scorch marks along the edges of the bathtub extending haphazardly across the bathroom floor, where piles of ash and tattered fabric: what once were Kaji's clothes lay bare. No one could deny, the place was a mess.

Kaji's eyes flutter open as he regards his surroundings, realising that last night was not a dream, he hadn't been imagining it, he really was on fire.

'It was real.' He says as he looks himself over, noticing that he hadn't obtained any burn marks. Aside from his scorched surroundings, there was absolutely no evidence that he was ever on fire.

He assists himself out of the bathtub, placing each of his hands on either side of the tub before stepping out. Kaji becomes motionless as he struggles to figure out what to do, he didn't believe this messed up situation could get any worse until it did. Hono sleepily walks into the bathroom, her eyes barely open as she places what appears to be neatly folded clothes onto the bathroom bench. She rubs her face as she walks towards him, still adjusting to the new day.

'AAHH.......' She shrieks as she locks eyes with Kaji, startled by the scene in front of her. She was in no way prepared to be mentally scarred by the unruly sight of her brother naked. 'Why are you in here? What happened?' She asks, scanning the room and noticing the state of the place.

He collapses, back into the bathtub, splashing water all over himself as he lands with a thud. He miserably tries to cover himself, not wanting people to see him like this, let alone his sister. He watches as Hono backs away from the tub and covers her eyes, everything just feels awkward.

'I uhh.'

'Well?' She demanded.

'Uhh.'

Hono looks around the room, disgusted by the state it is in. 'Why is everything burnt? Why are you still here?'

He looks at her, trying to find the words to explain this disaster without sounding like a madman. The burning sensation... the bedsheets... his clothes... I was on fire, I set myself on fire, he wanted to say, but he knew no one would believe that.

'You remember how I tried to show you that burnt leaf yesterday?'

'A lot of nothing? Yes.' She snaps back in retort.

'Last night I set myself on fire.'

She looks at him like he's an idiot. She found it very difficult to believe this whole mess could have been spontaneous, yet Kaji was known to do stupid stuff all the time.

'Well that was stupid. Why would you do that?' She asked with a change in her tone.

'It was an accident.' He barks back.

'Yeah. Anyway... Put some pants on. Father is mad.'

Without a moment's thought, he bolts out of the bathtub, rushing towards the folded clothes on the bathroom bench before snatching the shorts:

they were floral and feminine but Kaji had no room for complaint. He sprints out of the room still completely naked while making pathetic attempts to dress himself.

'HEY!! Agh gross.' Hono's voice echoed through the halls with disgust, but Kaji's mind was otherwise preoccupied. He knew that he had forgotten something. He was late for his duties.

†

The Palace grounds are surrounded by foliage , gardens and lush green trees. There is a lengthy stone pathway heading through the garden and up a small but tall mountain.

Kaji runs along the stone pathway in Hono's loose pink floral shorts. He scurries past the gardens and reaches the stone steps that ascend up the mountain. He bounds up the steps and as he gets halfway he realises that he had never once run up these steps before. He was exhausted. His mind was so preoccupied on simply reaching his destination that he had missed out on one of the only things he enjoys about this job: the breathtaking view of the ever expanding sky soaring over the glistening vibrant blue of the ocean and the luscious greenery of the surrounding islands. Even so, Kaji did not have time to appreciate nature's beauty, instead he kept running up the mountain to meet his furious father in order to assist in cleaning a garden gazebo and a dumb rock.

As he reaches the top of the mountain and approaches the entrance of the gazebo, he is greeted by an angry muscular man. He tries to hold back his fear, reminding himself that it's just a dumb rock and garden, but he can't stop his nerves. He was exceptionally late and he had to face the consequences of his actions.

'Oh… uh. Hello father.' He says, trying to keep his voice steady and himself from shaking.

'Where have you been?!' Sanmos asks furiously.

Kaji takes a step back, looking past his father as he surveys the shrine's surroundings. Most of the work had appeared to have already been done. The white stone building was bright, shiny, and clean. The fruit vines that were growing along the pillars had been pruned back, and the red clay tiles had been polished. The fruit bushes around the edges of the gazebo had also been pruned, watered and picked, with the fruit meticulously placed in a basket by the large almost translucent, luminescent great rune stone in the centre of the gazebo. The great rune stone is a translucent red and is covered in carvings of deity runes, although it had yet to be cleaned and polished.

Most breathtaking of all was what consistently circulated the great rune stone: several pools of flowing crystalline water.

'Why are you wearing Hono's shorts? Are you a woman?' He barks at Kaji, while shrouding him in his shadow.

Kaji opens his mouth to speak, trying to find the right words to explain what had happened and why he was late, but deep down he knew Sanmos would not care nor believe him. None of it seemed real and his sister's shorts certainly weren't helping.

'Shut up!' He barks, before Kaji could make another sound. 'I have been here since four in the morning, Tohroshatan. Four in the morning.' He takes a deep breath and softens his tone as he looks Kaji in the eyes. 'What were you doing?'

'Listen! I'm twenty two... This is the first time that I have ever been late.' He says solemnly, raising his voice to accentuate his point before being abruptly interrupted by a callous palm to the face.

Sanmos's expression grows more cross and rugged as his heavy tempered eyes stare directly into Kajio's soul. 'Don't you dare speak that way to me boy.' He quietly yet angrily commands before throwing a broom at Kaji and pushing his way past him. 'When you're done here you have the burn marks you left all over the palace to clean up. And when you are done with that, you have history to study.'

Kaji collects the broom off of the floor, stopping himself from rubbing his face or showing any sign of torment. He did not want to show his father that he could be hurt by him. 'By the way, grow up and start acting like you are twenty two and stop dressing like a woman. I did not raise a queer or a pathetic little boy who has accidents. NOW MOVE IT!!' Sanmos shouts. Kaji controls his breathing so as to not get angry, and makes his way towards a bucket full of clean rags. He walks over to the fountain connecting to the stream and he wets the rag before moving to the great rune stone.

'I am watching you, Tohroshatan. Do not miss a spot.'

'Yes father.' He acknowledges while rolling his eyes with his back turned.

As he approaches the stone a new vision invades his thoughts. It's that haunting monstrous place again. He's running through the black forest. Strong winds form around him, propelling him forward through the forest. Soon enough the wind becomes an electrically charged storm, forcing him to move at a superhuman speed.

As the vision continues, Kaji's right shoulder catches fire. Anxiety pulses through him as he catches sight of it. He quickly gets out of his father's peripheral before hitting himself repeatedly with the wet rag in an attempt to extinguish the flames. He manages to snuff himself out but not without a considerable amount of steam.

'That is why it needs to be done everyday.' Sanmos says, having definitely heard the sizzling sound. Luckily for Kaji, he was under the full belief that it was radiating from the rune stone.

Kaji nods behind the runestone where his father can not see him. He does not say a word as his mind is too focused on remaining hidden.

'What was that?' Sanmos asks with a firm but calm tone.

'Yes Father.'

'Hmm.'

Kaji's visions persist as he starts to clean the surface of the great rune stone. He watches the odd man practically fly through the black forest. More parts of Kaji's body catch fire, although, in smaller patches as the visions continue without his consent.

'Ahh no no no.' He whispers to himself while trying not to panic as he hits himself with the wet rag in order to extinguish the flames.

'Hmm, what was that?' Sanmos questions while searching his surroundings. He can see puffs of steam around the great rune stone. He starts to build suspicion that something is not quite right with Kaji.

'Nothing father, I am just really cleaning this rock you know.' He says as he continues to hit himself with the wet rag and traces around the stone so his father could not see him.

Sanmos starts to walk around the great rune stone towards Kaji, knowing full well that something isn't right. He knows he's harsh on his son but it is for good reason. Kaji is the last person besides himself with any blood relation to this great rune stone, one day he will reveal the importance and on that day he will learn, there are no sick days.

'Tohroshatan… You know this STONE is sacred right?' He asks as he watches him clean the rune of Bamapana high up on the stone.

Kaji almost falls over, startled as he sees his father standing by him. He grabs the rag and bucket and makes an effort to act casual as he moves to a different part of the stone, out of his father's sight.

'Yeah, I know.' He acknowledges as he starts to clean the rune of Ahriman.

'Then why are you hiding?' He asks, following Kaji around the rune stone.

He walks back around the stone, showing himself to his father. His shoulders were on fire but he was too concerned about his father to notice. He doesn't want to disappoint his father again or be hit by his unforgiving hand. He looks at his father who is staring back at him wide eyed. He takes no notice of his fathers change in body language, he needed to be casual.

'See? Nothing is wrong.'

'Why is your shoulder on fire?'

'Huh?'

'Why. is. Your. shoulder. On. fire?' Sanmos asks again.

He ignores the burning pain coming and going in waves as he pats his shoulder with the wet rag, extinguishing himself once again, all while paying his full attention to his father.

'I think we are done here.' Sanmos says.

'Yes father.' He says, turning his gaze to the ground. He feels defeated, he can never make his father proud and now he has something more to worry about. This new fire has let down himself, his family, and worst of all his bloodline.

'You can go and study your history now near some water.' Sanmos says in a much calmer tone, he can see Kaji is stressed, however he cannot let Kaji's fire near the sacred gardens and the great rune stone, not until he has it under control.

'Uhh.' He felt more confused, why is his father being so nice. A few moments before he swore he was going to die.

'Go and study, I must talk with your mother.' He says calmly, meeting Kaji's eyes again. He felt concerned but proud. His son, who much like himself belongs to one of the imperial bloodlines, going back thousands of years, is a sacred dreamer: one of the most honourable things to become. But he knows dreamers always have trouble with their new powers once acquired and realises that it will take time to get used to.

'Uhh.' He vocalises, feeling unsure about the situation.

'I need to talk to your mother, go. And. Study.' Sanmos says. 'Off you go.'

'Yes father.'

Kaji, still holding the rag and bucket, steps away from the great rune stone and walks towards the entrance. He places his rag in the dirty rag bucket and places the bucket of water next to the exit. He leaves the Gazebo and slowly walks down the steps, his body now more relaxed yet still being forced to deal with the spontaneous flames.

Sanmos watches him leave and walk down the mountain before inspecting the great rune stone. The stone is unfinished but he needs to see if the parts Kaji did were done well.

'Huh…' Sanmos says impressed, noting that certain spots of the rune stone were cleaned beautifully. 'Good job Tohroshatan'

He takes a moment to himself before tending to the other half of the great rune stone. As he cleans he thinks to himself that maybe he should be less harsh on Kaji, although he reminds himself that he is the last hope for the bloodline. There is no one else.

'Is it possible that Tohroshatan was touched by a dreamer? Or he has become one?' He pondered to himself.

†

The black forest is dark, clammy, wet and muddy. The humidity is so thick, the air feels like a pool of water and the trees are so thick, light has trouble getting through.

Ookonan is running through the forest, he has all his belongings in his backpack and his battered sword strapped to his side. As he runs through, he jumps over the thick roots and pushes through the mud as though it is nothing. He dodges any of the black slime that tries to follow and he moves his strong body along the forest with some ease pushing through his fatigue.

'I must keep going, ignore all around, and keep moving.' He thinks to himself.

As his stress and fatigue increases he sees a new vision of Kaji. He is getting abused by his father and he is cleaning an enormous red gem covered in carvings. He watches Kaji clean the stone and extinguish himself and as Kaji extinguishes, the strong winds form around him, the same ones that formed when he fought the brood mother.

He tries to think nothing of it, however he begins to brew a storm around himself, lightning sparks around his hands and the wind moves around him collecting up some of the fog with it.

'How am I doing this?' He asks himself.

The wind propels him forward at a superhuman speed and each step he takes he feels like he is temporarily flying.

'Okay now I know the brood mother happened, I had a lot of witnesses and they spoke about it again when we got back.'

He launches himself forward, temporarily flying and landing softly on the ground. He continues to dodge the trees around him and the strong winds around him blast the slime and mud away.

'The brood mother incident was not a fluke then. This is permanent. I can live with these powers. This is amazing and greatly convenient.'

A demonic jumps at him from a tree above and obliterates itself, shredding itself into pieces from the strong winds now gaining an electrical charge.

'Must keep going, I can't lose focus, I must keep going....' He mutters to himself.

As he pushes forward he can finally see an exit, he can see some light coming through the trees ahead, he forces himself to continue running. The light is illuminating the trees creating streaks of light coming towards him.

'There is light, Keep going and get out, let's go.'

He continues running, moving out of the way of the trees, blasting away mud and slime. Once he gets closer to the end he feels himself flying, the air and landing is lighter. But before he knew it, he had left the forest and he flies into the air before crashing to the ground.

He has crash landed into a strong moonlit grassy field. He looks back at the black forest, it almost looks like a thick black wall made of a black gas. The trees are thick and the roots stop as soon as the land turns grassy.

He gets up and brushes himself off, he looks back at the forest. The trees are some of the tallest he has ever seen, but as he can hear the demonics scream inside the forest, he wonders why anyone would choose to live there. The screams are so quiet and dampened from the thick atmosphere that he knows the people in there he may never hear from again.

'I am glad to be out of there.' He breathes. He turns to the grass land and moonlight and takes a deep breath. His storm finally disappears and he can see the beauty of the sky and land. 'It is funny how such beauty can come with so much chaos.'

Chapter 5

The Mirish Capital night markets are always magical. The colours, smells and sounds overwhelm the senses as the market is filled with food stalls, hand crafted goods and clothing stalls from the other islands.

Fire dancing performers are at the beach doing feats of acrobatics, eating flame and dancing. Dreamers would wander through the markets, giving and offering their blessings of the gods they are champions to along with handmade gifts to those who worship their deities.

As Kaji walks he doesn't let anything get in his way even his favourite street performers aren't garnering his attention tonight no Kaji was on a mission. He pushes through the crowds of people determined for a particular stall.

It's more crowded than usual as people from the other islands closest to the capitol travel over to buy and sell. He has quick glances at stalls, he sees both familiar and new things but nothing that he is after. He wants starch lollies, the soft sweets made of potato starches, sometimes yams and always covered in a powder. But it was too crowded tonight to find them. But there! A stranger was eating one. He pushes past people to approach the stranger, he needed to find that stall.

'Hey. uh. Apologies for disrupting you. But do you know where the starch lolly stall is?' He asks the stranger.

'Just down there to your left.' The stranger says, mouth full of the starch sweet.

'Thanks.' He says, quickly wandering off and back to pushing through the crowd.

✝

Hono and Yua remain at the less crowded part of the market, near the water and dancers. Hono waits impatiently looking out at the water, calm with very few waves tonight. She watches people gather around the beach area, sitting on benches and the sand as performers prepare for their next routine.

She turns back to her mother who is holding a shopping basket, filling it with assortments of fruits that are available at the stall. mangoes, dragon fruits, kiwi, grapes, and a tikimata, a spiky fruit with a hard shell and a soft cake-like consistency on the inside. Yua is always keen to buy fruits that are not available on the capitol island whenever the markets are on.

Hono turns back around to watch the performers as she waits for her mother impatiently. As enjoyable as the markets are, it's painfully boring to be around her mother when she would much rather be with her brother or friends.

'Where do you think Tohro has gone mum?'

'Hmm.' Yua vocalises Having paid no attention to what Hono had asked.

'Mum.' She grunts, turning to face her mother, leaning on a sana-melon. She sees that she is just casually grabbing more fruit and still not paying much attention to her.

Yua knocks on the skin of the sana-melon Hono was leaning on then places it in her basket, under the belief Hono might want it while she continues to admire and grab fruit completely in her own world.

'Mum…. Mum…. muuuuuummm.' She pesters.

'Hmm. what?' Yua asks, now leaving her trance and coming back into the reality of the Mirish capitol markets.

'Where is Tohro?' Hono asks, leaning on one leg, raising her eyebrows and pursing her lips.

'Where do you think?' She asks without glancing Hono's way.

'Huh?' She questioned, knowing she is missing something obvious. How was she supposed to know where Tohroshatan went? She thought to herself.

'He would always be looking for lollies, especially starch lollies.'

'Oh right…' She said, now realising the obvious and feeling stupid about it.

'You know this Hono…' She sighs, turning to look at her dark skin glowing from the fire performance, she gives Hono a look, unsure if she legitimately forgot or if she was pulling her usual jokes. 'What are you trying to do?'

'Nothing… I'm not doing anything.' Hono grunts, lowering her voice.

'Okay good. If you want him go and find him. I'm going to continue getting groceries.'

'Okay.'

†

The starch lolly stall vendor is sorting out several skewers into rows. He is grabbing the pink starch lolly blocks and covers them in sugar powder before sliding them onto the skewers. Kaji watches the vendor put the lollies out on display, his pupils are wide and his mouth is watering, the vendor has his full attention.

'How many would you like?' The vendor asks.

'OI… TOHRO!!' Someone shouted before he could answer. He quickly scans his surroundings, looking through the packed crowd of people. There. He spots his sister waving at him.

'I would like two skewers please.' He says, turning back to the vendor. He points specifically at the skewed pink blocks the vendor had just finished making and put out on display.

'That would be five mirtus.' The vendor says holding out his hand.

Kaji reaches into his pocket and pulls out a hand full of coins made of different materials, copper, quarts, shells, amber. He picks out the coins adding up to five mirtus and hands it over to the vendor, who smiles at him and hands over the two skewers of starch lolly.

'Why did you run off?' She asks him as she approaches him.

'It's the markets, it's good to look around and see what there is, look what I found.' He says while handing over one of the skewers to her.

'Thanks… but that's no excuse for leaving me alone with mum.' She says, accepting the sweet from him. 'Did you want to go and see the fire dancers?'

He looks over at the dancers, the male and female performers are throwing and spinning fire with perfect elegance and control. It didn't seem too bad but he does not feel comfortable with fire in his current situation of accidents. He's keen, until one of the performers spat their alcohol on their flame, creating a blast into the sky.

'I. I don't feel completely comfortable around fire at the moment.'

'Heh!' She scoffs. 'Come on! Time to relax and watch the show! They are the best part of the week!'

'Alright.'

She grabs his arm and drags him through the crowded walkways, she barely notices his resistance, his pullback to not go. He grips tightly on his sweets as he is dragged through the markets towards the waterfront. He didn't come to the markets to get this delicacy of sweet chewy love.

Once they reach the sand, he stops moving. He can now see the performers in all their glory, the bright orange flames illuminating every part of them, the ambers fluttering in the air and the acrobatics the compliment it.

He didn't want to be there, he could feel his stomach in his throat. His heart, pounding like it's about to escape from his chest. It's too much, he can't help but think about his recent combustion.

Hono looks back at him and yanks him forward, snapping him out of his short trance. He follows her to a log to sit down on, but the trance returns as a female performer does a backflip kicking fire into a flame circle around herself. He's fearful of it, but also fascinated of it.

Hono yanks him again, pulling him out of the trance once more. He looks around taking in some deep breaths and sits down next to her.

'You seem really out of place lately... What is going on?'

'When I was late to clean the stone-.'

'Did father hit you? He was pretty mad.' She asks quickly, cutting him off.

'Yes but that is besides the point...'

She takes a deep breath. 'Then what is it? What's wrong?' She demanded as thoughts started running through her head. Has he been studying too much? Is he putting too much pressure on himself?

He takes a deep breath, thinking to himself how he could tell her about this morning, but a fire dancer gets close to him. His stomach tightens as he watches the flames move past himself, he feels unsure of himself but he knows the fire in his body is real.

'I was probably dreaming, but I'm not too sure. I swear I was catching fire... constantly.' He tries to explain.

'Ever since that incident in the courtyard with the tree; you have been constantly talking about fire.' She puts a hand on his shoulder. 'You need to relax bro.'

He turns his gaze to her and he can't help but agree with her. He does need to relax, but he somehow needs to stop thinking about fire which would be impossible with the fire performers dancing along the beach. He leans back and takes a bite of his starch lolly, he then places his left hand on his lap.

'Okay… I will try to relax.' He says as he watches the performers with his sister.

He tries to relax and just watch as the performance goes on, but the more he sees the fire the more he feels an impending doom. He looks at his sweets, pink starchy and delicious. He takes a bite and looks down at his feet.

It's too late, he sees the visions. He can see the world again through someone else's eyes, he can see the tall grass and its sways with the soft wind, he can see the morning sun and he can see the thick black band of trees a few kilometres away. But not only that he can feel everything this person is feeling, the blades of grass brushing up against him, the cold air but also the mild heat of the sun.

He knows what's to come with the vision starting, he can feel his heat racing and breathing is becoming an effort. He looks up at the night sky and at the stars. Problem is, he can see the embers of the fire dance between the stars as his eyes start to glow an orange amber as he turns his gaze back to watch the dancers.

†

Ookonan walks through the thick long grass, parallel to the black forest. Conscious of his surroundings and ensuring he steps into the open patches of dirt, helping him to see and predict more of his surroundings.

He walks along the patchy dirt path between the tall blades of grass, completely lost in his own world. His thoughts are concise and clear as he thinks about his next move. But this is interrupted as visions begin.

He feels the strangers emotions take over, anxiety, fear and a burning sensation through his body. He tries to remain calm as he sees the unusual looking people walking around him, people he has never seen before and he feels a further surge of anxiety seeing one of these people dance with fire get close to him.

He tries to ignore the visions blocking most of his real vision as he scans the grassland in broad daylight for any demonics. Not a single one in near sight.

His right hand sparks as he tries to avoid the fire dancers, but panic sets in as they spit ethanol on their flames creating explosions into the sky. He tries to get away, punching and kicking the air, forgetting that he is completely alone.

Wind brews around him as his panic continues and his right hand starts to spark. He falls backwards still punching and kicking the dancers, blasting the sky with a strike of lighting.

'AHHH.' He screams, pushing himself away from the dancers who are smiling at him. They throw their fire into the air and bow, concluding that part of the act.

As the dancers turn away, the visions start to fade along with all the senses and feelings the strange man was feeling. He slowly gets back to his feet and scans his surroundings. Still alone, yet he can't help himself but still feel embarrassed by the experience.

'Ristinos ee bastille shoolled lävisi bäästo gïntèskä.'
(*I better start running so no one notices what happened and finds me.*)
He says in Euro Hondonian to himself.

He has another brief look around and begins to run along the path between the tall grass, trying not to think about what had just happened.

†

Kaji remains seated next to Hono still watching the fire dancers, but feeling like he cannot move as one hand grips the log and the other of the skewer of the starch lolly he has now finished. The visions of the other land and mysterious man start to fade, but as he watches the performers he still feels uncomfortable. He doesn't understand why, as their control of the flames are flawless.

The tightness in his chest starts to loosen as the visions disappear and he comes back to full reality. He notices a dancer looking at him, he grips the skewer and log tighter, a performer noticing him was not helping.

'DUDE! ARE YOU OKAY?' The performer shouts, dropping his staff onto the sand before rushing over to him.

A couple more performers stopped what they were initially doing. They all stare at him, mouths open wide eyed. Two of them run off to their equipment while the others try and distract the crowd of people before anyone else notices what is happening.

Hono watches the action, confused about why they are getting so much attention. She looks at the staffs and strings sitting on the sand still on fire, she looks back over at Kaji, he's just as confused.

'Did someone get you?' The performer asks him as the other dancers come over with first aid supplies.

'What no… why?' He asks, completely confused by the situation as he watches some chaos unfold as the performers surround him.

The dancers around him look at each other, panicked. 'Who lit him on fire?!' The first respondent called out to the dancers.

'I don't know!' Another shouted back, pulling a wet rag out of a bucket of water he brought over with him.

The dancers pull a wet rag out of a bucket of water to place on him. Hono watches them intently. She looks at the wet rag then down at her brother. She sees it. Hot red flames around his hand and arm. Unbelievable, he wasn't making things up.

'TOHRO YOU"RE ON FIRE' She screams.

'Don't panic whatever you do, do not panic.' The performer says to Hono and Kaji.

He looks at Hono wide eyed, then down at his lap. He sees the red glow as his gaze turns to his hand holding the skewer. He's on fire and the skewer is nowhere to be seen. He looks up at the performer who wraps his arm in the wet rag, extinguishing him.

He realised where the burning sensation was coming from which he ignored, like his flesh is searing. He is unable to tell whether his skin is unharmed with the wet rag covering him, but now that is all he is thinking about and what his life is now.

'So you weren't making it up… Tohro! You weren't dreaming.'

'Okay so this is real.' He breathes.

'What's real? Are you okay?' A performer asks.

'Don't worry about it, he's going through changes.' Hono says.

Chapter 6

The grassland stretches on for kilometres all around him, two kilometres to his right is the black forest stretching on for kilometres either way looking almost like a black ribbon. Then on the other side of him is just the vastly open grassy field, filled with hills and sparsely placed trees that goes on until the horizon.

Ookonan looks up at the sky, squinting as he tries to figure out where he is. He knows which way is north as the sun is on a forty five degree angle from the highest point in the sky, but he does not recognise any part of the land.

He is exhausted and has been walking non stop for almost two days, he stumbles through the grass dragging his feet along with him. His boots are thickly covered in mud, dust and grass from the days of walking.

'It is day two of this lot of grass. I am not complaining but I am not sure where I am.' He breathes heavily to himself.

He squints his eyes as he looks out at the distance. The horizon out in the field looks almost blank in all directions, except the black forest and a small structure that sits right on the horizon. Too small to make out what it is, a castle? A village? A city? A fortress? A giant rock?

'I think I was at that town a little too long.' He says to himself looking back over at the black forest. He catches his breath. 'It is a fair while until nightfall. I should be okay out here…'

A feeling of frustration sweeps over him. He tenses his jaw as he looks at the small structure on the horizon, it could be anything. A ruin from ancient people?

'I just need to figure out where I am… How could I be so ignorant about that yesterday?' He says to himself as he comes to a stop. He takes in a deep breath and looks down at his feet. Filthy. He is exhausted, he can feel his fatigue deep into his bones. He takes another look at his surroundings. Stressing about being lost is going to get him nowhere, he thought to himself.

The sun is at its highest, if a mountain were in its direction, it would be completely covered. He thinks to himself that, right now in this location might be the safest its going to be.

He looks for a clear patch of dirt next to the tall thick tuft of grass, he places his backpack on the ground and sits himself down next to a tall thick tuft of grass.

He leans forward, opens his backpack and goes through the inner well organised pockets. He has sacks pinned to the sides, one side for teas, one for dried foods and one for spices. At the back of the bag closest to the straps are his cooking utensils including a couple sized pots and pans.

He opens a pocket on the side of the bag and pulls out a metal teapot, a metal cup and a bladder of water from the other side of the bag.

'I could really go for a cup of tea… buuut setting a fire to boil water in my teapot may be a bad idea.' He says quietly to himself.

He leans back again and closes his eyes. All he wants to do is relax for a moment and rest, but the persistent urge to drink tea remains. He opens his eyes and sits up. He looks at his teapot and cup, yes a cup of tea will be made.

He stands up and looks around. The field is empty with an exception of a couple of trees and hills. The grass sways softly in the wind and the only sound he can hear are the blades of grass rubbing against each other. He looks back over at the black forest, the distance is far, the area itself is quiet. He can hear nothing coming from that direction even with his elven ears.

I'm near no tree for a demonic to be hiding from the sun, I should be safe out here. He thinks to himself. He looks over at the structure on the horizon again, that will be the place to go once rested, he thinks to himself.

The silence is uncomfortable, almost no sound that his elven hearing can pick up, he can theoretically hear a baby crying from a kilometre away.

But rest is important, can't get so fatigued that collapsing around demonics is inevitable, he thinks to himself.

He sits back down and looks around himself. There are a few sticks, a single branch and a couple of chewed bones in his near proximity and a lot of dry grass. He bundles it together and layers them, making a little box. Good enough to get air flow and sturdy enough to hold the teapot. He then stuffs it with dry grass.

He places his teapot on top of the little structure, then opens the bladder of water and fills the teapot. He takes out some flint and steel from an outside pocket of his bag and strikes the grass under the little structure lighting it up in a smoky flame.

He puts the lid on the teapot and leans back on the thick tall grass. Now realising how tired he is, he closes his eyes and takes a moment to himself. He thinks about the village and those people, most of whom willingly live in such a dangerous place. Who decided such a dumb place to live? Their so-called leader Scott?

He leans himself further into thought and into a dreamlike state. He has many questions about the past couple of days. Sudden powers or abilities which he has never seen before, whether it's a fluke, he just doesn't know. How many other people have had this happen to them? So many questions run through his mind that he thinks about what his mother would say to him when she was alive.

Sometimes you just need to slow down and have a cup of tea. The world may be a shithole, but it's easier to forget and rest when you have a hot brew in your hands.

The teapot starts to rattle. He opens his eyes and sits back up. He pulls out three sacks of tea from his backpack. He opens each: raspberry leaves with dried raspberries, green sage leaves and chaga. He puts a little of each into the boiled teapot and lets it sit for a little while to brew.

He thinks to himself that he always makes new blends of tea. He likes the different flavours and feeling the tea gives and he loves collecting the different blends of tea across Hondon.

He reties the sacks and puts them back away back into his backpack. He holds on to his cup, eager for the tea. But instead closes his eyes once more to rest.

He thinks about the visions he's been having, how strange they have been. The land is no land he recognises. Is it the far south, is the far south easy going and fun? There was a view of the ocean so it couldn't be the sky islands.

He changes his thought, there is no point dwelling on the visions right now. He reminds himself of the structure on the horizon, he has never seen a settlement out in the open before, so it couldn't be a little village or a town, it would have to be a ruin he thought to himself. 'It could also be a tree,' he mutters.

He can smell the aroma of the tea. It's ready. He opens his eyes and sits back up and pours himself a cup of tea. He holds the cup in his hands. Warming his extremities, reminding him how cold the air really is.

He smiles at the tea and takes a sip. That sweet relief the tea gives, as though the world's problems have ended for its moment. The tea has a flavour of fruity sweetness of the raspberries, like a village cake and a savouriness of the sage, like a bowl of warm meaty stew and another flavour of smokiness from the chaga.

He feels the hot liquid go through his chest and into his stomach. It's a feeling of healing, the battle wounds and the sore joints feel at ease for this moment.

'I wish moments like this could last much longer.' He mutters to himself under his breath.

He stretches out his sore legs and leans back on the grass. It's time for a rest and at the safest time, in broad daylight. Once the tea is finished and once rested will be the time to put out the fire and head off again.

Chapter 7

Kaji walks alone through the imperial palace grounds carrying a leather and stone bound book. He avoids the stuff sparsely scattered around the grounds as he heads for the courtyard, where it all began a couple of days ago.

He steps into the courtyard from the archway entrance. He looks at the tree, which glows as the warm morning sunlight beams onto it, illuminating its bright, healthy green leaves, leaving spectacles of green light to bounce around the courtyard ground.

He eyes the roots of the massive tree, remembering the past few days and remembering that leaf. A singular leaf burning up from his touch causes him great distress, just one leaf. He walks over to the tree, eyeing the trunk and roots as he walks around it, trying to locate the minute bit of ash that was left. Nothing. It's gone.

'Hmm.' He vocalises, as he wonders why him, why was he given this curse of flame?

He moves his gaze upwards at the branch he was sitting on that day, the branch he sits on most days to study and get out of his room, there is nothing unusual about the branch he thinks to himself. He climbs the tree with the textbook in his hand and takes himself to the branch and sits himself down.

He opens the textbook to the index and runs his finger down. He thinks about the words he last heard the man speak: *Ristinos ee bastille shoolled lävisi bäästo gintèskä.*

'I need to know what language that vision was in…. That could be the key to ending this.' He mutters quietly to himself.

He finds the note that says:

Wham Hondon rok ma gaji-otto non shotu. Kutahon ila zhutah Ginetilaoch - goket
> *What the Hondonian language may sound like.* Page 68-70.

He turns the pages to page sixty eight. 'He has to be from Hondon…. He fought what looked like demons?' He says to himself unsure about what the monsters the man was fighting and the sludgy, slimy place he was in. The man fought smaller, skeletal-like zombie monsters and a bulbous one with tentacles. This must be the present day, the past would not look like that, he thinks to himself.

'The demons look too refined and the people he was with are tiny. But I can't throw away the idea that this could be a past life speaking to me.' He mutters quietly as he starts to read the page about Hondonian language. The page reads:

Gingi gubbamaa molamanogu rok to lang ramijish gaji-otto
The five big Hondonian languages and each of their potential sounds.

'There are five main Hondonian languages that are presumed to exist. Asian, European, African, American: north and south. And there are believed to be more Hondonian languages, for instance, people tied to a religion speak one whole language that is often entirely different to the main in their region.'

'Whoever wrote this… how would they know? It is impossible to know. No one has ever been to Hondon….' He whispers to himself, pausing momentarily to think.

But Hondon isn't real, it's just folklore to scare children about the powers of dreamers. Misbehave and be sent to Hondon for eternity, which is something people believed for centuries.

'Well… One dreamer claims he has been to Hondon… He is long dead now… I'm sure it was an overdose.' He mumbles quietly to himself as he turns the page to page seventy. Which reads:

Ila lemanb molamanogu ereoppa uragalm

Some European Hondonian phrases.
'I recognise none of these…' He mumbles as he scans the paper, becoming more frustrated as he reads through the phrases.

Kïïköönam (*Thank you*)
oo hôr dissak (*How are you*).
Täävëëshka, êyïï yëm ginä hôrëk (*How do I find the tavern*).
Trâmena corre (*Run, get out*).
Oos zäshisk gïntèskä (*Let no one find your spice*)

As he scans the phrases, he recognises a single word or the potentiality of a word he may have heard. He thinks back to the phrase the man said *Ristinos ee bastille shoolled lävisi bäästo gïntèskä.* He thinks about the phrase all while the word *gïnètskä* stands out.
'I recognise that word.' He says in a realisation, recognising that the man could truly be speaking Euro Hondonian.
'Ahh… G g. Gin?' He takes a breath as he attempts the word. 'Gin Tesk Kah?'
Confused as he looks at the word, unsure of its pronunciation, he decides to move to a different section. He turns back to the index and searches for the Euro Hondonian dictionary section. He turns the pages to the Euro Hondonian dictionary and runs his finger down until he finds the word gïnètskä. Its pronunciation in brackets [*Geen EH Tsk eh*]
'Geen EH Tsk eh. It seems to have many meanings. Direct translation is finds by none… What does he mean?'He thinks to himself aloud. 'Other translations for gïntèskä are, no one finds, found by none, no one finds me and no one finds it.' He reads aloud to himself.
He lets out a large exhale as he leans back on the trunk of the tree. He struggles to understand the translation of the Hondonian word. Find by none? No one finds? 'What does he mean?' He questions, feeling full of frustration of the language barrier of his vision.
'I feel stupid, I know some Euro Hondonian. I need a break. I don't know why I can't understand him.' He says to himself as he closes his book.

†

Kaji lays on his bed as the afternoon sun beams through the window, lighting up his bed area and bookshelves. The heat is obvious as he sweats as he lays motionless on his bed, staring at the curved ceiling.

A knock on the door disturbs his trance of hopelessness about his curse of flame. He turns his gaze over to the door, with very little interest of who it is, he looks back at the ceiling.

'Who is it?' he asks, hoping it wouldn't be his father.

'It's me.' His mother says softly as she opens the door ever so slightly to peek her head through. She sees him motionless, just staring at the ceiling. 'May I come in?'

'Yeah.' He says quietly.

She walks into his room, closing the door behind her and takes herself to his bed. She sits herself at the foot of his bed and looks around the room briefly. The room is clean and tidy with an exception of scattered scorch marks.

'Tohroshatan.' She says, turning her gaze over to him. 'You have been very off lately. Your father has spoken to me and word has gotten around about... Last night's incident.'

He says nothing and continues to stare at the ceiling. He wants it to end, he wishes the incident never happened, he still cannot understand why him. The thoughts, the anxiety, the feeling of loss and hopelessness is paralysing him.

'Tohro... You are putting too much pressure on yourself, you will take over your father one day and you have some new unsolicited changes. It's a lot, but you can't just lay and pity yourself.'

'I just don't know why this is happening. I can't solve it.'

'Tohroshatan... you may have been touched by a god'

'Gods aren't real.' He quickly interjects.

'Tell that to the dreamers.'

'They are on drugs half the time.'

She frowns at him, she's immensely proud of him but also pities him. Disappointed that he can't see that he will be the first Imperial Emperor Dreamer, the first Mirish Emperor to be touched by a god. No amount of self pity will reverse this or make it go away. But she pities him as there is now further pressure on him for his future and more potential targets on his back.

'Hmmm.' She softens her voice and calms down. 'Well... Tohroshatan... you know what helps you destress don't you?'

'Hmmm.'

'Go to training Tohroshatan.'

'I just want to lay here.' He says softly.

She sighs, trying to remain calm around him. She stands up and stands over him, maintaining control over her emotions. She's the mum, even a future leader is not the boss of his mum.

'Get up!'

'Do I have to?' He groans.

'Yes now. Or I am taking your books away.'

'Uughh.'He groans. He starts getting up. 'Okay. fine.'

'Good. Now go and work off that frustration.' She says, firmly.

Chapter 8

The trek through the grassy field feels everlasting, kilometre after kilometre Ookonan has traveled with the land looking almost the same as when he started. The only difference is that dusk is setting in and the structure can almost be made out for what it is.

He walks through the almost chest high grass, eyes keen on the structure. He is able to make out what it could potentially be, but so far it's nothing but tall wooden walls.

The soft breeze slowing down becomes painfully noticeable, halting the noisy swaying and brustling tall grass. He stops walking to scan his surroundings. His ears twitch to look for sounds as his eyes look to the sky. The sun is setting, the bright blue sky as it once was now a deep orange and purple, yet the land is disturbingly quiet.

He takes another step towards the structure. The crunch of the dirt and dry grass beneath his booth is deafeningly loud in comparison to the painfully quiet atmosphere. Every bit of movement he does is deafening to him.

He attempts to control his breathing to help articulate his hearing, the uncomfortability in his gut is telling him something is to come. A slight movement in the grass almost startles him. He snaps his head around to its direction, he could almost swear it was right next to him. He starts walking again towards the structure but with a hyperfocus on the sounds around himself.

Screams and gurgles of demonics suddenly fill the soundless air, it was deafening with the sudden loud noise. He rubs his ears to ease them as he looks over at the black forest, one a kilometre away from himself. But now the sun has set, the forest so dark and dank oozes black smog into the grasslands.

Must keep moving, he thought to himself as he began to tread carefully through the grass again. He keeps an eye and ear on the forest, anxiously looking for any demonics that might be roaming out into the grass. Beads of sweat begin forming on his forehead as his stress rises and the growls sporadically echo throughout the land.

A sudden loud scream booms through the air followed by a crowd of deep gurgling sounds. He forces himself to keep moving towards the structure. He doesn't want to know what's to come from the black forest but he turns his head to look. The thick black smog wall has broken and the demonics have been released. But he could not see any glowing eyes as of yet but that does not negate the heavy dread he is feeling in the pit of his stomach.

He quickly checks over his body, he's seasoned himself. His backpack is full of herbs and spices, there is no way he should be a target. But then it dawns on him, he towers over the tall grass, he can be easily seen by anything making him an easy target.

He tries his hardest to ignore the screams and gurgles, but it's impossible when he can see movement in the grass nearing him in multiple directions. 'Vekk they are getting close.'

A large gush of cold wind hits him from behind sending chills down his spine. He knows in his gut he is not in a good position and he feels stupid for not finding safety sooner. Another gush of wind hits him but this time some leaves from the black forest hit him as well before rolling on the dirt.

He turns his head slowly to look at the black forest. He's finding it more difficult to breathe as his stress rises, his face also getting wetter as he breaks out in cold sweat. The wind coming to a stop with the air becoming still increasing his discomfort. It is as though the world has slowed down, or the quiet before the storm.

But there! Hidden within the six foot tall grass are the glowing red eyes of a demonic staring at him. These eyes are hungry and they are following him wherever he moves. He looks back over to the forest and there, everywhere through the tall grass are the glowing red eyes of demonics, staring right at him. He glances back at the forest and the demonic screams start back up as the forest smog oozes out completely like it's a door opening ready to let out the demonics.

He walks faster attempting to keep low and hidden from the demonics, knowing his height will give him away 'Running will have them run… I must try and avoid that.' He thinks to himself while keeping an ear out for his increasingly more deadly surroundings, he keeps as quiet as he can as he continues forth. But there, the grass moves around him as something circles him like a large fish in dark water.

'Vekk they saw me.' He whispers to himself as he starts to pick up speed. But there peering through the grass directly in front of himself are the glowing hungry red eyes and a wide grin filled with long sharp rock like teeth.

He lets out an uncontrollable scream ' AHHH.' He was not expecting it to be right in front of him. He dodges around it and breaks out into a full sprint towards the structure, hoping he would not run into any more demonics. He ignores his fatigue and the pain in his ears from the deafening screams of the hoard of demonics that chase after him.

The dread he feels in the pit of his stomach as he feels his legs burning with fatigue, he can't force himself to go any faster. But the closer he gets to the structure the closer the demonics get to him. The only things that run through his head is his need for survival but also a tiny voice telling him it's now his end, he can't win.

'Why the Vekk are these clafarging things going after me? Why not stay in the clafarging dark forest?' He cries to himself. But as his adrenalin rises, a new vision begins.

Blurry as it may seem, unknown whether it's fatigue or sweat, he sees the peaceful training grounds in the hot daylight and a bunch of young people with features he finds unusual standing around or training. As he pushes through the long grass, he feels as though his lungs are on fire whether or not it's from the fading vision, he cannot tell. But as the vision fades and his vision returns, he can finally make out what the structure is.

It's a tall thick spiked wooden wall with additional sharpened stakes aiming outwards. It has several tall watchtowers built within the walls themselves. He eyes it, somewhat satisfied with what he has found, knowing if he gets there he can be safe from the swarm of demonics chasing him.

'I will get there, let me get there.' He weeps to himself.

The watch towers all light up as the guards spot Ookonan running towards them and the raid of demonics chasing close behind him. He can barely catch his breath, the fatigue is almost too much and his lungs are burning. 'Do not stop... do not stop... keep going.... I will not die... tonight.' He kept telling himself aloud as he pushed through the agony.

He finds himself slowing down even through his own force to continue. He cannot out run this horde. But as soon as a demonic hand touches him the visions start once more.

The hot training ground is more clear as he can see the training equipment, such as punching bags, dummies, targets, ropes as well as a large empty bricked ground to practice. He can see the people who look strange to him training or fighting each other, he finds it impossible to tell at this point. But he finds himself in the shoes of the strange man, sparring or fighting the other men. Intensely hot flames grow up this man's arms as he throws one of the men onto the ground.

But as this happens, electricity and strong winds start to brew around Ookonan. 'This will be interesting.' He breathes, turning his attention to the demonic who touched him, electrifying it before smashing its head in.

The storm grows around him, allowing him to move towards those large walls in no time. But once he nears, he turns his attention back towards the swarm of demonics that have been chasing him. He realises that he cannot let those demonics into whatever is behind those walls, he cannot let people get hurt.

'Thank you man of peace.' He says, thanking the visions as he prepares himself to fight the demonics running full sprint at him. He takes his time to catch his breath before he embraces the uncontrollable electric storm around himself. He tightens his fists as electricity concentrates there and in his chest.

'Time to end this.' He unsheathes his sword and moves towards the demonics, swinging his blade at one's head, destroying its upper body. Then quickly piercing the end of the blade towards two demonics running in line with each other. A huge burst of electricity shoots through the end of the sword, pulverising the demonics.

A demonic smiles eerily, before moving slowly towards him. Twitching as it moves. He spins, slicing the demonics's head off with his electrified sword, killing it before turning his attention towards the other herd coming at him.

The storm brews more violently as he gets more stressed. He jumps into the air, the storm bringing him higher. He brings his sword above his head as electricity bursts through his chest into the blade. As he comes back down to the earth, he slams himself and his sword down to the ground blasting the area around himself, obliterating five demonics and leaving a crater in the process.

'I love this gift of power.' He says under his breath as he turns himself to slash two demonics sprinting at himself with a burst of lighting, cutting them in half and blasting their charred bodies away into the distance.

He readjusts his stance, gritting his teeth while examining the remaining demonics within his sight. Still unsure how many there truly are, but it must end, he cannot keep this up and he does not know how much longer the power of storm will remain. But those few remaining demonics, with no humanity left or brains as it seems, fall into the crater that he created.

He lifts his sword into the air, pumping it with the electricity that moves through his veins and he waits for the moment to strike. He waits for any remaining demonics to fall into the crater before he strikes. Bang! He slams his sword into the ground electrifying the crater and a few metres from it, destroying the demonics within.

It's over, the demonic horde is over. He pulls his sword from the ground and resheaths it before he turns his attention back to the tall wooden walls. He's made it. He begins his final steps towards it. He can finally see the gate, but his vision blurs and as he takes his final steps towards it, his storm subsides and he collapses.

†

The Mir Capitol Imperial training grounds are one of the most used places in all of Mir. For a thousand years, it had stood as a bastion for honing the skills of a warrior. It's stone work while old and ancient is well maintained.

Kaji, Hono and their friends, Toakase, Alefosio and Koloa are present in the training grounds with two other people: a man, and a woman. They are all practising martial arts, a form specific to Mir. Very flowy with strong stances and harsh leg and arm strikes.

Kaji is in a narrow stance as he hits punching mitts with Koloa. He is stiff and anxious, still thinking about the events of the past couple of days.

'Tohro, you need to relax your body and move with the flow.' Koloa says to Kaji while holding up punching mitts.

Kaji grunts with frustration as he swings his arms to punch the mitts, left and right, as hard as he could. He forgets to use his hips and relax his shoulders, worsening his stress, physically and mentally.

'Tohro, relax.'

'I am relaxed.' Kaji snaps.

Koloa lowers his arms as he takes a step back from Kaji, breathing slowly and purposefully. He strives to keep his cool as he provides Kaji with no reaction.

'It really does not seem like it.' He firmly informs Kaji.

Kaji tenses up, feeling frustrated and annoyed, wanting to burn off some energy. He is sick of people telling him what to do today, especially when he just wants an escape from his own mind through smashing a few things.

'WELL I AM.' He exclaims lividly, raising his voice to make a point.

Koloa regards Kaji, challenging his stare. 'Okay, okay. Well, why don't we head over to the bags over there.' He says, trying to defuse the situation after noting that Kaji's anger and frustration is out of character.

'Alright.' Kaji says relaxing a little.

Kaji and Koloa walk across the training grounds, passing the women as they forge their arms and legs on one another. Proceeding further towards the punching bags, they cross Alefosio as he spars with another man. Alefosio is young yet large while the man he is sparring with is much smaller yet much quicker.

They finally arrive at the punching bags as Koloa reaches out for the nearest sack of sand. Koloa looks at Kaji with compassion and apprehension flicker in his eyes, he knows all Kaji wants to do is smash out his frustration and is in no state to train and practice technique at this moment.

'I will hold it for you so you have more force. Alright?'

'Alright.' Kaji nods.

He stares down the punching bag, sizing it up as he takes a steady breath. He starts to punch it hard. He thinks about some combinations using his fists, forearms and elbows as he makes an effort to remould the punching bag, breathing out with each and every strike. 'Remember to relax your body.' Koloa reminds Kaji calmly.

Kaji looks at Koloa as anger rises within him, unsatisfied with being told what to do again. I am relaxed, he thinks to himself as he strikes the bag with violent frustration.

'AGH. I am!!' He bellows.

Koloa sighs. 'You really aren't.'

'AHH.' Kaji shouts, fuming with anger as he strikes the sack of sand with a belligerent kick. A burst of pain shoots through his lower leg as his shin makes contact with the bag. 'Ahhh ha haa ow.' He cries.

Koloa lets go of the mitts and confronts Kaji to see if he is okay. He is hopping on one foot clutching at his leg and scrunching his face.

'Are you alright?'

'I'M FINE!' He shouts feeling the anger surge through him like an insatiable fire starting to spread.

Everyone in the training grounds stiffen, ceasing their activities. All the women stop forging their arms and legs and Alefosio stops sparring. They all glare at Kaji as he falls backwards holding his leg. He is oblivious to everyone's shocked and disgusted stares.

Hono drops what she is doing and walks over to Kaji and Koloa with clear revulsion, she isn't mad but she is not happy either. 'Tohro!! What are you doing!?' She calls out while still walking towards him. 'This isn't like you at all.'

'Shut up, everyone just shut up.' He lashes out.

Tense and shaking with rage, he slowly brings himself to his feet before walking over to Hono with his fists quivering. The fire inside of him is barely holding, he can feel the burn through his chest and down his arms. He speaks quietly with a clear indignation in his tone.

'Can I speak to you for a moment?' He asks Hono, now standing next to her.

'What is it?' She responds, clearly annoyed.

He takes a deep breath in an attempt to calm the fire. Noticing that everyone is still looking at him with Alefosio only just putting his sparring partner back on the ground, he looks back at Hono apprehensively and notices her facial expression.

'I can't get the fire out.' He says, quietly and ashamedly.

'Hmm?' She hums as she waits for the reason behind his behaviour

'I feel like I am burning inside, I can't think. All I feel is fire.'

She takes a breath and looks at him with her head tilted. 'Tohro... that is no excuse for what just happened.' She explains.

Kaji took a deep breath and held it. He thought of the flame within himself. He pictured it moving to his lungs before a burning feeling began in his chest, tickling the back of his throat. With a deep exhale a small amount of flames birthed from his open mouth but dissipated into the air just as quickly as they formed.

She surveys the training grounds, focusing on all of the concerned and frightened faces. She sighs and looks back at Kaji. 'What did you have in mind?' She asks him firmly.

'Sparring.' He counters as he breathes heavily with smoke emanating from each of his exhales.

Hono takes a deep breath and looks at Kaji. She frowns, noticing how deep his breaths are. 'You and I both know that, that is probably not a good idea.' She says to him candidly.

Kaji meets Hono's eyes as he loosens himself up. He studies the other people on the grounds, inhaling and exhaling slowly as he does so in an attempt to calm himself down.

'What did you have in mind?' He asks.

Hono sighs. 'I will have a talk with them and see what I can do.'

'Okay.'

Hono walks over towards the women, gesturing for Alefosio, Koloa and the other man to come over to her. Kaji stands, feeling the heat within his body rise. He tries to understand what they are saying but can't read their lips. He could see the gestures of the women, Alefosio nodding to Hono and Koloa gesturing in what appeared to be a serious explanation of his concerns of the situation. He could feel the fire within him but makes an effort to push it down while trying to concentrate on Hono.

She nods to everyone and they all line up in a row, women to one side and men to the other, as she walks back over to Kaji.

'So the plan is that you will fight the three guys over there, Alefosio, Koloa and Manu at once and us gals… will be watching and keeping an eye out.' She explains to him.

'Okay, that sounds good.'

'If we say stop. You must stop.' She firmly elaborates to Kaji.

'Got it.'

Kaji has his head down while holding his breath as he and his sister walk over to the others for Hono to briefly address everyone.

'He is aware of how it is going to go. Tohro into the middle.'

Kaji nods at Hono as he walks towards the middle of the training ground, the sun scorching hot and blaring fiercely against his face.

He can feel the fire in his lungs burning up as he positions himself into an attentive stance. He can feel the heat of the fire spreading through his arms and his legs as he stares at the other men with a blank face, trying to focus on the moment and extinguish his inner flame.

'Get ready.' Hono calls out. Kaji and the men get their guards up.

'Three, two, one… go.' She calls out.

Koloa moves towards Kaji, slowly and cautiously, while Alefosio and Manu stay behind to observe Kaji's reactions.

Koloa reaches Kaji, his body is loose as he bounces on his toes. He throws a hook punch at Kaji, as Kaji ducks and strikes him in the stomach with an upset punch.

Koloa wheezes and falls to his knees to catch his breath. Kaji turns around and sees Alefosio moving towards him, his guard is up as he throws a kick at him. Kaji was not expecting it and quickly jumps out of the way noticing that Manu had come at him from behind.

Kaji hastily jumps out of the way in an attempt to line them both up. Alefosio jumps to the side of Manu and throws a spinning heel kick at him. He blocks the kick and Alefosio follows up with a strong solid back kick.

Kaji jumps out of the way while blocking the kick, he follows up with a solid side-kick to Alefosio's liver. He collapses momentarily.

Manu jumps at Kaji, aimlessly throwing punches at him. He bounces on his toes and expertly dodges each opposing punch. He jumps back and forth while looking for an opening from Manu. He blocks a few punches thrown at him before jumping in with a side kick followed by a back kick at Manu.

Manu gets pushed back and slightly winded. Koloa and Alefosio collectively stand as they place their guards up, aiming at Kaji. They strike. Kaji dodges, reacting with a series of fast punches and sweeps, he gets a fragmented vision of the strange man who seems to be knackered. Sweat drips off of him as the fear consumes him. Nonetheless, he pushes through the pain.

Kaji felt everything Ookonan was feeling: the pain, the fear and the adrenaline. He tries not to panic but as he throws a strike his hand burns as hot as flame.

'NOT NOW!!' Kaji shrieked.

The women watching immediately notice the change in Kaji: this new fear, and the sudden surge of energy and heat radiating from him. Toakase turns to Hono and raises an eyebrow. She contemplates striding towards the heart of the grounds in order to put an end to the sparring but is held back by Hono, knowing that she will likely get badly hurt by Kaji's unpredictable flame.

Hono, who is at the end of her tether, steps forward in an attempt to end the sparring match. Kaji remains ruthlessly throwing strikes at Manu, unable to notice Hono. He moves speedily with tremendous power behind each of his strikes directed towards Manu, who is now only defending and attempting to get out of his way.

'STOP!' Hono howls, loud enough for the whole capital to hear.

Kaji is unable to hear anything around him. He feels the same fear Ookonan does, hearing the twisted screams, gurgles and growls of the demonics as they mix eerily with the intimate crackling and hissing sounds of a nearby electric storm.

He is now unaware of what is happening around him, feeling as though he is in Hondon with the demonics surrounding him and his adrenaline pumping wildly. He breathes out fire like a starving and furious dragon.

Manu, Koloa and Alefosio collectively step back in horror, befuddled by Kaji's unhinged behaviour. The women watch anxiously from the sidelines, looking at Hono for their next directives.

'Tohro, your sister called to stop.' Manu shouts with a stern tone.

Kaji's senses are narrowed: his sight tunnelled and his hearing almost non-existent. He is stuck in this twisted daydream as if his soul is lingering within these unknown formidable plains. He is unable to make out what is happening around him in actuality as he launches himself at Alefosio with a jumping kick to the chest followed by a strong and deep punch to the face.

He turns around, catching sight of various nightmarish demonics in the training ground, despite them not really being there. He launches himself at them, performing a roundhouse kick followed by a spinning heel kick, drawing large bursts of flame as he does it. Noticing that his strikes are resulting in nothing, he begins to panic.

He turns his head followed by the rest of his body. His friends, his family, his loved ones have all distorted, no longer recognising any familiar faces, instead what faces Kaji are the contorted faces of these hideous vile beasts with deep, crimson, blood-red eyes. He jumps into the air and throws a thick roaring flame at them followed by a spinning hook kick harming both Alefosio and his sister Hono.

Hono screams as the flames hit her in the face. She grabs her scorched face in pain as she falls to the ground, trying to protect herself. Toakase runs to Hono for support while Koloa launches himself at Kaji, knocking him to the ground. He pins Kaji's chest to the ground with the help of Alefosio.

Kaji screams: exhausted, pained, and afraid, as all he can see is the whirlwind of electricity and the macabre outlines of demonics. He feels helpless, shaking while being pinned to the ground, unable to truly tell where he is or what is going on.

The vision of Ookonan begins to fade, replaced with the training grounds in Mir. He scans his surroundings and recognises his friends: Koloa and Alefosio. He notices that they are holding him down, pinning him against the ground. He catches sight of Manu and the women standing along the edge of the grounds. From the peripheral's of Kaji's eyes, he discerns a girl who is crying intensely on the ground. She appears to be burnt, clutching at her burn wounds along her face.

What did I do? Kaji thought to himself in horror. Who is that and what did I do? He looks at Koloa and Alefosio, who are both covered in burns. He meets Manu's eyes before peering down and noticing that something had caused his arm to be almost incinerated. The girl who had been clutching her face gazes up at Kaji.

It was Hono. He looks at her, petrified and miserable, noting that her face is burned and blistered, around her left eye, ear and cheek. Realisation hits him like a tsunami of guilt as he begins to comprehend the fact that he has harmed the people he cares the most for. Tears start streaming down his now damp face uncontrollably with no care for mercy as his vision slowly becomes tunneled and his breathing becomes fractured. He couldn't forgive himself for bringing so much harm and destruction to this place of peace and, worst of all, to his family.

Chapter 9

He feels his body sinking, the weight of his arms and legs are too much to move. He feels himself sinking deeper into the abyss as darkness surrounds him. It's consuming him as he falls, his shoulders too heavy to hold up, it feels almost inescapable. This feeling was wrong, it needed to end.

Suddenly a light pierced the darkness. It stung at his eyes as the sinking feeling began to disappear as his body ascended towards the light rapidly. Ookonan had no idea what was going on. He began to hear voices, voices he did not know. They whispered and wondered and finally small snippets of conversation entered his fuzzy mind. 'Is this the one...' spoke a voice, its volume waning as he rushed to the light.

Another voice called out. 'It was him I saw it the demonics...' The female voice faded as the clanging sounds of a hammer against an anvil filled his head. Its sound rang and rang louder and louder as he rushed towards the surface. He began to feel his arms again as he saw the light and breached the surface.

Ookonan opens his eyes. He is in a room not familiar to him with a large window to the side of his bed. The natural light of the sun illuminates the room with golden light, enhanced by the golden plating of some of the furniture.

He slowly wakes and lets his eyes adjust to the room. He feels his feet resting on a footstool, his body being too big for the bed. He felt linen on his skin as his head lay against a large thick fluffy pillow. It was comfortable but it wasn't natural. He looks down at his body, noticing that his skin is clean, really clean, not sticky, sweaty or clammy.

But why is he naked? He thought as his vision cleared. He looks around the room, now seeing some of the furniture. Beautiful highly polished wooden furniture crafted with burl patterning. Gold plating or coating were present on some of the polished furniture. It is upholstered with fabrics of white, maroon, blue, yellow, purple, silver and gold. It's fascinating but he cannot recall how he got here.

He thought of his journey in the grassland, the days spent walking and having no idea where he was, the day spent walking to a structure set on the horizon. The last thing he remembers is fighting demonics while his body burned from the lack of rest, he remembers the storm he created to end the demonic raid, then nothing.

He sits himself up letting the blankets fall into his lap. The chatter outside gets louder as excited women watch him eagerly from the window. Trying to ignore them he scans the room for a better understanding of his surroundings. Beautiful wooden floors, walls and the ceiling have intricate patterns consisting of those same colours on the upholstered furniture. Whereas the floor is covered in fur mats for foot warmth.

He looks over at the women looking at him, their grins a source of discomfort as they stare at his bare naked chest. Scarred from his many battles have these women drooling over him. He quickly pulls the blankets back up to cover his torso.

Without getting up he quickly scans the room for his belongings, looking over at the corners of the room and beside the bed for his backpack and clothes. He leans over the side of the bed, nothing. Still holding the blankets close to him to avoid the gaze of the thirsty women he peaks over the front edge of the bed, also nothing.

'What is going on? Where are my clothes?' He questions while attempting to remain calm as he pulls himself back to bed.

In the midst of the discourse, someone knocks on the door. He snaps his head and looks at the door, Vekk! One of the women from the window is coming in, he thinks to himself in a moment of panic. He scans the room one last time in search of his belongings.

'I am coming in.' A male voice says from the other side.

'Uh… okay.' He calls back, calming down.

The door opens, a charming man walks in, closing the door behind himself. He is of average height for a human, similar to the men living in the black forest. He has thick dark hair, well shaped eyebrows complimenting his eyes and olive skin. His face is chiselled, a strong sharp jaw and a well shaped nose as though a god or deity shaped him themself.

He smiles at Ookonan as he walks over to the window. His clothing is much the same as the furniture, well crafted, but also in maroon, white, blue and yellow. He closes the curtains of the window which is followed by the vocalised groaning of disappointed women.

'Did you have a good sleep?'

Ookonan remains silent, still feeling uncomfortable with an additional feeling of dread, all he wants is his backpack and to leave. The most unsettling part for him is not only waking naked but having no recollection of how he got into the room.

'Well?' The man asks again.

'Uuhh.' Ookonan vocalises. Unsure on how to act around the charming man whose mannerisms are kind but also unusual to him.

'You have been asleep for more than a day, I would hope your sleep would be good.'

'How did I get here?'

'You were found passed out by some of the guards.'

'Why am I naked?'

'You allegedly saved the town from the demonics.' He says, ignoring the question as he gives Ookonan a warm smile.

'Do not avoid my question!.'

The man raises his perfect eyebrows and takes a step back. He smiles as he masks his feeling of intimidation towards Ookonan.

'Not thanking us?'

He sighs as he sits up, letting the blankets fall off his chest, exposing his toned body and battle scars. 'I need to be going. I was not intending on stopping here.' He says lying under his breath.

'We wanted to make sure you would be well rested, but we do not like people using our bed or other facilities being unclean.' He explains, adjusting his collar. 'So we cleaned you before putting you in bed.'

A discomfort comes over him about the man, something isn't sitting right with him about the kind treatment. He worries that they might want him for other means or to never let him leave. Why would they take his belongings?

'Do not worry, you were not asleep for very long.'

'You told me I was asleep for a couple days. But I am not worried.'
He lied. 'Well I need to stretch my legs after laying for so long.' He takes off
the covers and gets out of bed before the man is able to interject.

'Oh.' The man vocalises. He looks Ookonans body over, he's heavily
scarred from the battles he's endured, sharp and blunt weapons including
swords and claws. He stands motionless as Ookonan walks up to him,
towering over him.

'Where are my belongings? I would prefer to be on my way.'

'Your clothing is still being cleaned.' He says, taking a step away
from Ookonan.

Ookonan takes another half step towards him. He wasn't having it,
He looked down at the man who was staring straight at his chest.

'I would like to be covered and leaving.' He says firmly.

'I was hoping at the least you stay in bed until we are done.' He says
as he tilts his head back to look at him.

'I am leaving.'

The Man rushes to the door barring him from leaving. 'No no wait
wait.'

'Why?' Growled Ookonan, his patience completely gone at this point.

The man, reluctant and conservative looks down at Ookonan's crotch
then back up at his face. Intimidating. He smiles at him and works back his
charm. The women clearly heard Ookonan say he was just going to leave as
their chatter started up again with a lot of oos.

'I will grab your bag but your clothing is still being washed, there is a
lot of demon blood on it.'

Ookonan grunts at the man. Displeased with how long he has been
there and how long his possessions have been held from him, he is not going
to make life easy for the town if they will not let him leave. He walks away
from the man and faces the curtains of the window.

'Clearly by your size your clothing is not replaceable. Please let the
wash ladies clean your clothing.'

'Bring me my backpack.' He demanded. His tone is even and the
underlying threat clear.

'I will be right back.' He says in a confident and warm tone.

'Also.'

'Yes?' The man stops and looks over at Ookonan.

'If I find out that I am a prisoner.' He turns his head slightly over his
shoulder back around to look at the man. 'That would be incredibly bad news
for you.'

The man leaves the room, closing the door behind him with a slight click of the door handle. Once the footsteps face, Ookonan walks over to the window. He pulls back the curtain slightly and looks through.

The community is not like he's seen before, very green and grassy, people have their own little farms and gardens consisting of different crops. Livestock are in different mandated fenced areas with the exception of chickens roaming freely around the village. Small roads link homes and community areas together, he can see the people working together and just spending time together as though its a perfect little area seemingly without worry of the outside world.

He can see the outside walls from the window, strange how he was curious about this structure but now all that is on his mind is how to get out. The people have a strange reaction towards bodies which is an extremely uncomfortable feeling for him.

The door opens followed by the swift footsteps of the man. He turns around to see him holding his backpack, so large it makes him look like a child. He walks over to Ookonan and hands him the backpack which is strangely much lighter than it used to be. Which would explain how the man had such an easy time carrying it.

'Your backpack.'

'Obviously.' Ookonan grunts back. He opens it while maintaining full eye contact with the man. The bag is disorganised and messy with things very obviously missing. He searches for the items worth more than gold, his spice, tea and teapot.

'Where are my spices?' Ookonan demanded.

'I am not sure what you are talking about.' He lies.

He walks over to the man and stands over him this time with the goal of intimidation. The man slowly backed up as each of Ookonan's steps echoed on the wooden floors. The sound deep and heavy his eyes began to narrow as the man finally reached the wall with nowhere to go.

As this happened his eyes became unfocused as a new vision started. The world shifted and Ookonan suddenly found himself standing on the edge of a cliff overlooking the ocean. The water was dark and choppy and the stars in the sky above were ones he had never seen before. Then with a voice not of his own screamed a scream of anguish which tore from his throat shattering the vision in front of him. Returning him to reality, standing over the man who's back is pressed so far against the wall he may as well have become the wall.

'If you do not know where my spices went.' Ookonan began as a surge of wind started to pick up in the small room, rattling the window.

'Then I will raid your stocks until I have back what was taken.'

'Well we would not want to be bad hosts now do we?' The man shrieks.

'Bring me my spices and clothing immediately.'

'Yes… I will get you spices and see if they are done.'

✝

Upon return, the man has clean and neatly folded clothes as well as all that was stolen from Ookonan's backpack sitting on top. He walks over to Ookonan sitting on the bed and places it all next to him.

Ookonan goes through it all, it's all there. But also the clothes are mended as well as cleaned. The leather jacket has stitches through it, his shirt and pants have been patched, all the holes and tears are gone. But before putting his clothing back on, he goes through the stolen items, opening the pouches one by one. It's all there.

He puts on his clothes, and lets out a sign of relief knowing his belongings have been returned and he can safely return to the wilderness of Hondon. But one thing that perplexes him, why did they feel the need to steal his spice and teapot.

'I guess you will be off now.'

'Yes… Thank you for looking after me and I apologise for not trusting you.' Ookonan says to him while putting on his shirt, noticing how nice it smelled.

'I understand… Trust is a difficult thing in this world. But one other thing, there is going to be a feast tonight, I insist you stay for it.'

Chapter 10

Kaji walks alone in the forest along the cliffside, the waves of the sea are loud and destructive. The sound is enhanced by the waves smashing along the cliff wall, each wave leaving a cool sea mist that flows through the forest leaving spectacles and patterns of salt in its path. He can taste the salt in the air with every breath he takes as he steps along the cliff edge eyeing the Mirish sea and the other islands close by.

Deep in thought he thinks about his sister, the destruction he did to her. He couldn't bear to face her again after he inflicted those wounds on her. He wished he knew why he had been creating fire with his hands, he wished he knew why his body combusts but most of all, why him?

He can't get the thought of his sister's burned face out of his mind. I did that, I lost control, I hurt her and she may never see again, he thought to himself. He stares at the sea and the surrounding islands, he needs to leave.

The trees rustle, startling him. The last thing he needed at this moment was to be followed. He turns around to see who it is. It's just the nocturnal animals coming out for the night. 'Why is this happening?' He asks himself, holding back tears as he turns back to face the cliff. 'It's so painful… And it's destructive.'

Tears start forming in his eyes as he looks down at the waves more than twenty metres below his feet. He grips the rock with his toes, anger and frustration sweeps over him. How many more people are going to get hurt from his uncontrollable flame?

The visions begin yet again. He sees himself in a small room, the ceiling very low for his comfort and he stands above a little man with some fear in his eyes. He sees electricity sparking around his arms with small amounts of wind around him.

Kaji closes his eyes as he enters the vision world, no longer is he too big for the room, but he sees a tall naked man with blond hair, pointy ears and glowing lightning blue eyes. He towers over the man standing with his back on the wall, he seems to be threatening him but Kaji is in no headspace to be hearing any language but his own. He looks around the room, the size feels very normal except the design.

Kaji watches the smaller man leave the room and as he does his vision begins to fade. He opens his eyes which are now glowing a bright orangey red which illuminates the dusk around him as his body burns igniting his fingers and toes.

He grips the rock with his hot toes and clenches his fists. 'AAAAAAAAAAAAAAAAAAAAAHHHHHHHHHHHHHHHHHHHHHH.' He screams. Filling himself with more raw emotion he struggles to control, as the flame consumes his limbs.

He grits his teeth as his torso combusts, the burning flame consumes him, burning away his clothing as it replaces the blood in his veins with bright orange flame. He tries to hold himself back as pain consumes his body, but holding anything back has now become impossible.

"WHYYYYYYY!' He screams as heat explodes from him burning away the lichen on the rock he stands on and the small plants around him.

'AAAAAAAAAAAAAAAAAAAAAAAAAAAHHHHHHHHHHHHHHH HHHH.' He screams, throwing a ball of fire from his mouth at the sea which lands into the water disappearing with a large puff of steam.

It dawns on him, he looks down at his hands. It's happened again but far worse, he's a glowing ball of fire. That rage starts to dissipate as the rock he stands on begins to melt into hot lava sinking him into it.

'Ah ah shh noo.' He starts to panic. The more self aware he becomes of the fire in his veins the more pain he begins to feel. Realising that he cannot put out the fire he tries to step off the rock, now a sticky hot molten liquid that is slowly pouring off the cliff.

He tries to climb off, instead tripping on the cold untouched rock instead. The cold rock was shocking and painful. Like stepping onto ice. A new panic arises as he falls to the water, would the cold water kill him.

'AHHHHHHHHHHH.' He screams as his life flashes before his eyes.

He plummets into the water, extinguishing immediately into a puff of smoke, however the enormous amount of heat he produced softened the blow of the water as it boiled and bubbled the instant he touched it.

But if the shock of the cold water wasn't enough, the rough sea mixed with his heat throws him around, making it impossible for him to get air. It slams him into the cliff rocks knocking him out cold.

A bright red figure moved towards him as his normal dark complexion returned to his skin and the blood returned to his veins. Olive arms wrap around him and pull him away from the cliff rocks.

'Kaji Tohroshatan, today is not your time.' A powerful woman's voice said. The figure with long flowing bright red hair and colourful clothing holds him, taking him to the shoreline.

†

The morning sun beams through the gaps in the dazzling carmine red drawn curtains of the hospital room, in a perfect arch of yellow light. There are various brightly coloured flowers and plants dotted artfully around the room, clearly well cared for. The walls of the room are a greenish white, paired nicely with a light blue tiled floor.

Kaji rests on what should otherwise be a pleasant hospital bed, complete with a beige knitted blanket and soft white pillows. Instead, his eyes twitch uncontrollably and his eyelids dart wildly as he is stuck in some disturbing and unending nightmare.

The events of the previous twenty four hours play continuously in his head, like a broken visual record. The melting and the falling. The rock and the cliff.

'No... hm. Eh... noo.' He mumbles. All that he could see was his cursed flame, and the pure, unfiltered terror in his friend's and sister's eyes as he set the training ground aflame. I must be dead, he thought as the nightmare persisted.

The door gently opens, carrying the noise of the doctors, nurses and other hospital staff into the room. A nurse walks in with a tray of near frozen food and drink. Fruits, berries, fish and rice as well as an icy cold drink to pair with it all.

They approach Kaji, closing the door behind themself and allowing the noise to dissipate into silence. They place the tray on the table next to his bed, as they look at him wrapped precariously in the beige hospital blanket with his head sunk deep within the thick white pillow.

The nurse takes a step back, unsure of what to do as they notice Kaji twitching and groaning in his sleep with a hardened breath.

'Ahh.' The nurse vocalises, clearly lost. 'His Imperial highness Tohroshatan… I think it's time you woke up.' The nurse states as they nervously walk up to the side of Kaji's bed, acutely aware of what Kaji's stress has driven him to do over the past couple of days and fearful of the consequences in which disturbing his sleep might result. 'Tohroshatan…. Tohroshatan… Wake up…'

Kaji opens his eyes, his breathing still intense and his body still twitching. He starts examining the room, noticing that he is in an entirely different setting than what he had been expecting. Now somewhat aware of his surroundings, he steadiers his breathing in an attempt to calm himself.

'You are in hospital.' The nurse manages to get out with a soothing tone.

Kaji's eyes draw towards the nurse who is dressed in a traditional mirish skirt both men and women wear as well as a green top and their hair is wrapped up in a well fitted hat. He's trying to understand his own situation while contemplating whether or not he is still dreaming. 'How did I get here?' He inquires, his mind muddled.

'I will answer questions later, time for you to sit up and have something to eat.' They instruct while reaching for the tray on the table next to him.

Kaji sits and slides himself up the bed as the knitted blanket falls off him. He is dressed in a backless hospital gown made of rough beige fabric. The nurse's hands fasten around the dinner tray as they bring it closer to Kaji and place it gently on his lap. Presented neatly on the tray is a bowl of watery soup paired with a bun and a selection of saturated fruits, as well as a tall glass of water and a generous glass of juice. Everything presented on the tray appeared to be icy cold, as if it had all been deliberately cooled down. He did not know if this semi-frozen abomination would manage to stop the fire in his veins, but he did know that word had clearly spread like wildfire, with the entire hospital becoming aware of his newfound power.

Kaji looks at the tray before him with a deadpan expression, almost disgusted, as he pokes at the food with his finger.

'Make sure you at least have something to drink.' The nurse says, smiling, before leaving the room.

Kaji, still disgusted, stares down at his frosty food. Who eats frozen fruit let alone an icy soup? He thought to himself. He ignores the tray, instead looking around the room, truly examining it for the first time. He had never stayed overnight in the hospital before, and never anticipated to. The room itself was actually rather large and accommodating, with two arched windows, an entrance door, and a second more mysterious door which led to some unknown place.

Kaji scratches his temple inquisitively, trying to remember what had happened; how he had gotten to the hospital and why he was there in the first place. 'How did I get here? I remember...'

He runs his hands through his hair, grabbing at his scalp as a sensation overcomes him. It felt as if worms had invaded his brain, wriggling around and rewiring his mind. He sees himself walking through a forest off a cliff side. The waves below are soft but muffled as he couldn't bring himself to remember the sounds well. He recalled the sound of screaming. His own screaming. It was so piercingly loud that he couldn't even hear himself think. All of a sudden he was ablaze, with some flickering light surrounding him from head to toe: it was fire, and it was scorching. So scorching that he managed to melt the rock below him into some thick molten glass like material. It glowed bright shades of red and orange like flowing magma.

He tensed at the thought. 'I was at the coast last night. I remember the coast. But not how I got here.' He mutters to himself slowly while looking down at his hands.

'I really hope this was all just a dream...' He says to himself unsure how long he has been in this hospital room for 'Was I in a coma?'

The noise outside of Kaji's room became louder and more audible as voices appeared to get closer to the door. He strains his ears, allowing him to hear the conversation transpiring between the nurses and who could only be the doctor.

'I do not think he is safe to be around.' A voice says.

Kaji slides himself up the bed before leaning forward in an attempt to more successfully eavesdrop. Fear starts to spread throughout his body, crawling up to and into his brain. He is unsure what is going to happen nor what his future now holds.

'We should see, I think he needs some help.' The nurse who was looking after him says.

'Yes but he—' The voice attempted to say before the nurse cut them off.

'Enough, he has had some trauma. Let me speak with him.' The nurse says harshly to the voice speaking on the other side of the door.

More unintelligible muffles radiate from the other side of the door. Kaji's fear intensifies as the hospital staff talk about him behind his back. Uninvited thoughts invade his mind as he begins to worry about the possibility of being locked up and hidden away from the rest of the world, or worse: being sent off to the outskirts of Mir. Well aware that the meeting occurring outside of his door is in relation to him, he makes a desperate effort to make out what they could possibly be saying.

'Not another word. I will speak with him and I will be back.' The nurse says sternly, aimed towards the unknown voice on the other side of the door.

The nurse opens the door slowly, gently, and carefully, entering the room before closing it behind themself. 'Well good morning Tohroshatan.' They say, although it clearly isn't.

Kaji does not smile back. He is visibly worried and tense, concerned for what the future holds for him. He is unable to concentrate on the present moment, only his destructive new powers and its threat.

'Uuuhh.' He vocalised, unsure on how to respond.

The nurse hastily examines Kaji's report as they further approach him. Now standing next to him, she looks down at the tray in front of him noticing he had touched nothing. It was all still the same as when they brought it in for him, only the food and drinks were no longer icy.

'Not interested in eating are you?'

'How did I get here?' Kaji inquired, ignoring the comment on his lack of appetite.

The nurse takes a seat next to Kaji's bed. Finally acknowledging his question. It was obvious that he was stressed and attempting to put the pieces together.

'You were found at the beach.'

'Uh huh.' He vocalises while gripping the sides of his bed tighter.

The nurse takes a breath, they think for a moment on how to answer without causing him any further worry.

'You were completely naked and it looked like you had been passed out all night... Tohroshatan... When you were found they could not tell if you were alive or not or what was going on.'

He stares at the nurse wide eyed as his breathing becomes more heavy. Many thoughts start to travel through his head. He looks straight ahead at the greenish white wall and swallows his saliva. He tenses his jaw and takes a deep uncontrolled breath before asking his next question.

'How long have I been here?' He finally asks the nurse.

'Only a few hours, I was surprised you woke up when I went to wake you.' They confirmed with a calming voice.

Kaji's mouth begins to feel dry as his breathing becomes more jagged and deep. His stress is on the rise as his blood pressure starts to increase. 'I need to be left alone.' He announces, his voice shaky and far from stable.

'I need to ask you some questions, your Imperial Highness Tohroshatan.' The nurse declares, taken back by Kaji's directness. They remain seated and study Kaji without touching him.

The irises of Kaji's eyes start to glow a vibrant yet foreboding shade of orange as he struggles to control his own emotions. He looks directly at the nurse with an unreadable and equally unstable expression painted against his face.

'Please can it wait… I was hoping it was a dream…. It has to be a dream.'

'I do not think any of it was a dream. I will leave you be so you can take it all in.' The nurse says to Kaji.

The nurse removes their hand, as they stand. They nod at Kaji before walking towards the door, opening it and closing it behind as they exit.

He is now alone in the room, just him and his own thoughts. He scans the room briefly before looking down at both of his wrists, assuring himself that he has not yet been arrested.

'I am not sure why I had to check to see if I am tied up…' He mutters quietly to himself. 'Relieving to know I'm not.'

He scans the room again, this time searching for any form of clothing he could snatch for himself. Adjacent to his bed, he notices an empty chair with a pair of neatly folded and well looked after traditional Mirish trousers that had clearly been left behind by someone.

He convinces his aching body to get out of bed before walking towards the chair, swift and silent, keeping any eye on the door. His backside is bare from the backless gown, causing him to feel even more on edge and uncomfortable.

Kaji grabs hold of the pants and quickly slips them on, lifting the hospital gown as to gain access to the front of the pants in order to do up the rope around his waist. He allows the gown to drop over his newfound pants as he walks back to the bed and lies back down, pulling the covers back over himself in order to hide the fact that he is wearing someone else's pants.

Kaji stares at the ceiling, slipping back into the chaos of his own mind and being led astray by a cesspool of his own thoughts. He tenses as the memories of what had occurred the previous day cross his mind yet again. He sees the burning uncontrollable flames, reddish orange in colour and scorching in nature. The flashback consumes Kaji, almost as much as the inferno consumes the training grounds. He sees the flames brush across everyone as they reach out for his sister, igniting her.

Fresh blistering tears run down her now burnt face as Kaji is held down by his friends. Trapped in this miserable evocation, his breathing intensifies. 'No! No!.. Okay it can't be real.' He says to himself, wanting nothing more than for his words to be true.

He closes his eyes, focusing on his breathing for a brief moment, each and every inhale and exhale, slowing them down in an attempt to calm himself. He opens his eyes again and surveys the room, his breathing is more steady but his stress remains intense.

Lifting up his right arm, he examines his hand. He turns it around in order to look at the back of it as he concentrates deeply, thinking about the strange looking man in his vision and his mysterious powers. A new vision of the strange man invades Kaji's mind.

He is wandering down one of the many pathways in the grassland village and he seems to be escorting a small dirty child back to his home. Upon reaching the child's home. It's a beautifully carved wooden house but it just looks like a boring cabin to Kaji. It's colourful with serpents carved into the pillars and it's decorated with plenty of plants. He is greeted by a burly man with dark yellow teeth, a questionable figure who could only be the child's father.

Kaji snaps himself out of the vision as he notices a small flame appear on the palm of his hand. Dread fills his veins as he stares at the small flickering flame dancing on his hand. 'It was real. It all happened.' He says to himself, barely audible. He quickly turns his head and looks at the door as the scarlet flame on his palm extinguishes.

There is some loud muffling coming from the other side. Whoever is behind that door is clearly trying hard to either get themself into the room or thwart someone else from entering. Anxiety flushes over him as he begins to sweat steam. He leans closer towards the door, he could place who the voices belong to and understand what they were saying.

'I need to see my brother.' Hono demanded, raising her voice.

'Yes but you need to rest, you are hurt and he is clearly dangerous at the moment.' Responds the mysterious voice from earlier: masculine, deep, and equally as loud and stern.

'Yes and clearly it was an accident. I need to see him.' She demands, keeping her voice thunderous.

Kaji begins to panic as he swiftly gets out of bed without a second thought and moves towards the closest window. He fumbles around the edges of the window in dismay, searching for a latch as more sweat steams down his face. He finds the latch, sighing in relief before unhooking it in an effort to open the window and realising that there is another latch to unlatch. He continues to miserably fumble with the window as he keeps a steady eye on the door. Finally finding success in unlatching the window, he opens it as his ears remain attentive, listening to the conversation occurring outside of the door mere steps away.

'You can't go in there at this time!' A nurse shouts.

Kaji briskly jumps out the window, leaving no room for thought nor any trace that he was ever there to begin with, aside from a freshly open window. At this moment Hono bursts through the door with the nurse chasing after her.

She has gauze patches and bandages on the right side of her face and neck with a special compression holding it all together.

'YOU CANNOT BE IN HERE!' The nurse shouts assertively at Hono as they follow behind her. Hono pays no attention to the nurse as fear and anxiety build within her, she wants nothing more than to find her brother.

She searches around the room and notices the empty bed. Hono walks towards the window, noticing both latches have been undone with the window wide open. She looks back over at the nurse holding back her tears as her fear takes control of her, worrying the worst for her brother.

'Where is he?' she asks, her voice full of consternation and her eyes weary.

'I do not know.' The nurse exclaims, equally as shocked by his absence as Hono.

Chapter 11

The community of the grassland village is almost like no other, the people are happily and comfortably walking around their homes, enjoying the gardens between the houses and walking on stone paths, like there is no worry of the world outside of their wooden walls. Women chat to each other while carrying baskets of home grown fruits and vegetables as well as breads and pastries they have made. While the men dig up weeds, plant new plants and plow some of the yards.

Ookonan steps out of one of the buildings, his backpack strapped to his back with all his belongings on him. He scans his new surroundings, the place is beautiful but strange. Not a single person looked anxious about any disease or demonic. Just people having a good time but in segregated roles. The buildings are all small, wooden with a cozy feel to them but not a single one has spice rubbed into their pillars, windows, doors or entrances.

He steps out onto the road and starts his walk to where he hopes to find the exit to the place. As he treks through, he notices more unusual things. Children playing in the mud, large animals in fenced off areas and every house has some sort of paprika plant as an ornament, including reaper plants, at the home entrances also hung herbs, garlic and onions.

He keeps his eye on the wall as he walks along the road. He tries to ignore the people noticing him, waving at him and smiling at him. But his discomfort about the village increases as he can hear women giggling, the same women peering through the window where he slept.

'How do I get out of here?' He quietly asks himself, waving back at the women. 'Why do I feel uneasy in this place?'

He refers his gaze back at the wall as he continues along the road. Even in his tall stature, he struggles to find the exit. The noises of the chatter, the carts being pulled by large animals, the children playing and the insects chirping are too intense for him. He tries to tune it out and just follows a man pulling his cart, stacked with sacks of grains and vegetables from people's gardens. This cart should be leaving the village for trade, he thought to himself; But he is moving so slow with a wheel that is about to pop off.

He lags behind eyeing the wall for the exit, but a large building grabs his attention. In the centre of the village this long but also tall building sat, it has plants growing on its roof, it has large doors and large sloped log pillars that support the roof. The building itself is beautiful; it is colourful with engravings of plants, animals and people, the decorative beauty, the same colours as the room he slept in, gold, red, blue and purple but there are more like green.

A loud sudden noise of heavy items falling onto stone startle him. He looks back at the road to see that the wobbly wheel of the cart had fallen off along with the sacks of grain and some of the vegetables. The man who was pulling the cart stood there staring at the mess he created, apparently unsure on what to do. 'Why now?' He complained, seemingly giddy in his tone.

Ookonan rolls his eyes and huffs as he walks up to the villager, he looks around at the road and notices that the wheel has fallen off in a pothole. The pot hole was barely noticeable as it is filled with muddy water.

Ookonan rolls his eyes and reluctantly takes himself over to the man. 'Would you like a hand?'

'Well you are a kind large man you are.' The man says, curling his lips into a warm smile as he looks up at Ookonan.

'Uhh, I suppose…' Ookonan says, stepping away from the man. His stomach churns as the man smiles again at Ookonan but without blinking.

'Well you are very kind.' The man assured.

'You just looked like you needed help.'

He walks over to the wheel on the side of the road, he picks it up and takes it back over to the cart and reattaches it. He looks back at the man just staring at him, he hasn't bothered to pick up any of the sacks or goods. Ookonan sighs and rolls his eyes again, he picks up the heavy sacks of grain and reloads the cart as people watch. He tries to ignore them as he picks up the fruit and vegetables, chucking them onto the carriage.

The owner of the cart walks over to Ookonan, now no longer smiling. He finally picks up the remaining vegetables and places them into the cart after Ookonan finishes reloading it.

'What is your name?' He asks Ookonan.

Ookonan stiffens, he snaps his head to look at the man. His eyelid twitches with such an uncomfortable question. 'I do not give out my name to people that I do not know.'

'My name is Rodger, now we know each other.'

'It does not work like that.' He says, trying to hide his increasing anger and discomfort.

'Sure it does.'

'No, it does not.' He says, annoyed. He starts to walk away from Rodger to continue to follow the dirt road keeping an eye on the wall.

'Hey, where are you going?'

'I am leaving.'

He walks as quickly as he can away from Rodger and away from the small crowd, following the path around the large building. Keeping his eye on the wooden walls, more trouble arises. Of course, a villager is trying to manoeuvre a bisonbear with just a rope around its massive neck. Its large horns come close to piercing the villager when it shakes its head and it bears its large pointed teeth.

The bisonbear, unique to the north of Hondon, is far from its home of Kikkumari. He quickly looks around at the other animals within this village, there are chickens, piglickens, sheep, buffalants and more. But only one bisonbear and it was not happy, stamping the hooves on its back legs and trying to swipe with its massive claws on its front.

Ookonan grunts again seeing the chaos, he wants to ignore it and continue searching for the exit before realising that the chaos is happening twenty metres to large door like gates. The bisonbear scratches the ground with its large bear paws and it launches itself out of the grips of the villager throwing him face first onto the muddy ground.

It kicked and thrashed as it ran wild through the village in an uncontrollable fury. Ookonan without thinking takes action while annoyed that this village seems to have a constant drama. Almost like it's trying to keep him here.

'I was hoping I could just leave this place.' He says, stunned at the bad luck of the place, he feels like he isn't even allowed to be angry with the astounding mess the villagers seem to always be in. First a wheel, now a large animal. It's almost like the village is insistent on keeping him captive. He sighs a heavy breath before walking fearlessly over to the bisonbear, muttering to himself under his breath that these ânälääsïna don't know how to look after this animal, let alone respect it.

The bisonbear thrashes around through someone's small farm, throwing dirt and vegetation everywhere including all over the road and it kept this up until it saw some children playing on the road. It roars and sprints towards the children, who are oblivious to the danger coming towards them.

Without thinking, Ookonan sprints after the bisonbear, reaching for the remaining rope attached to its neck. Moments of life flash before his eyes, the children being trampled, life being destroyed, the horror in the villagers eyes as bones are crushed. As the bisonbear reaches the children, he grabs the rope and slams his heals into the ground pulling the beast with his might, stopping the bisonbear in its tracks.

'Time to calm down.' He says to the bisonbear as it attempts to pull him along. He gently directs the beast away from the children. 'Shhhh… shhhh. It is okay, no one is going to hurt you.' He says patting it gently on its neck, calming it down.

He looks back at the kids, quickly checking whether they are safe and unharmed before directing the bisonbear back to its enclosure. However, one child is sitting on the side of the road holding his knee. Tears forming in his eyes as he tries to hold back his cries.

'Mister!! Hey!' A child called out.

'What?' He responds abruptly and harshly.

'He has hurt himself.'

'Yeah, it does seem that way.' Ookonan states while walking away.

The hurt child watches Ookonan walk away, he can't hold it in anymore and lets out a howl. His cries, annoying as they are loud with large tears rolling down his dirty face. Ookonan sighs while rolling his eyes so hard he can see the inside of his head, he reluctantly turns around and squats down to have a closer look.

'It looks like you graze your knee.'

'I i i i it huuuuurrrrts.' He sobs.

'Yes… Clearly. Where would your house be? I will take you there.'

The child stands up snuffling, he wipes his eyes and nose before taking hold of Ookonan's giant hand. He points to his house, two houses away from where they currently stand. He picks up the child and carries him down the road to the house he pointed at, the largest of houses, avoiding all eye contact with the villagers.

He knocks on the front door. A large burly man, still short in stature next to Ookonan opens the door. He has a thick beard, broad shoulders and large muscles under his thick layer of fat. He is a middle aged man with thinning hair, yet he does not smell like a middle aged man. With breath of fresh manure and pheromones of armpit he greets Ookonan with open arms.

Ookonan looks at him blankly. 'Your child has hurt himself. It is just a graze, but he should be okay.'

'Thank you for looking after my son.' The burly man says, taking the child off Ookonan. He smiles at him with bright yellow teeth, almost unsettling as his clothes, the same colours at the large building across the road from his house and the bedroom Ookonan stayed at.

'Not a problem... I will be off now.'

'I insist you stay for a feast tonight.' The burly man says, putting his hand on Ookonan's upper arm.

'I would rather not, I would like to continue on my way.'

The burly man smiles at him, his foul smelling demonic breath seeps through his yellow teeth. His odour is insulting to the senses. It's like he has never heard of a wash, outside of the village he would probably be dead.

'In this town it is rude to decline. I must insist you stay for the feast we are having tonight.'

'Okay I will stay if I must.' He says taking a step back.

Chapter 12

The Mirish capital city is a dense clump of buildings with living units, businesses, back alleys and streets. For a small island the capital is a business hub for Mirish inhabitants, bring in clothing, old world trinkets, gadgets and their cultural cuisine.

Kaji runs past all of this, the narrow back alleys passages. The alleys are filthy, there are leaking pipes, the ground is covered in moss in some areas, the vents are letting out a greasy steam covering the ground and walls in a greasy residue.

He slows down to a walk. Out of breath he observes his area, trying to make sure he isn't being followed. His lungs are burning from the couple kilometres of running. He checks his body over for any flames before sitting himself down with his back against the wall.

He looks directly up at the sky as the back alley courtyard seems so dark, the sky is a bright clear blue with the light only touching the tops of the buildings making it seem like they are almost glowing whitish yellow.

'I'm not meant to be a dreamer.' He says, looking at his shaking hands. 'They're spiritual and have a higher purpose than me.'

He gets back to his feet and starts pacing as his mind wanders. The alley smelled like old musty socks soaked in urine and sweat. The smell by no means is helping him to calm down.

'I'm a terrible person.'

The alley begins to grow a bright orange and the temperature grows as though the place has been set aflame. He quickly looks at the direction of the light, wondering if it was a vent, a restaurant's kitchen. He checks himself over again, hoping it wasn't himself setting anything alight again. But he couldn't deny it, the alley was catching alight.

'Aaaahhh why now? I am not even having visions of you.' He shrieks, searching for a way to put out this new fire. He quickly looks around the exits of the alley to see if anyone was around or watching him.

Relieved to find that he is still alone he looks down at his hands, questioning how he started this orange glowing heat. But as he stressed about it, a ball of flame developed in his palm. It rolls off him and bounces along the ground towards the glowing amber heat.

'No no no no no.' He whispers, chasing after the ball of flame trying to put it out.

The flame hits the glowing amber heat and sticks to it. It sits still unmoved for a moment with nothing happening. He circles around it curiously as fire has never behaved like this before. But before he knew it, the glowing amber holds onto the flame and it moves quickly down the alley.

Kaji runs after the flame, turning corners as it does until they both come to a dead end. But once there was nowhere to go the flame stood still. He stares at it, terrified as his thoughts and imagination run wild. No wonder the fire is chaotic and destructive, it has a mind of its own he thought.

The flames burst into a tall heat, changing form to an ethereal glowing mass. Features as flowing red hair, long strong arms and a flowing red dress that spread out like a fiery flower. The hot glowing amber combined with the flame transformed into a woman.

She has a curious but unusual feature that Kaji has never seen in person, features that hes only seen in his visions. She has a straight nose thats thinner than his, strong broad shoulders and a youthful but womanly facial appearance.

The flames around her are controlled, as though they are truly a part of her. There is no destruction, its as though it's just life.

She steps towards him and as she does, he takes a step away. He isn't sure what this is, who she is. He isn't even sure if he is awake, alive or asleep.

'Kaji Tohroshatan, what are you doing?' The woman of fire asks. Her voice powerful and filled with a deep god like femininity.

'Who... Who are you?'

'I am the Goddess of hearth, home and family. I am an ancient Goddess known only as Hestia.'

'A. a.nd w.why are you h.h.here?'

She takes another step towards him leaving no trace of flame behind her. 'It was time I revealed myself to you, it seems I have caused you some problems this past week.'

'W.who are you?'

'Kaji Tohroshatan.' She takes another step towards him. 'You need to calm down.'

'Yeah... And why should I?' He asks, on the verge of panic.

'I have chosen you as my champion Kaji.'

'Champion? A -and my name is Tohroshatan.'

'Well... Kaji comes first in your name so I will call you Kaji.'

'It is just that-'

'Kaji, I have chosen you as my champion, I have granted you my powers, the power of hearth and fire.'

He takes a deep breath as an attempt to calm himself down, assertive, I must be assertive, he thought.

'Why have you given me this curse?'

'It is not a curse. More of a gift, you are more special than you realise Kaji.'

He did not have the energy to argue with what he believed to be a hallucination. All he could think about was what's next and what is to come of this.

Chapter 13

Two long thick wooden tables sit side by side with their accompanying long bench seats down in the common area. But a step above sitting at a different angle is another table as though it is for the leader of the village itself. Between the two main tables sits a long fire pit for warmth during the cold months. The interior of this longhouse is filled with lit horns and candles for light. The walls are covered with decorations, woven, carved and painted throughout.

The grassland villagers start to enter the longhouse hall, some are carrying large plates, baskets and bowls of food they have prepared. Each contains cooked vegetables, fresh fruits, meats and home made brews. And before long the tables were all stacked with the home foods they had prepared and brought in.

Ookonan ducks through the entrance doorway and enters into the grand hall. He looks around and is surprised how tall the ceiling is. He hasn't felt comfortable standing straight indoors for a long time. But this hight comfort doesn't negate his discomfort of the people in the village.

The chatter of the villagers all quietened down as soon as they noticed Ookonan. Every single one of them stared at him in complete silence. He felt seen and awkward, an uncomfortability he has never truly experienced before. But this awkward silence was broken once the annoying man with the broken cart walked up to him.

'Oh it is great to see you again.' Rodger said, curling up that smile.

'Ooh you are a big boy.' An older woman says, clearly without boundaries as she cannot keep her hands off him. She touches his lower belly and his upper thigh, she's fascinated by his height and where her hands seem to wander she assumes the same for his groin.

'Yes... I... Am...' He gently grabs hold of her wandering hand and takes a step away from her. But before he could walk away, she grabs his forearm.

'Well thank you so much for saving our village.' She says, squeezing and stroking his forearm, knowingly that he is uncomfortable but plays it off as an innocent old woman.

'Not... A... Problem...' He says to the woman pulling his arm and himself away from her and Rodger. He looks the tables up and down, in search for a seat closest to an exit. He walks up and down the tables, refusing to sit in the middle while avoiding the people where possible until he finds a seat next to a door. He awkwardly sits down, sliding his legs under the table.

He watches the villagers gather and some take their seats until one particular person he did not want to see again walks through the doors. The man who greeted him after he woke up in this damn village. The man spots him and smiles and immediately walks over to him and sits down.

'Well, it is great to see you here.'

'Yes I suppose it is... You lot will not seem to let me leave.' Ookonan mutters, refusing to look in his direction. He also could not understand why this man decided to sit next to him.

'Yes we do love our visitors.' He chuckles. 'I did not catch your name.'

'I do not give my name out to other people.' He says bluntly.

The man chuckles again as he looks around the hall. 'Well that there is Ruth' He says pointing at the older woman who was violating Ookonan. 'That is Mathew, that woman over there is Emily and over there is Rodger and he is Kenneth. And over there is Gary-'

Ookonan rolls his eyes as the man continues, he just wont shut up. 'This will not give you my name.' Ookonan cuts the man off.

'Oh... Well I am Aniuken just so you know.' He says, with a smile.

'That is nice.' He says, avoiding eye contact with him.

The villagers all start to find their seats while continuing their chatter. A gentleman takes a seat next to Ookonan and it was none other than Rodger whom Ookonan has been trying to avoid.

'Well it is nice of you to join us in our town feast, we have had a good harvest this month.' He says to Ookonan who is actively ignoring him. 'Oh my apologies, you continue to listen to them talk, they often have some good gossip.'

A bell chimes loudly throughout the hall leaving a lingering ring once it stopped. The chatter fades including the annoying men on either side of Ookonan who won't shut up. All the villagers stand in a daunting silence. Aniuken looks at Ookonan who remains seated.

'You need to stand up.'

'As you can tell I am still taller than most of you sitting down.' He says, refusing to move.

The large grotesque man who introduced himself as Lawence walks in from behind the head table, followed by his wife and child. He is well dressed for the occasion wearing herbs and gold. He grabs a tankard and raises it high to all the villagers cheerfully.

'What a pleasure to have you all here, with wonderful food, drink and enough to go around.' He smiles showing his yellow teeth. 'Haha yes, and it looks like we have a new accomplice to the table as well.' He directs his tankard to Ookonan. 'The man who makes me look small.' He says as the villagers all laugh.

'Today he rescued my little boy, and yesterday he rescued the whole village. Yes! Yes! He is a mysterious man, will not give out his name. Anyway, how great was this month's harvest? Look at all the beautiful food we have grown as a community. Tomorrow be sure to start preserving your food, as you know life is tough so we must all look after each other.'

Ookonan takes a drink while rolling his eyes at the leader and the villagers. That speech was ridiculous. He thought to himself.

'Anyway... Lets eat!!' Lawence shouts.

Aniuken leans to Ookonan and whispers in his ear. 'His name is Lawrence.'

The villagers all cheered again as they quickly shuffle to all sit down. The room was filled with noise clinking plates and cutlery, shuffling bums and the enormous amount of chatter between the people taking pride in their harvest.

'I rarely get to eat plants.' Ookonan muttered to himself while looking at all the food on the table. It's amazing to see so many fruits in one place, supposedly uncontaminated and the vibrant green vegetables look almost unrealistic.

'Yes we love growing our fruits and vegetables here, we occasionally eat meat but plants are easier for us.' Aniuken scoffs while looking up at Ookonan. He grabs a boiled beetroot and some cheese to put on his own plate.

'Why is that?'

Aniuken pauses for a moment, almost like he needs to think about the answer. It's like he's never had to think about it before. 'Meat must be hunted most of the time.' He finally said, putting a small piece of boiled beetroot in his mouth.

'So you lot never leave these walls?' Ookonan asks, taking a bite of some cornbread with some cheese and jam while still refusing to look at Aniuken.

'No, we have no reason to, it is safe here and we grow all that we need.' He explains.

Ookonan finishes off his cornbread while looking at the villagers, checking to see who is watching before he looks at his backpack between his legs. He quickly snatches some of the colourful foods and baked goods and shoves it into his backpack while acting inconspicuous. He looks over at the head table, Lawrence is stuffing his face while he laughs with his wife who is holding fruits in her hand seemingly trying to insist that he eats some rather than all the meat.

'Are you liking it here so far?' Rodger asks Ookonan

'It does seem nice here, you have nice food.' He says, glancing at him.

'Is that why you put some into your bag?'

He was shocked. How did Rodger notice? He was busy talking to the woman next to him about cake. 'Well-'

'It is okay, the food is good and you will probably want some for later.'

'Yes…' He says, unsure on how to explain himself. He grabs his drink and finishes it in one swig and places the cup back on the table. 'Where would your toilet be?'

'Just out that door.' He says, pointing to the door behind Ookonan.

He grabs his back and gets up from the table and turns towards the exit.

'Leaving are you?' Lawrence calls out, slamming his drink onto the table. The whole room falls silent and stares at Ookonan once more.

He looks at Lawrence twitching with an ugly fury as he scowls about being stopped yet again in a way to leave. He searches for words that wont make him suspicious of escaping and without showing off any of his anger. 'I am just off to the toilet.'

'Oh… Carry on then.' Lawrence says, calming down and turning back to eat.

The hall noise returns as the villagers turn back to each other to eat and chat. Ookonan walks through the doorway and down a small hallway. He wasn't sure what to expect but a long narrow hallway was not it and the further he went the worse it started to smell.

He was eventually greeted with a small door that has an intense odour, the smell of ammonia and rot is strong and it's arguably worse than the village in the black forest. He opens the door and a powerful whift punches him in the nose. His eyes water and his sinuses burn as he looks around the tiny room that contains only a small bench seat with a hole. The only window in sight was so small a rat probably wouldn't fit through.

He closes the door and quietly retraces his steps to see that there was another closes door on his right. He listens towards his left for the village feast. He opens the door and walks outside of the longhouse.

He looks around and wonders how he would get away fast from these people. But then. He remembered from earlier in the day. The bisonbear.

He sneaks through the village over to the pen where the bisonbear is kept. It's tied to a thick wooden post covered in clawmarks. He silently approaches the beast patting him on his thick shaggy neck before untying him. 'Come along with me. I need you.'

He walks himself and the bisonbear over to the entrance door-like gate, there are guards on either side of the entrance standing watch looking out little windows to the outside world. A large thick long block of wood latches the door-like gate shut, making it almost impossible for any demonic to break through.

'Vekk, vekk, how am I supposed to leave?' He says, stopping just over fifty metres from the exit. He scowls at the guards, before he approaches them, confident that he could take them both on if needed. He walks further up to the gate until one of the guards finally turns around.

'Where do you think you are going? And do you own that bisonbear?' One of the guards demands.

'I am not from here and I wish to leave, also this bisonbear is a gift from Lawrence.' Ookonan says twisting the truth.

'You must have a reason to leave, we can not just let you.'

'I have also been granted permission to go hunt for meat from Lawrence.' He lies.

The guards both look at Ookonan with disbelief. 'We will need proof.'

'Or I can crush you and destroy everything in this pathetic village.' He threatens. He stares at both of them through his eyebrows as electricity sparks around his forearms.

The guards intimidated both witnessed what he did the night of the demonics. Obliterating them with the power of storm. They both know he is not bluffing and he is more than capable of shredding the village to pieces. They both look at each other, they know what to do.

They open the gate as Ookonan gets onto the back of the bisonbear and directs it towards the opening gates. 'Thank you, and with all due respect. I hope to never see you again.' He says as he finally gets to exit this insane place. Once out into the grasslands Ookonan taps the bisonbear gently on his sides and holds onto the neck wool. 'Hya hya Go Go.'

The bisonbear launches itself into a full sprint, far and fast away from the village. Neither of them look back, neither of them want to go back.

Chapter 14

Ookonan and the bisonbear travel through a thick sparse misty forest where the moonlight pierces through the leaves, illuminating the grassy root covered ground with a soft blue light. But throughout this forest hides the conscious slime which watches and follows all that live that go near. The slime follows Ookonan and the bisonbear, but is too slow to keep up, it maintains just out of reach for its next meal.

'The air feels somewhat clear here.' Ookonan mutters quietly as he steps over tree roots, conscious of the threat of the slime but his mind focused on a clear area ahead.

The sounds of water flowing, moving and hitting rocks becomes apparent as they both near the clearing which is bright, blue and it looks like it's almost glowing. As they both get closer to the clearing the louder the water becomes. It's crashing on hard rocks but also softly flowing into streams, it sounds like a heap of small waterfalls, a small river stream but it connects into a larger body of water.

But before he knew it, he had finally reached the clearing. Expecting it to be an open field, much like the grasslands he had been traversing for several days. He is greeted by a massive lake, the size of a small ocean. The moon light illuminated the whole body of water a soft blue as it reflects the clear sky, the lake looks almost as though it's glowing.

'Sometimes I hate how beautiful something can be… it is just so deceiving.' He mutters softly to himself as he pats the bisonbears neck, feeling some form of affection for it. 'I like you though.'

He takes in a deep breath, feeling the clean air fill his lungs as he admires the almost glowing lake. He takes in the view and stares right out into the horizon, barely any land is present there with the exception of some mountains wrapping part of the lake like a fjord. But the flat horizon of the water catches his eye, the beauty of the glowing lake is cut short.

A violent lightning storm is developing and dancing right on flat of the horizon. All he could do is watch, as it abruptly changes course. It rushes over to him at an unnaturally fast rate, growing in size as it moves the water in the lake around it.

'Hmm. What do you know?' He mutters as the storm nears him. Sparks of electricity develop inside of it as strong winds rush around it and the black clouds and rain dance inside and above it.

The storm subsided as quickly as it reached Ookonan, compressing into a small ball of electricity, wind and rain which suddenly exploded in a downward force of lightning forcing an electrified windy explosion in all directions. He quickly jumps back in shock of its strange behaviour. He keeps an eye on the strange storm, now seeing something new hidden inside of it.

Loose fabrics whip around in the fading storm eventually revealing an electrified man inside. He is dressed in loose unusual clothing which Ookonan has never seen before, especially in the west of Hondon. The man is dressed in layers of fabrics wrapped in a specific way but colours that seem unusual for a storm.

His trousers are loose flowing like the wind but are red. His top is well fitted but a light blue and a long red silk belt which is embroidered in an otherworldly material that glows like the lightning of the sky is wrapped around his torso, keeping his clothing fitted and well together. He has long black flowing hair on the top of his head and his eyes glow like the bluish white lighting he was conducting. He's a fascinating looking man with facial features that are most common in the east of Hondon.

Ookonan slowly gets to his feet, his eyes remaining peeled on the strange man now walking on the rough water towards him. Almost every aspect about this man blows Ookonan's mind. Everything about him is unique and god-like, he cannot tell if this is reality or a hallucination and he really is still stuck in the grassland village.

'Ookonan… It is time I revealed myself to you.' The man says, as he walks up to him. He stands more than a head length shorter than Ookonan, which surprises him as he would expect someone of extraordinary power like this to be somehow bigger.

'Who might you be and how do you know my name?! I never give out my name!' Ookonan demanded, shocked, that this unreal man knew his name. He has to be sleeping, there is no chance this is real he thought to himself.

'I am Susanoo. I am an ancient god of a land that no longer exists.' He says, as he lifts himself up in the air to be at Ookonan's eye level.

'I have seen and met crazy all over this land. You expect me to believe that you are a god of a dead land?' Ookonan says, staring at SuSano as though he is insane. Nothing can be trusted and he still cannot tell whether it's real or not.

'If this land is so crazy then why would it be false that I am a god of a dead land?' SuSanoo asked calmly.

He keeps eye contact with Ookonan who is unsure how to react. He isn't used to people who are smaller than himself being stronger in any way let alone not being intimidated by himself in some way. He feels unsure about everything, but there is one truth SuSanoo has said, if this chaotic land is crazy then it is possible for a man to be from a dead land.

'Why are you here? How do you know my name?' Ookonan demanded. 'I better not be unconscious at that crazy village.' He mutters under his breath.

'Ookonan you are completely awake. I have chosen you as my champion-'

'What does that even mean?' Ookonan demanded, cutting him off.

'I have granted you the powers of storm. I have chosen you as my champion for a great destiny!' Susanop explained, as he started to lose his patience with the stubborn man.

'Do you expect me to believe any of that?' He laughed in complete disbelief. Gods do not exist let alone someone choosing him or valuing him.

'You are a very important individual.' He stated firmly to Ookonan who continued to laugh over him. 'MORE THAN YOU CAN EVER REALISE!' He shouted as he began to lose his temper.

'Sure, if you say so.' Ookonan states as his laughter dies off and his face turns to a scowl.

SuSanoo's patients had now been tested, he could not believe the stubbornness of this giant buffoon. Any person from one thousand years or more ago would have been awestruck to stand before a god and filled with pride and honour to be granted such a gift. Any normal person in this present day would also have felt honoured, but not Ookonan and this frustrated him.

SuSanoo has had enough. He strikes lightning onto the ground and brews a storm around himself. His eyes glow a bright whitish blue as water and lighting rush around him. He throws an electrified strong wind at Ookonan, throwing him a few metres away and onto his back.

'Can you see the power of storm?!'

Ookonan effortlessly gets back to his feet, now enraged with SuSanoo he launches himself at him throwing a king punch at him. To which SuSanoo quickly evades and parries, throwing Ookonan back onto the rocky ground.

'This is meaningless!! The land is not saveable and there is no other land!' He shouts angrily at Susanoo.

He ignores Ookonan's remark and remains in the air, supported by his strong lightning storm. He conjures lightning around his left arm as he lifts it into the air before throwing charged bolts of lighting at Ookonan.

'This solves nothing, those other times were accidents!!' Ookonan shouts angrily as he dodges every bolt of lighting SuSanoo throws at him.

Fury grows in SuSanoo as the storm grows stronger, he charges a much larger bolt and throws it at Ookonan, hitting him in the shoulder.

'Oof.' He grunts. 'I am not the person you are looking for.'

Becoming more enraged, SuSanoo bends the lake water around himself, electrifying it with powerful winds. His eyes start to spark as his fury grows. He conjures massive powerful bolts of glowing blue electricity in both hands to throw at Ookonan.

Bolt after bolt he threw at Ookonan, every strike missing and instead smashing fiery holes in the ground. As anxiety pumps through Ookonan's veins, a storm much like SuSanoo's but on a smaller scale brews around him.

Electricity forms around his right hand as tension in the air rises. 'ENOUGH!' He shouts, throwing his hand out to block SuSanoo. Accidentally shooting a large bolt of lightning at him which was then followed by a small but powerful force of wind. Ookonan looks at his hand, shocked.

He turns his gaze back to SuSanoo. His eyes turned the glowing whitish blue, matching SuSanoo's. It's his turn now. He throws bolt after bolt as the powerful god until one finally hits. Stunned and in belief that he has the upper hand he throws several more. But to no avail, SuSanoo was not hurt or touched, every electrical storm strike he absorbed.

'Do you still believe that those powers were a dream?' He asks as he gets into Ookonan's face.

Ookonan couldn't bring himself to speak. The words couldn't even be forced out, he felt as though he's in shock. The mysterious floating man could not be harmed and any power thrown at him he absorbed it like a sock absorbing moisture.

'I have chosen you as my champion Ookonan. You have a large destiny in front of you. You are likely the most important person in all of Hondon.'

'I do not think I will ever see myself as important.' Ookonan says finally getting words out. Not one part of the last week feels believable and this most certainly feels the least.

'Your first task is to head towards Fatencia province...' Susanoo instructed ignoring Ookonan's comment about himself. 'You must find Kaji Tohroshatan.'

'Which direction is that?'

'You will need to cross this lake as Fatencia is on the other side.' SuSanoo says, pointing at the now barely visible horizon.

'Can I take this Bisonbear? He is convenient and good company.'

'You will need to bend the wind and storms below the both of you.' He says, acknowledging Ookonan's question. He subsides his storm and places his feet onto the earth. 'Ookonan you must trust me. I will be assisting you and granting you full control of these powers tonight.'

'This is real? The past week has not been a dream?'

SuSanoo bends the air beneath his feet to get back up to Ookonan's eye level. ' Pain confirms reality. Correct?'

Ookonan nods, agreeing with the unearthly man. He thinks back to the pain he felt while fighting the broodmother, the painful fatigue while trekking through the grasslands, the demonics attacking. It must be real then.

But before he knew it. SuSanoo places a hand onto his chest. Huge bursts of pulsing electricity pump into his heart. It's a sharp burning feeling that pumps through his veins. He feels the storm brewing in his stomach and lungs, the winds around him and the electricity throughout his body. He closes his eyes to embrace the electrical power and once embraced the pain goes away.

Once done, SuSanoo moves away from him. He lowers himself onto the lake water and once he touches it a burst of electricity consumes him before he vanishes in a puff of electrical wind. Leaving Ookonan and the bisonbear alone once more.

Ookonan felt the new set of determination run through his veins. Still unsure how to achieve what is expected, but the first step is to get himself and the bisonbear across the lake. He opens his eyes, sparks of electricity burst through the eyes. Glowing the bright blue of lightning, he bends a powerful storm around himself and the bisonbear.

Chapter 15

Kaji walks along the shoreline during the cool early morning. The sun has just risen above the horizon leaving a lot of the surrounding islands still in the dark. The seabreeze feels chilly on his exposed skin as he still only wears the same pair of pants he stole from the hospital and nothing else. He looks up at the cliffs by the beach, the whole edge of the cliff is melted and now looks like glass. He did not realise how destructive he could be in a fit of rage, the thought eats at him. He could never face his sister again.

'Well… you wanted to meet here.' He says loudly while waiting for the fiery woman to show up. He looks out at the water and the brother and sister islands, feeling some sense of hope that his newfound power will be solved or at the very least controlled.

A sudden burst of bright crimson fire appears near him, lighting up the beach for a brief moment before dying away revealing the fiery red haired woman he met earlier, Hestia. 'Kaji, it is time I told you about your destiny.' She says calmly, as she walks over to him.

'Why did you choose me?' He asks, turning to face her.

'I chose you due to your love for your family and you would do anything for those you love. There is more to it, but I cannot tell you what it is at this time.'

'Your powers…' He trails off.

'Yes, you have the power of hearth and fire and through me you can manipulate flame.' She explains. Her tone remains calm as though nothing fazes her, not even his disastrous accidents.

'Yes but how can I control it?'

She puts a hand on his shoulder, her skin is hot like heated iron or a volcano. She lights herself up becoming hotter, so hot he can feel the pumping through his veins. Her eyes became a bright orange filled with swirls of fire and as this happened Kaji's eyes did exactly the same. His body became a furnace but unlike Hestia, it's agonising for him. But soon the pain fades while the flame still pumps throughout his body and once the pain is gone she lets go.

'I have fully transferred myself onto you.' She says to him with a warm smile. She turns to look at the sea, appreciating the view. 'Look at the horizon and I want you to throw a ball of fire.'

Following Hestia's instructions and without a word, he faces the horizon and focuses his energy onto his hand. And without much thought, he throws a ball of fire out into the distance, it felt satisfying and effortless. He couldn't believe it, for the first time since his powers struck, he has some form of control.

He looks at his hand, no pain, no burns, no destruction and his pants are still on. 'I did not see any vision. My line of sight was clear. Everything is clear.' He looks at Hestia. 'How did you do that?'

'Kaji, I need you to listen very carefully.' She says, her face and tone turning serious.

Taken aback from her change of tone from calm to serious, he turns his undivided attention to her. Whatever she has to say must be of the utmost importance. He looks her in her fiery eyes as she says to him. 'You need to find Ookonan.'

Shocked, he takes a step back expecting her to say something else. 'Ookonan? Who is Ookonan?' He asks, confused and wondering how he would even find Ookonan.

'You are directly connected with Ookonan. He is in Hondon'

'Hondon? How will I get there? And who is Ookonan?' He questions. No soul has ever reached Hondon or even gotten past the Australian, New Zealand and Antarctic ridges and told the tale. How could he possibly get to Hondon and what kind of name is Ookonan? Who even names their kid that?

'I will take you to Hondon, but you must find Ookonan.' She says, her voice filled with serious grim as she ignores his other question. 'I wish you the very best Kaji.' She takes a step back from him, preparing herself with hot flame.

'Wait!!' He protested.

She blasts him with hot flame, engulfing his whole body in a bright crimson red that lights up the entire beach. But once the flames die away, Kaji is nowhere to be seen. The only thing left are his footprints. Hestia takes a brief moment to look at the melted cliff and the ocean before engulfing herself in flames and disappearing also.

†

The Hondonian province is dark and icy cold as the night has set in. The roads are covered in icy mud and the buildings are made of wood and have a red residue rubbed into them along with herbs hanging from any opening available.

Shivering people walk around this town, either closing shops, walking into warmer buildings and even a few adjust the hanging herbs and rub in more of the red stuff into the buildings. But then, startling everyone in a near proximity a bright crimson ball of flame temporarily heats and illuminates the town. But as quickly as the fire appears it disappears leaving behind Kaji.

He scans his surroundings, all the people here look strange to him, much like the people in his visions. He tries to relax himself in the strange new world but he was not expecting the place to be so cold. After he takes one step on the new land, he feels the cold radiate through his foot and shoot through his leg. He's never felt so cold in his life.

'Hmm so this is Hondon? It does not seem that bad?' He finds himself questioning. He looks at the people. Every single one of them are staring at him as though he is this strange alien or that he is naked. Several of them retreat into nearby buildings after looking at him. Some of these people stared at him in awe, this man appeared in a ball of fire.

Kaji gives them a quick wave before walking away. These people all look so strange to him but still look like people, unlike the rumours of Hondon that he heard about. Expecting them all to look like hideous monsters. But he is on a mission, he must find Ookonan, but unsure where to go or which direction is even north. All that's on his mind is 'must find Ookonan'.

'I was always told that Hondon is full of monsters.' He quietly mutters to himself, wandering through the village, observing people rub the red paste onto the outsides of the buildings before rushing inside. But then out in the distance, gurgling screeches with the sounds of scratching and screams echo through the village.

'Okkay. So the rumours are true. There may be monsters in Hondon.' He whispers to himself as he listens to the horrifying noises. He could feel his heartbeat rise and his blood boil as he stood, watching people dropping whatever they were doing to sprint to a nearby building.

One person stands in their doorway ushering people inside as the demonic screams get louder. They notice Kaji standing still on the icy cold road, just watching instead of running to a building. 'Inütri trâmina farsïs gelitîshj tehmis!' (*quick get inside! They are coming!*). They shouted.

He looks over at the person standing at the door shouting at him in Hondonian. 'I need to scratch up on my Hondonian.' He mutters to himself, struggling to translate in his head what they just said. 'Sorry what was that?' He shouted back.

'Cenäoo lëhäsöömm pelob trâmina farsïs.' (*Don't let them see you, quick get in!*). They shouted at him, urging him to get inside of the building.

'Uuhh Okay You do you.' He calls back at them. Feeling as though he needs a little time to adjust to Hondon to get into the headspace of speaking in Hondonian.

Sloshing running footsteps are now audible throughout the village along with the gurgling screams becoming almost deafening. The slam of the door startles Kaji, he turns back to the people who were shouting at him to see the door has now been shut. He looks around the village to see all the windows have been blocked off with these wooden doors.

He looks back down the street, confused to see human-like figures walking towards him. He wasn't sure what he was looking at, to him it looks like a bunch of disadvantaged people desperate for help. But as the horde got closer he can see they look almost skeletal with long sharp fingers. As they notice Kaji standing there watching them, they stop walking. Their red glowing eyes light up the street.

All of them smile at him, their sharp rock-like teeth are not a sight he has ever witnessed and those glowing eyes are a thing of nightmares that would never exist in Mir. The demonics all scream an eardrum bursting gurgling howl before they sprint at him with an inhuman twitching way. He now realises the people retreating into the buildings had nothing to do with himself and the people screaming at him were in fact urging him to get inside. He now realises a little too late that the supernatural is far more normal in Hondon than Mir.

'Well I guess the rumours about Hondon are true.' He says to himself as he bravely and stupidly prepares to fight these things alone. He gets into a fighting stance just in time for a demonic to launch itself at him.

He quickly jumps out of the way and watches the demonic tumble past him. He watches it get itself back onto its feet. It eyes him hungrily with a sharp wide toothy smile and the glowing red eyes now forever burned into Kaji's mind.

He thinks back to a few minutes ago when he was back home in Mir and the woman of fire Hestia was talking to him. A ball of fire develops in his hand and before he knew it, he has thrown it at the demonic.

'Eeeeeeeeeeeaaaaaaaaaaaaaaaaaaahhhhhhhhhhh.' The demonic screams as it falls back onto the icy muddy road.

'Well, they do not like fire... I should be fine. But I must find Ookonan.'

†

Ookonan takes in a deep breath, filling his lungs with the Fatencia provence air as he and the bisonbear arrive at the lake shoreline. The air is wet and frigid, irritating his throat. But he couldn't think about that right at this moment, the more important matter is that it's now night and demonics roam and he needs to find a Mirish man.

But of course, a few steps on land the scratching gurgling screams echo nearby. 'Well apparently he is here somewhere. I just hope he is not stupid enough to be near the demonics.' He mutters to himself as a feeling of dread sinks to his stomach as he faces the direction of the demonic screams. But before he knew it an explosion of bright red fire burst into the sky.

'Looks like I found him.' He mutters to himself, annoyed that he may have to save the foreign man and already fail the vague quest SuSano had given him. He jolts the bisonbears sides and rides it a few hundred metres in the direction of the noise and blast until he finds the well seasoned Fatencia village.

He rushes down the road until he is faced with a hoard of demonics and a half naked man fighting them alone. A lot of this just doesn't make much sense to him. The town is extremely well seasoned with different forms of spice powder and hung herbs, why would the demonics come into this town? He pushes that thought aside, he jumps off the bisonbear and rushes over to the man to help out.

He unsheathed his sword and charged at the demonics surrounding the mysterious man. He slashes at some demonics legs, cutting them off and forcing it onto the ground. The demonic screams, bearing its long sharp teeth at him. He then stabs it through the back and stomps on its head, crushing it.

The mysterious man looks at him, horrified. He watches Ookonan stab, kick and slash the demonics before blasting them with lightning. He lights his upper body on fire and blasts the demonics behind Ookonan with balls of flame. He's amazed with Ookonan's athleticism and his ability to keep up with the monsters. But before he knew it, Ookonan was staring at him, he looked fierce and frightening.

Ookonan stares down the demonic behind the man who isn't paying enough attention to his surroundings. He throws his sword right through its head, killing it instantly.

'Sahalatoh teleha.' (*thank you*). The man says to him.

'Huh?' Ookonan grunts. Unsure whether the man is insulting him or thanking him. But there is no time to question the man. He quickly pulls his sword from the demonics skull. A fresh storm brews around him with strong winds with bolts of electricity. He turns to demonic running at him, twitching in its agro state.

He blasts it with a large bolt of lightning and at the same time the mysterious man blasts it with a stream of fire. It cooks from the inside out, but it keeps moving towards him with sheer determination before crumbling into ash and charcoal onto the muddy ground.

The mysterious man looks at Ookonan, as though he realises something but unsure of what. He stands and watches Ookonan blast a few demonics with more lightning. But the looks was cut short as he quickly reacts to a demonic slashing at him.

The mysterious man grabs the demonic's head with both his bare hands and blasts it with hot flames. It was the craziest thing Ookonan has ever seen a human do before. The demonic screams as it's being held by the man as it cooks from the inside.

This man is insane, there is no way this is the Mirish man named Kaji that he is looking for. He takes a step away from the mysterious man and waits for him to turn off his fire.

Once the last demonic is dead, the mysterious man turns his attention to Ookonan. He also waits for his storm to die away as his flame slowly fades and his body cools down.

'Who are you? What is your name?' Ookonan asks, as he calmly walks over to the mysterious man.

He looks up at Ookonan, in awe. But struggles to understand him. There is far too much going on to be translating Euro Hondonian at this moment.

'I… Not… Hondonian well.' He attempts to say back.

Ookonan quickly scans the area, he feels they both need to be alone for the next question. 'I am looking for a Kaji.' He says quietly. 'From Mir.' He whispers.

'I. am… Kaji Tohroshatan.' The mysterious man responds while pointing at himself.

Ookonan takes a step away. He is in awe. Finally putting a face to the visions, finally seeing the power of the man in his visions in person. The man who has saved him on many occasions without meaning to.

'Ookonan, find I need.' Kaji says as he tries to understand the Hondonian man.

'I do not know how you found that name Kaji. But I was sent to find you.'

'A god sent you? Me you visions have?' He asked, struggling with the language.

'Yes, I had visions of you. With your anger and fire.'

Kaji also couldn't believe it. Finally a face with his visions. The electricity, the monsters. But never did he think that this man would be a giant or have purple eyes and pointy ears.

'First time we meet, Ookonan meet you is nice. Hestia I have been sent.' Unsure of a proper greeting or how Hondonians greet. But before he knew it. Ookonan grabs a hold of his right hand firmly and shakes it.

Chapter 16

People of many backgrounds sit in silence in the warm well furnished tavern. Every person anxiously remains still as they listen to the screaming, growling and gurgling of the demonics outside. Some people tried to continue to eat and drink but it's difficult to stomach not knowing whether it will be your last night with a conscience.

But suddenly the last scream of the demonic raid came to an abrupt end. Every person inside the tavern freezes, shocked about the sudden silence.

The tavern manager breaks this silence with their footsteps on the hard wooden floors as they walk over to the barred entrance. The entrance door is barred by two thick wooden beams that are heavily seasoned with spice and the door frame itself has herbs hanging above it. The tavern manager opens a little peephole door to safely inspect the outside.

'It looks like the demonic raid has ended. Much sooner than normal.' The manager announces. The tavern breaks into an abrupt cheer. The manager removes the thick wooden beams from the door and opens it to shout.

'TAVERN IS BACK OPEN!!'

Workers from behind the front counter get back to work, setting up the brick oven and getting baked goods ready like bread in the traditional Fatencia style. Another worker sets up the charcoal grill and pit to cook the raised meat while another worker gets a bucket of soapy water to clean the front entrance.

Heavy footsteps walk up the steps leading to the front door and before anyone knew it, the door swung open and two filthy men covered in mud and demonic blood step inside. The first customers since the demonic raid. An exceptionally tall half elven fellow ducks under the doorframe and steps inside followed by a much smaller half naked man who follows. It's Ookonan and Kaji.

'You must be tired coming all that way. We also need to get you new clothing.' Ookonan says to Kaji as they walk into the entrance mudroom spot. The floor is polished and freshly cleaned. There are racks filled with filthy outdoor coats and little open lockers for shoes and contaminated clothing.

'Megalasan ma lemba sohlo-mang.' (*Speak more slowly*).

'This place seems nice...' Ookonan says slowly as he looks around at the tavern. The warm light of fire and wood has an extremely welcoming appeal for him.

'You must clean yourself before using this room naked man.' The manager snaps as Kaji goes to take a step onto the main tavern floor. 'You must clean your skin and take off your filthy clothes. Demonic blood and filth should never enter the clean place.'

A large barrel of soapy water sits by some hot coals away from the clothing racks and shelves. Ookonan takes off his boots, backpack and jacket and places them next to the barrel of water. He proceeds to wash his exposed skin and hair before washing his backpack, jacket and boots. He looks over at Kaji who stands awkwardly in the wash entrance, absolutely smothered in blood and mud. He gestures him over to the barrel of warm soapy water to clean himself.

He reluctantly walks over to the water and looks himself over. He's filthy, the black demonic blood and the reddish mud is caked on him. He dips his arms into the water and feels its warmth which almost feels hot after fighting in the ice. He scrubs the filth off his arms, face and torso, leaving behind a watery muddy mess in the washroom entry. He took no notice of the mess he left behind, the only thought that was in his head was if people were watching him, he couldn't help but feel extremely uncomfortable with the thought of not only people watching him have a bath but having a bath in a communal space of eating. Insanity.

Ookonan looks him over, seeing a clean Kaji for the first time. But his eyes drift to his muddy demonic blood soaked pants. 'Hmm.' He vocalises as he walks over to the front counter. 'Hi.' He says, getting someone's attention. 'Do you happen to have a spare room and any clothes?'

'Room yes… Clothes… Why do you ask?' The worker asks as they fill up tankards with lager.

'My friend here.' He says pointing at Kaji who stands awkwardly in the washroom entrance. 'Has travelled far and has had his belongings raided. Do you have any spare clothing?'

'How much are you willing to pay?' Putting the now filled tankard onto the bench. 'For the room-'

'And clothing?' Ookonan asks, cutting them off.

'Yes…' They sigh while taking a step away from the bench to cross their arms. 'The room and the clothing.'

'I have some spices and gold weighing me down.'

'What kind of spice do you have?'

He walks back over to his backpack and pulls out two leather sacks. 'I have paprika and a smaller amount of reaper.' He says, holding them up for the worker to see.

'I will take the reaper…' They say holding out their hand. 'The hotter the spice the better at deterring the demonics.'

'Agreed' He says, putting the paprika back in his backpack before walking back over to the counter. 'So the room and clothing.'

The worker looks over at the entrance to see Kaji now attempting to wash his filthy pants. They look back at Ookonan and sigh, there is no immediate fix for those pants. 'I will be right back with the clothing.' They say before walking off.

'Alright.'

'Ookonan!!' A loud deep voice boomed through the tavern.

He looks around for the familiar voice, it was most certainly not Kaji who is attempting to dry himself. It also was not coming from behind the counter. He eventually looks downwards to see a short stocky and muscular man smiling at him.

He has a large thick beard, a large nose and broad shoulders. He wears a dark blue linen shirt, leather pants and no shoes. He looks to be middle aged, within his late thirties or early forties.

'My man!! How are you?!' He enthusiastically asks, holding out a hand for Ookonan.

'Hey Buruk. Same, same, nothing has changed.' He responds, grabbing Buruk's hand.

'I will reserve us a table, we should have a drink.' He says cheerfully. As he walks away, the worker returns with some old worn brown leather clothing which they hand to Ookonan.

114

'Thank you.' He says, taking the clothing off him before taking himself back over to Kaji. 'Kaji you are clean enough.'

As he hands the acquired clothing over to Kaji, Buruk walks up to the both of them. Smiling broadly as he's excited to have a drink with an old friend. 'Ookonan, I have just booked a booth for us to have a few pints of lager.'

'I would love to have a drink with you Buruk, but I am in need of some good rest and my friend here has travelled a long distance.'

'Ookonan, since when do you travel with other people?' He scoffs. Raising his eyebrows at the strange new man Ookonan seems to be with.

'I do not. But we have been given a very important quest... Apparently.'

He raises another eyebrow at him in disbelief. He turns his attention to Kaji and looks him over as though he's sizing him up. He holds out a hand with a bright grin. 'Who might you be?'

Kaji looks at the short thick hand, unsure what to do. He looks the short man over having never seen someone like him before. Little people exist in Mir but this individual looks different to him. His thick limbs make his own look long and lanky, his thick bearded face makes his own look childlike, he's unsure how to feel about it. 'I am Kaji Tohroshatan.' He finally says.

'Kaji!!' He says loudly and enthusiastically. He hits him on the back and gestures to the tavern floor. 'I have reserved us all a table, so we shall drink!'

Ookonan puts a hand on Kaji's shoulder and directs Kaji away from Buruk and the tavern staff. They both walk to the other side of the tavern, backpack in hand. Once alone, Ookonan opens up his backpack and pulls out some gold, other worldly trinkets, bracelets with a round top with small parts, rings and coins.

'Are you hungry?' Ookonan asks him.

He looks at Ookonan for a short while trying to translate the Euro Hondonian question to Mirish. He thinks the words said to him in his head (*Deher dissak oo?*) while translating them. He looks at the trinkets Ookonan is holding and his other hand on the counter of the tavern.

'Uuuuhhh... Yes?' He eventually says, still unsure what was said to him.

Ookonan takes himself back over to the counter. 'Hey, we would like to order some food.'

'What would you like?' A worker asks, walking over to him.

'Whatever this can buy?' He places the gold trinkets onto the counter.

'Pizza wrap or Pizza?'

'Oh! Pizza wrap tonémash ka?' Kaji blurts out, excited for something he recognises, a food that over the course of one thousand years still has not changed much.

'Alright I will bring it over to you shortly.'

He frowns at Kaji, he wanted to know what else might be available before realising there were only two options for tonight and all toppings or stuffings are chosen by the staff. He looks over at the worker and nods before grabbing Kaji by the upper arm and taking him somewhere more private, out of the public eye and ear.

'Kaji, when we go outside tomorrow. You need to wear that clothing… It is one of the most important things to survive.' He says in a soft and stern tone. He tries to collect his thoughts in case the foreign man doesn't understand and he needs to reexplain in another language somehow.

He listens to Ookonan's quiet words as he looks around the tavern. Mostly looking for the short muscular man. There are a lot of unclothed people scattered around as though it's normal. Just eating and socialising with their friends. Not everyone is unclothed, some are in underwear and some are wearing light clothing like it went under heavy sturdy wear. 'Naked people? Many people naked? Why? No cares, why?'

'Clothing protects from the land.' He sighs, unsure how someone cannot understand this. He quickly scans his surroundings before proceeding to further answer the question. No one can know Kaji is from Mir, he thinks to himself. 'You do not want too much of the land getting on you, it will turn you. You need to value clothing.'

'Sooo… The naked people?' Kaji asks, still holding his new clothes.

'Do you wear contaminated or filth indoors?'

'No.'

'Then why do it here? Filth should never be brought into a building. What if you get someone sick? What if that sickness changes them?'

Kaji looks at him bewildered. How could a bit of mud make anyone sick? This is madness and the naked people sitting at tables, eating, drinking and socialising is disgusting but also how do they have no shame? He thought to himself. Over an hour in Hondon and everything is far from what he expected.

'Here in Hondon most people do not care about other people's bodies. Unless they look sick.' Ookonan says, leaning in to whisper in his ear.

'Food is ready. I will take it over.' The staff member called out to Ookonan and Kaji.

He steps away from Kaji and walks back over to the counter. Kaji stands still momentarily still unsure about how to take on Hondon's strange customs. All of this would be considered to be the utmost disrespect back home in Mir.

'Thank you. I can take it.' Ookonan says as he grabs the plates of sliced up Pizza wraps. He looks over at Kaji and gestures with his nose to follow him as he walks to the back of the tavern.

'Whatever you do. Do not accept Buruk's drinking challenge.'

Kaji looks up at Ookonan, acknowledging the sound that came from him, but still unable to completely understand what he is talking about. Once they both arrive at the booth, Buruk is sitting alone, he is relaxed with a massive grin on his face as multiple bottles, tankards and pints of alcohol sit on the table in front of him.

'Nice of you to finally join!' He says loudly and cheerfully as they both take a seat at the booth with him. Ookonan then searches for a clear area on the table so he can place the plate of food on so he and Kaji can enjoy a meal.

'Drink, so many.' Kaji says in awe but also shock. Not a single person back home could or would drink this much. Not even Toakase.

'Yes! Down for a challenge?' He asks enthusiastically as he slams his hands on the table, causing it to wobble and some of the drinks to spill slightly.

'Do not do it Kaji.'

Buruk grabs the largest cup of lager that he could. He lefts it with two hands and downs it with large mouthfuls, sure not to spill or waste any. He drank a litre of lager in ten seconds, wasting nothing. He slams the empty stein onto the table before eyeing Kaji with a wide toothy grin.

'How? How? You did that? How?' Kaji asks, astounded that this little man drank so much so quickly and cleanly. Was there more body under that beard?

Buruk bursts out with laughter. 'Hahahahaaa I am a dwarf!!!!' His voice booms as he looks at Kaji suspiciously with disbelief. 'You should know we are the best drinkers. Here, have this!' He says handing Kaji a shot of absinthe.

He takes the small glass of liquid from Buruk. He looks back at Ookonan who is taking a slice of the pizza wrap. He looks back at him wide eyed and shaking his head. 'Do not do it.' He mouths before taking a bite of the food.

Kaji quickly downs the shot. He then takes a tankard and drinks the ale as fast as he can. 'Finished.' He says, slamming the tankard back onto the table.

Ookonan takes another slice of the pizza wrap while rolling his eyes at Kaji and Buruk, waiting for the chaos to unfold. He could not believe Kaji's stupidity when he explicitly told him not to drink with him. And Buruk for bringing a full bottle of absinthe, twelve beers, twelve ales, a full bottle of reaper whisky, two full bottles of vodka. No one besides a Dwarf would ever drink this much.

'HA! One pint and a shot! Here have another.' Buruk shouts while holding back a laugh as he hands Kaji a shot of reaper whisky.

Kaji accepts the shot and downs it as fast as he could while Buruk watches eagerly for a reaction and Ookonan does his best to ignore the two of them. 'Aaahhh maang oh-wah.' (Spicy) He says, trying to cool down his mouth.

Ookonan rolls his eyes. What did he expect with reaper whisky? He looks over at Buruk and notices that he has finished five steins and half the bottle of absinthe to himself. 'You will not beat him in drinking, he has already drunk five steins...' Ookonan says, leaning into Kaji. 'You have... Hhhh'

'Yeah!' Kaji says, pointing to his empty glasses and tankards on his side. 'One pint and a bit... Three shots... Great I am.' Kaji slurs.

Ookonan looks at the table and all the empty cups. 'Two shots and... Yes one and a half steins... Well done' He says, patting Kaji on the back.

Buruk bursts into a loud laughter seeing Kaji get drunk so quickly and easily compared to most people who challenge him.

†

Kaji lays motionless in bed staring at the ceiling. The world is spinning and he feels unbearably nauseous. It did not help his case to continue drinking even after two more pints. He looks over at Ookonan who is preparing himself for bed.

Ookonan pulls out a soft pair of pants from his backpack and lays them on the mattress. He starts to undress his upper body, neatly placing his jacket and outer shirt on the bed covers.

'Sick I feel.' Kaji complained.

'I did warn you not to drink with a dwarf.'

Kaji laid there wondering how Ookonan can feel fine in the cold room. The blankets were not enough for him as he wraps himself up with all three blankets available. 'Well he had drinks there ready…' He responds, struggling to keep warm while he also feels his mouth fill with saliva as the nausea worsens. 'Rude it is to say no.' He tries to argue as he holds back vomit.

'Hmmmm.' Ookonan vocalises as he takes off his undershirt. 'He could have drunk that whole lot on his own… He is a dwarf, Kaji.'

'Ahhgg, meaning I not know…' He said under his breath, now struggling not only with keeping vomit down but trying to translate and speak Euro Hondonian as the world started to spin faster.

'Do you not have Dwarves in Mir?' He asks, trying to picture this land, filled with people like Kaji and no demonics, it's so foreign for him and almost impossible to properly picture.

'No…'

'Hmmm, interesting.' He places his now clean boots next to his bed. He undoes his belt and takes off his sword and other pieces attached. He places it all next to his backpack and boots. Lastly he takes off his pants to fold and put away.

As soon as the pants come off, Kaji dry heaps and covers his eyes. Ookonan was not wearing any underwear and he was not prepared to see anyone's manhood. 'AHH Ookonan!!?!'

'You are ashamed of bodies?'

'No. Just is.'

'What? You are intimidated? Ashamed? A body is a body.' He says as he puts his soft pants on.

'Mir, do not, people. No show.' He badly attempts to explain. 'Naked, rude.'

'I do not understand how it is rude.' Ookonan says, now finally getting into bed. 'It is just a body… If you are intimidated I will do it more often in front of you.'

'Intimidated, not.' He says feeling embarrassed about the moment.

Ookonan lays flat on his back with the blankets piled on him for the weight, the only thing that irritates him is his feet laying off the edge of the bed. 'If you say so.'

They both lay in silence, neither of them are used to sleeping in the same room with someone else, especially not a stranger. 'First night this is. Away from family…' Kaji finally said, breaking the awkward silence. 'This far I have never been before.' Coming to the realisation that he is on the other side of the world.

'Did you ever wander far?'

'How you mean?'

'I mean, did you ever travel far from home? Just for the sake of it, I mean, exploring or uhh.'

'I, to forest and beach I go.'

'How far was that to your family?'

The room fell silent again, this was never something he has ever had to think about before, especially when the nausea was just getting worse by the second. The island itself is not very big and he's never left it until now. As part of the imperial family he was under some strict guidelines about where he can and cannot go. Everything had to be pre-organised.

'At most. Ten kilometres.'

'Only ten kilometres?' Ookonan giggled.

'Parents strict really I have.' He protests.

'Oh… That is not something I can relate to.' Ookonan said softly. 'You are doing surprisingly well with your Hondonian.'

A lump in Kaji's throat starts forcing its way up. He tries to force it back down as the last thing he wanted to do was get up in the cold and or throw up. 'Yes… Continents unite I studied in case…' He trails off, unable to finish what he wanted to say. He quickly sits up as the urge to vomit is now unbearable.

'It is not perfect.'

Without another word, Kaji throws himself out of bed. He runs to the door and gets out of the room as fast as he possibly could. 'Ta-ah na nasalam ka?' (*Where is the toilet*). He asks someone, now no longer able to process Euro Hondonian as all that's on his mind is, don't make a mess.

'What language are you speaking?'

Ookonan now comfortable in bed, he watches the door, anticipating what is to unfold. Never challenge a dwarf or accept the challenge from a dwarf in a drinking game. No one ever wins. The thought is quickly interrupted with the wet pouring sound of liquid hitting the ground.

'Clafarging Vekk!! WHY!!!'

'I did warn him… Do not challenge a Dwarf.' Ookonan said as he rolled over and fell to sleep.

Chapter 17

Kaji lays sprawled out in bed still fast asleep although the sun has risen, his mouth gaping as drool drips down a corner of his mouth. His breath soft as he sleeps peacefully forgetting that he is not in his own bed let alone his home island.

Ookonan is up and only wearing his day time pants as he makes the bed, smoothing out the sheets and fluffing up the pillow as he waits impatiently for Kaji to wake. He places his backpack on the bed and sits next to it as he begins to sort through its contents, double checking to see if everything is still there before putting his neatly folded nighttime pants into his backpack.

He sits and looks at Kaji, wondering to himself how long he normally sleeps for and how long do Mirish people sleep. The sun has barely risen, it's time to get up. He slips on his clean boots while keeping an eye on Kaji.

'Hey! Hey! Kaji! Wake up!' He shouts.

'Eahhgg ssssvv.' Kaji groaned, remaining fast asleep.

'Kaji! Wake! Up!' He stares at him for a moment, still no budge or sign of awakening. 'You have until the count of three! One! Two!' Ookonan says, taking his right boot off. 'Three!' Ookonan says calmly, throwing the boot at Kaji's belly.

'OOhhhfff.' Kaji grunted, waking almost instantaneously from the sheer force of the boot. He sits up with haste and scurries to the back of the bed, placing his back against the wall while holding the blankets up towards his chest. He makes an anxious effort to survey the room while his freshly awoken eyes manage to adjust, trying to figure out what had hit him.

Ookonan walks over to Kaji and grabs his boot off the bed, slipping it on and raising his eyebrows at him.

'THAT HURT!' Kaji blurted out loudly as he looked up at Ookonan. 'Ajore imhimja imajo.' *I forgot that I'm here.*

'Get up!' Ookonan demanded.

'Uhh, my head hurts.' Kaji complained, grabbing his head.

'You did try to outdrink a dwarf last night... I have never seen someone fail so miserably.'

'Yeah... Today planned what is?'

Ookonan says nothing, he nods at the new clothes for Kaji at the base of the bed. He looks back at Kaji and raises his eyebrows.

'Well, downstairs I will meet you then.' Kaji says, looking at his new clothes. The last thing he wanted to do was to get changed let alone get naked in front of someone else, especially someone he barely knows.

'You will want your pants you slept in as a spare. Hand them over, I will pack them away.' Ookonan instructs Kaji who remains unmoved.

'No... Change I will later.' He insisted.

'You are intimidated by me?'

'No. No. I am not.' He says, getting out of bed.

'Take off your pants so I can put them away and put your new clothes on!'

'O.o.Okay.' He says. He takes off his pants and awkwardly hands them to Ookonan before rushing over to his new clothes. In a panic, he struggles to unfold them and figure out which ones are the pants. He looks over at Ookonan to see that he is preoccupied with rearranging his backpack.

Ookonan looks over at Kaji after packing away his spare pants and rearranging his backpack to see Kaji has thrown his spare clothes on the floor and is rushing miserably to find the pants.

'Calm down. There is nothing to be ashamed of.'

After finally managing to identify the pants, Kaji notices that Ookonan has finished with his backpack so he hurriedly puts one leg in and yanks them up as quickly as he can, failing to realise that he forgot about the other leg.

'I will meet you downstairs.' Ookonan says, grabbing his backpack and walking out the room, closing the door behind himself.

He pulls the pants back down and places his other leg in the second hole and yanks them back up as fast as he could, falling over in the process.

†

Downstairs in the tavern people sit along the long tables socialising with morning alcoholic beverages and questionable breakfast foods. The people chatted about their plans for the day, whether it's cleaning the demonic blood and reseasoning the buildings, their crops, harvesting lumber for repairs and buildings and anything they may be trading.

Ookonan walks down the wooden stairs into the bright and warm tavern. Golden beams of light pierce through strung herbs that hang around the window opening. Ookonan smiled, knowing these people knew how to keep the corruption at bay utilising their herbs and spice well.

He walks up to the front counter to see how busy the place really is during the day. Multiple staff members work behind the counter rather than just the three last night. He watches one person grab a bucket of clean water and a mop to clean the front entrance of the demonic blood or any mud. He turns his attention back to the counter and the kitchen behind it. Staff were mixing a cauldron of soup, putting things in and out of the large oven and making herbal drinks next to some hot coals.

'Hello.' He says, trying to get attention from at least one staff member. But none hear him from the loud chatter of the tavern hall, the screaming kettles, the crushing of ingredients of the mortal and pestle for tea.

'Hello!' He called out again, successfully getting the attention of a staff member.

'Just a moment.' The staff member calls out. They pour hot water into a teapot filled with crushed herbs. Ookonan nods respectfully at them, acknowledging how busy they are as he watches them pour the hot herbal tea into four cups before putting them on a tray with a loaf of bread.

'How can I help you?'

'What do you do for breakfast?'

'Oi!! Where are our hot drinks?!' A tavern goer rudely shouts at the staff member.

'It is coming your way.' The staff member shouts back. They turn their attention back to Ookonan with their hands on the counter. 'What do you have to offer?'

'I have some gold, silver, and copper coins as well as some salt.'

'One silver, one copper and half a spoon of salt will get you a small meal and a hot drink.'

He puts down his back pack and opens up a pocket on the side, removing two bags. One that jingles with coins and the other more dense with salt. He pulls out two silver and two copper coins, he then grabs a spoon off the counter and scoops up a full spoonful of salt.

'Twice that will be two small meals and two hot drinks?'

'Yes. We have porridge with a side of mushrooms and beans or we have mashed yams with minced meat and sauce.'

'Uhh, the second.' he said, unsure which is the better option.

'And what drink? Flower or herb tea?'

'Flower tea.' He said looking over at the dusty herbs and the dried flowers.

The staff member clears their throat and looks back up at Ookonan. 'Before I make it, that will be two silver, two copper and a spoon of salt.'

He hands them the coins and the spoonful of salt. The server takes the coins and hands him a larger spoon. He pours the salt onto the spoon and digs out another spoonful to fill the spoon. The staff member takes the spoon as he reties the sack of salt and puts the valuables back into his backpack.

The server then hands him a wooden card painted a bright red with a Euro Hondonian number carved into it. He thanks the staff member and walks off to one of the long tables. He takes a seat facing the stairs which Kaji will eventually come down.

'It will not be too long.' The staff member says to Ookonan walking past with the four hot drinks.

'Alright.' Ookonan says looking over his shoulder as the staff member walks behind him. He watches the staff member carry the four hot drinks over to the angry rude customer at the back of the tavern near the fireplace. He is a large man with thin arms and patchy facial hair and with him sit two thin women. One is dressed in light weight clothing while the other is barely wearing anything at all, just some cloth wrapped around her chest.

Ookonan looks back at his hands as he waits for Kaji to get down stairs. He hasn't bothered to look at his hands in a long time, heavily calloused, broken nails and bruised knuckles.

He looks back up and over at the wooden stairs to see Kaji awkwardly walking down them in his new clothes. Leather pants, linen shirt with a leather jacket, he is holding his new boots. He scans the room in search for Ookonan, truly seeing how different Hondon is to Mir.

The place is packed, most people this time are wearing some form of clothing which was far more preferable for him. He looks up at the roof to see a window opening that wraps around a higher part of the roof filling the hall with fresh air and sunlight. Every window opening has herbs hung around them and the smell mixed in with the fresh cooking is overpowering for him.

He walks over to the Ookonan who easily stands out as the tallest man in the room and takes a seat next to him. Besides the overpowering smells, his new clothing feels tight and restrictive unlike the loose flowing clothing of Mir he is used to.

'Hi... Long I took. Sorry.' He said, pulling at the crotch and back of the pants, he tries to get comfortable in his pants but the more he moves while seated the more restricted his thighs and shoulders feel.

'I have ordered you some food and a hot drink, it should be here soon.'

'Well... uhh thank you.' He says, crossing his arms to lean on the table. The leather stretched tightly across his back. He starts feeling worried that his new clothes will rip, exposing him in front of everyone again.

Ookonan raises an eyebrow at Kaji, he notices how uncomfortable he looks in his clothes. He wonders if he is still feeling insecure about earlier. But there are important issues he must briefly discuss with Kaji.

'So... Things you might need to learn around here.'

'Know what I need to?' He asked, looking up at Ookonan.

Ookonan leans into Kaji, ensuring no one can hear what he was about to say. Hondon is dangerous, even local people never feel safe. He thought.

He leans into Kaji as closely as he can. He needs to make sure what he is about to say only stays between himself and Kaji. 'No one can know where you are from. No one.'

'Why?'

'It may be best if we do not find out.'

He leans back, placing his hands onto his lap. 'Say if you so.' he said, confused about why it matters.

'I say so.' Ookonan said firmly.

The staff member walks up to them with two plates of food. They place the hot food in front of both Ookonan and Kaji. 'Your drinks will not be too long away.' The staff member said before walking back to the front.

'Thank you.' Ookonan said, pushing a plate over to Kaji.

Kaji looks down at the food, it looks horrifying. Steaming mashed mess of purple potatoes with bits of minced meat throughout. He looks over at Ookonan, horrified to see him scooping this purple monstrosity into his mouth.

'This you eat?'

'There is not much better. You can go hungry if you want.'

'Do food better get in ho-'

'No, get used to it.' Ookonan quickly interjected.

Kaji sits there and moves his food around, unsure whether he could stomach it at the moment. He looks back at Ookonan who takes another large spoonful of the mashed mess, seemingly enjoying it.

The staff member walks back over holding two large steaming tankards of hot tea which they place in front of Ookonan.

'Thank you.' Ookonan says. He looks over at Kaji and places a tankard in front of him. He looks down at Kaji's plate, nothing has been touched. 'You might want to start eatin. Long road ahead.' He says, gesturing at the plate with his spoon.

'Go we where?'

'Not sure. I was not told what we must do.' He admitted.

'Ookonan! My Man!' A loud grungy voice called out.

Ookonan is smacked on his lower back. He looks around to see Buruk taking a seat next to him. The bearded man smiles at him and seems to be genuinely excited to see he's still around in the tavern.

'What are you still doing here?!' Buruk asks.

'Well, I decided to stay the night.' He said, putting a spoonful of the purple monstrosity into his mouth then washing it down with a mouthful of tea.

Buruk moves his attention over to Kaji, he raises his bushy brows at him, smiling behind his thick beard. 'How are you feeling, little fella?'

'Little?!' Kaji squeaks, offended at the remark the short bearded man said. Where he's from he is average in size and height.

Ookonan finished the last of his food. He smacks his hand on the table and twists himself to look at Buruk, scowling at him, hoping he could eat his hot breakfast in peace. 'What do you need, Buruk?' He asked firmly.

'I thought you travel alone.' Buruk said, suspicious of Kaji.

Ookonan takes another mouthful of tea. He's in disbelief of this man, who or what he travels with is no one's business. 'I have been and I made a friend along the way… Kaji here, who stupidly challenged you last night is from the east and decided to tag along… He has been lonely and for all you know I have been as well.'

'Right… Right.' Buruk said in disbelief.

'What did you need Buruk?'

'I am after an artefact.' Buruk said, softening his voice.

'When are you not Buruk?'

Intrigued by the conflict of the interesting looking men, Kaji finally scoops some of the purple mashed mess into his mouth. The texture is mush, it has an almost indescribable flavour he has never had before, the only thing he could make out was the flavour of a starchy yam that's been overcooked. He forces himself to swallow and hold it down in his stomach.

'That is a fair point Ookonan.' Buruk says, folding his arms. 'I am willing to pay very well for this artefact.' He says calmly and softly.

'What are you offering?'

'Spices, herbs and maybe some new weaponry.'

Ookonan takes a moment, he leans back and looks at Kaji who is gagging at every mouthful of the purple monstrosity; he's taking a mouthful of tea with every spoonful. It may be harder to hide where Kaji is really from, he thinks to himself.

'What is this artefact?' Ookonan asked quietly, turning back to look at Buruk.

'It is believed this was owned by Odin himself.'

Kaji chokes at the remark and finds himself coughing. He quickly drinks some of the tea to calm his taste buds and throat before going back to the disgusting food.

'This is the horn of purification.' Buruk continues as though he didn't notice Kaji coughing. He leans into Ookonan to speak quietly. 'I would like to have it.'

'Can you tell me about it? Where is it?' Ookonan asks.

'Legend has it that Odin made this horn himself. He removed it from a fierce bison. A pure bison if you have heard of it. Somehow not mixed with anything. Not a bear, not a bird. Pure bison.'

'Get to the point.'

'He hollowed out the horn and he carved his runes in it. Binding it with gold. But it was not complete. He then took the horn to his son Baldr to have it blessed with purity.' He leans into Ookonan and deepens his voice. 'This horn is believed to purify water instantly. It is believed to purify any drinking beverage. Do you have any idea how pure my beer will be?'

'Where will we find it?'

'You will find it north east of here, guarded by a monster of enormous proportion. I can not explain much on its location except it is north east of here. It rings a sound like no other and the area around it should be filled with life like no other. The demonics can not harm it.' Buruk explains.

'We will get this horn, but we will eat first.' Ookonan says, looking over at Kaji.

Chapter 18

People are sweeping the ashes and any debris of sorts off the roads, clearing the roads and moving the demonic corpses onto carts to allow foot or cart traffic as people start their day in the Fatencia provence. To start the day cleaning is the beginning of a potentially good day in most of Hondon. The village survived.

Now that the sun is out it is noticeable how colourful the road the tavern lives on really is. The trees are green with bits of orange, yellow and red within their leaves and bark. The wooden buildings are brown with patches of red from the spices being rubbed into its surfaces. The roads are reddish in colour, but not from the demonic blood. The roads are gravely and muddy with a coat of spice which is obvious in some areas. Not one building has glass in the windows as all are wooden window doors that open during the day when the demonics are hiding.

There are an abundance of animals around the village. Most unique to Hondon much like hybrids of animals of the past, pre-cataclysm. There are piglickens and buffalants amongst the dogs, cats and goats that live around the place.

The tavern door swings open and Ookonan and Kaji step outside. They both survey the village noticing different things. Ookonan takes note of the seasoned buildings while Kaji pays attention to the people setting up their shop stalls and doing their chores.

'Hey… Hey, tall man.' A young woman calls out. Ookonan quickly turns around to face her. 'Was that your bisonbear?' She asked?

'Yes… where is he?'

'He looked unhappy and a little lost. So, we took him over to our stable. Come. follow me.'

Both Ookonan and Kaji follow the woman across the street and into an open stable. Ookonan is immediately greeted by the bisonbear who had a comfortable haystack to himself as well as some water and a large bowl of leftover meat from the tavern.

Kaji stands awestruck with the magnificent beast. Animals like this just simply do not exist in Mir. He walks up to the bisonbear and pets its side whilst talking to it in Mirish.

'Hey… How much for some rope? To use as a rein for the bisonbear.'Ookonan asks.

'What do you have to trade?'

He takes off his backpack and pulls out a gold coin and a silver wrist chain.'Would this be enough?'

'Throw in a copper coin or some herbs and you have a deal.'

Ookonan quickly scrambles back through the pocket and pulls out three different sized copper coins. He holds them out for her to choose the largest of the three. He hands over the gold coins and silver wrist chain to her. The woman walks away for a brief moment and returns with a thick sturdy rope coiled in a neat bundle.

'This should be long enough and strong. Would you like me to attach it?'

'That would be great if you could.'

The woman walks over to the bisonbear's horns with the rope. Ookonan turns his attention away back to the tavern. Exiting the tavern was Buruk himself, the stocky dwarf walks down the steps and out onto the muddy street. Curious about what he's doing and why he is holding a clean folded piece of paper, Ookonan walks over to him.

'Buruk, what are you doing? Are you checking to see if we are both on our way to retrieve the horn?'

'Ahh, Ookonan my man! No, I forgot to give you the coordinates and instructions on how to retrieve it.' He hands Ookonan the folded piece of paper. 'What is that little brown boy doing over there with the bisonbear. Only savages handle those beasts.'

'Should I start referring to you as 'dwarf' then rather than your name?'

'HA! Ookonan, you would not dare.'

Ookonan takes the note from him and walks back over to Kaji. He opens it and reads:

Ookonan! The artefact is located in the grey forest, approximately six kilometres east from here. Remember I do not like to be kept waiting, I will be waiting with Galbor and Amadar in the tavern for your return.

'Hmm. It is not too far from here but the Vatpik did not tell me how little time we have.'

'Are we riding on that?' Kaji asked, pointing at the bisonbear.

'Yes! And we have a small window of time if I want to get paid!! Uuugh'. He gestures Kaji towards the bisonbear. 'Get a move on Kaji, we do not have much time.'

'Did not ask Buruk, for time why? Time we have?'

'The VatPik was pissing me off but now we have less now. Move! Get on!'

Kaji lifts himself up onto the bisonbear, sitting himself right on the hump of its upper back. He grabs hold of the wool and waits for Ookonan to get on. Ookonan grabs the reins which are tied around its large horns and walks it out onto the street before getting on himself.

†

No tree in sight is alive within this grey forest. Almost all the grey in sight is a thick grey clay like mud but also the completely lifeless trees that fill the full proximity of view. The whole forest is a skeleton. Nothing was moving except the swaying and rattling of the dead trees and nothing can be heard except the creaking of old dead wood.

Ookonan, Kaji ride the bisonbear through the cold icy forest. The bisonbear's feet sink into the mud with every step, but thankfully its thick fur protects him from the freezing mud unlike what it would do to Kaji and Ookonan.

'We are what for looking?' Kaji asks as he looks around the forest, finding himself looking at a depressing soulless death or the bright blue sky for some colour.

'Look for a sign of life or something gold. Look for colour that is not the sky.'

Kaji scoffed and bursted out laughing. 'Hahahah. Life?' He has only seen trees so dead in Mir that have been sun bleached after being dead for so many years.

'If what is said by Buruk is real, a small portion of the land around it should be alive.'

'Right... magic real make it seem like.' Kaji says, calming down.

'Seems that way. But we have been granted god powers.' He says scanning the area to still see nothing but the same colour, grey. 'Were you not transported here from Mir? Would that not be magic?'

Kaji thinks about that for a moment, realising the truth that has just been said to him. He did teleport to Hondon after meeting an actual god. It is possible to see life in this lifeless forest being formed by an object. 'For this, give you what?'

'What do you mean? I do not understand you.'

'This now, to get horn. Reward?'

'Spices usually. Sometimes something tasty.'

'Tasty. You know not.' He said recalling what they had for breakfast. 'Spice why?'

'Spice has many uses around Hondon. The biggest use is repelling demonics. The spicier the spice the better the repellent. Often the best is paprika but... reaper is the best and rarest nowadays.'

'Interesting...' Kaji takes a short moment to absorb and translate in his head what Ookonan just said to him. He wanders to himself how long it will take for him to better understand Hondonian. 'Paprika, just food in Mir.' He finally responds.

'Only food?' He asked surprised. 'Everything has more than one use.'

'Yes, not heard paprika repelling. Only weak.'

'Not even for bugs? But, demonics are sometimes weak I suppose.'

'Work, that will not. Other plants do.'

Ookonan ignores Kaji's remark and continues to lead the bisonbear forward through what seems like a neverending and painfully grey, dead forest. But he notices something disturbing. Some of the husks of what used to be trees are starting to get covered in demonic slime. He directs the bisonbear towards the slime. The slime follows life wherever it goes with a soul goal to destroy it, the most logical thing he could think to do would be to follow it.

'Longer how much?' Kaji now realising he can't take the soulless grey much longer, his eyes are beginning to feel numb, his body cold and his head aches.

'This is the type of land you must be patient with. You must be patient and... But ready.'

'Ready what for?'

'Anything can happen.'

'Understand I do, but life how long?'

'You need to stop complaining. Life is not easy, it will never get easier but right now you need patience.' He explains while trying not to get frustrated.

As they continue to follow the slime, colour begins to appear. The greens and browns within the dense grey. Kaji tugs on Ookonan's right arm attempting to grab his attention and direct them both towards the subtle colour.

'Ookonan, look!'

'What do you see? What is it?' He asks, continuing to look straight ahead through the deathly maddening grey.

'Green!' Kaji said, pointing to the right.

Ookonan looks to his left, but still only sees the lifeless grey. He does see some subtle bits of green but is unable to tell whether it's his own imagination or if it's really there. 'I can not see what you are seeing. But, I will turn that way anyway in case you really can see the leaves. It might not be real Kaji.'

He directs the bisonbear to the right, towards the green leaves Kaji can see. As they all continue in the direction where Kaji can see the colour, the ground around them slowly becomes firmer and livelier, allowing the bisonbear more stability and to move faster through the forest.

'I still can not see.'

'You told me to be patient.' Kaji quickly interjects.

'Hmm. Use my words against me.'

The ground became firmer and browner as they continued along Kaji's path. The trees closer to the artefact started to show some form of life as their leaves became greener and larger the closer they got to it while the lifeless grey started to diminish.

'Green you see? Finally?

'Yes. You were right. This time.' Ookonan agreed. He felt both relieved that it was the right way but also annoyed that Kaji, who has been in Hondon for not even a day, was right. The grey plays tricks on the mind and the blind.

The grey now fully diminished, new sounds of animals can be heard as well as beautiful sights of vines, saplings and sprouts can be seen all around them. 'Buruk was not making something up to get me killed.' Ookonan said, sighing with relief.

'He did that?' Kaji asked, astonished that someone would consider giving them a job just to kill them and that someone would even accept.

'He is devious and often can not be trusted. He in the past has sent me on deadly missions.' Ookonan admitted.

'Accept. Did you why?'

'I was desperate.'

'Desperate. No one that much.'

'You do not know Hondon at all then.' Ookonan said grimly.

'I from Mir!' He said, turning himself around to face Ookonan, looking at him as though he was an idiot.

'Hmm, yes.'

'Getting close are we?'

'I believe so.'

'Off we move and for it we hunt?' Kaji asks Ookonan.

'Get off the bisonbear? That might be wise.' Ookonan says, pulling the bisonbear to a stop.

Kaji pulls his left leg to his chest and slides off the right side of the bisonbear, landing on the solid ground which felt soft under his feet. He looks around for the most colourful area of the forest before proceeding towards a large patch of brightly coloured flowers.

'Kaji, be careful. It may look beautiful but you are in Hondon.' Ookonan says softly to him.

'Yes. Careful I will be. Down you not, why?'

'Our transport will run off. Check the most colourful place.' Ookonan says, pointing to a bed of flowers that appeared to have a large rock in the centre. 'Over there.'

He looks over in the direction Ookonan is pointing. There are more flowers than the other patch, with a large moss covered rock in the centre. But what's more interesting is that the trees surrounding it are also in bloom. The scents coming from that direction are divine, sweet, fruity and like sweets that could be found throughout the marketplace of home.

Without much of a second thought, Kaji carefully treads over to the rock while Ookonan watched with the bisonbear. 'What are you doing?' Ookonan asks, wondering why he is stepping so carefully in what looks like a choreographed sequence towards the centre stone.

'Unpredictable Hondon is?'

'Yes. Why are you doing that?'

'Demons to not upset.'

Ookonan watches anxiously, the antics are not only frustrating him but he is finding it painful to watch someone else do a job meant for himself. 'Do not be ridiculous. Get there faster!'

'Down calm!' He shouts back as he reaches the centre stone. He runs his fingers over its surface as he circles around it, investigating it but unsure what he is actually searching for.

'I can not find it.'

'Search for a hidden compartment.' Ookonan shouts as he keeps an ear out for any unusual sounds within the somehow lively but dead forest.

Kaji feels around the rock on the lower edges, rough all over with sharp points and edges. He moves his hands closer to the plants at the base of the stone. There it is a sharp straight line. He traces his fingers along it, feeling all its corners forming a rectangle.

'Something I found!' He shouts excitedly. He pulls out a perfectly carved rectangle block of rock.

Ookonan doesn't respond, he is too preoccupied listening out for any dangers. But there, he can hear it. Deep growls and heavy footsteps that got louder as Kaji shouted at him.

'If you have found anything Kaji, hurry up!'

Kaji slides his hand into the rectangular hole and leans into it as far as he can. The rock itself is practically hollow. He feels his way round to feel a lot of moss and a lot of mushrooms. He keeps searching until he feels something smooth and cone like with the exception of some patterned textures on it. He gently grabs hold of it and pulls it out of the rock.

He holds it in both his hands, it's beautiful. The horn itself is beautifully polished, the attached metal is carved with beautiful craftsmanship. He can't help but admire its beauty.

Ookonan gives a nervous smile as he watches the trees behind Kaji fall over one by one. Buruk wasn't lying but neither of them had time to celebrate. The deep rumble of the monster hiding within the grey forest can now be heard from Kaji himself. The scream deafening to all that can hear it.

'Ignore the flowers! Run! Get on here fast!' Ookonan screams.

He holds the horn with one hand. He leaps over the stone and sprints as fast as he can over to Ookonan and the bisonbear. He tries to hand Ookonan the horn, but he ignores it and grabs him by the arm, lifting him onto the back of the bisonbear instead. While Kaji is awkwardly adjusting himself into a better position, Ookonan whips the reins while directing the bisonbear to the opposite direction towards the destruction.

Chapter 19

The unbearable density of the greyness of the dead forest has returned, feeling more unbearably dead than ever before as it surrounds and almost suffocates Ookonan, Kaji and the bisonbear.

Anxiety slowly yet assuredly builds within Kaji and Ookonan as they ride the bisonbear back into the thick unbearably grey mud. The small pockets of life slowly vanished behind them as they rode further and further into the suffocating density of the colourless environment.

The withered bark of the skeletal trees started to decay or disappear entirely the further away from the centre they traveled. There wasn't a spec of life present within any of the foliage surrounding them. Concerningly, the monster was still out of sight due to the intensifying greyness of this environment, the only sign that they could rely upon were the numerous fallen tree branches which were snapped and almost obliterated, an unsightly image which could have only been caused by the undead giant.

Ookonan glanced down at Kaji who was leaning against the back of the bisonbear. He noticed the tension and anxiety building up within Kaji's body and he was still firmly holding onto the horn of Odin, although he didn't look pleased about it.

Ookonan disregards Kaji as his eyes closely examine his surroundings, specifically what was in front of him. He tries to peer through the grey forest, looking beyond the ever expanding population of macabrely shrivelled trees, searching for the opening of the colourless soulsucking hollowground. He turns his head, looking behind himself as the bisonbear continues to slowly charge forward through the thick mud. Trees begin collapsing left, right, and centre as they smash into the ashen sludge below, spraying the thick grey goop in all directions. Although, the undead giant: the reason behind all this chaos is still not visible.

'We may have to face this thing... The mud is too thick!'

Kaji's stomach sinks as he digests Ookonan's statement. He looks over his shoulder in an effort to search for the undead giant who was actively destroying these skeletal trees, although all his eyes could recognise was the grey debris being thrown around the lifeless forest. He glances over his other shoulder towards Ookonan who appears to be scanning the barren and desolate woodlands for something, anything that could be used against the undead giant.

'CRAZY ARE YOU?!' Kaji shouts at Ookonan with unfiltered horror.

Without a word, Ookonan fixed his gaze on Kaji, handing him the ropes of the bisonbear before turning himself around to face the back of them. Kaji does not take the ropes, leaving them to instead hang and partially flap in the wind.

'Take the rope Kaji!' Ookonan vehemently instructs as his eyes scan through the debris, searching for any sign of colour in this monochrome abyss.

'What?'

'TAKE THE ROPE!! I NEED TO LOOK FOR IT!' Ookonan demands with dire urgency.

Kaji makes an effort to balance himself on the bisonbear while reaching for the rope. As he leaned further to grab it, a large stick covered completely in grey mud flew at him, striking the sleeve of his leather jacket. Pushing his reluctance aside, he took hold of the rope while managing to maintain a tight grip onto Odin's horn with his other hand.

While this is happening, Ookonan sits facing backwards on the bisonbear, watching the trees plummet into the thick mud below.

'I can not see what it is yet. Do not let us stop moving! We have a chance of getting away!'

'A chance!' Kaji squealed. 'Get out alive we might not?!' He shouted at Ookonan, trying to remember his Euro Hondonian language even through all of this stress.

Ookonan looks over his shoulder towards Kaji who appears to be concentrating on the grey path ahead.

'You are in Hondon... There is always a chance of death!'

'Yes!! I gathered!' He shouted in retort while directing the bisonbear through a clear passage of lifeless trees. The grey mud seemed to get thicker and deeper through the clear passage, forcing the bisonbear to move slower and become fatigued.

Ookonan maintains his position on the back of the bisonbear as he disregards Kaji and proceeds his search for any visible outline of the monster that has been chasing them. He could see a faint silhouette of a large creature who appeared to be smashing the ground and creating a spray of mud before knocking over yet another shriveled tree skeleton.

'How are we going Kaji?'

'Stuck we get, tired he is Ookonan...' He responds while patting the bisonbear on the back of the head. 'Die we will.' He expresses with evident trepidation.

'Remember we have been granted god powers.' Ookonan retaliates while still maintaining his position facing the back of the bisonbear.

'Yes!. Use them I do not know.'

Ookonan finally caught sight of the undead giant that is chasing them. It is a gnarly creature, larger than the withered trees it is forcing itself through. It has glowing red eyes that can be faintly seen through the overgrowth of fungus enveloping its body. Covered with mushroom heads and what appears to be mycelium, splotches of red, white, black, and purple paint the body of the monster.

Its head is puffy and grotesque, resembling a clump of mangled mushrooms growing from a small skull. All Ookonan could distinguish from the behemoth's barely recognisable face were its razor sharp teeth, everything else was either hidden or entirely non-existent.

'No....' Ookonan exclaims with barely a whisper. His eyes are plagued with horror as his attention is infatuated by the demonic. He takes a heavy breath before exhaling and turning towards Kaji.

'Is what?' Kaji asks uneasily.

Ookonan anxiously surveys their surroundings, making a miserable effort to not show his fear. 'How well can you control fire Kaji?'

'Ookonan! Is what? Attacks up what?!' Kaji snaps back, annoyed at Ookonan with his transparency. I have been placed in Hondon doomed to my death within a day. He thought.

Ookonan catches his breath in an effort to further calm himself as he hesitantly turns his focus away from the fungal monstrosity getting closer to them in order to glare down at Kaji. He takes another deep breath. 'We are facing a yähris thoren..' He says in a thunderous tone while exhaling.

'Yes…?' Kaji asks, confused and looking for more clarity on what exactly the demonic is and what it is capable of.

Ookonan does not answer Kaji, instead he slips into the chasm of his own mind, lost in thought as his eyes go glassy. What will destroy this soul sucking abomination's rampage, and worst of all was it releasing spores? He turns his head towards the demonic which is moving closer at a rapid rate. It tears a skeletal tree from their dwindling roots and tosses it far enough that it lands next to the bisonbear, Ookonan, and Kaji.

Kaji jumps in shock, only just maintaining his balance onto the creature beneath him. He turns his head and looks behind himself, at long last seeing the grotesque monster who appeared to be made of fungus. Its giant mushroom head seemed to smile at him, baring its eerily sharp teeth as it screamed senselessly before smashing into and biting a tree, consuming the muddy grey wood.

'THAT CREATURE YOU EXPECT ME TO KNOW?!' Kaji cries at the top of his voice.

'Can you keep your fire at only your upper body?'

'I know not!'

Ookonan takes off his backpack and places it on his lap. He opens the top compartment and quickly pushes a few things aside. He examines Kaji, still trying to keep his fear at bay and prevent it from showing.

'Take off your clothes!' He demanded.

'WHAT!?'

'This is a fungus demonic. We are doomed if it comes too close to us. You need to set the place on fire!'

'Okay!' He said hesitantly, trying not to panic anymore than he already was. He takes off his beaten leather jacket and hands it to Ookonan who impatiently snatches it off of him. Kaji, although reluctantly, proceeds to take off his shirt and hand it to him along with the horn.

Ookonan hurriedly stores them away in his backpack before fastening the compartment shut. He assists Kaji with moving towards the back of the bisonbear as he switches positions with him, taking control of the ropes.

'Use your powers Ookonan. Disabled once is, use yours.' Kaji suggests while setting his hands on fire and moving closer towards the back of the bisonbear.

Ookonan places his backpack on his back and takes charge of the bisonbear.

'Yes! I will!'

Kaji nods at Ookonan as the fire trickles up his arms and expands across his chest and upper back. He observes the yähris thoren as it moves towards them, mangling trees under its feet, screaming and baring its long, sharp, and pointy teeth.

He hurls a fireball at the yähris thoren, missing miserably as it slams against the dead tree next to it, lighting it on fire almost instantly. Shaking with visible fear, Kaji hurls another ball of fire at the fungal demonic. Missing again as it slams against another lifeless tree.

'Blast the whole place, set the whole place on fire!' Ookonan thanklessly demands.

The yähris thoren rips another perished tree from its roots before savagely chomping down on it, feasting on the dull bark and the monochromic mud.

Kaji squints at the yähris thoren. He charges another fireball in his hand while waiting for a brief moment of inactivity from the demonic. He launches the fireball, pelting it against the monster's enormous chest and igniting it in a surge of flames. The yähris thoren stumbles back momentarily but seems incapable of feeling any pain. He hurls another fireball towards the monstrosity, striking it in what should be its face. The demonic stumbles further but remains resistant to pain, showing no sign of agony.

'Ookonan, fire not used to. Us out get.'

'Hold it off, give me a moment, I am not used to mine as well.'

He throws another ball of fire, which inadvertently splits into two. One travels behind the fungal demonic, striking it on the back, while the other lands on the dead tree next to it setting it alight in a bright blaze of madness. He charges another ball of fire with both of his hands.

He releases it as it flies towards the demonic at almost terminal velocity, hitting it in the upper chest and lower face. Flames spread across its body, forcing its movement to become more and more stagnant. The yähris thoren reaches out for a withered tree but the fire causes the shriveled wood to spontaneously combust, triggering the flames to burn hotter, brighter, and faster across the body of the monster.

Experiencing an agonising searing sensation from the red hot flames flaring along its body, the yähris thoren screams in misery and anger, launching itself towards Ookonan, Kaji and the bisonbear. Ookonan lets go of the ropes, charging his arms with electricity. Almost instantly, wind whirls around himself and the moisture from the mud surrounding the demonic is drained, trapping it in a motionless state.

'I have it.' He declares in almost a whisper while turning back around to face the front of the bisonbear. 'Hold it off and let me concentrate.'

'Got it.'

Ookonan brews a powerful storm around the three of them, draining the water from the mud, pushing the dirt and debris away from the bisonbear and summoning a whirlwind underneath the creature, forcing it to levitate. He looks over his shoulder, catching sight of Kaji blasting fireball after fireball at the fungal demonic, cooking it and rendering it immobile.

Ookonan pitches a substantial bolt of vibrant blue lighting at the monster, illuminating it in various sparks of almost lethal electricity. Closely following this scene, he musters a strong blast of wind, effortlessly launching himself, Kaji and the bisonbear forward through the skeletal trees of the barren colour-deprived forest and away from the yähris thoren.

Chapter 20

The afternoon is young as the people of Fatencia are finishing off their lunches or awakening from their mid-day naps, ready to get on with their day. It had been just over four hours since Ookonan and Kaji left on the bisonbear to retrieve Odin's horn, although it felt like an eternity as they were filthy, exhausted, and ready to collapse. The three of them were artlessly covered from head to toe in thick grey mud as if they had been rolling around in the stuff.

Ookonan dismounts the bisonbear, firmly stepping onto the dirt road of the town entrance, while Kaji slides off, clumsily collapsing onto the ground. He is still not wearing anything on his upper body aside from the soot in which his arms, chest, and back are enveloped in, leaving the townspeople to avoid him at all costs.

Once free from the weight of Ookonan and Kaji, the bisonbear wanders over towards the stables and collapses on the ground with a grunt. The stablehands move towards the exhausted beast with haste. They are holding several buckets of water, some for washing the filth off of the brute and some for resolving the animals' evident dehydration.

As the bisonbear walked off and collapsed, Kaji searched his surroundings, looking for nothing in particular. The sky is elated and clear, painting the backdrop of this intimate provincetown town a bright and energising shade of blue. People are wandering the town, working on chores he finds unusual, such as: hanging up new herbs and replacing old ones, repairing roofs and parts of buildings, mending the roads, feeding the livestock and pruning and watering gardens which are filled with an exotic mix of herbs, chilli plants and vegetables.

Ookonan ignores what is happening around them as he makes his way towards the tavern, up the stairs, and past the people rubbing spice into the verandah posts. He pauses at the door and turns around to glance at Kaji who is unmoved from his position on the road. He notices how filthy he is before reminding himself that he has something more important to deal with: the dwarf.

'Are you coming?'

Kaji cranes his neck to look up at Ookonan. He feels unsure about going inside the tavern, especially when he is covered in grey mud and what seems to be charcoal from the fire he started. Noticing that Ookonan looks furious, he cautiously runs up the steps towards him.

'Come in. We will face Buruk together and you will learn how it works around here.' He says while reaching for the door handle-latch.

'You mean in-'

'Do not draw attention to where you are from.' He snaps harshly at Kaji, cutting him off.

Kaji nods in apprehension. Ookonan is the first to walk through the tavern door, finding himself in the all too familiar wash room, although he was distinctly too filthy for the soapy water they had on hand. He gestures to Kaji to enter.

Kaji slowly yet assuredly enters the tavern. He feels awkward and filthy, an awful mix. He studied the wash station with disconcert and thought to himself: there is absolutely no way that this barrel of water would be capable of dealing with this amount of filth and grime.

The tavern manager inspects the both of them, from head to toe, while standing at the counter. Their face drops as they notice the sheer amount of grey sludge encompassing their bodies.

'NO. NO. No…' The tavern manager barked. 'Both of you! Get cleaned up before you get served.' They ordered, strongly encouraging them to leave and get cleansed at the bath house.

'We are looking for someone.' Ookonan said, ignoring the tavern manager's request.

'You will not be getting served until you both are clean!'

'We are looking for one of your clients.' Ookonan continued in a much more strident tone, showing zero care for the establishment's rules. He had something of greater importance and urgency occupying his mind.

'Get cleaned up. Now. Go to the bath house and get cleaned up. Then we can talk.' The barkeep demanded, acknowledging what Ookonan was saying but refusing to provide an ounce of help until the both of them were disinfected.

'He sent us on a suicide mission!' Ookonan declared, further raising his voice, compelling the tavern to grow silent. His tone was coarse and rough, like a chainsaw. 'We are looking for a dwarf.'

The tiniest smidge of empathy and apprehension strikes the tavern manager as he ceases his attempts to pressure Ookonan and Kaji into cleansing themselves. Plenty of quests and job offers happen within this tavern, each of them as unusual and deadly as the last.

'We have a lot of dwarves come through here… Be a little more specific.'

Ookonan looks around the room and notices that all eyes are on him, people have even stopped feasting. The room is as silent and still as a grave.

'We are looking for Buruk Fireflayer.' He discloses with evident frustration varnishing his expression.

'Who might that be?' The tavern manager inquires as they place down the tankard they were cleaning and polishing. They lean against the bar countertop, peering at Ookonan and Kaji.

Ookonan grunts as he takes off his mud smothered boots. He carelessly places them next to the barrel of soapy water before steadily removing his leather jacket which was splattered with the grey mud from the debris of the yähris thoren. He places the leather jacket over his boots and proceeds to trudge over to the tavern manager. He reaches the front counter and unapologetically towers over the barkeep.

'He is a short but rather large man with a thick red beard. He would have paid you well with trinkets and spices.' He says with a calm tone, placing his decrepit and fatigued hands on the counter. Veins were popping out of the back of his palm as well as his along his forearms, yet his face and neck remained relatively smooth.

'Y-y-yes I do remember him.' The tavern manager recalls while heedfully taking a step back from Ookonan. 'He left in a hurry.'

'When did he leave?' Ookonan interrogates through gritted teeth. The tavern manager clams up, feeling threatened and frightened by Ookonan's sheer size. Ookonan impatiently waits for a response but comes to the conclusion that he wasn't going to receive one. 'Are you hiding something?' He pried.

'No…' The barkeep utters with hesitation, clearly withholding information.

'Well?'

'He left about three to four hours ago.' The tavern manager confesses, taking a few more carefully placed steps away from Ookonan.

Ookonan tenses up as massive thickset veins pulsate down his hands, neck and face. He turns towards Kaji, locking eyes with him as his breathing intensifies and his facial expression heavies. He felt a burning itch between his shoulder blades and an insatiable need to break something, scream, or carry out a mix of the two. Walking back to Kaji, he stood utterly motionless in the wash room.

'It looks like I will be eating a dwarf.' He declared, feeling sick to his core.

'W-w-well we still can not serve you until you are clean.' The tavern manager articulated as they trembled, standing far behind the bar counter, doubtlessly fearful of Ookonan.

Ookonan turned around to face the tavern manager. 'I am not interested in anything but Buruk.' He said firmly, his voice riddled with anger.

'I-I-I m-may have o-o-overheard-'

'Do you know where he went?' Ookonan asked, cutting off the barkeep.

'He mentioned Brogan.'

'I apologise for my disturbance in your tavern…' Ookonan expressed, staring at them through his eyebrows. He takes a breath and turns to the barrel of soapy water before picking up his belongings. 'It looks like I will be heading to Brogan.'

He quickly slips on his boots and shows himself to the door with Kaji following closely behind. Kaji closes the door as the two of them exit the tavern. They meticulously yet hurriedly make their way down the verandah steps before heading towards the stables where the bisonbear is catching up on some well earned rest.

Ookonan meanders over to one of the stable posts before punching it with great aggravation, causing the whole stable to shake like a small earthquake. He looks down at his hands as he makes an effort to relax them.

'I was so stupid.' He says while turning to Look at Kaji. 'I let my guard down and put both of us in danger… FOR NOTHING!! WE GOT NOTHING!!'

'Ookonan. Calm down.'

'CALM DOWN!? I AM ALMOST OUT OF SPICE! IT WAS STOLEN!' Ookonan shouts with unclouded frustration. 'Do not say anything about it. Do not.' He says through gritted teeth.

'Not I will. Something I ask must.'

'What?!'

'Dirty I am. How cleaned? Before Brogan.' Kaji asked, still covered from head to toe with the soot and the thick grey mud.

Ookonan glances at Kaji, noting his sheer discomfort and underlying repugnance with his body's current condition. Ookonan takes a deep breath and makes every effort to relax his body.

'Let us get cleaned first then we will be heading to Brogan.'

He takes out his leather coin pouch from his backpack and walks over to the stable girl. Kaji ambles onwards towards the bath house as Ookonan offers the girl a couple of coins. Fastening his pouch shut, he places it back into his backpack as he catches up to Kaji and the two of them saunter towards the bath house together.

Chapter 21

Rolling hills compose the unruly green grasslands. Across these hills, trees are sparsely scattered and an assortment of colourful flowers are found amongst the grass. It had been one unbearably slow day since Ookonan, Kaji, and the bisonbear had left the Fatencia Province, and Kaji had become irritable and restless.

'Aaaaaaaaaaahhhhhhhg.' Kaji groans, boredom inching into his voice.

'What is it?' Ookonan asks, not really interested.

'Take much long will this be?'

Ookonan sighs, frustrated with Kaji's stupidity. 'Are you clafargin kidding me?'

Kaji glances at Ookonan with muddled eyes, clearly nothing behind them. 'Long this home it takes never.'

'You lived on a small island in Mir! THIS IS HONDON!! You clafarg!'

'Yes… Right…' Kaji acknowledges feeling slightly humiliated. Gazing back out towards the rolling hills, he finds himself wondering just how long the land goes on. Having been to almost every location on the Mir capital island, this was the first one where he couldn't see some form of coastline. 'I not been one for land study.' He confesses.

'Be quiet.' Ookonan disgruntledly demands.

Kaji could feel his whole body tense up as he surveyed the area. He wasn't quite yet sure how the demonics worked, he had only been in Hondon for a couple of days. To him they were a twisted mystery wrapped inside of an even more twisted mystery. What happened yesterday could just as easily happen any day, including today he grimly thought to himself as the hairs on the back of his neck raised.

'What did you hear?' He whispers to Ookonan, remaining vigilant.

'Only you… Now shut up. I want some quiet.' He barked at Kaji.

Kaji's shoulders drop as a conflicting wave of embarrassment and annoyance gets the better of him. Defeated, he slouches against the back of the bisonbear.

†

Another day had passed since the motley group had left the province of Fatencia. Dragging his paws and hooves along a muddy dirt path riddled with overgrown bushes and disproportionate patches of grass, the exhausted bisonbear was clearly drained from carrying the considerable weight of Kaji and Ookonan for hours at a time without any form of break. Heeding no attention to the steady rain falling from the dark grey sky above, Kaji, Ookonan, and the bisonbear are all soaked to the skin as they travel along the muddy pathway. Contrarily, small creatures scurry across the path in desperate search for shelter. Forcing the bisonbear forward without much care for its wellbeing, all Ookonan can think about is getting to Buruk as fast as possible.

'It is okay Rangi…' Kaji whispers, running his hand gently through the fur of the bisonbear's neck. 'We should stop soon.' He says to Ookonan.

Ignoring Kaji, Ookonan tugs at the ropes attached to the creature with heightened force, leaving the bisonbear no choice but to continue on the arduous trek.

'Ookonan…' Kaji calls. No response. Comprehending that Ookonan might not be able to hear him while lost in his own thoughts, Kaji calls again, raising his voice. 'Ookonan!' He sighs, realisation dawning upon him that Ookonan is deliberately ignoring him. 'Rangi is tired! We need to let him rest! We have not eaten in over a day!'

Kaji pauses for a moment before turning around to confront Ookonan who appears expressionless as he focuses on the path ahead.

'OOKONAN!' Kaji shouts in an unmistakable attempt to capture Ookonan's attention. Failing, he reaches for the ropes with the intent to tear them out of Ookonan's grasp. Playing the defensive, Ookonan whacks Kaji harshly against the side of his temple and whips the ropes, forcing the bisonbear to remain in motion.

He grunts at Kaji, exasperated with his endless complaints and pointless remarks.

Kaji's sympathetic eyes meet those of the bisonbear who visibly wobbles with exhaustion. Enraged by the giant who does not seem to understand fatigue, Kaji shouts, his tone loud and sharp. 'OOKONAN STOP!' Raindrops drip from Ookonan's face and down his jacket as his hair lays flat on his head, almost getting in his eyes.

'What!?' He barks, tilting his head to look down at Kaji.

'Stop! Rest, Rangi rest he needs.' He pleads.

Ookonan sighs. 'Who the vekk is Rangi?' He asks.

Kaji gently pats the bisonbear on its shoulder and looks back up at Ookonan. 'This is Ragni. Rest he needs. Keep going he can not.'

'We must continue. There is no rest here in Hondon Kaji. How do you not understand that yet.' He says firmly under his breath.

'Remember. Rangi animal is and rest he needs, you like or no.' Kaji remarks, fighting for the wellbeing of his newfound friend.

'Why are you calling him Rangi.' He asks, clearly irritated. 'He does not have a name, he does not need a name.'

Suddenly, the bisonbear comes to a complete stop, its legs shaking violently as they buckle under the pressure and collapse to the ground. Uncomfortable and in a considerable amount of pain, the bisonbear grunts as it lays on the muddy path, feeling as if it is knocking at death's door.

'Fine. we will rest.' Ookonan grunts, despising the fact that Kaji was right for once. 'His name will not be Rangi. If anything it will be Björn.'

Ookonan gets off the bisonbear and slumps himself against the filthy, wet, and slimy ground. Taking off his backpack, he places it on his lap before leaning back on the bisonbear. His eyes wander towards Kaji who gracelessly slides off the bisonbear and sits next to its broad head.

'Do not get attached to him.' Ookonan enjoins, looking back down at his backpack. 'He is nothing but spare food.'

Kaji glances over at Ookonan, sick to his core with disgust. He couldn't bring himself to believe that he heard what he had just heard. Does he not care about other sentient life? Has he eaten other pets before? Kaji thought to himself, fighting the urge to scream at Ookonan or throw up, neither of which he was convinced would bring much good.

'Cover we make? For rain?' Kaji asks, deciding to ignore Ookonan's out of pocket statement.

'No. We will be leaving as soon as Björn is rested. Rest up.'

†

Afternoon becomes night and soon thereafter, night becomes morning as a further day passes. It has now been three days since Ookonan, Kaji and the bisonbear left the quaint province town of Fatencia. Beneath their feet unfurls an expanse of strange layered rocks as they find themselves walking through a stone-strewn field scattered with ancient long-rusted pieces of metal and foreign vine-encrusted formations of stone and metal.

Maintaining a firm grip onto the rope attached to the bisonbear, Ookonan appears to be acutely alert of his surroundings, paying close attention to the path ahead of him and the unusual yet ageless structures surrounding him. All he could think about is getting to Buruk. On the other hand, Kaji wanders along a vine covered track ahead, relishing in the sunlight after spending so many hours in the rain.

Kaji spins around to look up at Ookonan who maintains a steady pace, steering the bisonbear and paying little attention to Kaji.

'How do you do this?' Kaji asks while walking backwards.

'What do you mean?' He counters, glancing down at Kaji.

Tripping over a stone along the path, Kaji recovers quickly, collecting himself and trying to make the mistake seem purposeful. Slowing down, he continues walking backwards in the same direction as his eyes meet Ookonan's.

'How do you walk so far and continue to walk?' He asks, noticing that Ookonan's breath is quiet and controlled despite the fact that they have both been walking for hours.

'You just have to keep going...' He says, tugging at the bisonbear a little. 'It is do or die. No exceptions.'

Kaji kicks a pebble and watches it skip along the path as he forces himself to keep moving. He can feel the muscles within his legs burning as if they had ignited into flames. Realising that the possibility of that happening was higher than zero, he looks down at his legs, and to his relief finds no smoke, flames, or any other form of fire. Instead, he notices that his leather boots are barely recognisable as they are now covered with dry and cracked mud and miscellaneous debris.

'Tired, my legs are.' Kaji whined.

'I need to care why?' Ookonan retorted, rolling his eyes.

Feeling the burning sensation of fatigue build throughout his body, Kaji further slows his pace and starts dragging his feet.

'Can I get on Rangi's back?'

'No! Bjorn needs a break from us.' Ookonan snaps.

The two of them continue in silence, stepping over ancient bricks, metals, and vines that seemed to stretch everywhere, with only the sound of dragging feet and heavy breathing filling the air.

As Ookonan remains utterly focused on the task ahead, Kaji's attention wanders towards the bisonbear who is similarly dragging their feet, exhausted and ready to call it quits.

Glancing down at Kaji for the briefest of moments, Ookonan notes that Kaji is lagging behind and staring almost yearningly at the bisonbear.

'Do not think about it!' He snapped. 'Keep moving '

'Converse may we, to distract at least from pain?'

'I am not into conversation.'

Chapter 22

The imperial palace living room is unique in its own sense, floors made of stone and hardwood, walls made of hardwood, paper and stone; the ceiling is tall with smooth thin hardwood beams that spiral upwards. In the centre of the room sits an indented square shaped lounge area, a hardwood short square table sits in the centre with thick square cushions placed around it fit for cross legged seating.

Hono sits alone in the quiet room. She has gauzes and bandages on her face along with her neck and arm. She sits motionless, staring with her good eye at her hot cup of untouched tea.

With the sound of scuffling feet, the door opens. A servant walks in followed by a doctor carrying a large leather case.

'Your Imperial Highness. The doctor is here to see you.' The servant said, bowing at Hono.

'Your Imperial Highness.' The doctor said taking a bow.

As the doctor walks over to Hono, the servant turns to leave the room.

'Before you leave. Get me a bowl of water.' The doctor instructs.

The servant nods their head to the doctor and leaves the room. The doctor places down their leather case on the ground next to a cushion before taking a seat next to Hono.

'How have you been your Highness?'

'Worried.' She says blankly.

'Don't worry, I'm sure your wounds are looking good.' The doctor says opening the leather case.

'I don't care about the burns. I honestly couldn't care.'

The doctor takes out fresh gauze and bandages and places it all on the table. 'Then what's bothering you?'

She turns her gaze away from them and looks at the fresh gauzes, bandages and serums laid out on the table next to her tea. 'I haven't seen him since this happened.'

'Seen who?'

She looks back at them, dumbfounded. What a stupid question. 'My brother.'

'But, didn't he do this to you?'

Another stupid question. 'Didn't I tell you that I don't care what I look like?'

'But...'

The doctor was cut off with the servant walking back in with a bowl of water. They stood still waiting for someone to say something or to give some sort of instruction.

'Thank you, just place it on the table.' Hono said.

'You may go now.' The doctor says to the servant.

'No.' Hono looks at the servant. 'I would like you to stay. Take a seat.'

The servant nods and sits across from them both. The doctor looks at Hono with very little understanding. Why would you want a servant near you? Why would I want a grubby servant near me?

The doctor puts a clean cloth into the bowl of water and lets it soak. He takes it out and places it onto the gauzes on Hono's face and lets it rest. She reaches for the servant's hand and holds it while she waits for the doctor to do their thing.

'Weren't we talking about your brother? Why would you want anything to do with him after he did this to you?'

'He is my brother. Do you honestly think he did this on purpose?'

'No, but he should have been careful.' The doctor says while removing the wet cloth and the gauze on Hono's face.

The doctor removes the bandages and is not gentle about it, she winces in pain as minor tears happen to her wounds. They put the used gauze next to the bowl of water and go for the gauzes around her eye.

'Careful? There is some irony there.'

'How do you mean?' The doctor asks, revealing her eye. It's red but not opaque or creamy in colour. She's finally able to see out of it after a week.

'Do you think dreamers would have any control of their new abilities when they were first blessed?' She asks, ignoring the question.

'No. But.'

'Exactly.'

The doctor opens the serum and puts it all over Hono's wounds before opening a jar of ointment and putting a generous amount on the burns. They grab fresh gauze and begin to patch her up.

'I was warned you would always have something to say, you're the sassy type.'

'Shut up and do your job.' She snaps.

†

Sunlight pierced through the arched openings of the white stone gazebo, the plants were swaying and bouncing with the soft wind and the water still running throughout the small streams and pools. The great rune stone glimmers in the sunlight, glowing red and letting the light bounce off the stone walls and roof of the gazebo.

The runes carved in the great rune stone are all visible, clean and clear, with the runes of Anahita, Gaiya, Whiro-te-tipua, Chernobog, Malsumis and Hundun. But on the side of the Great Rune Stone is a golden glowing crack over a now unrecognisable rune.

Chapter 23

Ookonan and Kaji ride the bisonbear through some ancient city ruins. Crumbled bricks, concrete and beams of rusty metal scatter the place in some unorganised piles. Some old structures remain. Some of which look like brick boxes without a roof or they have massive holes in the walls and some of the structures look like towers of old rusted metal beams which stretch into the sky.

The roads or what used to be are made of scattered pieces of asphalt with some areas being mostly intact and some areas of road seemed to used to be scattered brick if it wasn't covered in layers of dirt. Large trees have taken up some of the areas with large and thick roots growing through the remains of structures, rubble and roads. Moss and small plants grow in between old crevices left of the structures and any area which has a lot of dirt.

Kaji observes the ancient city skeleton as he moves through with Ookonan on the bisonbear. He's amazed at the thick vines growing up the tall structures, the moss covering the surfaces and the ferns growing from any crevice available. But there was one thing that was bothering him, the lack of sound in the air.

Every step the bisonbear took, every rolling leaf, every loud breath or movement of clothing echoes through. It was almost like a crackling sound in some cases followed by the creaking of the towering ancient metal structures, but the lack of animal or demonic noises he finds disturbing.

'Quiet too it is.'

'Hmm?' Ookonan vocalised, barely acknowledging Kaji or his existence. He is too focused on what is ahead and getting there fast enough before nightfall. All that is on his mind is getting to that dwarf.

'Quiet too it is.'

'What do you mean?' Ookonan asked, finally acknowledging Kaji.

'Sounds should be there.' He says, gesturing to the ancient decayed structures. 'Nothing there is. Mir night time no water sound except.'

Ookonan scans the ancient ruins attempting to look in the direction he is pointing, trying to understand what he is going on about. He just cannot understand why he is complaining about how quiet a place is during the day. Until it dawned on him, there are probably no demonics in Mir and the likelihood of anything trying to kill you is slim.

'It is normal for the day to be quiet in Hondon. But still keep an ear out for any unusual sounds.'

Kaji feels a little more at ease now knowing that the day is quiet unlike in his homeworld where it's the opposite. But there was still an uncomfortable feeling in his stomach, the sounds he could hear aren't birds or other animals; that every sound is bad news.

'Will do.' He says to Ookonan.

The two of them continued on through the skeleton city in silence. The sounds heard are those of the bisonbear, which still echo through the metal beams and standing concrete or brick walls.

The bisonbear takes a step over a large metal beam laying across the ancient asphalt. The moss covered rusted beam lays as a reminder of the great cataclysm which almost destroyed everything. A large gush of wind blows through the city, hitting the three of them. Kaji's anxiety increases yet again as he watches the tall beams sway and creek with the wind.

The wind howls as it rushes through the structures. The leaves on the trees and vines rustle, echoing through once more.

'Hear that did you?'

'That is leaves. Only leaves.' Ookonan mutters under his breath.

Kaji holds his breath as he scans the area. He sees the dry brown leaves rolling along the road, making him feel somewhat at ease again. He looked up at the metal beams and he could see them swaying with the wind like a tall tree.

Ookonan keeps his eyes on the road and both ears pierced on his surroundings, listening to the bisonbears footsteps, the creaking of the metal beams and any unusual movement within the shadows.

Kaji observes the area around them in awe as Ookonan directs the bisonbear over a bridge that is miraculously still standing after one thousand years. They cross the bridge over a wide ditch filled with rocks, ferns, small bushes and other plants as well as other interesting objects.

A massive rusted wheel like structure lays in the ditch, like a giant metal wheel for a cart, surrounded by more rusted, moss covered metal beams. But as they get to the other side of the massive ditch, they are greeted with more ancient structures, some that are mostly still standing made of interlocked stone. But the structure that catches Kaji's eye is the structure that looks like an ancient relic.

It's also made of moss covered stone, but the inside is filled with old metal structures that are like toothed wheels that are interlocked. But as they move to the other side, the glass remains after all those years, it has two pointy things that lay on the ground but the glass itself is a circle with twelve points. The detail of this thing fascinates Kaji, his imagination wanders how it would have looked pre cataclysm.

Much to Ookonan's care as his primary goal is to move through this ancient hole as quickly as possible. Kaji continues to look around the land, fascinated by what these skeleton structures could have looked like, what the sand that scatters the place really is.

His fascination was cut short when he felt his stomach growl and rumble. It felt painful as he forgot he really only gets to eat once a day as Ookonan really rations the food as much as possible.

'Ookonan...Ookonan.'

'What is it now?' He asks, glancing down at Kaji.

Kaji holds his stomach and looks up at Ookonan, his stomach aches and is growling as he notices his hunger, he realised he hasn't gone without food for this long before.

'When stop we eat?' He asks, looking up at Ookonan while grabbing his stomach.

'Cute...' Ookonan scoffs. 'We are not stopping.'

Kaji scans the area and listens to the sounds of the leaves, the creaking of the trees and metal structures. The only growling he could hear was his own stomach and the only movement he could see was the swaying of trees, small plants, leaves, the bisonbear and himself.

'Danger, it seems not here-'

'There is never anything safe around here.'He snaps. 'When we find something more out and open we might stop.'

'Might stop?'

'Harden up Kaji...' He says under his breath. He feels annoyed that he wont listen to him when he knows this land better than anyone and he keeps insisting on some form of rest. Soon he will harden up and learn to ignore pain.

Kaji turns to look at Ookonan, he can see his frowning and glancing down at him. He almost wonders if he feels anything at all.

'Hungry, you not feel?' He asks Ookonan, turning to look at him. He could see that he was looking down at him frowning.

'Do not be stupid. Hold the pain and move on.' He snaps harshly.

'Want you not to eat? why?'

'Will you wait? You are so clarfargin annoying. Wait until I believe it is safer to sit down and eat will you!' He says becoming increasingly more frustrated. He jolts the ropes to get the bisonbear to move a little faster.

†

A woman sits in the middle of the room by some small piles of white sand and in front of a small fire. She is wearing bright armour that has intricate patterns on its edges and a thick green cloak with golden and silver stitching. Beneath the cloak she wears leather plates, intertwined in an interlocked pattern across her body. Her forearms are guarded with leather cuffs with gloves that have pressed patterns of dragons and vines.

She wears leather trousers with thick stitches holding it together along with a thick green crotch cape with the same patterns on it. It's all held together with belts made of leather and metal around her waist and torso. But her final thing is her high leather boots plated with metal along the toes and shins.

The woman has exquisite features of those from the south of Hondon. Her face seems soft but with a sharp jawline, she has magical fluffy purple hair that is styled in a mohawk with dight braids along the sides of her head held in place with metal. She has long pointy ears covered in piercings. Her skin is dark and she has what looks like a green tattoo going up her neck and her eyes are a deep forest green like the plants around the crumbled building.

She sits in the middle of the ruins of an ancient building, cooking a rodent over some hot coals. She turns it over and juices came out of its charred cracked skin.

159

Salivating, she takes it off the hot coals and takes a bite. She savours the bite, probably her first and probably last meal of the day. As she places the meat on a cleaned rock, her ears twitch as she can hear faint steps outside of her hiding spot.

She throws her cloak around herself and quietly retreats to the bushes so as not to be seen by whatever is about to walk past. She keeps eyes peeled between the leaves as she waits.

Walking along the road outside of the ruins is a bison bear with two men on its back. A large blond hair tan skin man who appears to be half elf and a smaller dark man with unusual facial features and curly black hair. She observes them noticing strange differences in them, the larger man seemed intent on something, while the smaller man seemed curious and other worldly.

The smaller dark man grabs his stomach and looks in her direction, it's almost as though he is looking right at her. She freezes in place as to not be seen but takes the opportunity to scan his features. He has a stronger jaw, a wide nose, dark fiery eyes. He has the most beautiful eyes she has ever seen.

'Ookonan. Ookonan' He says.

She freezes in place, holding her breath. She could feel her heart pounding on her chest wall as she held her breath in an attempt to not make a sound. The last thing she needed was to be spotted or seen.

'What is it now?'

'When stop we eat??' He asks, looking away from her direction.

She lets out her breath, relieved she was not spotted. Finding it unusual that he potentially didn't smell her food. She backs away from the bushes and moves back to her spot. She sits down and picks up her meat and takes another bite, deciding they are not important or what she is looking for.

'Harden up Kaji.' The big man said.

Kaji, she thought. That is not a name that is used around here, or in Hondon. It could be from the east, but again it is not a name that Hondonian people use. She quickly munches down her food while twitching her ear to listen to them.

'Hungry, you not feel?' Kaji asked.

'Do not be stupid. Hold the pain and move on.'

She quickly eats around the bones, while listening to the unusual man's words, trying to understand him.

'Will you wait? You are so clarfargin annoying. Wait until I believe it is safer to sit down and eat will you!'

She breaks up the bones and throws them into the fire. She quickly shakes out the blanket and rolls it up and gathers her few belongings and ties them together before heading off. She has a feeling these are the men she is looking for and decides to follow.

Chapter 24

Buruk and his two acquaintances Amadar and Galbor are travelling by cart with an oversized muscular alpaca-deer pulling them along. On the back of their cart are bags, crates and wooden boxes stacked high, filled with teas, herbs, spices as well as trinkets, treasures and old technology of the ancient world pre cataclysm.

The land they are travelling through is pale green and grassy, there are hills of different sizes all around and many cliffs stacked on top of each other in jagged patterns. Much of the land has been squished and compressed throughout the grassy highland. It is filled with hills and cliffs and some surviving corners of buildings still stand throughout, which look like many small pyramids.

Islands float in the sky above, all of different shapes and sizes. Although they are scattered, some of the smaller islands are connected to the larger islands through a section of vines. The larger islands float in a circular perimeter as though they are tethered to the earth by an anchor.

Each island in the sky is unique in its shape, size and climate. Some are covered in snow and ice and some are covered in fire and lava whereas most islands are covered with lush green forestry. The largest island is almost cone in shape with the bottom coming to a sharp tip while the top is glowing gold with beautiful greenery. The sides of this island have gold and copper piping and what appears to be windows within the pointed rock, each with its own mini garden.

'What do you think holds the sky islands in place?' Amadar asks. An Androgynous elf who looks neither male nor female, yet looks like both. They have the smoothest face of the three of them and they have long hair that changes colour based on their emotion.

'Magic.' Galbor bursts out while looking at Amadar as though they are stupid. 'What else? How else would they be in the sky?'

Buruk raises his eyebrows and looks at the two elves, disappointed in the lack of brain cells between them, no one who sees something on a regular basis would question it. He thought to himself.

'Why are you two talking about the sky islands?' He asks, butting into the conversation. 'You see them often… very regularly. Why would you question their function?' He asks, looking at the elves either side of himself. 'Let us just hope that we get to Brogan with ease.'

'So you can give your wife some of the trinkets you have found?' Amadar asks, looking down at Buruk.

'Of course. She is the best blacksmith and inventor of all the land!' He boasts.

'So why did you not wait for Ookonan to come back with the horn?' Galbor asks Buruk, almost disgusted about leaving him but curious for Buruks motives.

'Amadar. Galbor.' Buruk says without giving either of the elves eye contact. 'I am not someone who trusts people easily. Would you both agree? Now Ookonan was with a new. Strange. And interesting fella. Do we not agree?' He asks looking up at both the elves. Both are silent.

'Odin's horn does not exist. It is not real. If they manage to find it. Then we have a problem. Besides having to pay him, I do not trust him. That interesting little man Ookonan was with is not his boyfriend… He is otherworldly, he is not from around here… Ookonan is not one for travelling with other people. Whatever Ookonan is doing, it could destroy me, it could ruin my plans and I do not want him getting in my way.' Buruk confesses.

Both elves glance at each other with raised eyebrows, neither of them felt comfortable with Buruk's excuse for his treatment of Ookonan. He has always been of great value doing dangerous tasks in exchange for spice, but never did they think Buruk intended on killing him.

Chapter 25

Ookonan and Kaji ride the bisonbear slowly into a large square opening, with crumbled structures of stone and metal and the surrounding area has piles of white sand and translucent small pebbles. The place is overgrown with tall trees, scattered around the place and thick shrubs and vines covering ancient structures along with thick amounts of moss covering shaded areas.

In the centre of the square lies a fallen damaged metal statue of which looks to be a man riding a horse now covered in moss and the exposed metal oxidised. Piles of rock and dirt are scattered across the small open space with grass and small saplings growing out of any open crevice.

Ookonan directs the bisonbear to the clearest spot of the square and scans the area, looking for any disruptions in the plants and ancient structures while also listening to any suspicious or unusual sounds. He slides himself off the bisonbear, landing on hard ground with a thick layer of white sand. He walks around the bisonbear investigating the ground and the surrounding area more closely. He takes off his backpack and places it on the ground next to the bisonbear before gesturing Kaji to get on the ground.

He clears some of the sand in a circular patch on the ground while he watches Kaji slide off the bisonbear and land softly on the white sand. Kaji stretches his back and twists himself side to side while stretching his arms and legs while watching Ookonan clear a little area curiously.

'I am going to need you to search for something that can be burned, we are going to need to start a small fire to cook our food.'

'Fire power I have remembered.' He says to Ookonan while pointing at himself.

'I suggest you rest it. ' Ookonan snaps. All he could think about for fire and powers is that neither of them can control it properly at this point, neither of them know how to properly turn it on or off or what actually activates it other than adrenaline.

'Kiðlamääne.' He says, pointing at dried leaves, sticks and small logs around the place. He squats down to his backpack and opens it to go through the contents. He takes out his teapot and a cup, he places them next to his backpack. He goes back through his backpack, searching the side pockets on the inside and out for a spare cup.

'Hmmm, I only have one cup gross… We will have to share.' He says as he goes back through the backpack and takes out the leather sacks of tea and other dried ingredients as well as the bladder of water.

'Soup…' He says looking at the ingredients laid out on the sand. 'I do not have any dried meat.'

After a couple of minutes, Kaji walks back over to Ookonan with a fist full of dried leaves and a large handful of old sticks. He stands over him, watching him fill a teapot up with water, he looks at the ground next to him, there sits a steel pot and a metal cup.

'Set up the sticks and set a fire for us. We are going to have to share.' He says, pointing at the cup.

'Otislaka. Bowl and the cup you sô kamji search.' He says, wondering how Ookonan forgets every time they stop to rest. 'My own I will get.'

'Set up the fire.' Ookonan snaps, pointing at the area he cleared.

Kaji walks over to a spot near the bisonbear and Ookonan's backpack, he squats down and starts stacking the sticks in a box shape with the leaves in the centre, he lights his thumb on fire and sets the sticks alight.

Ookonan fills the small pot with some dried vegetables and the few fresh ones he has left of the grassland village and pours in some water, he places a lid on the pot and puts the pot on the fire before taking a seat next to it.

'Hotter, I can make do. Go to faster it will.'

'I think that would be a very bad idea and I would very much like to keep my pot. Let us just sit for a moment.'

The two of them sit by the fire waiting for the water to boil before cooking the food. Kaji draws pictures in the sand out of boredom while Ookonan just sits patiently.

Once the water has boiled, Ookonan replaces the pot with his teapot on the fire. He places the pot in front of himself and Kaji and scoops some of the soup into a bowl. But before handing him the bowl he places his leather sacks of tea out in front of them.

'What kind of tea would you like?'

'You and tea, why?'

'It is relaxing and I can take a moment of peace. Try it... You will calm down.' He says, pushing the sacks of tea towards Kaji. 'Have a smell and see which one you like.'

Kaji goes through each individual sack of tea, smelling and inspecting their contents. Some had earthy scents while others had a grassy or creamy scent, a lot like the smell of home. But the smell and look was a satisfying floral aroma, the sack is filled with little flowers, it smells delicious.

'This one... Flowers I like.'

'Camomile. Perfect. Be prepared to relax.' He says, with some enthusiasm.

'Hondon, not sure how relax you do... See we shall.'

Ookonan raises his eyebrows at Kaji's remark, he hands him the pot of vegetables with a spoon and keeps the bowl for himself. He looks at Kaji, his eyes wide as he picks up the spoon, he shovels the soup into his mouth and devours it so quickly he is unsure how he could enjoy any of the Hondonian flavours. He looks back at the bowl he holds in one hand, mostly water but the vegetables have rehydrated enough for sustenance. He slurps the soup directly from his bowl, enjoying every moment of it. But when he looks back over at Kaji, he sees him scoffing it as though he hasn't eaten anything in days.

'Slow down.' He grunts. 'Give yourself a chance to hold it in.'

Kaji looks at him while slurping on a spoonful of soup with an already full mouth. He isn't used to eating only once a day, it's almost tortuous to him. Back home in Mir, there is never any need to conserve food. While slurping the soup, he watches Ookonan take off the lid of the teapot and put in some of the camomile flowers. His eyes widen about the thought of drinking flowers, it just sounds amazing.

Once kaji finishes the pot of soupy vegetables, he places the pot and spoon in front of himself. He leans back, taking in a deep breath of satisfaction while patting himself on the belly.

'The tea should be ready soon.' Ookonan says, still slurping up his vegetables.

The teapot starts to whistle. Ookonan puts down his bowl of soup and takes the teapot off the hot coals. He pours the hot tea into the cup and hands it to Kaji.

'Sahalatoh teleha.' (*Thank you*). He says, grabbing the cup with both hands. He blows the steam off the tea and inhales the aroma. The smell is floral and the tea, although hot, is light and delicate. He feels almost instantly relaxed after his first mouthful and it was as though the world has stopped for that moment.

He sits back, now having some kind of understanding of why Ookonan loves his tea so much and why he always insists on having tea when it is time to rest before continuing on the journey.

'Good?' He asks Kaji, watching him enjoy the cup.

'Tis good.' He says taking another mouthful.

An abrupt rustle in a bush disturbs Ookonan, his ears twitching in its direction. He stops what he's doing and listens carefully, his superior elven ears picking up the subtle breathing of someone hiding. He puts his bowl of soup down and gets to his feet.

'Is it what?'

'There is someone watching us…' He says, turning his head to look back at Kaji. 'I believe they have been following us.'

As he neared the bush another abrupt rustle happened. Whoever or whatever is hiding there seems fearful as its breathing becomes heavier. It tries to hold it's breath, but cannot as the big man approaches. He peers through the bush, but sees nothing but a suspicious shiny piece or metal, out of place for the ruins of this city.

He grunts and rips out the leaves and branches of the bushes until the shiny piece of metal is more exposed, revealing a shoulder plate which quickly moves away. He continues to move and pull out more of the bush until he sees the face of an elven woman.

She is wearing shiny metal plated armour, fixed up with green and gold fabric. She has exceptionally dark skin but with the most vibrant fluffy purple hair fixed in place with jewels. Her ears are longer than Ookonans, ending in a long point and she has piercings all down each of her ears.

He forcefully grabs her, dragging her out of the bush into the open. But as she tries to hit and kick him, he turns her around to face Kaji, while he locks her arms in place behind her.

'Who are you? Why are you following us?'

'Let me go!' She shouted.

He looks over at Kaji, he nods at his bag and beacons him over with it. Kaji walks over to his backpack and tries to lift it. What is he carrying? It is ridiculously heavy.

'On the side pocket I have some rope.'

He opens the side pocket and pulls two small but neatly bound bits of rope. He closes the pocket and takes them over to Ookonan now coming to the realisation how tall this woman is. He backs away and sits by his cup of tea.

'I will ask you one more time. Who are you and why are you following us?' He snarls through gritted teeth as he ties her wrists together.

'I overheard you talking here in old London so I followed because you…' She says looking over at Kaji. 'I believe you are not from here… I think I know more about you two than either of you know about yourselves.'

Chapter 26

Ookonan, still maintaining a tight grip on the woman, has bound her arms together tightly as Kaji watched while leaning on the bisonbear. He's mesmerised by her, one of the most beautiful women he has seen in his entire life. Her fluffy purple hair is mesmerising even her eyebrows and eyelashes are purple. Her facial features are unique and her ears are far longer and pointier than Ookonans. He just can't keep his eyes off her.

He continues to drink his delicious cup of tea as he watches Ookonan force the woman to sit down. He's unsure why he's being so harsh to her. He tries to focus on his tea and drink that instead until Ookonan finally speaks again.

'Who are you!' Ookonan snarled, looking the woman over.

'I will not answer to you.' She snapped back firmly.

He squats down to her level and he looks at her long pointy ears, flicking one. The rings on her pierced ears wobble and rattle against each other. 'Why are your ears so long and pointy?'

'Are you joking?!' She scoffs while trying not to laugh. 'Are you serious right now?! Have you looked at yourself?!'

'I rarely see elves far from their city and I never see them alone... So you could be a fake.'

'You are an elf!' She snaps back at him.

Frustrated, he stands up and takes a few steps away from her. 'How do you know who we are?' He snaps back at her, changing the subject.

'I do not know who you are.' She tries to hide how intimidated she feels over Ookonan. She looks over at Kaji. 'He is not from around here. His name is unique.'

'Why are you interested in him?' He asks firmly, deepening his voice.

'I will not be giving you information on myself, my missions or my purpose.'

Kaji, feeling like a lost dog in this situation, quickly finishes his tea and puts down the cup. 'Ookonan, tea of cup you want?'

Ookonan's face turns bright red as he looks over at Kaji. 'Shut up! Drink some more tea.'

'So, you are Ookonan.' She smirks.

Ookonan freezes, his heart sinks as a strange woman now knows his name. He has no idea what her purpose is, who she is or her intentions. The thought of her intentions to have her way with himself and Kaji terrifies him. For all he knows, she wants to kill Kaji. 'Who are you?' He asks again.

'That is none of your business.'

'Hello.' Kaji blurts out. 'Kaji, I am-'

'Never introduce yourself to strangers.' Ookonan quickly interjects, throwing the water bladder at him. He turns his attention back to the mysterious woman. 'Especially if she is hiding something.'

'I know who Kaji is for the most part.' She says, rolling her eyes at Ookonan. 'He is not from this land.'

'How do you know his name!' He snaps, trying to control his temper.

'He just said his name. Are you diarog? But I overheard the both of you talking further in this skeleton city of old london.'

He looks over at Kaji and gestures to his backpack with his chin. 'Pack the bag and Bjön.'

'His name is Rangi.' Kaji says, picking up Ookonan's belongings off the ground.

The woman sits still and watches the two of them pack Ookonan's backpack and bicker over the name of the bisonbear. She looks over at the bisonbear who lays on its belly trying to relax. It's majestic, she thinks to herself. Mesmerised by its thick wooly coat, its large horns, a cow-like nose but the face of a bear, large bear claws but hooves on its back legs, it's huge. But another peculiar thing gets to her, that behind its eyes is a long life but a lot of pain.

'It is Björn, do not get too attached to him.' He says getting more frustrated.

Snapped out of her moment by Ookonan claiming the name is Bjön again, she recognises the long life of pain was not by Ookonan whatsoever. But she fell sick of the bickering over the majestic beast. 'I can find his real name, you know.' She loudly interjects.

'You are not moving anywhere.' Ookonan says firmly, looking over his shoulder at the woman. He turns his attention back to his belongings and packs his backpack in his particular order.

The woman sighs at the boys, her legs aren't bound it would be easy for her to escape. But that will not bring trust. Ookonan seems like the type who would kidnap her all over again anyway. She gets to her feet and walks over to the bisonbear.

Ookonan, seeing her walk over to the bisonbear goes to stop her. But before he could do anything, she sits herself down and places her face on the beast. her eyes turn bright white as she breathes out softly.

†

The atmosphere is static and foggy, seeing in this world is difficult, as though we are in a distant burned memory. But then things slowly begin to appear in puffs of white smoke. revealing a land of ice with the usual Hondonian decay. Black soil with ice scattered across it as large chunks and frost.

A decayed memory revives as a small village from the frostlands appears. There are wood and skin huts all around and every one has some form of spice rubbed into it and herbs hanging anywhere where they could be hung. This is quickly interrupted as a young person walks through the fog and up close until their face clears revealing a young girl with long black braided hair that is decorated with beads and fur.

'Come on Yuma.' She says hugging the fog. 'Yes, you are a beautiful boy.'

The girl walks away towards a wooden hut, the fog follows her closely and stops at the door. The girl opens the door and walks in as the fog looks down at the ground seeing two large fluffy bear-like paws. The fog looks back up to see the girl holding a pot of honey out, she's smiling as she pulls a spoon out. A large bear-like paw grabs the spoon.

She reaches in for cuddles and scratches the fog as it eats the honey off the spoon. But things drastically turned dark. When the girl moved away from Yuma, he looks around. The village is in a deathly chaos.

The dreaded gurgling sound everyone from Hondon knows. The sound of demonics have arrived. The girl looks terrified. Yuma, the fog tries to grab her and take her away. Then the fog grew, the memory burned. All that can be seen are the people of the village running in terror, demonics eating corpses. The dreaded slime and the kumdria slither its way in consuming all that lays in its path.

All that's seen is death, demonics slashing at other bisonbears left the fog screaming. The veins of the people turned black as the black slime poured from their mouth. The fog is the sole survivor.

Out in the distance he sees a black hooded figure, but the memory facedes and the fog thickens, transforming it into the face of Aniuken.

'You seem lost.' He says, with care, all he wants to do is help.'Come along with me.'

The fog becomes thick once more showing the face of Ookonan. 'Come along with me. I need you.' The fog becomes thicker once more as the vision fades into nothing.

†

She sits up, her eyes still completely white. She suddenly breathes back in as the green of her eyes returns. 'His name is Yuma.'

A sudden respect from Ookonan was almost earned. He's fascinated by what happened, did she just read the bisonbears past? What did she even see?

'What just happened?' Kaji asks, taking a step away feeling fearful of the woman.

'His name is Yuma and he is originally from the north. A little bit older than he looks.'

'You did not answer the question.' Ookonan says, managing to maintain a calm. 'What just happened?'

'I just had a brief vision of his life. Yuma is from the northern frostlands. It is likely his village was destroyed.'

He raises an eyebrow at her, unsure whether to believe her or not. But from current events and her eyes turning completely white, he has no reason not to believe her. He walks over to Kaji and grabs his backpack. 'Yes. Anyway, we must all be heading off. Kaji, did you pack everything away?'

'Yes.' He says, looking up at Ookonan. 'Grabbed everything I did.'

'Good, we must all be off.'

'Great.' The woman says standing up. 'So you can release me now.' She says showing Ookonan her bound hands.

'No. You are coming with us.' He says, blankly.

Her stomach drops once those words exited his mouth. Anxiety starts running through her veins. She feels as though she knows them but she knows nothing of Ookonan's intentions. She has her own mission she must accomplish, she has a destiny to fulfil.

'I can not go with you… I am on-'

'For the safety of Kaji, you are coming with us.' He interjects cutting her off. 'You know too much about us and you are hiding too much from us.' He points at Kaji. 'As much as I do not like him, he can not die.'

She takes a step back, looking over at Kaji who seems oblivious to their conversation as though he doesn't fully understand him. He stands there scratching Yuma's neck. She turns her attention back to Ookonan.'I have an artefact I must find.'

'You should have thought of that before you started stalking us.' He says, grabbing her upper arm, directing them over to Yuma. He grabs the rein and gets him to his feet, he gestures kaji with his chin to get up. He then boosts the woman up to sit behind Kaji before putting his backpack on and getting up himself.

'Can we get the artefact first? It is important.'

'We are not falling for that again. We are heading to Brogan.'

Chapter 27

Stars dance aimlessly around the boundless sky, encompassing the inviting luminescent moon and stars twinkling elegantly. The indigo blue of this starry night time sky gracefully backdrops the capital island of Mir where Hono and her three friends: Toakase, Alefosio, and Koloa, are wandering the drawn out streets holding lamps, still in desperate search of Kaji.

The typically animated metropolis feels strangely quiet and almost intimate tonight with the only noises being those of the bats flying overhead, the crickets hiding amongst the grass, and the waves as they crash against the sand of a nearby beach.

'We still have not checked the beaches, cliffs, and forests.' Hono vocalises, clearly beginning to feel hopeless in the search for her brother.

'Yes true…' Toakase sighs. 'We should check there soon, we have not finished back alleys.'

'Yes, Toakase. We will check there next.' Hono confirms, still scanning the streets with great scrutiny.

Alefosio, thinking he might have heard something get knocked over nearby, comes to a halt and peers down a dark alley. He surveys the passageway in firm belief that he might find something.

Toakase approaches Alefosio and gently places her hand on his shoulder. He remains unwavering, searching the dark alley for even the smallest of signs leading to Kaji's presence, while Hono and Koloa proceed down the street past them.

'We will find him.'

Alefosio takes a hitched breath and looks at Toakase. His rough and rugged face almost sheds a tear, feeling indisputably overwhelmed and irreparably helpless. 'I hope so.' He says, his voice barely a whisper as he looks over at the other two.

'TOHRO…' Hono shouts, raising her voice louder than she ever thought possible. 'TOHROSHATAN!!'

Alefosio and Toakase briskly catch up to Hono and Koloa, being met with a question riddled with hope. 'Any luck?' Hono asks them.

'No…' Toakase sighs. 'Hono, it is getting late. Should we try searching some more tomorrow?'

'I am going to keep searching… I cannot sleep.'

Koloa takes a deep breath and walks in front of Hono. His exhausted eyes meet her mournful eyes as he delicately places his hands on her shoulders in an effort to comfort her.

'We will find Tohro, we will do everything we can to find him.'

Hono lowers her head, taking a breath and holding back the storm of tears that so desperately want to break free. Instead, she pushes aside her fear and worry, even just for the slightest of moments and leans in to give Koloa a hug, thankful for the company. Letting go of Koloa, she takes a step away from him, still trying to burrow her emotions. She hopes and believes that he is here somewhere on this island.

'Thank you.' She says to Koloa with full sincerity.

'We should all split up and search the island and meet back at the training ground in the morning.' Toakase suggests.

'That is a good idea.' Alefosio agrees. He looks over at Hono, in an effort to discern her stance. 'We can cover much more ground much more quickly to find him.'

Koloa and Hono nod in accordance.

'So we will meet up at the training ground at what time?' Hono asks.

'Make it as soon as you notice the sun rising.' Koloa says, taking a few steps back.

'Five in the morning, six at the latest.' Toakase instructs. 'Got it.'

Hono takes a steady breath. 'Thank you guys so much.' She expresses earnestly, her voice barely audible as she fights the urge to ball her eyes out.

'We will find Tohro.' Alefosio assures.

'One of us will tonight.' Toakase reassures.

All four of them take a definite step closer to each other as they extend their arms, forming an impenetrable group hug. Dropping their arms in unison and smiling, Hono, Koloa, Toakase, and Alefosio take a step away from each other as they start walking in opposite directions to further the search for Kaji.

'Do not stress. He will be found.' Koloa promises.

Hono continues down the dimly lit street and heads towards the forest and cliffs by the beach. She turns and walks down an alley between some houses.

The alleyway has a stone path along its base and fences either side, covered with a mixture of unruly ferns, fruit vines, and other small miscellaneous plants. As she walked through the alley, she could smell the scent of salt becoming stronger and stronger. Goosebumps invaded her legs, arms, and neck as the air became chilly, misty, and thick.

Reaching the mouth of the forest, Hono struggles to see through the increasingly thick ocean mist. Despite the best efforts of the velvet moonlight, beaming through the thick trees and hot lantern's illuminative light, neither were enough to cut through the thick salty fog.

Stepping onto the thick juniper green grass of the forest floor, she can feel the damp leaves fallen from one of many trees under her feet. The forest is immense yet sparse, with moss covered boulders lying between trees of differing sizes, colours and styles. There are very few ferns and miscellaneous plants scattered senselessly throughout the biome.

She carefully inhales and feels the cold moist air fill her lungs. She can feel the frosty mist clawing against her sweat steeped skin making her feel clammy and uneasy as if her already subsisting stress wasn't worse enough.

'Okay Tohro, I have not checked this forest yet…' She exhales, taking a few more determined steps into the dense forest. 'This is by the beach you were found at…' Hono explains, finding reason for her own actions while feeling the anxiety filter through her veins.

'Please just be here crying like a baby.'

She heedfully patrols the forest, shining her lantern against the forest floor and scanning for any footprints. Stepping slowly through the forest and over countless rocks, she calls out for her brother in hopes that he might be nearby.

'TOHRO!'

She comes to a sudden stop, trying yet failing to keep her breath stable and silent. She makes an effort to scan the forest for any movement or unexpected noises, but all she can hear is her own panicked breathing.

All she could bring herself to fathoming was the fact that her brother was dead, or at least the all too real possibility that he was. She dreaded the idea of finding his corpse, so much so that her breathing would become tighter and more strenuous and her chest would begin to simultaneously burn and sting feverishly every time that thought invaded her mind. Shoving her thoughts aside, she inevitably saved herself from a foreseeable heart attack as she proceeded to walk through the murky woodlands, grasping tightly onto any last speckle of hope she had left.

Startlingly, in the distance, the snapping of a branch is heard followed by a series of heavy footsteps. Hono silences herself through holding her breath before meticulously surveying the area and making a desperate effort to concentrate on the nearby footsteps.

'Please let that be you.' She whispers to herself while taking a breath.

She purposefully strides towards the direction of the footsteps, wishing that she would find her brother on the other end of them. She could feel her heartbeat pounding on the inside of her chest as she managed to hold back the cyclone of emotions that dreadfully wanted to push forward and engulf her.

'TOHRO!.... TOHRO!!!!'

The footsteps, seemingly heavy and uncoordinated as if from more than one person, appear to increase in speed, moving closer and closer towards her.

'TOHRO IF THAT IS YOU, FOLLOW MY VOICE!!'

'Hey!. What are you doing out here?' A gravely masculine voice calls out.

'I am coming to you!'

Two shadowy figures approach her. She can discern the faces of the men under the dying light of her lantern. They are both wearing uniforms accustomed to the authorities of the capitol island, however, she recognises neither of them. One of the men is larger, more muscular, and has a round face while the other is a much skinnier man who is slightly darker.

'Princess Hono....?' The burlier of the men asks, shocked to see the imperial princess of Mir out in the middle of the forest this deep into the night.

'WHY!?' She screams, devastated that the footsteps didn't lead to her brother and wanting nothing more in this moment than to curl into a ball and hide away from the world. 'Why did it have to be you guys?' She asks in a barely audible tone.

'We are sorry…' The skinnier authority says, confused as to why she is in the midst of the forest. 'What are you doing out here?'

She takes a deep breath and looks up at the men, struggling with great difficulty to contain the raw emotions wanting so badly to break free. 'I am looking for my brother. Have you even been looking?'

'Hono… We are sorry to tell you… But we cannot find him anywhere…' The larger man states apprehensively.

'You are just not looking!' She says, collapsing to the ground and allowing her emotions to surge forward, taking full control of her mind. 'I WOULD NOT BE OUT HERE SEARCHING IF YOU DID YOUR JOB!' Tears relentlessly stream down her now damp face.

'Your Imperial Highness… We are doing our best. But he is nowhere to be found. In the morning we will be sending out messages to the other islands.'

'Just…' She tries to speak, but more tears unapologetically pour down her wet face, making her voice shaky and unstable.

'We promise. Now head home. Get some rest.' The skinnier man says, trying to comfort and reassure her, however clearly failing.

A few moments pass before an abrupt high pitched sound breaks the silence, followed closely by the sound of nearby movement. It sounded wet and slimy in the worst of ways, as if a massive slug was passing by. Despite her grief-driven emotional state, Hono's instincts kicked in as she immediately turned around and moved her lantern towards the direction of the noise, revealing a dark grotesque goo-like substance on the side of a tree. It smelt like a rotting corpse.

'Take a note of this.' The larger man says to the skinnier before turning to look at Hono stubbornly. 'Head home now. Come on, we need to move.'

Hono ditches the men as they look between each other and the strange substance. She bolts through the woodlands and out of the forest, while making an effort to control the tears which continue to fall down her face without remorse.

Chapter 28

The prepossessing islands, as if defying gravity, remain hovering in the sky. Now painted a stunningly royal purple, this early nighttime sky hosts a multitude of glistening stars as the sun, now merely a vivid red in the horizon, has been replaced by the shimmering moon.

The light reflected from the moon and the stars shine brightly between the sky islands, making the land appear as if it is almost glowing.

As Buruk, Amadar, and Galbor travel under the sky islands, through the ancient remains of the pyramid structures, they look up in awe. Although they have made this trip many times before, seeing the whales, dolphins, and fish swimming amongst the sky never loses its magic, it never gets old. Watching the islands move so close to the ground that they could almost touch them by reaching up is always a satisfying feeling for Amadar.

'This is so beautiful.' Amadar gasped, stunned by the beauty.

Buruk leans back on the seat of the carriage, tilting his head as he looks up at the sky. He sighs with satisfaction and reverence as his eyes meet the glimmering stars above. Strange yet beautiful, he had a clear, breath-taking view of the milky way as a family of whales flew past.

'Do you think we can stop here for the night and leave at dawn?' Galbor asks.

'It is not really safe to stay near the sky islands for long.' Amadar calmly explains, keeping an eye on the sky, mesmerised by the whales dancing overhead and the fish swimming around the islands.

Galbor glances at Amadar who is reaching for the sky as various fish of differing sizes, mostly small, swim around their fingers. 'What do you know Amadar?' He scoffs. 'You are a ânälääsïna.'

Buruk sits up and begrudgingly looks over at Galbor, raising an eyebrow. 'As we can agree that Amadar is not the brightest person. We shall not call them an ânälääsïna... just a bit rude.'

Amadar straightens themself before glaring at both Buruk and Galbor, feeling annoyed and frustrated with the both of them. 'We should leave. I can not remember if it is fairy season.'

'Fairy season?' Galbor scoffs. 'You have to be joking?!'

'You know fairies live on the sky islands?' Amadar pressed, getting increasingly more frustrated.

'What is your point?'

'It is not safe. We need to move on.' Amadar declared with a certain urgency in their tone.

'Alright! Now.' Buruk challenges, gesturing to the sky islands above and looking at Amadar. 'Do you see any fairies?'

'N-no.' Amadar mutters, flustered as they raise an eyebrow at Buruk as though he were an idiot.

'Can you see anything around us dangerous?'

'No...'

'Is there a kumdria?'

'No-'

'So what is the problem?'

'The fairies live on the sky islands...' Amadar discloses, finally getting a word in through Buruk's taunts. 'They also kill dwarves for fun.'

'You are so dim witted.' Buruk laughs at Amadar, a loud and hearty noise, before he catches his breath. 'Of no offence.' Buruk pats them on the shoulder, a playful yet demeaning gesture.

In the distance, a loud horn is blown, echoing through the grassy highlands and bouncing off the three sided pyramids. Amadar crosses their arms, smugly glancing over at Buruk and Galbor who are both looking around for the hornblower wide-eyed.

Loud, ear-piercing screams from hundreds, maybe even thousands of beings are suddenly heard from overhead in the sky islands. Following the screams, creatures began filling the air, swarming around the island like small insects. Humanoid in appearance, these beings all bore a large set of wings, differing in size and shape, dependant upon the island in which they came from.

Some of the strange, airborne creatures appear to have large insect-like wings and bug-like armour, while others have large bat-like wings and are covered in a great deal of fur and what appears to be armour consisting of leather and metal. In the distance, the almost humanoid creatures dive off of the island, flying across the purple sky in an effort to hunt for one of many fish, while others appear to be socialising with each other.

Galbor stares at the sky in horror before looking at Amadar, his face flooded with shame, he simply couldn't bring himself to believe that the young individual he always deemed as stupid was actually right. Were the harrowing rumours of fairies real? He silently thought to himself, getting more and more anxious by the second.

'Well it looks like it is hunting season for the fairies...' Amadar expresses dreadfully. 'With no offence, Buruk. But you are an easy target.' Buruk's muscles tense as he moves back in his seat with great caution.

More fairies start jumping off the sky island in the masses. Some are flying towards the pyramids while others are flying low to the ground, and as the fairies get closer and closer to them, the ungodly sound of screeches and screams become almost deafening.

Buruk, stiff with fear, looks over at Amadar, hoping they aren't right about himself being an easy target. His eyes continue wandering, glaring at the precious cargo surrounding them: the carriage stacked high with spices, trinkets and old world technology.

'Protect the riches!' Buruk shouts at Amadar and Galbor.

'Forget the riches, Hide!' Amadar shrieks, clearly anxious.

Buruk turns to Amadar, feeling simultaneously infuriated and petrified, however, reminding himself that the last thing he wants is to lose three months worth of work from a fairy attack. He grabs Amadar by the collar of their shirt, pulling their face closer to his.

'I will not let my riches go. Protect the riches! That is an order.' He bellows through gritted teeth. Locking his glowering eyes on Galbor, the unfiltered mixture of frustration, determination, and trepidation intensify within them as he maintains a firm grip on Amadar's collar. 'What are you doin' just sitting there? Protect the riches!' He bellows, his tone gravelly and remorseless. Letting go of Amadar, he shoves them against the rough wooden ground of the carriage.

Galbor stares back at Buruk wide-eyed before looking over at the cargo. He scans the carriage for the blanket, grabbing it upon finding it alongside a line of rope. Throwing the blanket over the cargo, he jumps off the carriage with haste in order to tie it down.

Nerves build within him as he looks overhead towards the fairies, noticing that a few have spotted them. They are tall, lean and muscular beings. Their faces look particularly humanoid with large eyes.

One fairy is covered with brightly-coloured feathers all over its body. Its face is smooth with human-like skin and its wings are more than three times the length of its body. It has four limbs, similar to that of a human, however, their fingernails and toenails resemble long, sharpened talons.

Flying next to it is another fairy, this one is covered with colourful amour and fur in between each plate. It has fuzzy antennas and human-like fluffy hair. Its wings are large, resembling that of a dragonfly's and it has large bug-like eyes, hexagonal in shape and put together like a fly or a praying mantis.

Galbor's face drops in horror, his eyes fixated upon the fairies flying nearby, too close for comfort. Goosebumps start invading his skin, starting with his arms before crawling down the rest of his body as he notices that one of the fairies is considerably larger than he is.

He glances over at Buruk to see Amadar trying to drag him off the carriage. Buruk is kicking and whaling like a child, caring only about the cargo rather than his crew. He eventually turns himself around and hits Amadar hard in the temple, knocking them out.

Amadar lets go of Buruk and falls flat on their back, hitting their head hard on the ground with a loud thud. In turn, alerting the fairies to their direction and towards Buruk. He freezes and glances at Galbor as the fairies fly up high into the sky.

Realising that the fairies are flying away rather than closer, Buruk takes a breath of relief. He looks down at Amadar who is lying almost lifeless against the ground before allowing his eyes to wander back towards the road ahead, glaring at the animal that has stopped pulling the carriage.

In the blink of an eye, the fairies that appeared to be flying away swoop back down with vicious haste, straight towards the carriage, screeching as they do. The twisted insectoid fairy swoops Buruk, forcing him to stumble backwards before falling head first onto the seat of the carriage.

'Do something you idiot?!' He commands Galbor, staring at him with a mixture of rage and fear burning within his eyes. Galbor grabs a blunt heavy weapon, an old world solid cylinder piece of metal with gears at one end from the carriage, preparing for the fight of his life.

Buruk stares back up at the deceitfully inviting purple sky before being met face to face with a feathered fairy with large piercing eyes. Towering over him, its face, although humanoid, has strange features, resembling that of a bird.

Buruk tenses up, becoming forcibly motionless, unsure of what to do next and even more unsure if he will ever see the light of another day.

†

Alefosio, Koloa and Toakase stand together in the middle of the training grounds, all exhausted with a look of defeat. Not one of them found anything, no tracks, no book, nothing that could trace Kaji. They huddle together as the sun rises bringing in the cool morning light.

'Has anyone seen Hono yet?' Alefosio asks, his mind racing about whether or not he would see his best friend again.

Koloa and Toakase both shake their heads as they look at the large young man trying desperately to keep his composure. He has deep bags under his eyes, he looks like he hasn't slept in days.

'No, I have not.' Koloa mutters.

'Did anyone find any evidence of Tohro?' Toakase asks, letting out a deep breath.

'I found nothing… It is like he just disappeared.' Alefosio says, holding back tears.

The three of them stand in a deafening silence. Not one of them knows what to do or how to comfort one another at this moment. There is just numbness between them.

'Where did you both look last night?' Alefosio asked the other two. 'I went along the beach and forest north of town.'

'I looked through the forest west of town.' Koloa responds softly.

'I went south of town and I found nothing.' Toakase responds.

The pitter patter of quick footsteps with heavy breathing breaks the awkward silence. The three look towards the direction of the sound to see Hono running towards them. Alefosio briefly lightens up until they see her face more clearly. Tears have been running down one cheek of her face, her eyes are weltering red and her face is puffy.

They all move over to her, each of them expecting the worst. Unsure if Hono is missing her brother or if she has found something.

'Hono, what did you find?' Toakase asks.

'I found nothing... The authorities found me and did not like me being out. They can't find him and are contacting other islands.'

'Contacting the other islands will solve nothing.' Alefosio states.

Hono bursts into tears. All she could think is the unlikelihood of ever seeing her brother again, she thinks the worst and he took matters into his own hands. She blames herself, thinking she could have stepped in and stopped him or given him bags to let out his frustrations on instead.

'I think he is gone... My brother is gone.' She sobs, collapsing to the ground.

Koloa squats down and wraps his long arms around her, all he could think to do is comfort her. No words can help this situation. Toakase and Alefosio both follow and squat down to the ground and wrap their arms around Hono, leaning into her as sobs grow uncontrollable.

Chapter 29

The milky way overhead is bright and visible as the sun finally sets. Yuma carries Ookonan, Kaji and the strange and still very mysterious woman on his back through the evening. Visible in the distance are pyramids alight by the gleam of the moon.

Appearing for the most part flat, the land bears host to a multitude of cliffs and crevices from the great continental change during the cataclysm. Above the crevices in the sky float several land masses of differing sizes which are thoroughly surrounded by fish, whales, stingrays and sharks.

Ookonan maintains control over Yuma the bisonbear and is actively brewing a storm around them, bending the air and allowing Yuma to move faster while not only keeping him lighter on his feet but saving his joints from the weight of everyone.

The ancient structures they travel through slowly start turning into three sided tetrahedron pyramids. A good chunk of these structures stand clean but look newly built while the older ones are or were overgrown with vegetation. Some of these structures have collapsed from the large array of ridges and crevices across the unforgiving land. Meanwhile, a large number of the pyramids have been built around the many crevasse suggesting some were recently built.

Yuma effortlessly and swiftly carries everyone through the spaces between the pyramids. He gallops along the ground and jumps off the tilted sides of the pyramids with his powerful paws when pathways get too rigid or narrow, utilising the countless tetrahedron structures to get up and down the vast amount of cliffs and crevices.

The mysterious woman surveys the land as she unwillingly travels with Ookonan, Kaji and Yuma. She can see the sky islands from where they are.

She leans back, careful to not graze against Ookonan while she keeps her eyes peeled on the floating islands above her and the holes, cracks and crevices in the ground also sporadically at her near below her, scanning surroundings for any holes, cracks and crevices in the ancient structures for anything that will come out at night.

'Be careful not to steer Yuma to those islands in the sky.' She suggests to Ookonan.

Kaji quickly turns his head and looks at the woman. 'Why? Fall will they?' He asks her, distracted by her sheer beauty. Her long pointy ears, her purple fluffy hair, her forest green eyes and her dark complexion.

'No they will not fall, they are tethered to the earth and the moon. It holds them in the sky but lets them travel.' She gently explains to him.

'Oh…' He vocalises. Unable to grasp everything she said, he quickly gazes forward again.

Ookonan peers over at the sky islands. He can see the countless fish, who despite differing in size, appear to be in peaceful unison as they swim in groups across the distant sky. Whales swim and twirl between islands as though they are playing, while hunting for fish. Beautiful is their voice as they sing to each other which echoes through the pyramid highlands. He takes in the magnificence of the whale songs and the sky island, his senses feeling relaxed and at peace as his eyes begin drifting. Remembering where he is, being carried through the ancient wreckage by Yuma, he hastily shakes it off and refocuses himself to continue bending the wind around them.

'Amazing…' Kaji muttered under his breath as he saw, heard and felt everything Ookonan had a moment ago.

The woman peers down at Kaji, raising her eyebrows, silently questioning whether or not he has seen fish in the sky before. While Ookonan refuses to interject or question as he understands how he could find it amazing.

A colourful fish swims up to the group which weaves between them. Kaji's gaze follows the colorful scales of the fish, taking his eyes off the path and islands as they fill with awe. Questions filled his mind at a thousand kilometres an hour, such as: how could the little fish stay afloat in the air without wings or feathers.

'Do they not have sky fish where you are from?' The woman questioned.

'No.' He responds without taking his eye off the peculiar creature.

'Where are you from?' She interrogated in an effort to understand him.

'Ask you do, why you keep?'

At this point Ookonan's focus dwindles, causing the wind around them to slow down. The frustration he feels with the mysterious woman grows on him as she keeps questioning and trying to find more about Kaji, leaving him to feel more unsure about Kaji's safety as they further trek through Hondon.

The woman, noticing the wind around them had slowed down after her question, turns her head to look at Ookonan. She sees his deep purple eyes staring right at her. But she hopes he won't think too much into it.

'Why are you so interested?' Ookonan firmly asked.

She holds her composure now knowing he most definitely noticed. The last thing she wanted to do is leave him to believe she could be intimidated. 'Whoever has not seen the sky fish would not be from here. I am curious.' She admitted.

Kaji stops looking at the fish and turns his attention to both Ookonan and the woman. He tries to keep himself from being too agitated especially as he's unsure whether or not he hears the language correctly. 'This place, from I am not. I already said.' He bluntly states.

The woman sighs a deep breath as she leans back and frowns. She feels disgruntled with both of them, Ookonan's constant suspicion of her and Kaji's mystery. She feels the wind pick back up as Ookonan refocuses himself and Kaji goes back to observing life in the sky.

She takes some time to herself and waits for the right moment. She keeps a keen ear on Ookonan and an eye on Kaji. Waiting for Ookonan's frustrated breath to slow down as his mind focuses back on Yuma and his storm. She then just has to wait for the moment that Kaji returns to his aloof self, watching the life in the sky.

Once they both reach that point she then puts her face on Kaji's exposed skin. Her eyes turn a bright white as she transcends into his world and life. She can hear the crashing waves of the sea and she can see a multitude of islands.

The mysterious woman is transported into Kaji's bedroom, his marvellous bookshelves around his bed, the window that lets in the cool ocean breeze and the stacks of books and papers at his desk. She notices him sitting at his desk, hands on head in a miserable effort to bring himself to deep concentration. This was interrupted as a young girl entered the room. She looks to be around the age of twelve and her appearance is very similar to that of Kaji's but with long wavy black hair and loose airy colourful clothing without shoes.

She looks over Kaji's shoulder and grabs a considerably large book with a Mirish title in large bold letters. The woman squints her white eyes as she tries to understand what the title of the book says, but it's not in any language that she can recognise.

'Hondonian languages, what linguistics presume to be? Really?' The girl says. The woman takes a step back from this remark, thankful it was read out loud as she can always understand spoken language in a vision.

Kaji turns around to face the girl, he looks several years younger: no older than sixteen or seventeen in age. His cheeks are chubbier and his eyes are rounder, larger, and back to his normal blackish brown colour.

'It is interesting Hono… You have Euro Hondonian, then sections of African Hondonian. South Americas seems to be mostly the ancient language spanish. It's interesting. Don't judge me.' He explains in a calm and playful tone.

'I am judging.' She scoffs as she leaves the room.

As the girl leaves, the visions fog consumes and transforms. She finds herself following Kaji up the stairs of a mountain towards a marble gazebo where in the centre sits the translucent red engraved rock. She watches Kaji grab his rags to clean it as she comes to realise what it is. The legendary rune stone.

The fog quickly shifts once more. A spark is struck and the fog catches fire. She remains as calm as she could be, understanding that visions are oftentimes messy. The flamed fog fades leaving her in a fiery land and in the distance there is what appears to be an erupting volcano.

There are demonics of all sorts, including fairies, humans, dwarves, gnomes, elves and animals. The salamander slime known as the kumdria and its dessert counterpart the ubakara amongst other monstrosities roam in hordes across the land.

Dragons fill the land, sky, water and lava. The woman could see nothing but the pure chaos of the planet. Fear and dread fills her heart as she tries to figure out what is going on until out of nowhere Kaji shoots up into the sky with bright fiery wings. It is as though he is pure flame and nothing can touch him. His eyes glow a bright orange as the fire moves around him and before she could figure out what is happening the fog engulfs everything.

†

She feels a rough hand on the collar of her cloak which yanks her back. As her skin loses contact with Kaji's, the forest green colour returns to her eyes. She quickly surveys her surroundings seeing that fairies have now filled the sky ready to hunt the fish that swim through the bright night sky.

She brusquely looks around for whatever dared to pull her from Kaji so roughly by the neck. Noticing that the wind around them had practically faded, with only the faintest of breezes present, she turns her eyes to look at Ookonan who is staring back at her with his own deep purple eyes, an undoubtable anger painting his face.

'What were you doing?' He interrogates.

'I was just looking.'

'What did you see?!' He presses through gritted teeth.

'Kaji must be protected at all costs. He is far more valuable than I anticipated. I always thought Mir was a legend. I did not expect it to be real.'

Kaji snaps his head around to look at Ookonan and the woman. 'Huh. What?' He mumbled, unsure of how much he might have missed. 'Mir I did not say I was.'

'You did… Without meaning to.' She admits.

Ookonan grunts at her remark as he tries to refocus on Yuma. As he directs him through the tetrahedron pyramids and bend, folded land, a loud high pitched almost womanly scream becomes audible, almost startling him. He stops the storm around them completely and pulls Yuma to a stop.

'Did either of you hear that?'

'What?' She snaps.

'There is a scream.'

He gazes down at Kaji. He's no longer watching and feeling what's around him. He's merely staring in the direction of the scream. 'You are coming with me and we are going to help who is in need.' Ookonan announced as he pulled Yuma to a complete stop between several pyramids. 'Kaji.'

'Yes I am ready.' He also announced, snapping his head around to face Ookonan. 'Come I will.'

'No Kaji, you are staying here and looking after...' He sighs heavily as if the words or name he is about to utter brings him a great deal of pain. 'Yuma... And the stuff.'

He slides off Yuma and passes his backpack to Kaji. 'You are coming with me.' He firmly instructed the woman as he turned his gaze towards her.

'Are you going to unbound me?' She asked as she jumped off Yuma.

'No.' He says, grabbing her shoulder. He leads her away from Kaji and Yuma, between the pyramids and towards the sound of screaming. However more screams overlap the original. They sound like loud screeches mixed with an unusual chatter as they approach the more open plain, closer to the sky islands. The sky is filled with fairies of varying shapes, sizes and colours, most of which are hunting and socialising with each other as they fly around the strikingly strange yet beautiful airborne marine life and their islands.

Ookonan firmly takes hold of the woman's arm as he surveys their surroundings. He sees a familiar and peculiar carriage with cargo piled high only a few hundred metres from them. Flying around it, taunting the individuals trying to keep guard are a small swarm of fairies.

Eyeing the fairies, the woman is horrified by the attack but more so that she knows Ookonan is going to drag them both head first into the chaos to rescue the people guarding the carriage. Her intuition about him was correct. He pulls her along as he runs to the chaos at the carriage, but she doesn't resist, she wants to help as much as he does with the exception of valuing her own life more.

'This is suicide. I hope you know that.'

Once Ookonan arrives at the carriage, he realises it's not just anyone's carriage, it's Buruks. The fairies have overwhelmed him so much he's now given up trying to protect his carriage as he grips any handle or f beam on the side while trying to hold on for dear life. He eventually pulls himself under the carriage and grips the axle with all his might while the fairies take turns grabbing at him, scratching him and trying to get a grip of him. They collectively taunt him, laugh at him and mock him.

'A dwarf... We need to help! He is in grave danger.' The woman shouts at Ookonan. She feels helpless to do anything as her hands are bound tightly behind her back, but she still has control over her legs and she can still convince Ookonan to let her loose.

'Buruk...' He grunts through gritted teeth. 'Go and check on the fallen. Buruk is mine.'

†

Kaji sits alone with Yuma, chatting with the bisonbear while listening to the screams and chaos of the fairies. 'Trakänö-tâmýâ žaluh-na ashha mos annamah-sam etamil.' (*interesting how they couldn't take us with them*). He mutters as he pats Yuma's head and neck. Yuma gazes back at him and huffs before resting his chin on his paw. 'Otislaka.' (*I know*).

He gazes at the pyramids and their uniqueness, each one different yet similar in its own way, whether colour, cracks, age and some had holes or square like windows. The main thing that made them the same was each of them only had three faces, a tetrahedron. Kaji looks closer at the ancient structures, now seeing the fine details etched into their walls. But he failed to notice the cracks getting darker and the slime oozing out as he turned his focus on the restless Yuma.

The slime became almost obvious as it slowly poured from the cracks and open holes. But from an ancient window crawled out a large salamander-like creature. It has slick slimy black skin where black slime seemed to secrete from, its face is round, its eyes are as dark as its body and its mouth is full of short pointy teeth. It crawls its way out of the hole in the pyramid and seamlessly slides down the side as more of these creatures crawl out of the cracks to make their way over to Kaji and Yuma.

Oblivious to the inevitable death that crawls towards him, Kaji remains leaning on Yuma and watching the life in the night sky. He loses himself as he watches the majestic backdrop above, but as the whales danced to their own transcendent song the salamanders known as the kumdria got closer and the slime pulsed nearer and nearer like a matrix of vein-like arms reaching for himself and Yuma.

The hairs on the back of Kaji's neck stood on end as he could feel something was not right. He turns his attention away from the majestic whale swirling through the sky to quickly survey his surroundings. His heart skips a beat as he now sees the danger surrounding himself. The pulsating slime and several large slimy salamander creatures known as the Kumdra stared hungrily at him.

The creatures all have four short limbs, a large wide almost flat head with a large set of small pointy teeth, a wide body and a slimy liquid-like tail. The Kumdria closed to him bears its teeth as it readied itself to attack.

'AAHHH.' Kaji screams with a startled yelp. He jumps away from it, alerting Yuma to the danger of the encroaching monsters and slime. He scans the pyramids once more to see slime spilling out of every crack and crevice. He's surrounded and there isn't any way himself or Yuma could escape.

†

The fairies have the carriage under siege as they circle it in the air, each of them taking turns swooping down to claw Buruk as he attempts to seek cover under the carriage. The fairies giggle amongst themselves after flying near the terrified dwarf or the elvan man tethered to the carriage as he swings his fist and a pipe wildly at them.

'AAAAHHHH NO NO NO. GET AWAY!' Buruk screams as a feathered fairy managed to get a tight grip on his ankle.

Its grip is too strong for him to shake or kick off as every struggle or fight he put out results in its grip growing tighter and tighter. The claw-like hand of the fairy eventually started pulling him out from under the carriage. Its sharp talons sticking into his leg as he desperately tries to hold onto the axle.

'AHHHH...' He screams as he loses grip on the axel. He punches his fingers into the dirt as a desperate attempt to stay on the ground, but as he left claw marks in the dirt, the fairy was successful in dragging him out from under the carriage. 'VEKK VEKK!!'

The fairy lifts him up to show its giggling and cheerful friends. While Buruk hangs by his ankle, he struggles like a defenceless rabbit trying to use its core strength to reach up to the hand holding onto it. He wanted nothing more at this moment than to force its hand open to let him go.

'UNTIE ME!' The woman screams at Ookonan as she sprints over to him.

'Can I trust you?' He asks.

'You do not have a choice right now. You need to save that Dwarf and I need to help those elves. Untie me now!' She demanded.

He briskly unties one of her hands. Once freed, she sprints to Galbor and Amadar to assist them with the fairy swarm.

'AAAAAAAAAAAAAAAHHHHHHHHHHHHHHHHHHH.' Buruk screams as he is taken into the air.

Ookonan sprints after him. A breeze spins around him as he jumps onto the carriage and launches himself into the sky towards the colourful feathered fairy and Buruk. As his adrenalin spiked the storm around him grew stronger, empowering his superhuman force to keep up with Buruk and the fairy.

†

The slime smelt putrid, like sweet garbage mixed with chemically dissolving rotting meat. The closer it got to them both the more distressed Yuma got, as though he knew exactly what it was capable of while Kaji broke out in a cold sweat as he tried to think his way out.

As the Kumdria neared them, completely surrounding them, all Yuma could do was whimper and whine as he feared the inevitable, while Kaji felt the dreaded burn from within. All he could think about was fire. He lit up a hand and reached for the aggressive pulsating slime which shrieks and retreats from the slightest touch.

'Asi anala na ami na malusin.' (*It hates fire*). He quietly mutters to himself now realising there is a way out of this for both himself and Yuma. 'Natish enen ima zulakh' (*I can do this*).

He removes Ookonan's backpack and his new leather jacket. He straps them both onto Yuma's back before proceeding with his fiery plan. He turns his attention over to the Kumdria closest to Yuma and blasts it with a ball of fire.

He knew he had no real control of his power yet and as his emotions took control, the fear and the rising adrenaline and anxiety to protect Yuma. The flames quickly spread throughout his body, burning away anything he wore. He takes a step onto the slime which both withers and retreats from the flame.

Approaching the Kumdria with his charging glowing hands, he blasts it with a hot ball of fire, knocking it back. It squirms and wriggles as he blasts it several more times until it is nothing more than a simple pile of ash. He turns his attention to the flowing slime exiting from the pyramids and the remaining Kumdria creeping up on Yuma. He blasts the pyramids, igniting the slime in all directions before running back over to Yuma to blast the remaining Kumdria.

'HHHAAAAAA!' He shouts as he destroys every bit of corruption that comes towards them. Leaving the area in a black charred ashen mess.

Once the slime retreated and the last of the Kumdria ran away, his flame died off leaving him mostly naked with the exception of some of the leather of his pants remaining. He walks over to Yuma, climbs up onto his back and collapses from exhaustion.

†

The fairy maintains a tight grip on Buruk's leg, holding him like he is some type of toy as he takes him high into the air, above the sky islands within reach of the whales. It's satisfied with the height it flew up to, knowing Ookonan would not be able to reach it. It can now begin the real fun with the little man. Lifting Buruk to its eye level, the fairy stares deep into his eyes and straight into his soul.

Buruk fearfully eyed the fairy, believing this feathery face will be the last face he will ever see. The fairy smiles at him, showing beautiful clean white teeth as it holds him out ready to let go. And just like that, it releases its clawed bird-like hand and let's go.

Buruk feels his stomach drop and his heart leap into his throat. He watches the island grow closer and closer as he falls. He closes his eyes, not bearing to look at the ground coming towards him. He lets his body go as his life flashes before his eyes.

Ookonan retries his jump from the carriage. Sprinting as fast as he can, he jumps up onto the carriage and launches himself yet again into the sky. His storm brewing around him as the adrenaline pumps through his veins. The strong winds lift him high into the air, high enough to catch the falling man.

Without a word, Ookonan snatches him from the sky. Now hyper focused on how to land from his inhuman jump he does not notice Buruk's new smell. He lands on the ground, denting the soil and skidding to a stop.

He put Buruk on the ground as the adrenaline allowed him to continue to pump the storm out and bend it around himself. Buruk meanwhile flops onto the ground unable to comprehend he is still alive.

Sparks of electricity twist around Ookonan's limbs as his eyes glow bright and he watches the fairies swarm around them in the sky. He bends the strong winds around himself while the electricity dances within the winds and before long, he unleashes the electric storm into the sky.

Fairies are hit left right and centre from the blustery tempestuous electric storm. They bicker with each other and grab those injured by Ookonan's storm until they eventually leave everyone on the ground and fly back to the islands.

Ookonan lowers his storm as the adrenaline and anxiety fades before turning his attention to Buruk laying on the rocky soil. 'So you sent me and Kaji on a suicide mission?!' He interrogated.

Buruk rushes to his feet and scurries away from him. He brushes himself off and attempts to play himself cool while it becomes clear to himself that he soiled his pants.

'Ookonan. Ookonan. Look, we had a bad night tonight, why not let it go?'

'Why send us to get a horn if you were not going to pay us... Did you want me to die!?'

'No. no. look-'

As Buruk tries to speak and explain himself, Yuma barges in and tackles Ookonan and while doing so Kaji flies off him along with the leather jacket and backpack. He lands shoulder first onto the grassy ground a few metres from Buruk and Ookonan.

'I guess it is your lucky day Buruk...' Ookonan grunted as he grabbed his backpack and gave Yuma some love. 'But you will be coming with us.'

He walks over to Kaji who has gained some sort of consciousness. 'What happened to you?'

'Slime black, crock. Set fire everything to.' Was all he could get out in his semi conscious daze.

Ookonan hauls him back onto Yuma's back, giving him some time to rest as he directs them back over to the carriage. Amadar still lays unconscious on the ground while Galbor eyed everyone with shame. The mysterious woman however was more interested in Kaji laying in burned leather rags on Yuma.

'What happened to his clothes?' She exclaimed, eyeing his body.

'If I find that you have not come to Brogan... I will do things you will hate... I have the horn by the way. I might keep it.' Ookonan firmly announces to Buruk, ignoring the woman's remarks to Kaji.

'We will be heading to Brogan...' He confirms to Ookonan while trying to avoid eye contact.'Amadar needs medical help.'

'Good I hope to see you there.'

Chapter 30

The sun slowly rises from behind the horizon as dawn approaches the highlands. Above the cliffs and hills the sky begins to light up a mild orange with cool blues above it. As the group, Ookonan, Kaji, the mysterious elven woman, Yuma, Buruk and his companions reach the top of the hill a massive stone wall with an almost equally as large drawbridge appears.

Ookonan, Kaji and the mysterious elven woman walk next to Yuma. His tired legs could no longer handle carrying so much weight. Kaji brushes his hand along the tall colourful wild flowers, captivated by their unique beauty while Ookonan is preoccupied by holding onto Yuma while keeping a close eye on the mysterious woman as well as Buruk and his crew.

Buruk rides his carriage with Galbor sitting next to him on the front seat while Amadar is falling in and out unconscious and tied up on the back with the cargo. The bull-deer seemingly unbothered by previous events pulls them a few metres ahead of Ookonan and the rest.

'Around to is nice here.' Kaji remarks, Observing the highlands, the flowers, the jagged cliff landscapes while also oblivious to his own exhaustion as well as everyone else's irritability.

Ookonan grunts at his remark. Buruk and Galbor ignore him as they are too preoccupied in their own exhaustion and irritability. But for Buruk, almost being killed by fairies as well as the guilt eating at him for his treatment of Amadar is all that's on his mind. While the elven woman eyed everyone, repealed by their behaviour.

Having overheard what Kaji had muttered. Galbor gets off the carriage and walks over to him. Curious about the human. His features he's never seen before in any part of Hondon. 'What is nice around here?' He asks, curious to know more about him, hoping he would say more about himself.

'The colours.' He replies looking up at Galbor blankly.

'Oh.' He vocalises. Disappointed, he walks back to the carriage and takes a seat back next to Buruk.

As everyone nears the stone walls a massive abyss appears around it. As the stone walls stretch from east to west, the abyss follows like a giant cliff like a mote. The walls appear to be sitting on a floating island trapped in a cliff surrounded hole. The elven woman looks up at the drawbridge gate anxiously as they all get closer. She looks at Ookonan who is eyeing the bridge and walls thinking of a way to run ahead without being caught.

'There it is…' Ookonan breathes, startling her and distracting her from her plan. 'We have almost reached Brogan.' He mutters tirelessly.

She and Kaji look up at the architectural structures that can now be seen from behind the wall. Especially the elven palace which is plated in gold, but also materials of blue, purple while the rest is made of a white marble. What can be seen of the palace itself are intricate structures of unique shapes, designs and offset towers. An incredible sight for anyone who has never seen Brogan.

'Architecturally amazing.' Kaji breathes in awe.

'This is an elven city.' Buruk states, looking over at Kaji. 'They do take their architecture very seriously.'

'I see, they do, yes.' He said, unwilling to give Buruk eye contact as he caught up to his carriage.

'They do not take it kindly to humans.' Buruk says, cracking a small smile behind his thick beard.

'Are you not human?' Kaji asked surprised as he quickly turned his head to look at Buruk.

'No. I am a Dwarf.' He says, smiling slyly. 'We are racially known to be the best smiths around.'

Kaji anxiously looks back at the giant walls and drawbridge of the protected city. Anxiety sweeps over him as he turns to look at Ookonan for reassurance. He no longer wanted to enter the city as much as he curiously wanted to see what's behind the giant stone walls.

'Take no notice of him.' Ookonan grunts.

Awkward silence falls over them as they continue their walk toward the mote crevice. But once it was one hundred metres away, the elven woman sprinted off ahead of everyone.

'Where are you going?' He calls out.

'Ahead!' She shouts back. She maintains her focus on the drawbridge as she nears the deep canyon mote until she meets a large carved out spot that circles the cliff edge. It's about a metre deep and full of long sharp dagger like spikes, preventing anyone from gaining unsolicited access. She pulls back her cloak and removes a small carved horn from her belt, she places it on her lips and blows.

A loud high pitched sound exits it . It echoes through the abyss, bouncing off the great stone walls creating a long crackling bouncing echo that moves through the highlands. Once the noise finally dies off, the drawbridge starts to lower. Its giant great chains creek as it holds the heavy bridge as it lowers onto the sharp daggers in front of her making a huge booming echo as it lands.

Behind the drawbridge reveals a dense city behind another large metal gate. The houses and businesses are tightly packed together and in most cases fused together as one building. But this was all very normal for most everyone intending to enter with the exception of Ookonan and Kaji. She runs across the bridge, keen to get into Brogan before everyone else. The metal gate is lifted as she crosses.

Once she reaches the other side, she is greeted by two tall muscular elven guards. They are tall enough to make Ookonan seem short. Their uniforms are made of woven and knitted cloth of purple, crimson red and black under some leather and metal plated armour.

'Your-' A guard tries to say as they go to bow.

'Act casual around me.' She quickly interjects, stopping any formalities of the guards. 'A group will be following me. The half naked one. Let him in. Just send him to quarantine in the palace.'

'But A-'

'Do not say my name. You should be aware of the prophecy foretold. He is the one. Send him to quarantine.' She demanded. She looks back at the group following behind her. All of them are already halfway across the bridge. She looks back at the guards and gives them a nod before running off into Brogan.

'Aagneya was in a hurry.' A guard says, getting swiftly whacked by another.

'So her name is Aagneya…' Ookonan says slowly, while turning his gaze towards Kaji.

'Aagneya?' Kaji asks.

'Yep.'

Before anyone could proceed, one of the guards steps in front of them. He turns his attention to Ookonan and Kaji, remembering what the elven woman Aagneya had instructed himself. 'What is your purpose?' He asks firmly.

Buruk whips the reins of the bull-deer and pulls up as close to the guard as he could. He stands up onto the seat before speaking. 'I am the husband of the Smith Greybeard Fireflayer and everyone else is with me.' He interjects, speaking loud enough for the guards to take their eyes off Ookonan and Kaji. 'The two pureblood elves are citizens of Brogan, the other two saved my life and wish to visit my family and myself.'

'Yes I am well aware of the infamous Buruk.' The guard says, looking down at him. Even standing on his carriage seat, he's still not tall enough to meet eye to eye with a Brogan military elf. 'I need to know if anyone has been sick lately.'

'No I have not been sick as of late. I always carry spice and treat wounds when I get one.' Ookonan respectfully addressed the guard. He then points at Kaji. 'He, he is always on fire and is not sick.'

The guard inspects Ookonan and checks all exposed skin as well as his leather outer clothing, checking for spice. He then looks for any anomalies on him, such as any changes in the eyes, a rash or skin discolouration. He finds nothing, but does not give the same attention to Kaji.

'You are clean half breed.'

'Great. What about him?' Ookonan demands while pointing to Kaji, to be swiftly ignored by the guard.

'She needs medical treatment. What happened?' The guard said, turning their attention to Amadar strapped to the back of Buruk's carriage.

'Amadar is not a she.' Buruk rudely interrupts.

'Right… Well he needs me-'

'Not a HE, either.' Buruk rudely interjects once more.

'Before I arrest you or plummet you to the ground. Buruk, I suggest someone lets me know what happened to this individual.' The guard says slowly, while trying to keep his cool.

'Fairy attack.' Ookonan quickly says.

'Clafargin vekk. How did you survive? Especially you Buruk, I heard they like to take small races into the sky to drop them.'

'I would say it was a miracle how you survived but I would be lying.' The other guard says.

The guards turn to each other for a moment and very quietly exchange information with each other about Buruk and his crew as well as Ookonan. Once they are satisfied, one of them signals the guards in watch towers to lift the drawbridge back up.

'You are all free to go.' The guard says. But as soon as they all turn to leave, he places his hand on Kaji's shoulder. 'Except you.'

'What do you mean?' Ookonan demanded.

'He does not have protective clothing for the outside world, so he is required for quarantine.'

'Then we will leave.'

'Too late. The bridge has been lifted. Now you must comply with us or we will throw you into the abyss.'

'Do as they say Ookonan, it is really not worth messing with the Brogan army. He will be fine. Come with me and meet my wife.' Buruk says, grabbing Ookonan's hand.

Buruk rides on his carriage with Galbor on his side and Amadar strapped on the cargo. They are slowly waking and groaning in pain. Buruk maintains control over the bull-deer pulling his carriage through the busy street close to central Brogan while Ookonan lags slightly behind walking with Yuma.

The city of Brogan is nothing like what Ookonan had imagined. He never knew what to picture within a protected city especially as he has only ever been around struggling villages. The road itself is made of stone which is not a sight he is used to, but not walking in bloody spicy mud so far is pleasant. On either side of the stone road are drainage channels that run the full length of the road and each doorway has a little bridge across the channel. He looks around at the buildings, they are all old, crooked and so close together that some don't even have a gap inbetween, they are fused together as one building.

The buildings aren't made of a single material, usually wood like the villages he visits, but a multitude of materials. Wood, stone, brick, metal, fabric, mud or plaster and clay. And most of the buildings are made of a combination of all, some of the buildings are made of materials from pre-cataclysm, a material known as plastic as well as unrefined materials from the pre-cataclysmic era that has an unknown unrecognisable language that no Hondonian understands.

Buruk pulls his carriage over at a larger house that happens to have two bridges unlike everyone else. A bridge for the front door and one for a little port for his carriage. He gets off and awkwardly walks over to Ookonan.

'I guess you can come inside. Your pet can sit in the port with my carriage.'

'And what would she say about betrayal?' Ookonan grunts back.

Amadar groans loudly attempting to sit up. Ookonan looks over at them and their face has gotten swollen and they have no idea what's going on

'I will take them to hospital.' Buruk says with a deep croaky voice.

'Great. You have a hospital here.' Ookonan snaps.

'Look.' Buruk takes a step back with his palms up at Ookonan. He's unsure how to respond and nothing he will say will make anything okay. 'I did not know Odin's horn is real.' He says, somehow hoping that would help him weasel his way out.

'So you tried to kill us?'

'No… No… Uh.' He stutters.

'Why did you betray me?'

'Well… I did not want to pay you.' He says, smiling awkwardly.

Ookonan growls and picks him up by the beard. Nothing he could say would make anything better, but he needed a real response. He needs to know why. 'Then why send us!?' He shouts into Buruk's face.

'I-I-I did not realise I could not pay.' He stuttered.

'LIAR!!' He shouted, drawing attention to himself and Buruk from the public. People started opening their doors and windows to see what was going on and if the guards would do anything about it. 'WHY DID YOU BETRAY ME?!' He continued to shout, ignoring the public eye.

'I-I did not trust the brown foreign man… I-I could never pay you.' He stutters in fear.

'YOU SENT US TO OUR DEATHS BECAUSE YOU DO NOT LIKE SOMEONE'S SKIN?!' He shouted furiously into Buruk's face.

'WHAT DO YOU THINK YOU ARE DOING?!' A deep feminine voice shouts loudly.

With flared nostrils, Ookonan turns his head towards the voice. All the people who came out to watch scattered from view and all windows quickly shut as he looked around. Everyone left except a small dwarven woman with her hands on her hips.

'HMM?' She vocalised. Everything about her face looked normal, but she has patchy alopecia on her head and she is wearing worn clothing, a leather apron and worn gloves with holes in them.

'This man sent myself and my new acquaintances to our death because he is a racist!'

The dwarven woman turns her furious gaze from Ookonan to Buruk. 'Put. Him. Down.' She says firmly.

Ookonan slowly lowers Buruk to the ground, letting his feet touch the pavement first before dropping him. As soon as Ookonan moves away, the woman grabs Buruk by the ear and drags him over to herself. 'What do you think you are doing sending others to do your dirty work and not pay them?' She asks him. The way she speaks to him is as though she is his mother, but Buruk very much looks older. Buruk did not want to answer, she tugs roughly on his ear again, refusing to let him go without an answer. 'Where do you think you are going? You apologise right now.'

'How are you supposed to trust someone who is not from this land?' He asks pathetically.

'So you tried to kill them?'

He stumbles with the question, still nothing can defend his actions. Nothing he says will get him out of trouble. He looks down at his scuffed boots and kicks the ground.

She lets go of him and pushes him aside. She walks over to the carriage to inspect the cargo but to her further disgust and surprise she sees Amadar in a terrible state.

'Buruk now explain this.' She said firmly, pointing at Amadar. 'What happened?'

'Well Grey… We were attacked by fairies.'

'You are lucky to be alive! You are an irresponsible vatpik and Amadar looks close to death.' Disgusted is only half of her feelings, she did not know what to do with the idiots. She looks at Ookonan. 'Grab Amadar for me.'

Ookonan nods and unties Amadar and throws them over his shoulder. But Grey has another idea when she looks over at Galbor standing awkwardly in shame.

'Actually. Galbor, you can carry them as you were irresponsible enough to drive through fairy territory. How much of a ânälääsïna do any of you have to be to go through fairy territory? During their hunting season? I thought you both knew better.'

'What! No.' Galbor attempted to protest.

'I do not want to hear it.'

He takes Amadar off Ookonan and puts them over his shoulder and follows Grey down the street, leaving Ookonan alone with Buruk.

Chapter 31

Aagneya approaches the grand golden, titanium and copper gates, made of twistings of metal into intricate patterns. Cloaked guards still as statues while holding sharp weapons. The guards stiffen up and move their weapons to the front of their bodies facing downwards. The guard on the right turns his gaze towards her while keeping a straight face, showing no emotion.

'Your highness Princess Aagneya.' He says, bowing his head.

'At ease.' She says as she approaches the guards, straightening herself into a military stance.

'Your highness, you have arrived home sooner than expected.'

'I have my reasons.' She says as she looks through the royal gates and at her home. The royal Brogan palace sits on its own floating island surrounded by a deep canyon mote and the only access to it is across the heavily guarded bridge.

'Open gate for Princess Aagneya!' He shouts loudly.

The masterly crafted gate starts to swing open, just wide enough for her to walk through. Stepping through, she starts making her way across the bridge as the gate starts to shut behind her. Walking across the bridge, several guards wait either side of the grand doors to the palace. Made out of dark wood and decorated with thick beams of metal, the doors stand over five metres tall and three metres wide. Opening briefly, just long enough for

Aagneya to enter the palace, the metal beams slide and latch back into place, closing the door behind her.

The palace interior is grand and open. The floors are made of marble with crystal inlays, the windows are colourful with images of Brogan royalty and its conquests. There are intricate and detailed statues of Brogan royalty, each made of its own material and at the end of the grand room are three large chairs which have a blue carpet, patterned with purple colouring as well as copper, gold and silver leading up to them.

As she has done a thousand times before, Aaeneya makes her way past the sizable royal throne composed of stone, before turning right towards rows of statues of high class figures, but two specific ones always stand out to her. A marble one of a large muscular elf who has chiselled features and holds a large sword down at his feet. The other statue is a tall woman with much softer features, she looks strikingly like Aagneya herself. This statue is made with ebony stone and she wears a long flowing cloak down past her feet. She moves on from them and steps through the wooden door that rests between them.

As she reaches the top of the staircase, she is greeted with an all too familiar dome like library. The roof is comprised entirely of glass, allowing natural light to seep into the room. Several bookcases wrap around the room and flow to the brim with books, and in the heart of this haven, four large cushions are artfully placed.

Sitting next to each other on the cushions, each holding a book are King Tolibane and Queen Mebatikual. King Tolibane is a tall and pale man with formidable purple eyes and thin blond hair paired with an equally thin beard and a chiselled jaw.

His wife, Queen Mebatikual, on other hand is a tall elven woman with skin as dark as ebony wood. She has dark eyes, long pointed ears, and soft black hair.

'Amma… Anpa.' Aagneya says, greeting her parents.

'Aagneya…' King Tolibane says, his eyes still glued to the pages of his book. 'You will address myself first. Then your mother…' He states firmly. 'Have you forgotten something?'

'Why must I address you before Amma?' She asks her father, fighting the urge to argue with him.

'Because I am the king, I am the head and I come first… Now Aagneya, you have forgotten something.'

Without another word, she approaches her father and kneels. She grabs his right hand and kisses the royal ring before placing the back of his hand to her forehead. She then turns to her mother and does the same.

She gets back to her feet and stands like a soldier, hands behind her back and up straight. Waiting for her fathers approval.

'You may tell us the issue now.' He says, while still reading his book and not giving her the time of day.

'Yes. Well.'

'Why are you back so soon?' Her mother, Queen Mebatikual asks before she even has a chance to explain. 'You were going to Fatencia which is weeks away on foot. You have only been gone four -'

'Yes well, I have good news and I have bad news.' Aagneya tries to get to the point as she feels her body tense.

'Well, what is it?' Tolibane snaps.

'The bad news is… I did not find the Horn'

'No one expected you to find it. No one has in millenniums.' He explains boredly.

'Presumably.' Mebatikual comments.

'Hmf. It likely never existed.' Tolibane comments as he turns a page in his book.

'I have found the other half of the Prophecy…' Aagneya butts in. 'Mir is real. He is from Mir.'

'Mir does not exist.' Tolibane scoffs.

'He's here in Brogan.' She quickly interjects. 'His acquaintance brought me back here before I can -'

'Get to the point.'

Flustered, she takes a short moment to herself to get the words out. 'I can prove it, I can go and get him.'

Mebatikual puts her book down. She stands up and walks over to Aagneya. 'Aagneya… Sweetie.' She says putting the palm of her hand on her cheek. 'Just because there are stories of old prophecies, it does not mean they are real.'

'You know some people have been blessed by a god, and you know I see visions of truth at times when I am touched… you know I have been blessed by a god.'

'Yes we are both well aware of that.' Mebatikual says, attempting to be motherly and gentle with Aagneya.

'Then understand what I saw.'

'We do understand that you have a very active imagination.'

'I saw a great red rock made of unknown material-'

'This is not-'

'Strange people not from this world-'

'Enough.'

'Great wings of fire and-'

'ENOUGH!' Mebatikual shouts.

Aagneya stops talking and stiffens. They never listen, neither of them care. All she can ever do is remain silent and invisible around them both.

'OUT!' Tolibane shouts.

She nods and quietly leaves. Nothing will convince the two stubborn idiots, she thought. She needs to find Kaji.

†

Aagneya storms through the palace, infuriated with her ill informed, airheaded, insufferable parents. As she walks through the corridors she eyes the guards that patrol, searching for the right one to question. But there, standing alone and off duty stands a guard admiring the statues and paintings on display.

'On guard!' She loudly and assertively calls out.

The guard becomes startled, quickly turns around and more to their surprise to see Aagneya. They quickly straighten themself and salute.

'Your royal highness. I-I'

'At ease. What is so special about the art you are looking at? Why do you admire it?

'The history behind it and the intricate details.'

'Are you on duty right now?'

The guard freezes, now caught admiring art instead of patrolling the palace as instructed. 'Y-Yes. Do not-'

'I do not care.' She says bluntly. 'Take me to the foreign man in quarantine.'

The guard quickly straightens themself. They bow to Aagneya before turning around. Strictly marching down the corridor towards the palace dungeons. She follows them closely behind as they move down a spiral staircase until they both reach a guarded gate.

'What is your reason to be here? The gate guard asks.

'The princess wishes to see the quarantined.'

'Not without permission from the king.'

Aagneya steps forward and gets into the gate guard's face. She has had enough of stupidity, enough of her parents and especially enough of her father. 'I put him in here and if you do not let me through I will have you thrown into the abyss, which I will personally do myself.'

'But you might get sick.'

'Use. Your. Head.' She snapped. 'If he was sick, would I let him into Brogan?'

Neither guard knew how to respond. They both know Aagneya is not someone to bluff, so they both stand aside and open the gate to the palace dungeon. Without a word, she walks through the dungeon entrance and into the corridor filled with rows of closed doors. Each door has its own little window to check on either patients or prisoners.

She inspects each window, seeing things she never thought to see. People cuddling their knees as they sat on the floor or their bed, people smacking their head against the wall, people strapped to their beds as they screamed or called for help. Every person within a cell was alone and isolated. Not every room had someone, but every room was dirty. She kept looking until she found it. The only human sitting alone and lighting his hands on fire to keep warm.

She steps away from the door for a moment, realising she cannot just say the name he associated himself with. She takes a moment to just think about the vision she had of him, trying to remember the name he goes by.

'Toh…' She whispers to herself as she recalls the name.

'To… Toh. Ro… Sha. Tan……. Tohro… Sha… Tan…. Tohroshatan… That was his name in the vision.' She whispers. She peers back through the small window. He just sits, looking lost as he practices manipulating the fire with his hand. 'Tohro… Tohroshatan.' She says a little louder.

She sees him twitch to the name. He briefly looks around, almost confused about whether or not someone did call his real name. He seems almost perky but also frightened by hearing it.

'Tohroshatan!' She calls out.

He perks up again, but this time he stands up. He investigates the practically empty room with no avail before deciding to walk to the door. He cannot tell whether it's his imagination or if something is going to happen to him. Fear starts sweeping over him, his body lighting up and getting hotter by the second as he slowly approaches the door to peer through the window.

As he peers through the window, Aagneya steps in front. Still frightened, he felt unsure whether to trust her. After getting to Brogan, the first thing that happened was he was escorted to what is essentially a prison under the palace.

'Kaji, hey. I will get you out.'

'Trust you how? Aagneya.'

'I will explain later. I need to get you out.'

He needed answers and answers fast. How did Ookonan get through untouched? How did everyone get through but himself? Why was he thrown into prison? He wasn't happy and he will not follow her anywhere until she explains herself right away.

'No. Now tell me.' He demanded.

'Well first, how did you know my name?' She asked, knowing she never once gave out her name to either Ookonan or himself.

'Said name by authority.' He quickly said. Hoping she would understand his broken Euro Hondonian.

'Well.' She said looking further displeased with the guards. 'I asked them to put you into quarantine, because you would be left out in the fields outside the gate.' She takes a deep breath as she tries to calm herself. 'I will explain further when no one is listening, right now I need to get you out.'

He listens to her words, slowly translating them in his head. She seemed genuine and is always going on about her purpose. He slowly puts himself out as he takes a step away from the door while waiting for her to open it to let him out.

'Well, will you come with me then Kaji?' She asked a little more firmly.

'If door opens.'

Aagneya calls the guard over and instructs them to unlock and open the door. The guard slowly creeks open the door. And before they knew it, Aagneya and Kaji were face to face again. But he was a bit more taken aback than anyone was expecting. He was not expecting her in any way to be wearing different clothing.

'Follow me.' She instructs.

He steps out into the freezing corridor and follows her all the way down until they are met at the gate once more. She leads him up the spiral staircase and through the palace until she decides to open a secret passage behind a large painting.

Once alone, in a small shelved trophy room. she felt more comfortable to question him on things. Things like the prophecy foretold and why she had him put into the quarantine. 'Kaji. Are you aware of a prophecy?'

He raises his eyebrows. Confused about why they are alone, why a question about a prophecy and why they are both in a secret room in a palace. It all felt suspicious and strange to him. 'Hondon I was sent to. Reason not known really. Prophecy… Not know…' He tried explaining.

'Prison. Why?'

'I just said why.'

'Information new. Now there is prophecy.' He needed to know. He needs to know if she wants him captive.

'I had you put in because you would not be granted entrance to Brogan. I know you are not contaminated, but.' She said getting a little more intense as she spoke. 'You are from Mir, you are the second half of the prophecy foretold. I needed you in the city, so I did what I had to.'

He wasn't sure how to react to her explanation, but he knew there was some trust he could have in her.

'Come with me.' She said, grabbing his hand.

✝

With a firm grip on Kaji's hand, Aagneya leads him up a spiral staircase until they both reach a wooden door leading back into the dome library where her parents remain seated on the cushions in the centre of the room.

'Anpa… Amma… This is Kaji.' She announces to her parents, showing him off in the centre of the room.

'Aagneya, what is the meaning of this?' King Tolibane asks sternly, annoyed with her for not only interrupting him and his wife again, however, with her for having the audacity to bring a stranger into the private library dome.

'This is the man from Mir.' She explains, making him feel like he is like some sort of trophy.

'Aagneya, he is unusual but this does not prove anything.' Mebatikual says unable to take her eyes off Kaji.

'Amma…. He is from Mir. I am telling you he is from Mir.' She turns to Kaji and gestures to her parents. 'Kaji, say something.'

'Are you aware of the fact that you are wearing nothing in front of the King, Queen and Princess of Brogan?' Tolibane snaps at him.

Kaji pensively takes a step back, shocked by the statement. He turns towards Aagneya, befuddled. 'Princess, you are?'

'Yes…' She says, her tone conveying great frustration. 'Say something or do I have to-'

'Hi?' He says to Aagneya's parents, feeling uncomfortable and out of place. 'People away from home call me Kaji.'

'Your full name is Kaji Tohroshatan…' She says, feeling increasingly exasperated with both her parents and Kaji.

'Your family does not have a family name, you were granted that name from someone blessed by a god who is really old. You mend a big red rock-'

'How do you know all this?' He asked, cutting her off.

Tolibane and Mebatikual both place their books down after hearing Kaji unintentionally confirm all the information Aagneya blurted out about him in a moment of frustration, fascinated by the disgrace standing in front of them.

'You can trust us. If you are who Aagneya says you are, you will not be harmed.' Mebatikual assured.

Kaji sighs. 'Told I have been, speak to none for my safety… I am from Mir.'

'The prophecy is real…Who or what sent you?' She asks, looking back at him.

'I was sent by Hestia to find Ookonan.' He says, wanting nothing more than to leave.

Hearing this, Aagneya's heart drops as she looks over at Kaji. Believing her whole life that the second half of the prophecy was herself, she watched her life's meaning crumble in front of her in the span of two seconds, unable to do anything about it.

Chapter 32

Guards patrol the palace grounds and all around the small mountain the palace lives on. The palace is small, but grand and takes up some of the mountain. The palace itself is unique, being made of wood stone and marble, it has sculptures, plants and fruit trees surrounding it and its grounds. But one of the most interesting places of this palace are the meeting grounds, a large open courtyard overseeing a cliffside. .

It has a couple of stone seats locked in place on its grand marble and granite floor surface along with artistically placed potted plants and vines growing around some of the stone structures marking its area.

Connecting directly to the back of the palace is a long and tall staircase going up the mountain, leading to a white marble gazebo at the very top and within the marble gazebo is the great rune stone. Imperial guards patrol the grounds, not only to protect the imperial family but to stop anyone from climbing those stairs day and night.

Two guards patrolling the palace are walking side by side down the path towards the meeting ground. Once they arrive they both put hoods and a mask on before stepping onto the stone surface, they walk to the cliff edge and look out to the rest of the island. They nod at each other and walk out of the meeting grounds from where they came and out of the imperial grounds.

Those guards continue their walk until they reach the centre of a field where the stars are all visible. They are then greeted by three hooded and masked authorities. There was a moment of silence before anyone said anything.

'Is everyone here?' One of the palace guards asks. 'There should be five people in this meeting. No identities should be used.'

'Agreed.'

'There should be two guards and three authorities.' The second palace guard says.

'Then everyone is here. It's time for us to move to our meeting place.' The first guard says looking at those who are present.

As the five hooded and masked figures walk off in the southern direction, the hidden Toakase lets out her breath. She couldn't believe what she had just witnessed, five anonymous figures that are palace guards and authorities meeting up in secret.

Being sure not to draw attention to herself. She watches them walk off before she quietly exits her hiding spot to follow them closely behind.

While keeping her distance, she moves behind any tree or wall that comes her way as she watches where they are going. She quickly and quietly scurries after them when they turn a corner disappearing behind a cliff wall. But once she reaches it, to her surprise is a flight of stairs she's never seen before.

She quickly looks behind herself before proceeding to see if she is being followed. She slowly follows them down the stairs keeping a fair distance, following the stairs around the cliff curve until they come to a stop.

One of them holds open a door while the others enter a secret area within the cliff. Seeing this made her question herself whether Hono or anyone knew about a secret area built into the cliff wall. Once the door shuts, she moves as quickly and as quietly as she could down to the door. She wasn't sure what to expect but an ancient rusty metal door was not it.

She wondered how she never knew the door existed before, or even the flight of stairs. She brushes the thought away and puts her ear to the door. The interior echoed as the voices are all loud and clear through the door, like a reverb sound, almost cave like. She can hear everything including the five people walking around, grabbing and moving things like paper and other materials.

'We have some things to discuss about the disappearance of his imperial highness Tohroshatan.'

'It is presumed he has taken his own life. We promised his family that we will contact the other islands and that is what we intend on doing.' One of the Authorities says.

The room seems to have gone silent, she can hear slight scuffling of feet and more moving of paper along with items of different weights and materials being placed on a table or shelf. She puts a hand on her other ear to block out the sounds of waves, brustling leaves and nocturnal animals. She wants to hear the whole conversation, for better or worse, this could be good gossip for Hono, or this could be a disaster waiting to happen.

'We will not be contacting the other islands. That family are hiding something important and powerful and we need to know what it is.' A voice that sounds like one of the palace guards says.

The thought of juicy gossip while getting high with Hono gets discarded, what she's hearing is far worse than she thought it would be. Her stomach sinks and she begins to feel nauseous but she can't move away yet.

'Not only that but the gangs of the other islands are starting to revolt.'

'There are five main factions who want power over Mir and that power starts on this island.' A deeper voice says. 'And I think we can agree it should start with us.'

'So what of imperial Kaji?'

'He is dead.' The deeper voice says firmly. 'There is no point looking for a suicide.'

'We know where we stand in this and we will slowly start taking action.'

Toakase realises she can't listen to much more of this, she quietly stands up and takes a step away from the door. She feels like she is going to be sick and she needs to get away before anything comes up alerting them to her. All she could think about was Hono and that she will never see her friend Tohro ever again. But most of all, their aim is to kill her best friend's family.

She quietly runs back the way she came, sick to her core. She needs to alert Hono, but she needs to wait until morning. Once she feels safe out of ear shot, she sprints home.

Chapter 33

The crowded and busy streets of Brogan are lively, colourful and full of interesting people, stalls, shops and animals. The locals barge their way through to get to the freshly cooked street foods and some are desperate to sell whatever they may have at home, oftentimes handmade crafts.

'Get your fresh hobtatoes here freshly picked!' A stall vendor enthusiastically shouts as people rush to them.

'Onion, sweet onions, tall onions and all you can find's!' Another shouts as they hold up bunches of wilted onions high in the air before being swarmed by even more people.

'Twice... SOLD! To the maiden with the bonnet!'

The Brogan streets are a cacophony of noise, shops, vendors, people. The lot. Ookonan with his companion Yuma pushed their way through the crowd. He glances at Yuma and he can see the tension rising in his eyes. It seemed they were of the same mind as it was far too loud and visually overwhelming for the both of them. Ookonan is fine with small towns and trading posts, but he has never once been in a big city before and clearly neither has Yuma.

Ookonan spotted an alley not too far off from where they both stood. He directs himself and Yuma towards it to ease their senses and before Yuma takes out his displeasures on the crowd. As they walked down the street the number of people drastically decreased as compared to where they were.

Trudging down the path, something catches Ookonan's attention, a sacred animal. Standing in front of him is a piglickon, peck licking between the pavement stones. Noticing movement nearby, the piglickon stands upright and turns its head to look at them. Its head resembles that of a pig, yet with a beak and feathers, its feet are hooved, it has small wings and is covered with brown and pink feathers.

However, the piglickon catches Yuma's eye also. His pupils dilate as the sacred animal studies him. But before anything else could happen, Ookonan quickly directs them both away from the creature.

Struggling to navigate the city, he starts to walk faster. He has never felt lost before, he has always thought of himself as someone who could easily navigate the world, finding small towns, ancient ruins or places and wonders to temporarily relax before moving on.

Taking a deep breath out of frustration, he comes to a stop to survey the area in the hopes of noticing anything that resembles smoke or a forge. He held onto the slightest hope that maybe Yuma might know something. Instead he sees the people of Brogan doing their daily chores: hanging washing out of their windows, sweeping their doorways and hitting their rugs. He notices that a lot of these people are setting up stalls right at their front doors, to sell fruits, vegetables, hand crafted items and other questionable things.

'Yes this sauce will fill you up for sure! N No more hunger pains!' A stall vender enthusiastically shouts in an attempt to advertise his brown questionable beverage.

'What are the ingredients?' A Brogan citizen asks.

'Well that is a secret.' The vendor boasts.

'Rumour has it you put sewer water and rat poop in bottles and sell it.' A Brogan child says.

'What!' The first potential customer shouts, disgusted.

Ookonan walks past, deciding that he needs to avoid a lot of the vendors. He looks around for anyone who might not be busy so he can ask for directions. Until finally he finds an elven man standing alone on the side of the road. He has a glass bottle in his hand, consisting of what could only be alcohol, and he looks like he's been bathing in the so-called sauce a vendor was selling.

He approaches the elven man, hoping to not catch a whiff of what he was ingesting or even worse, his lack of hygiene. 'Hello, uhh do-'

'What?' The man grunts as he sluggishly turns to look at Ookonan.

'Would you happen to know where Greybeard's forge is?'

'Did you mean the shop or did you mean the forge itself?'

He rubs the back of his head. 'Whichever one Greybeard would be in.'

The stranger's eyes dart to either side of the street as though he's looking for something. Once clear, he perks up and sluggishly walks over to Ookonan. Taking several mouthfuls of the questionable amber liquid, he mutters to himself about losing his job. He wraps an arm around Ookonan, and as he does, Yuma looks him dead in the eye. He bears his teeth and snarls. Too drunk to notice Yuma's distaste in him, he walks with Ookonan and Yuma down the street before finally giving directions on where to go.

'Alrigh, alrigh. So. you want to go down this stree, then take a left, then a right then straight. You got this? Now the forge where that clafargn dwarf is, is by the palace. Don't go near the entrance of the palace. You wll be killed. Anwyay it's on the same street as the palace.'

'Uhh.' Ookonan vocalises as he tries to take any of the directions in.

'You got that righ?' He asks while taking another swig of the peculiar liqueur. 'Alrigh, alrigh. Remember, it is the end of this street, then is a left, then righ, then straigh until you see the *palace*, then is a left.'

'Thank you.' Ookonan says, scurrying off before he can either give more directions or vomit on him.

'No worries.' The man says as he continues to follow them.

Yuma, agitated and disgusted with the questionable odour of the man, aggressively turns around. He lowers his stance and bears his teeth, conveying one crystal clear message: keep away.

'Kay, kay, I wll go.' He said with his hands up. Once he turns to leave Ookonan alone, Yuma turns back around and continues to walk through the Brogan streets with him.

Ookonan and Yuma follow the road much like the drunk directed until the road sharply ends in two directions: the left and the right. Ookonan directs himself and Yuma leftward into another painfully crowded street. Realising that the drunk man did not state which right to take, Ookonan takes himself and Yuma into the first right he spots.

He sighs in relief after spotting the palace in clear view at the end of the almost empty street. Approaching the end of the road, he could see the vast colours and architectural details in the grand building. Multiple towers, archways, and bridges composed of purples, golds, coppers and silvers. He's never seen anything like it in his life. But upon exiting the street to the palace road, he could now see the palace is floating on its own island, hovering in a chasm.

He looked to his left and about twenty metres from him he could see smoke. He directs himself and Yuma towards it and the closer they got the more obvious it became that they were in the right place for finding Greybeard as the noise of her hammer hitting hot iron radiated throughout the street.

The forge shop was not an open place like he is used to seeing in small towns, but instead is a large self-contained building with several large chimneys and various windows of differing shapes and sizes. The building itself is unique to Greybeard, containing warm colours, and desirable materials, such as: dark hardwood, copper, iron, stone and concrete.

He grabs the large brass knocker and knocks on the sizable wooden door. Each knock booming through the building.

'Just a moment.' A voice calls out.

The hammering of iron comes to a stop and footsteps approach the door. A heavy geared latch unlocks the door and it slowly opens, however, only part way. Standing on the other side of the door was none other than the dwarven woman who scalded him about Buruk, her husband.

She is styled in a woven singlet, the only fabric article in her entire outfit. Everything else she was wearing appeared to consist of leather, from overalls, to thick boots and her own hand crafted gloves. She also dons round metal framed goggles for her eyes, while the rest of her head remains uncovered, patchy and bald. He wondered why she didn't cover it when working with hot metal.

'Oh. Pleasure to see you again. Are you here to scald my husband more?'

'Uhh, yeah. Hi. Uuuuhhh Buruk sent me to see you, he said that you could maybe help me with my bisonbear.' He said awkwardly.

'Did he now?' She asks, unamused.

'Yeah, what happened between me and Buruk will not happen again.'

'He is an idiot, but he is my idiot.' she says as she opens the door wider. 'Come on in.' She gestures them inside and Ookonan follows suit.

Once Yuma has entered, she closes the large door, latching it shut.

Ookonan looks around, the place is marvellous. Filled with all the unusual trinkets Buruk has found throughout Hondon over the years. A lot of the old relics appear to have been pulled apart with a select few having been chosen for modification.

Her actual forge is huge, it's a large elevated pit, held together by a rock wall. It sits next to the shop's wall and lying above it, wrapping around said wall is a metal chimney. Multiple iron rods sit in the hot glowing coals. Less than a metre from the forge are two heightened step ladders and an anvil which is a little too high up for Greybeard herself.

'Hey, big man. Come and help me out over here.'

Ookonan manoeuvres towards Greybeard who is standing in the corner of the shop. There are piles of seemingly stale seasoned wood and some stacks of old hide. She is picking up the piles of hide and is stacking them over one of her shoulders. Ookoan, following suit, begins picking up the seasoned wood before stacking them all onto his shoulders.

He follows Greybeard through the shop as she throws the hides up onto a workbench. Stepping onto a stool for better access, she pushes some of her projects, all in differing stages of completion, to the side to clear some space for her to lay the hide out flat.

'You can put the wood under this bench. Keep clearing that corner for your companion to have a place to lay down.'

He places the wood on the ground and moves them under the workbench before walking back over to the corner. Noticing two large ancient steel beams sitting in the corner, he picks them up and heaves them over his shoulder.

'Where would you like these?'

She looks up from the bench and peers over at him. 'Oh those! Put them by the forge, I can use them for forging weaponry.'

He walks over to the forge, looking into the hot coals. It wasn't as mesmerising as he had hoped. Some say they see visions in the flames. He didn't. He puts the heavy beams next to the forge and out of Greybeard's way.

'Is that corner clear now?' She asks.

'Yes it is. Except for some dried up grass or hay.'

'Oh good. Your companion has somewhere to lay down now.' She says without glancing in his direction.

Ookonan walks back over to Yuma who stands uncomfortably still in the front entrance of the shop. He directs him over to the corner where Yuma lays down on the hay and rests his head on his paws. Ookonan gives him a quick scratch behind the ears before taking himself back over to Greybeard.

'Did you need help?'

'Pass me that leather bag.' She says pointing towards a colourful bag sitting on the other side of the bench. He picks it up and places it next to her. 'Thank you. That will be all for now.'

'Oh.' He says awkwardly.

She opens the bag, but to Ookonan's surprise, she doesn't go through it, instead she rolls it out revealing a lot of different and intricate tools he has never seen before. She pulls out a crescent shaped blade, which to Ookonan looks like an odd looking chisel. She begins to shave off the fur from one of the hides to reveal the leather she will use.

'Would you like some parts to be fuzzy or all smooth? Some parts fuzzy should help with cold weather or really hot weather.'

'I do not know.' He admitted. 'My friend who I now travel with combusts every now and then.'

'On fire?'

'Yeah.'

'You elves are a strange bunch, he will get used to it. I will add the fur anyway because as you know, it does get cold.'

'He is not an elf. He is a dark human from the east.'

'Great. I will get started on the design and I will keep an eye out for him.' She says grabbing some chalk to mark out shapes and areas on the exposed leather. She looks over at Yuma, realising that every companion is different. She grabs a notebook and a pen sitting on the bench and starts to come up with some different designs that would be comfortable for Yuma himself but will be good enough for a nomad like Ookonan.

'Thank you Greybeard.' He says, walking off to find a broom or frankly anything that would help keep himself busy.

'I will be adding areas to place items, much like spices. Pockets and the sort.'

'Make it however your heart desires… I really appreciate it.' He says as he found the broom. He begins to sweep up the shop, it's incredibly dusty like it hasn't been cleaned or swept in months.

'Oh thank you. I have not had time to clean, Amadar usually helps around the forge.' Greybeard said, looking up at Ookonan.

Before either of them could make any progress, the booming knock of the brass knuckle echoes throughout the shop. 'Do you mind getting that for me?' She asks, remaining focused on her work.

Ookonan heads towards the door as the ambient noise from the outside world grows stronger and stronger, distinctly the voices on the other side of the door. .

'She said he will be in here.' A loud voice said confidently.

'Are you sure?' A second voice asked in uncertainty.

'Yes I am sure! Drop that! Why would you buy anything from that vendor? That is sewer water!'

Ookonan looks back over at Greybear who is laser focused on her work. He turns back towards the door before grabbing hold of the handle and unlocking the latch. Upon the heavy door slowly opening, two palace guards are revealed, both dressed in their colourful uniforms.

'Ahh, you must be the halfbreed we are after.' The confident guard said.

Ignoring the halfbreed remark, Ookonan opens the door wider and looks over at Greybeard again. 'Why are you after me?'

'We will get to that in a moment. Greybeard... Master smith.' The guard called out.

'Yes? What is it?' She asked, unfazed by the palace guards at her doorstep and unmoved by their authority.

'May we enter?'

She waves them in without giving them so much as a glance as she marks out the hide. They both step into the shop and the last one to enter closes the door behind themself. Both of them keep their distance from Yuma who is uncomfortable and alert from their presence.

'What is the issue?'

'We have been given orders by the princess for this halfbreed here to come to the palace.' The more confident of the guards says as they walk around the shop, examining all of the projects Greybeard has started.

Placing her tools down, she looks up at both the guards with distaste. 'I do not appreciate anyone coming into my shop spewing racist words or hatred.'

'Well, by order of the princess, this unknown man assisting you is required to go to the palace.'

'Me?'

'Yes, you.'

'What would the princess want with me?' He asked, suspicious of the request.

'She did not disclose.' The guard said bluntly.

He looks over at Greybeard who has started to pick up her tools again. 'You better go, the royals here are not those who should be challenged.' She said, getting back to work.

Accepting defeat, his eyes wander back over towards the guards, where he finds the overly confident guard gesturing towards the door. He reluctantly yet accordingly leaves the shop with them both.

†

Two guards enter as the marvellous palace doors open, each standing either side of the walkway. Ookonan soon follows, walking into the grand entrance. He surveys his surroundings much like a curious child, having never seen architecture or art like this around Hondon let alone materials used for building like this. As soon as he starts to walk down the hall the doors close behind him.

He snaps his head back to look at the doors which are now completely shut and the guards who still stand motionless. The regal throne catches his immediate attention, finding a dark skinned woman sitting there. His belief was that in Brogan the royals would be light skinned, but the closer he got to the throne the clearer the woman became. It was none other than Aagneya.

'What are you doing sitting on the throne?' He interrogated, failing to hide his disgust.

She smiles at him as she looks him dead in the eye. Jumps off the throne, she starts to walk in a dance-like stride before storming angrily towards him. She's fierce, powerful and has an uncanny fury about her.

'I summoned you here.' She stated as she stopped a few metres from him.

'So that is why you ran off and kept yourself a secret?' He pressed, failing to hold back his own frustration.

'It looks like we all have secrets. Ookonan. Come and walk with me.' She turns back around and briskly walks towards a well decorated double door.

Ookonan follows her towards the door which a guard opens for them. He then follows her through the walkway and down a corridor while maintaining his distance. Art delicately suffocates the palace, with sculptures, paintings and tapestries all depicting different qualities of Brogan and its accomplishments. From its grand fountain on the top of the palace to wars that have been fought.

But, one painting in particular catches his eye. He feels an uncanny sense of familiarity about it, yet still feels foreign. The painting itself depicts the Brogan elvan army led by the king. They appear to be slaughtering a village of smaller humans who sport furs and decorate themselves in the colours of blue and red. The land they stand on is an icy forest smothered with hibernating trees. What makes him particularly uncomfortable is that the pyramids, Brogan itself and any surrounding area is nowhere to be seen and the people themselves, although familiar to him, are defenceless against the Brogan army.

'What is so interesting about this painting?' Aagneya asks, breaking his concentration. She notices a little sadness in his desolate eyes, but there is no time to properly interrogate. 'Let's go!' She urged, gesturing him to keep following her.

He rolls his eyes as he shakes off the uneasy feeling the painting created within him. He continues to follow her through the palace until she takes him to a plain unmarked door.

She opens the door letting both herself and Ookonan in. Behind the door is a small room with a single arched window. On one wall are shelves, filled with chemicals, ornaments and books and on the other wall sits a stone fireplace that is filled with charcoal and ash. In the centre of the room sits a small round wooden table with a couple of wooden seats. But most surprising of all was Kaji who was sitting on one of the seats looking up at both of them, waiting for something to happen.

'How did you... Why are you here Kaji?'

'Locked away I was. Then...' He points at Aagneya. 'Me here took.'

The door closes behind them, startling the already tense Ookonan and Kaji. Ookonan turns around and looks at Aagneya who is staring back at him with a sharp dagger-like glare. 'How can you!?' She screeches at him. 'How can you!? You!? You of all people be of the prophecy?!'

'I am really lost now.' Ookonan admits as he looks into her fierce glowing green eyes.

'You are his second half!?' She shrieked, half a question and half a statement as she pointed at Kaji. 'You with him are meant to end the chaos of this world! You!?' She could not understand how someone like Ookonan, a lost loner of a brute, could be important.

'You are a princess but why are you upset about this?' He questions, disgusted by her entitlement. 'And what do you know about a prophecy? How did you know about this?'

'Scholars have written about the prophecy...' She tenses, gritting her teeth as she talks to a dimwitted buffoon, her frustration increasing tenfold. 'How can you not know about the prophecy?'

'Do you really think the world is going to get better?' He probes as his temper rises in response to the unsolicited confrontation.

'How can a savage like you be chosen? How can someone with no knowledge of the prophecy be chosen?'

'Now you attack my character?'

'Judged my chatacter, whole time you have!' Kaji interrupts, standing up and walking over to Ookonan and Aagneya. 'Talk of prophecy, what is?

And you!' He says raising his voice as he turns his attention to Aagneya. 'You talk about, you should been chosen! Fix the world! I know Brogan people suffer, starve.' He grills, feeling the fire in his chest yearning to escape.

'HOW CAN YOU TALK? YOU ARE FROM A LAND OF PEACE! A LAND WITH NO CHAOS! HOW CAN YOU SPEAK? YOU HAVE LIVED A LIFE OF PRIVILEGE - THE BOTH OF YOU!' Ookonan shouts back, his voice loud, gravelly, and intense.

'I would have found the artefact to start cleaning the land if you did not kidnap me!' Aagneya snaps back.

Ookonan feels his blood start to boil as electricity pumps through his veins. He tries to hold it back, but the tips of his fingers begin sparking and flickering. He takes off his backpack and places it on the table, opening it and quickly rummaging through its contents.

'Is this what you are looking for?' He asks, removing Odin's horn from his backpack and roughly shoves it into Aagneya's hands. 'This is what almost got us killed! And you!-' He says, turning his attention to Kaji. 'Do not speak of suffrage in Hondon when you are from Mir!'

'YOU THINK MIR SO GREAT? CIVIL WAR HAS BEEN BREWING FOR FIFTEEN YEARS! OTHER ISLANDS HAVE ALSO REPORTED A GREAT BLACK ROT THAT IS SPREADING!' He rages, breathing flames out of his nose.

As electricity starts to spark around his body, he takes a deep breath in an attempt to calm himself. 'Who has time to fight?! This is stupid! I am leaving.'

'You can not leave.' Aagneya demands as she places herself in front of the door, blocking Ookonan's path.

Ookonan closes his backpack before putting it back on and making his way to the door. 'Watch me. I am leaving.' He snarls. She could feel the electricity brushing across her skin as he shoved his way past her, leaving the door open and a trail of soft wind as he left.

She feels everything all at once: anger, frustration, bewilderment, disgust. She could not believe that he of all people was chosen as the Hondonian half of the prophecy. She looks down at the horn she holds in her hands, a perfect ivory, bronze and gold artefact with shapes and runes carved into it.

Her eyes trace back towards Kaji whose shoulders are on fire as his head steams. 'You are on fire Kaji.'

He pats the flames out and takes a deep breath in a failed attempt to calm himself. 'I need some air.' He says, walking towards the door.

'Remember, he is nothing and you are the most valuable person alive.' She makes an effort to reassure him as he leaves the room.

†

The streets directly outside of the palace are calm and quiet unlike the streets a couple of blocks away. Greybeard sits with her feet elevated, enjoying a much needed and well deserved break with a hot beverage.

But something catches her eye, the grand palace doors are opening and someone too small to be an elf storms out. She sits up and finishes her cup of tea with haste as she watches him cross the bridge to the main city of Brogan. Putting down her cup, she quickly moves towards him.

'Hello. Did you happen to travel with a man known as Buruk? And that other one?'

He turns to look at her, confused by why some stranger is talking to him at all. 'Buruk? Man who tried to kill?'

'I suppose. Who was the tall blond one you traveled with?'

'Ookonan you mean?'

'Yes! Do you know where he went?'

'Gone.' He says as walks off, clearly in no mood for conversation.

'It is okay. I had not had the chance to meet you.' She said, understanding that he is experiencing some difficulties and frustrations which he needs to deal with. 'Why not come with me? I need help with my forge, you can release your frustrations and anger in here.'

She gestures for him to follow her a few metres to her shop. The most unique building on the street besides of course the palace itself. She opens the large door and he follows her inside.

'There is a pit of fire in here.' She said as she closed the shop door, latching it shut. 'Go over to it, I will show you what to do.'

Kaji wanders over to the forge and glances at the hot coals. Images suddenly jump out at him from deep within the flames. Visions of pyramids, fire and power. But also of things he has not ever seen before. A dragon, fairies in a palace high in the sky and the slaughter of people.

'I did not catch your name earlier, Galbor mentioned it but I may have forgotten.' Greybeard states as she sets up her anvil.

'I get called Kaji.' He says, looking away from the flames uneasily and back at Greybeard. 'Used you feel? At times I mean?'

'Sometimes I feel Buruk does but then he goes on his way but always brings me back something from the old world. So it's okay. What happened?'

225

'This prophecy. Aagneya says prophecy, me, a fight happened. Ookonan left.' He attempts to explain in his broken Hondonian. But the anger and upset he feels intensifies and expands, igniting his hands and his shoulders.

'OH! I have not seen a human with abilities before!' She admits. 'I have an idea.'

She grabs a chunk of metal she has been having trouble forging and puts it under the hot coals. 'I want you to release your anger where I put that material.'

'Hotter you want?' Astounded that she wants him to release his flames indoors, let alone on an already scorching pit.

'Yes. It is not hot enough for me to work with.'

He takes a steady step towards the forge and closes his eyes. His body shaking and steaming with the conjoined and muddled anger he has been feeling towards not only Ookonan, however, being left in Hondon, being used and likely never seeing his family again. He takes a deep breath in, aiming a hand at the spot Greybeard requested. He then opens his eyes, breathes out and releases.

A considerable fireball blasts into the forge, heating up everything inside and only leaving him more upset with the lack of control he has.

Greybeard puts a hand on his arm, startling him again. He looks over at her and to his surprise, she is wearing her protective goggles and thick leather gloves.

'That was amazing. It also heated up the metal how I wanted too.' She said, unfazed with the additional flames around the shop. She grabs her tongs and pulls out the tough material. She starts to shape it on the anvil and with some success she was able to forge the material that has been frustrating her for what felt like forever.

She gently and attentively places it back into the forge and covers it with coals once again before turning her attention back to Kaji. 'Luckily only around the forge caught a little fire. Or we would have been in trouble. Now I need you to take a deep breath and think about something that made you feel that everything is alright, it could be a drink, a happy time, an adventure. Something that made you feel calm.'

She leaves him with that thought for a moment while she puts out the little flames scattered around the forge. 'Push away the emotion, it has happened and it can not be changed.'

He nods at her and turns his attention back to the forge. 'I got it…'

He takes a deep steady breath and thinks about his first cup of chamomile tea and the feeling it gave him as the fear of Hondon eased. He then thought about going swimming with his friends and his sister, not a single problem in the world bothered him then, it was a much easier time.

He opens his eyes and releases a breath as tears begin to form. He aims his hand at the same spot and relaxes his body. A stream of hot flame sprayed the coals turning them a hot glowing white. For the first time since these powers made themselves apparent, he had control.

As he lets go of it all the flame comes to a complete stop. He looks at Greybeard who has a bright smile on her face, he couldn't believe it, he truly had control of his flame. 'Thank you.'

'I am always here to help the friends of my friends. Well I need some help around here for the time being and we can practise until Ookonan comes back or if Aagneya needs you for whatever reason.'

'Good, I can do that. Thank you.'

Chapter 34

The sun starts to rise over the island's horizon, basking the ocean in a beautiful orange light as Toakase makes her way across a path enclosed by flowering plants covered in dew. Approaching the Mir capitol palace entrance, she notices the imperial guards patrolling the grounds. She looks around with a sense of distrust in all of them. Keeping a keen eye on the guards, she makes an effort to walk past them without need for confrontation but is abruptly stopped in her tracks.

'Oi! What is your business here?' The guard rudely asked.

She turns around, smiling and raising her eyebrows. 'I am Hono's best friend…' She says with a nonchalant attitude riddled with sass. 'What is your business here?'

'What makes you think I believe you are the Emperor's Daughter's best friend?'

She tilts her head, perplexed with the guard's stupidity. The guards should all know who she is, she thought to herself. 'You must be new here, let me in and you won't be fired for incompetence.'

'You. you can not do that…. No you are making it up.' The guard says feeling shocked and appalled.

'Let me in and you will not have to find out.' She playfully retorts, memorising the guards face, unable to determine whether they were one of the masked figures in the meeting.

Tensing up, the guard ushers her through the grounds towards the palace, intent on keeping a steady distance away from her. The guard slowly wanders off to continue to patrol the grounds of the palace.

'Thank you… I will let Hono know about you.' She says loudly as the guard slowly wanders off to continue their patrol of the palace grounds.

She runs along a stone path towards the building, stepping up the steps with haste before slowing her pace as she approaches the front door. She reaches for the metal door knocker and strikes it four times, each knock louder than the last.

She stands by the sizable door impatiently waiting as she places her ear against the surface, trying to listen for any footsteps. To her dismay, she is unable to hear whether anyone was coming to the door or not.

As further impatience grows within her, she strikes the door knocker five more times, letting it echo throughout the residence. As she places her ear against the door once more, she can hear the sound of faint footsteps coming from inside the residence.

Reaching for the door knocker, she strikes it again three times and is startled as the door swings open. She stumbles forward, falling slightly onto the person who opened the door.

'Toakase. How pleasant it is to see you…' A servant says, opening the door a little further. 'You are not the most patient person I have met. What are you doing up at this hour?'

'Good to see you too.' She says with a bit of sass. 'Is Hono awake?'

The servant sighs, disappointed in Toakase for not knowing that the imperial family women aren't typically awake this early in the morning. 'It is five thirty in the morning. No she is not.'

'Can you or I wake her?' Toakase asked, seemingly stressed.

'No!'

'Aaahhh….' She groans, stumbling around at the entrance.

'Her Imperial Highness Hono is due for training a little later this morning…' The servant says while rubbing their eyebrows. 'Just let her rest, she really needs it.'

'It. Can. Not. Wait…' She says slowly, purposefully drawing out her words in order to add emphasis to her statement. She places her hand on the door and leans forward, preventing the servant from closing it. 'Is Yua or Sanmos awake? Can I tell them instead?'

The servant raises their eyebrows at Toakase as though she must be insane. Having little patience left, they start closing the door on her. As the door almost completely closes, Yua walks over to the servant, sounding both annoyed and sleepy.

'What is this about?' Yua asks. She reopens the door, finding the agitated and clearly stressed face of Toakase. Knowing that Toakase is rarely awake at this time in the morning and understanding that something drastic must have happened, she tries to contain her annoyance.

Toakase looks at the servant then around the grounds at the guards. She looks back over at Yua and takes a deep breath.

'This needs to be mentioned in private.' She urged Yua.

'Can it wait?' Yua asks, gesturing to the servant to move along.

'No it can not.' She says, pushing past Yua and letting herself into the palace. She closes the door behind herself and takes another breath.

She surveys the palace entrance, noticing the thick drawn curtains and the minimalist interior. She walks down the hall despite Yua's growing exasperation, before making her way through an archway on the left into the family living room.

In the centre of the family living room were some steps leading to large cushions in a square formation surrounding a short wooden table. Towards the right side of the room a small water fountain is found amongst various rocks, and surrounding the walls of the room are numerous shelves holding countless spellbinding books, enough to make any academic jealous.

Toakase walks down the steps and sits on one of the cushions where she can face the entrance. She taps her leg nervously as all her brain could fathom was the horrible news she was about to deliver to Yua and Sanmos.

'Toakase… care to tell me why you are here so early?' Yua impatiently presses as she follows her into the room and sits down on a cushion facing her.

Toakase takes in a deep breath and slowly breathes out, worried that Yua might be suspecting that she had smoked kava. 'I was at a park yesterday. Just chilling, doing nothing.'

'HA! Nothing?' Sanmos scoffs while walking into the room holding two cups of water. He makes his way over to the steps leading down to the lower cushions and sits next to Yua, handing her one of the cups of water.

Yua smiles at Sanmos and takes the cup of water he handed her. She puts her hand on his knee and turns back to Toakase, noticing her tapping her leg seemingly anxious which was unusual for her.

'Yes. Anyway.' She says, trying to ignore Sanmos's scoff. 'I was in the bushes when three authorities and two guards who I think are yours turned up.'

'They stood in a circle and spoke of a secret hideout and organisation they are making.' She tries to collect her thoughts as she notices Yua and Sanmos lean forward, their eyebrows raised and their cups of water lowered to their laps. 'Something did not sit right with me, when they moved off I followed them.'

'Yes, yes - get to the point.' Sanmos interrupted.

'I followed them to a cliffside by some stairs by the beach, there is a door there. I listened in and they said they are contacting the other islands, not to find Tohro but to start a war... with you...'

Sanmos places his cup of water on the table and rubs his temples, displeased and unconvinced. 'You expect me to believe that?' He asks as his temper rises.

'Not at first no... But they have put down Tohro as a suicide and they have discontinued their search...' She tries to explain as Sanmos' Dark skin seemingly starts turning a vermillion shade of red.

'There is something you look after every morning. Hono and Tohro have mentioned it. They want to overthrow you for it... They think you are hiding a great power.'

Yua raises an eyebrow at Toakase, now wondering just how much Kava she had smoked last night. She looks over at Sanmos who seems unsure of his emotions and how to handle himself.

'It is just a family tradition to mend and polish the stone and to care for the garden... it holds nothing powerful.' Yua explains, looking back at Toakase.

'That will not convince them of anything... I did not listen to the whole lot as I did not want to get caught... I came to you as soon as I could.' She explains while trying not to allow her stress to muddle her words.

'Thank you Toakase for informing us of this...' Yua says as her eyes meet those of Sanmos which appear to hold the largest amount of stress she had ever seen him exhibit.

Chapter 35

Ookonan moves through the highlands alone and with nothing but his backpack dangling precariously across his shoulders. He is now several kilometres from Brogan and has not looked back since the confrontation. His senses remain alert as he watches the sun slowly set, leaving the sky to turn a beautiful crimson red that fades into a purple.

As he reaches the top of a hill, he notices a small village towards the bottom. He squats down to rest but also to remain hidden as he keeps his ears peeled for any suspicious noises. He waits for the candles or any light source to come on in any of the buildings but as the sky grows darker, nothing happens.

He takes in a deep breath of air through his nose, but instead of smelling the crisp leaves, dirt and grass, there was a rotten smell of decomposition. Whatever it was, it was nearby and although the scent was faint it still burnt his nostrils.

Realising that something wasn't quite right, he stood back up and made his way down the hill and towards the unsettling village.

The stench grew stronger with every step he took towards the village, almost overpowering his senses and forcing him to feel nauseous. It was unbearable, somehow worse than that of the black forest.

As he finally entered the village, much to his own surprise it felt significantly colder than where he was moments prior, on top of the hill. His curiosity had him wondering how and why until he stepped into what could have only been the main road. He looks down at his foot that has sunk into thick cold mud.

But was it mud? He quickly opens one of the side pockets of his backpack and pulls out a match. He lights it and shines the light onto the road, and much to his own horror, none of what he is standing in is mud. It's a mixture of decaying flesh, blood, bones and organs. No wonder the place stank.

He surveys the dark street as he begins his journey through, listening for any faint sounds as he watches for any potential movement before deciding to investigate one of the buildings. He treads carefully towards its verandah and runs a finger down a post. He smells his finger, investigating it before wiping it clean on his pants and moving on.

'There is no spice... Only decay... It is not looking good here.'

He wanders back out to the middle of the blood-ridden road, trying his hardest to scan his surroundings. Listening for any sounds that might be coming from inside any of the buildings. One building catches his attention. From inside it emits a faint spongy, wet and airy noise mixed with what sounds like sobbing.

He takes himself over to the house, but the first step he took onto the steps loudly squelched, which echoed through the village. He cringes at the thought of something hearing him. He takes the remainder of the steps as carefully as possible until he has reached the front door.

The rancid odour is now overwhelming his senses, he can feel it in his sinuses violating his airways. He brushes his hand over the door, checking for seasoning. But yet again all he got was the same black sediment. He brought his hand to his nose to only smell the mild musky scent of mould, which was overpowered by the rancid smell of rot.

A sharp creaking noise suddenly echoes from the building across the road where he once stood, investigating the verandah. He snaps his head around attempting to see the building in better light. Nothing. Only the dark wood of the building, empty hollow windows and the so-called mud splattered everywhere.

He turns his attention back to the damp mouldy door. He takes hold of the door handle and slowly opens the door. Its loud creaks felt deafening and upon the door opening, he noticed every surface of the room had a dark wet slimy surface. It covers the floor, runs down the walls and drips off the ceiling. He thought he had seen it all when he saw the large pulsating lump of flesh sitting in the far corner of the room. The noise it made was unlike anything he had ever heard. It seemed to be struggling to breathe.

He took a single step into the room then. 'Aahh…. Ooooahh.' A tortured voice calls out from the same direction as the pulsating giant flesh clump.

'Do not come in… You are too late…' Another whispered.

'What happened?' Ookonan inquired, stepping out of the room with one foot.

'There is an acadius in here… Leave while you can.' The voice says, trying not to choke on its own blood.

'How did this happen? What is an acadius?' Ookonan questioned as calmly and quietly as he could.

'They stole our spice. We were unprepared, gggchaaah……The ball of flesh…….The acadius is absorbing me…. Leave……. I do not have much time left…………. Ghichagh………. Leave.' The tortured voice urged as it choked and struggled.

He steps away from the doorway and back down the steps, out onto the road as the choking and struggling turned into gurgles, growls and screams.

'EEEEEEAAAAAAHHHHHH.' It screamed loudly through the open door, echoing through the village.

His stomach drops and his chest feels heavy as he surveys the village for any movement that could have been alerted by the scream. He tries to control his breathing as the stench is now suffocating. Every breath counts.

He notices a faint amount of colour penetrating through the darkness against the building at the far end of the road. Taking himself towards the building, he examines the entrance, finding that this time there is no door, just a rectangular void of pure darkness.

He steps onto the verandah and up to the entryway opening. He peers into the house and takes a moment in an attempt to let his eyes adjust, even though his ears are picking up everything. Scuttering and shuffling footsteps on a slimy sticky surface, biting and chewing on hard objects like bone with decaying flesh still attached.

But once his eyes adjusted, he could finally see what state the house seemed to be in. The walls have holes and scratches throughout, like a struggle until it was an embracement. Broken furniture thrown around and like the other place, a black sticky surface spread across the floor but only partially up the walls.

He ducks under the doorframe and steps inside, onto the sticky floor. Each and every step he took felt like sticky velcro beneath his feet. He tried to be quiet in order to avoid being noticed and potentially swarmed, but he was clearly failing.

As he progressed through the monstrosity of a house, the chewing and gnawing got louder and this time there were unsatisfied grunts. He tries to keep an eye on the floor to watch where he stepped, avoiding any bones or broken wood. Next to his foot was a slimy chewed on human rib cage in which he had missed by less than an inch.

Just around the corner squats what appears to be a seemingly normal person from behind, chewing on a mangled corpse. It rips the rotting liver out of the body and takes a large bite out of it, grunting as it enjoys its meal.

Wide eyed, Ookonan steps away, mortified by what he is witnessing. He holds his breath, maintaining eye contact with the barely human monster as he walks backwards, trying to escape from this all too real nightmare. He forgets about the littered sticky floor, leading him to step back onto the ribcage he carefully avoided moments earlier. The crunching noise of the bone beneath his feet fills the room, alerting the monster inside.

Frozen in place, Ookonan waits for its next move, hoping it would think the sharp sound was nothing. Instead, it stops eating and drops what was in its hands as it snaps its head around and stares directly at Ookonan, right into his soul.

He desperately hopes it cannot see all too well in the dark, at least not yet as its face is still mostly human. But the change was obvious as its eyes brightened with a yellowish orange glow. It tilts its head at him and grins, showing off the shifting in its teeth, longer and pointier as it loses its enamel structure and gains more of a rockier form. Black sludge begins to ooze out of its mouth through its now eerily unhuman smile.

'How long ago did you change?' He interrogates, attempting to tap into its humanity.

It tilts its head to the side in some sort of attempt to understand him. While growling it scutters towards Ookonan on all fours. 'Eeeeeggggggrrrrrhrhhhh.'

'You are still young and fresh... Your face is still human...' He quickly steps out of and away from the ribcage and slowly yet steadily makes his way towards the door while maintaining close eye contact on the half human monster. 'My guess you got corrupted a week ago.' He says, still trying to tap into its humanity, but also attempting to find out what happened.

'You are too late… I am so hungry… Eeehhhhgggerrrrr…' Trying to grasp onto any last fraction of humanity it had left, the halfling struggled to get words out through the constant sticky ooze that permeated its mouth. 'We were taken si…. Ahhhhh… six days ago… I got hungry… So hungry…'

'When did the hunger for flesh start?' He asks, trying to maintain a distance between himself and the halfling demonic.

'Two days ago… heeehh… heeeehhhh….' It screeched, finally giving into the irresistible demonic urges. 'You are so fresh… I could really go for some FRESH MEAT!!!'

Ookonan dashes towards the exit, avoiding the halflings' launch attack by mere millimetres. But as he reaches the front door, he is caved in by an almost fully formed demonic. Its smile swells from ear to ear, displaying its long sharp rock like teeth, Its skin excretes the black sticky slime and its eyes glow a bright crimson red. Almost no human qualities remain.

'Aaaaaa aa aa aa aa.' It growled in an odd clicking tone.

'Lemicölään.' He muttered under his breath.

'We tried….' The halfling responded with a gruesome smile, flaunting its blackish white teeth. 'But the hunger… Impossible to resist… Eeeeehhhhh… Especially… When fresh… Meat… Presents itself…'

Ookonan steps away from the exit while drawing his sword, readying himself for a grisly fight. Despite the darkness encompassing him, he can still see both demonics twitching, drooling and bearing their grotesque teeth, so he positions himself where they are both somewhat in his line of sight.

The more twisted of the two launches itself at Ookonan. He quickly reacts to it, blocking its bite with the blade of his sword which he jams into the corners of its mouth. He was so close to the vile monstrosity for comfort that he found himself noticing distinct things about it. Its eyes were still mostly human, it still had some clumps of hair on its head, as well as a humanoid nose and some patches of human skin which was bruised or necrotic around the edges.

'Aaaaahhhhh.' The mature demonic screams, pulling itself off the blade and clutching its mouth in pain as viscid blood pours from its fresh wound.

It snaps its head back to look up at Ookonan. 'AAAAAHHHH.' It screams as it claws at its head, turning its jaw side to side to adjust it, causing more blood to pour erratically from its mouth.

Ookonan readies himself as their crimson eyes lock onto him. The demonic gives a sharp grin before launching towards Ookonan who lowers his stance and sweeps his sword at its shins With exorbitant speed, he drives the blade in an upwards motion, slicing an arm clean off the shoulder of the demonic before it collapses onto the ground.

It flops around on the floor for a mere moment before getting back onto its feet, ignoring the pain pulsating through its body. It stumbles on broken legs towards Ookonan, reaching for him with its one remaining hand as its bones crunch with every step.

'AAAahhhhhahahahahaha NOTHING BEATS HUNGER... And you are so fresh.'

Ookonan ignores the taunts of the halfling as he avoids its attacks while trying to maintain focus on the more formed and injured demonic. He tightens his grip on his battered sword and waits for the opportunity to strike.

As the halfling jumps at him, he dashes out of the way, causing the monster to fall into a heap of broken furniture. He spins around in a lowered stance and slices the more formed demonics head clean off. Blood oozes from the demonic's neck as it falls onto the black sticky floor below. Its head barely rolls as what was once a red glow in its eyes fades to nothing.

The halfling crawls out from the broken furniture and slowly gets to its feet. Now with several puncture wounds, it smiles at Ookonan through bared teeth. Its shoulders are rolled over and its breathing heavily as it stares him down through its eyebrows ready for a fight.

'You are next!!' Ookonan fiercely grunts, now directing his attention towards the halfling. He feels fear rise within his chest as he stares down this monster while contemplating ways to escape the sickening house. But the last thing he can do is give into his fear or even worse, let the demonic know about said fear.

'I am okay with that... But just so you know... I have been calling the others... Good luck trying to leave!!! AAAAAHHH HAHAHAHAHA.' The halfling laughs as it starts taking steps towards Ookonan. It twitches and shakes uncontrollably as the guilt and empathy of his little remaining humanity tries to push through with no luck. Simultaneously the demonic pushes just as hard, burrowing humanity deep down, where it will never see the light of day again, replaced by an overwhelming excitement for their first hunted meal

Ookonan's chest begins to feel electric as his heart beats faster. His lungs feel the strong winds, it's like a storm is brewing in his chest. Sparks start forming around his hands and forearms. This gives him an idea. Before the halfling makes its first move, he takes a deep breath and fills his lungs up all the way, fighting against his instincts of not inhaling the stench.

The monster goes to launch itself at him, and in response, he blows the storm out of his lungs. Strong winds pick up the halfling and throw it against a wall, winding it on impact. Ookonan takes this opportunity to race towards the exit.

Ducking under the doorway and jumping out of the verandah, Ookonan is thankful to be out of the hazardous house, although his surroundings including the filthy wet road underneath his feet are no less sinister. He takes a brief moment to catch his breath as he attempts to survey the area for his next move.

'EEEEAAAAAAHHHHHH!' The halfling demonic screams.

He snaps his head back to watch for the halfling as scream intensifies. Suddenly, throughout the rotting village more demonic screams begin, one by one. He scans each building around him as demonics slowly start exiting them. Some walked out of the buildings, some fell out of windows and some crawled out of the underside or any other unfortunate opening.

He moves himself into the middle of the road, readying himself for an attack or a swarm and hoping to have even the slightest of advantages while he prepares for the worst. As the stakes rise so does his heartbeat, it's as though it wants to surge through his chest and escape his body. He closes his eyes and takes a few deep breaths as an attempt to calm himself before the attack. There can be no mistakes, he thinks to himself as a mistake from panic could end his life.

'YOU WILL NOT GET AWAY!!! WE ARE ALL HUNGRY!!' The halfling screams while stumbling down the stairs.

He grips his sword tighter while he blanks his mind from the increasing stress of all this chaos. This time in his cleared mind tries to think about his favourite tea. He takes in one more deep breath and thinks about the flavours of the tea, the feeling it gives him and the positive memories it brings back, as if transcending him into an entirely different realm, where nothing could ever go wrong. He opens his eyes which now glow a bright whitish blue like a lightning storm. He faces the demonic running towards him before charging at it.

As he nears it, he gets low and thrusts the sword through it diagonally. The battered weapon tears through its rib cage, shredding its corrupt flesh. Ripping the blade out of its chest, he sidekicks it in the mouth, shattering its teeth and snapping it where his blade did damage. It falls to the filthy wet ground and its glowing eyes fade into bleak nothingness.

He looks behind himself to see the horde of demonics slowly yet assuredly approaching. He feels the storm swirl within his lungs and embraces it. With electricity still sparking off of his hands, he twirls his free hand in a circular motion as he fills his lungs with more air. He turns around to face the horde that are making their way towards him, all are too far gone to see the glow of lightning He lets the air out of his lungs and pushes throws his hand forwards while maintaining the twirling motion. An electrified whirlwind is released from him and rapidly smashes into the demonics, throwing them backwards in multiple uncalculated directions. Impaling several onto broken building structures and breaking the bones of several more.

that wraps around his hand. He waits for the perfect moment, the closeness of the horde and the charge of his hand.

He takes a moment to catch his breath, refusing to let the stench of rot that's increasingly getting stronger by the minute distract him or invade his mind. The one thing that has been bothering him and getting under his skin is the constant laughter of the halfling who stands on the verandah, watching the fight unfold like some kind of demented show.

He turns his attention towards it only to see it stumble down the few steps connected to the verandah as if forgetting how to use its own legs. It hunches over as it struggles to coordinate and hold its changing body. It eyes Ookonan with its glowing amber eyes as black sludge oozes from its mouth.

'There is an acadius here… Just so you know MEAT! Hehehe.' It shouts and giggles at him.

Distracted by the halfling's uncoordinated display, Ookonan loses his clear mind and his thoughts about tea. The foul air makes his eyes water and he struggles to breathe. He surveys the area for a quick escape, noticing the halfling still creeping towards him but also the eight other demonics surrounding either side of him.

He harrows in on his mind and closes his eyes once more. He refocuses on tea, the aromas and flavour complexities. He reopens his eyes but to no avail, it's no longer working, he cannot regain control as he loses more time and even more energy to fight.

Reclosing his eyes, he finds himself thinking about something different. The time he spent rubbing spice into strangers homes as he traveled. Rescuing towns from the monstrosities of Hondon. The thoughts of the time that people were safe because he added his spice to areas they forgot to patch up. Children feeling safe like she or tea made him feel.

He opens his eyes again to find that the world around him has slowed down, almost to a stand still with the most minimalist of movements. His eyes glow like an electric typhoon as a blast of electrified watery air rushes around him. But before could see the demonics, a short hooded woman covered in mud walks up to him, her features are fairly young. She lifts up a hot steaming cup of tea. He shakes the thought away, closing his eyes again shortly and briefly to open them again and for the tea holding woman to no longer be seen. He turns his gaze over to the eight demonics running at him in slow motion.

He grips his sword tighter and thrusts the inordinately electrified blade into the chest of a demonic, frying it from the inside as he slams the blade downwards, cutting it almost in half before giving it the final blow of an electrified windbound hook punch to the side of its head. Obliterating it before it could comprehend anything ever happening to it.

He moves onto the next, thrusting the blade through its neck and into its skull with a simultaneous blast of wind, effortlessly obliterating it as well. Spinning around with his blade out flat, he throws a flat projectile of wind which slices a demonic clean in half.

As the storm around him gets stronger, he jumps high into the air. High enough to see the whole village. He can now see how many there are left, six in total including the halfling whose increasingly dwindling human side seems to be terrified.

'HHHAAAAAA!' He screams as he charges his sword, channeling all of his energy.

He dives back down towards the earth, creating a shockwave that drags the demonics in all directions, ripping them apart with both brute force and shrapnel. Few were impaled by the remnants of buildings. Two survived but were too badly injured to move from where they lay. One scrapes the ground with its remaining arm while the other just bites the air as it lays defeated and almost limbless. Surprisingly, the halfling remained untouched.

Ookonan stands back up and walks out of the small crater he created. Hyperfocused on the halfling, he makes his way over to it.

It cowers in fear as it tries to move itself away from Ookonan. 'Eeehh eeehhh...' It screeched as it tried crawling up the stairs. 'What are you?'

'You are asking me what I am?' He interrogated as he watched it sob. 'Did you not say you wanted to die?'

'No.... No...' It cried.

'The only humanity you have left is fear, no compassion, no empathy. Only the thought of easing a hunger you can not explain yourself.'

Before the halfling could say another word, he switched grip on his sword. He forces himself and the blade downwards with great momentum, slashing through its eye and puncturing through the back of its skull. Killing it almost instantly. He rips the weapon from its head and stands back up before giving it a final blow. Stomping on its grotesque bleeding head.

He turns his attention towards the two barely alive demonics who are laying in the mud. Nothing human left in them and apparently not even pain. But the hunger was still apparent as they hissed at him and reached for a bite.

'It would be great if you abominations did not exist.' He mutters. For good measure and to avoid more transformative demonic mutations, he curls his right leg up high and stomps down onto the demonics head, crushing it through the thick mud and he does the same to the other. Destroying what's left of them.

He steps around the mangled corpses in order to travel down the road he once came. Listening and observing for anything hiding that could jump out and attack. But once he neared the end of the village, he could hear the soft sobbing of a woman.

He comes to a stop to survey the area, listening closely for the direction of the cries. 'Where is this coming from?' He quietly asked himself. His ears twitch in the direction of the soft sobs leading him to cautiously and quietly follow. As it gets louder it leads him back to where he started, the house with the pulsating mass.

'Well, it looks like I will be meeting you.' He whispers to himself under the belief that he will be meeting the tormented voice that urged him to leave.

He cautiously approaches the steps, walking up them and onto the verandah before ducking under the doorframe and letting himself inside the home. Unsure if he's being lured or someone was in real need of saving, he had to do the unthinkable as he knew he would never rest soundly knowing there was a survivor he could have rescued.

As he ventured through the wrecked home the weeping grew louder, but it made a transparent effort to remain silent as if it were trying to hide from someone or something. He cautiously avoided the walls, not allowing the sticky slime to get on him, for if he did, he would transform into one of the monsters he just faught. The wet airy noise of the pulsating mass was painfully close by and he needed to avoid it.

As his eyes adjusted to the darkness, he was finally able to locate things within the building. Broken furniture, toppled over objects and a drenched fireplace. With this faint vision he could see the pulsating mass, its form resembled the likes of unformed bodies and faces in strange places.

Deliberately ignoring it, his focus is casted back onto the weeping which he believed he could finally locate. Behind a sideways-facing table in a corner lies a woman, curled up in a fetal position. It seems she made a shield or barricade between herself and the monstrosity on the other side of the room.

241

'Were you the one telling me to leave?' He asked her softly.

Startled, she quickly sits up, defensively backing herself closer against the wall while locking eyes with Ookonan. She has soft Euro features but it's evident that she's infected. She has discoloured skin and thick dark veins, which clearly have already started the process of pumping viscous black blood around her body, invading, battling and corrupting her otherwise human blood. Her hair is falling out in patches and there is a faint amber glow around her irises.

'No... He was absorbed into the acadius over there.' She answered quietly, her tone barely a whisper as she pointed in the direction of the pulsating mass with her chin. 'Please leave before it is ready.' She pleads.

Full of sympathy, all he wanted to do was comfort the poor woman during her final consciously human moments. As he inched closer to the table, she quickly interjects.

'Please... Do not come closer. I have been infected.' She weeped.

She removes an arm from her filthy coat to show him. It's pale with thick black veins. Her arms are heavily bruised and the tips of her fingers are black and pointed, like dry necrosis with claws.

'How did this happen?' He questioned.

'We were raided and they stole our supplies, and all our spice. We were left defenceless.' She tenses up as the black veins in her neck pulsate, forcing further demonic conversion that she forces back down. 'The demonics came sssss... There was only so much hiding we could do.'

'Why did you not leave?'

'The slime got everywhere...' She said, wincing in pain as more change is forced upon her, brightening her eyes and deepening the bruises. 'There was no leaving.' She finally got out as her teeth became ever so slightly pointy.

'Slime is rare around villages... It hates fire.' He mentioned, trying to make sense of it all.

'I. I am just as clueless as you... It was as if it was placed here... There was no getting rid of it...' She said as her eyes nervously landed upon the pulsating acadius. 'It created that... An acadius.'

Following her gaze, his own eyes meet the abomination again. The fused bodies are practically motionless aside from the pulses acting as a macabrely conjoined heartbeat. He looks back at the walls and the veins that map the place, realising much to his horror that they all connect to it.

'I am very sorry.' He said as his heart ached.

'What for?'

'I am sorry for what happened. It must have been horrible.' He takes a deep breath as he forces himself to keep it together. 'And I am sorry for what is about to happen.'

She shivers and tightens the jacket around herself in effort to get warm as the demonic blood strips away her body heat. She tightens her fists and tenses her body as she holds back an almost irresistible rage that pulsates through her, further brightening her eyes and sharpening her teeth.

'Once it sets in, there is no going back.' She admits through gritted teeth. 'Please make it painless.'

'Let us go and look at the sky one last time with some grass on your skin before you go.'

'Okay.' She sobs as she gets to her feet. She climbs over the table, but maintains a distance between herself and Ookonan. Following him out of the house and onto the rotting road, she chokes at what she sees. Her friends and family. Everyone she once knew and loved lay beneath her feet as mangled demonic corpses scattered across decomposed rot she could no longer identify.

He puts a hand on her back and guides her away from the tragedy and towards the grassy hill that overlooks the village. She fills her lungs with the fresh air, feeling the grass on her feet and the breeze on her skin. She hasn't felt any of this in days and it was comforting. It must be preserved, it cannot be corrupted like her once treasured home.

'I do not fear death anymore.' She says, feeling human as she embraces her senses.

'Why does it not scare you anymore?' He questioned her, noticing that she wasn't looking at him but rather the colourful star-filled sky.

'After getting infected, I learned that there are fates far worse than death. Losing who you are and what makes you, you. Your thoughts, memories, your likes and dislikes… You feel it fade and yourself turn to something else…' She trails off. She doesn't want to think about becoming a demonic.

'I understand.'

'Thank you.'

'Relax and let yourself go… I will bring the angels of death to you, whatever happens next will happen, but it will not be your fear.' He said in a calm, soft tone, trying to bring even the slightest comfort to her in her final moments.

Sitting on the thick grassy carpet of the hilltop, she lies flat on her back watching the stars glisten amongst the beautiful swirls of colour in the milky way galaxy. She closes her eyes and embraces the breeze, the nocturnal noises of various animals and the rustling of leaves. She grips the grass she lays on and feels the blades between her fingers.

As she embraces her senses Ookonan focuses his breath and lets the electricity flow around his fingertips. He lets her have her moment as he focuses on pushing his emotions to the side. He then kneels down next to her, he hovers his hand over her chest where her heart would be.

†

For the first time in weeks the night in Hondon is peaceful with the stars bright enough to light up the earth. Animals claw their way up trees, ready to rest, while terrestrial animals lay in the grassy fields for the first time in a long time.

A huge bolt of lightning strikes the earth from a distance, temporarily lighting up the land as though it were day. Only a few seconds later, the booming sound of thunder frightens the terrestrial animals, causing them to scutter and run away in several directions. As the thunder subsides, the howling of wolves is heard disrupting the silence.

Chapter 36

Ookonan sits near the very top of the tetrahedron pyramid, gazing out to the sky islands that bop and sway in the soft breeze. His eyes are dark and grim from his sleepless night as he watches the sky in a failed attempt to relax as he reminiscences in his own thoughts.

He attempts to clear his mind and think about nothing but what he sees in the sky and what he feels in his lungs. The clouds that float by in their interesting shapes, the cold air that feels his lungs, but it did nothing to deter his thoughts. 'Why is the world so beautiful yet so terrible?'

A small contained but powerful storm forms next to him, which quickly gets stronger and fills with a strong surge of lightning. Which transforms into a small electrified tornado on the top of the pyramid, which quickly disappears leaving behind SuSanoo.

'What is it now?' Ookonan grunts.

'Where is Kaji?' Susanoo interrogates.

'How should I know?' He responds, briefly glancing at SuSanoo. 'The princess of Brogan decided that I am nothing... She is not wrong but she suggested that I delivered Kaji to her.'

'Twagólüum.' SuSanoo scoffs. 'She knows nothing.'

'She spoke of a prophecy...'

Susanoo straightens himself before sitting on the air next to Ookonan. It's almost like he is sitting on a cloud. 'Have I mentioned the Prophecy to you before?'

'No...' Ookonan mutters under his breath. He turns his gaze to Susanoo. 'And you are not denying it.' He mutters, annoyed at the deity, he still has no idea why he and Kaji are connected and why either of them have powers.

'No Ookonan. I am not denying it, there is a prophecy.' He confesses. He waits for more questions Ookonan may have, to learn about his destiny. A path he cannot change or control as much as he might want to. .

'How does the princess of Brogan know about it?' He abruptly questions, more to SuSanoo's surprise. .

'It is interesting how the world found out. But the information was found by other champions and spread by Vassels.' He explains in a calm tone.

'There are other champions? And what are Vassels? Did you mean Vessels?' Ookonan interrogates. He wants answers but he has so many more questions.SuSanoo proceeds to tell the story of an ancient vassel, originally a champion of a god who falls to an unforeseeable corruption.

†

The sun is slowly setting behind sharp jagged peaks as a strong muscular man, burdened with heavy scars of a long life of battle walks along a tall cliff edge mountain path. His leather clothing is worn and frayed, his boots are barely holding together and his aged skin holds fresh weeping wounds of battle.

As he travels along the sharp jagged cliff,a sudden sharp pain hits him in the chest, painful enough that he feels like he has just been stabbed through his sternum. He grabs his chest, believing it's nothing more than his harsh battle and he forces himself to continue the trek through the mountainous valley. But the pain worsens as it turns into a feeling like hot iron knife that burns through him.

He collapses to his knees as his chest begins to glow. The pain, now unbearable even for a refined warrior with a lifetime of battle experience. He shuts his eyes and holds back his screams of pain, he couldn't let the corrupt land find him, regardless of the pain. But it was too much. He collapses and passes out face first into the hard soil and lays there momentarily.

He opens his eyes and sits back up and stares straight ahead as though he is looking at the land for the first time. The glow travels through his body, burning and scaring him until he eventually awakens. He sits himself back up, opening his now glowing eyes. But, there was no longer a person behind them as his face now remains blank.

He surveys the land as though he's looking at it for the first time. He can no longer recognise himself and the person he once was, is no longer present. It's as though he's been killed and replaced by another spirit or soul.

The glow of the body grows brighter and hotter and the body struggles to handle the agony. It leans back screaming as the original soul is consumed. It grips its face as the glow and agony radiates through the body until it's so bright it. illuminates the entire surrounding land, but as soon as it reaches its peak it slowly begins to subside.

Once the glow is gone along with all pain, the man he once was is gone. He slowly gets to his feet as the remaining glow in his eyes fade and he takes his first steps as the new fraudulent owner of the body. He stumbles and wobbles as he struggles with his first steps as he continues on the mountainous trek

†

SuSanoo peers into Ookonan's eyes, he hoped to tell him about it later, but uttering it forced him to explain some harsher realities of his forced path.'Yes there are other champions, there are other champions as there are other gods and these gods sometimes want people to represent them granting them powers. Some gods have other means and turning their champion to a Vassel.'

'What would a vassel be?' Ookonan questions.

'A vessel is something that contains something. Like a jar or a bottle. A vassal is ownership or control. Like owning some land or... A slave... This is why they are called vassels.'

'Vassels are gods who have taken over their champion...' Ookonan states as he gains an understanding.

'Yes. The protected towns and cities learned about the prophecy through champions and vassels. But not every god or deity is aware.'

Ookonan takes a deep breath and looks at the grass on the bottom of the pyramid. 'According to Brogan scholars of the princess, say I am not worthy... And I am worthless.' He mutters as the powerful feeling of despair and worthlessness floods him. He has never felt the world is savable, only corruption, chaos and bloodshed.

'What did she say?' Susanoo calmly asked.

'She said: "how could you be his second half? How could a savage like you be chosen?"' He catches himself getting emotional which he briskly shoves aside as he gazes up at the sharp pyramid horizon.

'Ookonan.Do you know why I chose you?' SuSanoo questioned in a sharp tone.

'No…' He responds as he takes in a deep breath to steady his voice. 'I do not.'

'I chose you, as you always put others before yourself even if you do not like them, much as you had been while taking care of Kaji. Why did you leave him behind?'

'His destiny is with the princess.' He states feeling as though he is confessing the truth to Susanoo.

'Did she say anything about a second half? Does she think she was meant to be the second half?' SuSanoo interrogated as his temper began to rise.

'Yes she does.'

'She is not the second half of Kaji… Unless she intends to marry him; prophecy she is not.'

'She said an uneducated savage like-'

'Education and savagery is irrelevant to my prophecy.' Susanoo snaps, completely losing his composure.

'Huh? You created the prophecy?' Ookonan was left shocked and conflicted. Learning the prophecy off a mortal not the god who chose him to fulfill it and now the god created said prophecy. He needs answers, real answers to the vagueness that's been thrust upon him.

'Yes. I did. I created the prophecy with my friend Hestia, Greek goddess of hearth. I am a god of Mir, but I searched for someone who is from Hondon. I needed someone who puts others ahead of themself.

Who has struggled through hardship, war, fear… And has seen death in the worst ways known. I chose you because you do not want to see others suffer the way you did, you put yourself in harm's way to help others, you live a life of honour and bravery and seek nothing in return. The life of a warrior nomad.'

'You are from Mir?'

'Yes.. I am.'

'Would it make sense that Hestia…The other god of prophecy is from Hondon?' Ookonan questions as he tries to piece the prophecy together.

'That is correct. Hestia is from Hondon.'

Ookonan takes a moment to himself as he attempts to understand. He looks at SuSanoo, now finally seeing him, his eastern features with his godly tones. His pale skin sparks with electricity and his clothing floats around him like a constant storm lives within. He looks back at his hands, tanned from the nomadic life, his nails are unkept and his skin holds heavy scarring from the Hondon land.

'Why did she choose Kaji?' He finally asks.

'She did not originally.'

'What do you mean?' He felt surprised by those words, as annoying as Kaji is, he was likely perfect for the prophecy.

'Hestia's sister tried to rush things. Things were getting worse and worse on earth. Hestia considered many Mirish people but she almost gave into the pressure of forcing things along. She considered a Mirish individual, someone of similar qualities to Kaji, but her sister jumped in. That champion was the first Mirish person to venture to Hondon and thanks to this them Kaji had access to the Hondonian language. Which Kaji has studied according to Hestia.'

'So Kaji was not chosen to begin with?'

'The Prophecy is old. Very, very old. Hestia considered she may have been wrong as time went on. Her sister's champion gifted Kaji his name and told her to keep an eye on him.'

'How does that answer the question of why she chose Kaji.'

'Ookonan you need to learn patience…' He says firmly as his voice rumbles his like thunder in his chest. 'For now that is your biggest downfall.'

'Kaji was chosen as someone who is from a culture of family. He is in line to be the emperor of Mir. He's been forced to focus on responsibility of unknown reasons… Reasons unknown to himself.' SuSanoo continued.

'He cares deeply for the people he loves and the people around him. He is very determined to leave the world a better place than how he found it… A lot like yourself.'

'We are the same yet completely different.' Ookonan states, trying to convey an understanding, Yet failing to find reasons of their shared purpose.

'Yes and no. You were chosen out of kindness and Kaji was chosen out of love. To put it simply.'

'How long did it take for you to choose me?'

'The entire one thousand years since the earth changed Hestia and I searched, from the cataclysmic start until you were a lonely young boy. Of all of Hondon you are one of a kind. There are plenty of people who have noble causes… Such as the righteous Aagneya… Her quest you disrupted in fear of Kaji's life was finding the horn to clean their water and grow food in Brogan.'

Ookonan's eyes widen as he catches the information Susanoo spoke. 'How do you know her name?'

'I watched closely and I did consider her. Another god ended up making her their champion, I will tell you about it.'

✝

Ten years ago.

The grand doors of the Brogan palace abruptly open, disturbing King Tolibane's court meeting. Two large elven guards march in dragging a young Aagneya between them towards the less than impressed Tolibane himself who sits on his throne and on the smaller to his right seats Queen Mebatikuel.

The few high ranking figures in the court stare in silence as Aagneya is forced towards her parents. Her mother refused to look at her as a foul disgust crossed her face while her father stared directly into her soul.

'Hello Amma. Hello Anpa.' Aagneya grins as she greets her parents. Her eyes are bloodshot and her pupils are dilated, but behind those eyes are not a single care in the world about her parents' approval.

'Take her away.' King Tolibane growled.

'No hello?' She sarcastically asked as the guards escorted her away.

She is dragged through the palace, down the cold corridors lined with the colours of purple, blue, copper and silver. The art scattered she has seen many times before are now invisible to her. She is dragged until a well crafted door engraved with the copper silver, purple and blue appears in front of her. A guard opens it before throwing her into the room and locking her in.

She stumbles through her room catching her footing as her legs feel wobbly and uncoordinated from a heavy day of drinking and drugs. She looks back at the door and smiles to herself as anger pumped through her veins.

She takes herself over to one of her dressers in her grand bedroom. She opens it and presses a hidden button which opens a secret compartment along the side which is filled with rolled papers stuffed with herbs. She removes one and stares at it for a short minute before searching the draws for something to use to light it.

As she lights a match, a bright and loud flash suddenly fills the room, startling her. She whips around, herb stick in mouth and lit match in hand. However, from the quick spinning and the heavy day drinking she found herself fighting for balance and struggling to see what had happened. Her blood pressure rises as she spots vines and leaves growing around the window, but as the light subsides and her vision returns to normal she sees a strange woman sitting on the window cill.

The woman is glowing with an unearthly aura. She has bright pale skin, braided ginger hair, green tattoo like patterns across her skin and her gown is otherworldly. The long dress is made of earthly elemental materials; water, wind, pants, rocks and dirt .

'Hello Aagneya.' The strange otherworldly woman says with a smile.

'How did you get in here?!' Aagneya barked, even while on her fun substances she cannot hold back her shock.

'I did not expect the princess to be taking something like that.' The woman stoically says as she gets off the window cill and makes her way over to Aagneya.

'Do you not like fun?' Aagneya playfully questioned, trying not to be annoyed with the woman while putting down the burned out match.

'Is that any way to address a god?' The woman calmly utters as her otherworldly dress lifts her to Aagneyas eye level.

Aagneya takes a step away from the woman while failing to hold back her own laughter, unsure how to respond to something like this. She is unable to tell whether she is dreaming, really drunk and high or whether her father has officially beaten her to death.

'I am the celtic goddess Danu.' She announces as she circles around her. 'Deity of Nature, Prosperity, wisdom, death and regeneration. I have selected you as my champion.'

'This is getting ridiculous.' Aagneya muttered as she finally lit her special herbs. She takes a deep puff and fills her lungs. She takes her time and holds it, truly feeling the next high hit, there is no way she will deal with this sober. She slowly lets the smoke leave her lungs before following up with her questions. 'Why would you choose me? The world is doomed anyway. Why should I care?'

'So what did you do today?' Danu questioned.

'I... Uuuuhhh... I.' She stumbles, unable to get a word out, unsure whether or not to trust this hallucination.

'You were stealing food, alcohol and other substances from the palace and giving it to the citizens while drunk.' Danu explains to her as though she may have forgotten her day or was too embarrassed to say.

'Judging me like my parents...' Aagneya condescendingly states while rolling her eyes and taking another puff. 'They only care for themself.'

'I have chosen you as my champion. As my representation. Your act today fed families who have not eaten a proper meal in weeks. I have chosen you to help restore the lands you live on. Do not let me down.'

Aagneya raises her eyebrows and takes another large inhale of her special herbs and blows the large cloud of smoke at Danu. 'Do not expect me to be proper about it.'

†

Ookonan takes a deep breath as he looks over at the sky islands. He takes a moment to himself and reflects on SuSano's story about her and how a few days ago when the fairy attack happened at those floating islands, she wanted to help and never ran from him. All she really wanted to do was to make Brogan a better place for the citizens.

'I learned she was not out to hurt Kaji well after we got there and I did not realise she had noble intentions.'

'Yes, Ookonan.You went to the last Village to find survivors and the night I granted you your powers when you fought the brood mother. You had nothing to gain from either of those experiences. Why did you help them?'

'Last night I wanted things to go back to the way they were. The village was not looking good, but I thought I might find a survivor unharmed. I could take them to another village or possibly Brogan. They would be safe and they can carry on with their life.' Ookonan explained.

'And what of the night I granted you the power of storm before you met me?'

'They clearly did not know what they were doing. They told me they were hunting every night with men dying every time with the demonics getting closer for every day they remained. The Vatpik who was taking them on their expeditions had no idea what he was doing and would often head back without them. A complete coward. They did not season their homes and they were not doing much of anything properly.'

Susanoo to Ookonan's words, taking in everything he says. He tries to understand why Ookonan sees himself as worthless, but all he is doing is explaining his own invisible importance without realising.

'I destroyed the swarm hunting them. I killed the brood mother and when we got back I showed them how to season their home. I hope they have left the black forest as I do not believe it will do them any good.'

'Do you believe Aagneya will do that?'

Ookonan was taken by surprise by the question, he's never been asked that before and he's never really thought about if anyone else would consider helping people the way he does. He has never thought about whether he was doing a good deed or if those deeds would get him rewards. He's never wanted rewards and he's never truly considered if other people would do the same as himself. He just wants to help whoever he can.

'Answer my question.' Susanoo demanded.

'No I do not believe she would do that... No one would do that unless they have a death wish.' He finally admitted to himself, now realising no one would go out of their way to season other peoples homes and kill demonics for them.

'Do you care for your life Ookonan?'

'Not as much as I care for others.'

Susanoo stands up and uses the air under his feet to lift him so he could stand straight on to Ookonan. 'That is why I chose you. Ookonan you are the most important person from Hondon. It does not matter your class, your bloodline, your education or your race. What matters is your character.' He smiles as he takes a step away from him. He couldn't help himself but to admire the large man. He knows he chose the right person.

The wind around him grew strong and powerful as water and electricity formed. It grows into a small contained typhoon and disappears as quickly as it had begun, leaving Ookonan alone on the pyramid once more.

'It is nice to hear that I am not unimportant.' Ookonan mutters to himself as he looks down at his hands, now appreciating his gifted power of storm a little more. 'First time I heard that one.'

He gets to his feet and slides down the pyramid. He walks through the pyramids running his hands across the ancient building remains as he takes himself out into the grassy plane near the sky islands and Brogan.

'Hmm... I suppose I better head back off to Brogan. I am not sure how I would get back in.' He admits as he gazes at the large city walls of Brogan out in the distance. But something peculiar catches his eye. A small child-like figure stands alone in the open plane.

The wind howls, the grass sways like ocean waves. The small figure stands there, appearing to have some sort of heavy breath as it watches him. As he steps out of the dense tetrahedron pyramids, the figure has not moved a muscle but he now has a clearer view of what it is. A small child.

'What are you doing standing out in the open like that?'

He continues to hike through the long grass, his eyes never leaving the figure that remains standing, unmoved and unbothered. It couldn't be a demonic as they only like the night and it's too human to be a ubakara.

'What are you?'

Chapter 37

Countless pieces of leather and fur are cut to size and mapped out in front of Greybeard who is sitting on a stool next to the lowered workbench. Standing next to the forge is Kaji who is breathing in deep and holding onto each breath for a few seconds before releasing them. As he does so a soft yet hot stream of fire expels from his hands into the forge.

Greybeard stands and takes a considerable step away from the workbench, examining all the pieces in which she has laid out before contemplating where she should start.

'Are pieces all ready?' Kaji asks, maintaining his calm focus on the fire while also keeping an eye on Greybeard.

'Yes I believe so.' She said while retaining eye contact with the leather pieces. She grabs out some twine and two needles and places them on the bench.

Looking up at Kaji and meeting his eyes, she takes off the goggles from the top of her head, and starts cleaning them with a cloth she pulled from her pocket. 'Now I believe tungsten, titanium threading should be used to hold this together.' She states as her gaze wanders past Kaji and towards the forge.

'Tungsten?'

'Yes, well. You are a fire man so it would make sense to have a heat resistant material. Until I find something better.'

'Makes sense.' He says, feeling unsure on what tungsten means in Mirish.

She places her hands on the bench in front of her and leans as if stretching in an undignified manner before making her way over to the other side of the room towards a large stack of shelves next to a moveable case of stairs. She walks up the stairs and peers at the words on each of the wooden boxes.

She brushes her hand over the boxes and pulls out an evidently hefty one labelled walaakil *(Tungsten)*, before eyeing another box of almost equal heft labelled darlifaa *(artefacts)*. She reaches into each box, pulling out rocks and cubes of tungsten and an artefact in the shape of a thin club with a ball on the end.

Sliding both boxes back in place, she makes her way down the steps before walking over to the forge where Kaji is standing. She places the rocks and the artefact into the hot fiery coals before leaning back and taking a deep breath as her eyes wander over towards Kaji. Wasting no time, she walks over to the sizable pile of coal near the forge. Grabbing a shovel, she pours two scoops of the jet black coal into the pit of ember fire.

Placing the shovel next to the cold coal, she walks back over to Kaji, looking up at him smiling as she places her goggles over her eyes. 'I need you to take a deep breath and clear your mind… Then I want you to open your eyes and aim your breath at the coal in the forge.'

He looks down at her and nods, taking a deep breath and closing his eyes. He focuses on the air filling his lungs before composedly opening his eyes. Aiming his hands at the forge, he breathes out, shooting a hot yet controlled stream of fire at the coals in the pit.

'You have got it… almost.' She says reassuringly, patting him on the back.

He nods at her without breaking focus from the task at hand, projecting his flames towards the tungsten ore and the titanium artefact. Reaching for the long tongs by the forge, Greybeard removes the red hot artefact from the pit of fire.

'Time for you to practise refined prediction flame to keep this material hot to shape.' She announces as she takes the glowing piece of metal to the anvil.

'I will give it a go.' He offers while watching Greybeard bash the anvil with a hammer, repeatedly hitting the metal artefact. 'Great.' She says, removing another tungsten rock from the forge and placing it on the anvil. She gestures Kaji over to her and points at the material on the anvil, it was glowing red hot like magma.

He takes a deep breath and looks at his hands as he makes an effort to centre himself before walking over to the anvil and standing in front of her. He breathes out, focusing on his index finger on his right hand, he closes his eyes. Reopening his eyes, he is greeted by a sharp and sweltering flame igniting from the edge of his finger.

Taking control of the flame, he aims it towards the the materials on the anvil, keeping them well heated as Greybeard moulds them with her hammer.

'Kaji, you have done well. This saddle for Yuma will be done very soon.' She states, drawing out the material and folding it over.

'How long do you think it will take?' He asks as Greybeard takes the drawn out material to what appears to be a winding machine. 'Well.' She gestured towards the workshop door. 'Have a look outside and tell me what time you think it is.'

Taking a breath, Kaji flicks his hand, extinguishing the miniature inferno. He walks towards the entrance of the building and opens the door.

Sticking his head out of the door, he is welcomed by the golden glow of the sun beaming against his face. He takes note of the fresh air, the relatively clear skies, and the sun shining behind the palace. The guards are patrolling the streets while countless residents head to their jobs. Meanwhile, vendors continue to make an effort to sell their questionable substances.

'I estimate it to be around seven o'clock maybe.' Kaji confirms as he heads back inside, closing the door behind himself.

'Huh?' She says, looking up as she notices the light beaming through the holes and cracks in the walls before her eyes meet the windows. 'Give me another five hours maybe.'

'Fast you work.' He says, taken aback. No one in Mir could work that fast, that precise or with the tools she is using.

'Yep that is me. When you are passionate about something. You tend to work harder and often faster. I also have no other projects at the moment.'

Kaji stumbles for a moment, scanning the workshop. He can see a pile of completed projects under a thick white blanket towards one side of the shop, while mounds of scrap metals, woods and other materials lay haphazardly towards the other side, and stacks of wooden boxes pile over each other towards the back.

'Uhhh.' He vocalises after clicking his tongue.

'Kaji.' She says slowly while looking up at him. 'Go out and explore for a bit. Get some fresh air.'

'Oh… okay.' He responds as he dusts himself off and walks towards the front of the workshop. Looking back at Greybeard who is hunched over the bench with her newly forged pins and thread, he opens the door.

'Bye.' He says as he walks out the door, closing it firmly behind him.

He takes a breath as he surveys either side of the street. Carriages carrying crates and jars manoeuvre their way through the bustling foot traffic. Kaji notes that more stalls appear to now be set up on either side of the road and more guards appear to have clocked into their patrol duties, ensuring that people stay clear of the palace stone wall and fence.

He takes a step away from Greybeard's shed and sees people trading home made food and crafted items using round pieces of metal as currency.

Standing awkwardly, he watches the street for a little longer before deciding where to go. To his expanding discomfort, he notices several people starting to stare at him, speeding along his decision.

He lowers his head as he starts to briskly walk down the street towards his right.

'Have an accident did you?' A stranger calls out to Kaji. Searching for the voice amongst the crowd of uneasy eyes, Kaji halts his movement.

'Yes I am talking to you Human.'

'Me?' Kaji asks, bewilderedly pointing at himself.

'You are the only human here…' The voice reveals itself from the crowd as a scruffy looking elven man approaches Kaji and towers over him. 'But because you have clearly already been beaten up. I might leave you.'

'I. ah. I' Kaji stutters. He starts to tense up as the dark yet seemingly playful eyes of the elf proceed to stare down at him almost as if staring directly into his soul, only made worse by the macabre pairing of an excessively widened grin. This stranger clearly wanted to inflict harm on him in some way and Kaji had little doubt that he would enjoy doing it.

His anxiety began to grow as the elf reached for his jacket. Buruk wasn't joking about how they treat humans, Kaji thought to himself.

Startlingly, a hand from behind firmly grasps his shoulder causing him to jump as if right out of his own skin. He feels his heart racing beneath his chest as he chokes on his own breath.

This unsettling figure who was only moments prior increasingly daunting becomes considerably less threatening as he places his hands in the air and takes a few shaky steps away in the opposite direction. 'Princess

Aagneya…' The stranger smiles. 'I am sorry I did not hurt him, I promise you.'

'Carry on.' She says domineeringly yet nonchalantly, gesturing the stranger away. 'Go away.'

The stranger takes a few more shaky steps in the opposite direction before turning around and bolting down the road, once again getting lost amongst the crowd. Once the stranger was out of Kaji's eyesight he turns around and looks up at Aagneya as his convoluted curiosity about her grows.

'How did you find me?'

'It was by chance.' She lied, as she grabbed his hand and looked him in the eye. Her own eyes were a deep forest green and a strong sense of fierceness was present within them.

'You need to come with me… I have a few things to show you. And you need new clothes.'

'I could really go for new clothes.' He admits.

'Lets go.' She says, gripping his hand tighter to lead him along the road.

†

Aagneya leads Kaji through an old hallway in the Brogan Palace where the sunlight beams through the windows allowing streams of light to bounce against the pristine walls. . The floorboards were made of old hardwood while the walls were made of thick stone with equally old wooden beams holding the roof up.

Kaji draws closely behind her, noting how broad her shoulders are, how fluffy and purple her hair is and how lean and muscular her build is.

Following Aagneya, he stops walking and turns to the right, being met with a plain hardwood door. She opens the door and swings it inwards before looking down at Kaji.

'After you.' She says, gesturing him through.

Walking through the door, he is followed by Aagneya who closes the door behind them. The passageway leads to a small room filled artfully with shelves, cupboards and crates. All of which appear to be filled with fabric and materials, including but not limited to a curious combination of spare clothes, fancy dresses and repaired armour.

'What is it you want to show me?' He asked, surveying the unfamiliar room.

'I am just getting you some new clothes...' She says as she inspects the shelves like she has done a thousand times before.

'They are not fireproof or fire resistant but you clearly need new clothes...' She expresses, pulling neatly folded clothes off the shelves. 'And a bath.'

She holds up a plain blue shirt and a pair of plain blue linen pants and reapproaches Kaji, holding them in front of him. 'Hold still, I need to make sure these are not too long for you. Humans are shorter than elves.' She explains as she holds out the pants in front of Kaji at his waist level. Unsure what to do, Kaji stands motionless as he watches her make an effort to measure the pants. The pant legs reach the floor with the ends dragging a few centimetres against the floor. 'Hmm. these are the smallest.'

'You will need to roll up the bottoms. Follow me. I will take you to the bathhouse.' She says, grabbing a pair of fresh underwear off a shelf.

'After you.' She says as she opens the door and gestures him back through it.

He nods and walks out of the room, with Aagneya following, closing the door behind them.

Chapter 38

Palace guards patrol the Mirish Imperial grounds in groups or pairs, ensuring not only their own safety but the safety of the Imperial family since the disappearance of Kaji and the so-called reckless behaviours of Hono and her friends. They each hold lanterns and march past one another, taking details of each patrolled area.

Two masked hooded figures lurk within the bushes, just out of sight of the guards. They watch the palace eagerly. Avoiding the torch and lantern light are two more masked hooded figures hide within the shadows of the palace.

They search for the two hidden within the bushes as they avoid the gaze of the guards. One of the figures hidden in the bush puts their hand up and waves, signaling the two hiding in the shadows of the palace. They swiftly make their way over to the bushes to meet up with the other two. Without a word they point to the path leading out of the imperial grounds.

All four of them make their move to leave the grounds while keeping to the shadows. Out of sight from the guards and out of hearing range until eventually they are out of the imperial grounds entirely.

All four of them peer back at the grounds, scanning for any lantern lights that aim in their direction. Once clear one of them gives the signal to continue. They run off into the darkness and the other three follow until they reach a small grass clearing about a kilometre from the grounds itself. Once all there, they catch their breath as they look each other down in an attempt to reassure that each person is who they think they are before someone finally speaks up.

'We are all here…' A young female's voice finally said under heavy breath. 'On the count of three, we will all take off our masks. One… Two… Three…'

She takes off the mask revealing herself to be Toakase. The other three take off their masks at slightly different times revealing Hono, Koloa and Alefosio.

'We are all here…' Toakase quietly states under a deep breath. 'Good.'

'What are we doing, still?' Alefosio questions as he looks at Toakase. 'I do not understand.'

'What do you mean? The masks or where we are going?' Hono quickly interjects.

'No… Well yes the masks but why?' He questions while feeling the dark plaster mask. He couldn't help but feel anxious and afraid about what everyone and himself were getting into. Whether this would find his best friend or whether Toakase has found a conspiracy that would result in their inevitable harm.

'We need to make sure our identities remain hidden. I am under the belief that a war will start… Or something… I don't know.. I just know we need to investigate.' Toakase half states and mumbles as she looks over Alefosio. All she knew was it wasn't good news, but articulation was never her strong suit.

He nods, unsure whether or not Toakase was far too out of her mind with her special herbs and it was a group of drunks having some fun or if there is some merit to her claim. But he's agreed to come along, any information about his best friend is information worth having.

'Alright. Masks on.' Hono commands in a whisper as she slips her mask back on. 'Toakase lead the way.'

They slip their masks back on and follow Toakase through the small grassy field towards a hidden bushy path of stone and gravel. Each of them attempt to keep their footsteps as silent as possible as they follow the increasingly narrow path. Until they reach a set of stone stairs that circle around the edge of a cliff.

The only one out of the four of them who wasn't phased about the stairs was Toakase. She turns to look back at her friends who stand crouched staring at the stairs. She silently waved at them to keep following her as there was no time for questions and she could not see their faces behind those masks to see what they could be thinking.

Before even reaching the bottom of the steps, Toakase looks through the creeping vines and thick ferns along the cliff in search of something. The three of them stare at her, seemingly confused behind those masks, which quickly fades when she quietly calls out.

'It is here...' Toakase states, with her arm behind some rocks and ferns.

The other three circle around her to see a reinforced rusty metal door, hidden by the overgrown vegetation on the side of the cliff.

Toakase puts her ear to the door to listen for anything inside. 'It sounds empty...' She whispers. She could hear the size of the room on the other side, large, hollow, cavelike and mostly empty. 'I think we should be good. What's the next move?'

'Let's open it.' Hono whispers, eager for answers. She grabs the rusted handle and attempts to move it. 'It's locked... Who knows how to pick locks?'

'I think I might know how. Do either of you girls have hairpins?' Koloa quietly asked as he steps past them for access to the door.

Hono slips her hand up her hood and removes one of her hair pins and hands it to him. She briefly tucks her hair behind her ear before pulling the hood a little further forward.

'Thanks.' He bends it into shape and prepares it in the lock. 'Do you have another? Best with two.'

She looks over at Toakase in the hopes she might have a hairpin herself, but all she did was shrug. Hono rolls her eyes and slides her hand back up her hood to remove another pin. She pulls it out which causes her hair to fall into a disorganised mess as she hands it over to Koloa.

'Thank you... You can put your hood back on.'

She feels her head with her hands, now realising that her hair has caused her hood to slip. She quickly pulls it back over her head as she watches him insert the pins into the ancient lock. He very gently pulls on one pin as he uses the other to move old pins into place, each with a click. To everyone's surprise the oxidised lock starts to turn, however with no luck unlocking the door, until he tries turning it the other way.

The latch clicks. 'Unlocked.' He whispers.

'Keep in mind, I do not know what is behind this door.' Toakase admits.

'Okay.' Hono whispers.

Koloa turns the door handle and slowly opens the ancient door. It creaks loudly as the rusty hinges painfully move the heavy door outwards revealing a spacious hidden cave like room within the cliff wall. It's filled with cave-like structures of jagged dripping limestone hiding ancient artifacts; old world metal boxes, soft toys turned to stone and inaccessible shelves filled with lime soaked or covered items. The cave walls curve in some areas and are rock in most with the exception of a couple of rusty metal walls with old world engravings or art, things the Mirish group did not understand.

The few present day things within the room are wooden shelves filled with scrolls, notes and books. A wooden notice board with letters, notes and pictures stuck to it.

The most noticeable thing in the room is the large round stone and metal table that sits in the centre of the room. It has a detailed three dimensional map of the entirety of Mir on it but the part that really grabs the group's eyes is that it's glowing and somewhat illuminating the cave.

Alefosio closes the door behind them and locks it, giving everyone a chance to take a breath and remove their masks. Toakase pulls out a lantern from under her cloak and a box of matches from her pocket. She lights it, allowing some light through the room for the others to navigate their way over to the table.

'Is that the islands?' Alefosio questions.

'Where?' Toakase asks.

'The glowy thing in the middle.'

'It looks like it. Let's have a look.' Hono says.

'Wait... Did everyone bring their lanterns?' Toakase buts in.

'Yes.'

'Yep.'

'Yeah.'

'Grab them out and light them.' She snaps, handing Koloa her matches.

As Koloa lights up his lantern, Hono makes her way over to the table with Alefosio. It's nothing they have ever seen before, light without flame or stars. The map itself is emitting light from an unknown power that has an annoying buzz only Alefosio and Toakase could hear.

'Yes, that's the islands.' Hono confirms as she takes the matches from Koloa.

'What are the cressents around the islands? Those large tall mountain-like islands that kind of like wrap the islands?' Alefosio further questions as he points to the Australia, New Zealand and Antarctica mountain ridges.

'Those are remains of lands that moved and formed to keep the islands safe. I was told.' Hono says.

He takes the matches from Hono, but takes his time before he lights his lantern. He studies the Mir continent, never had seen the islands on a map before or the continent as a whole. But something catches his eye. He studies the map to see coloured markers on major island cities on several of the major islands; Negal, Pline and Salagab are all marked with the brightest red.

'What do you think those markers mean?' He further questions.

'I believe they might be contacts.' Toakase states as she leans over the table, cautious about touching anything.

'Let's search the place and see if we can find evidence of anything like plans.' Hono cuts in. She lifts up her bright lantern, alerting Alefosio to light up his lantern already.

As Alefosio lights up his lantern, Koloa nods at Hono and turns his attention over to one of the bookshelves. Once Alefosio finally lights up his lantern he takes himself over to the papers, notes and pictures pinned to the wooden board.

Toakase walks around the table towards Hono, with her attention still on the map. She points to the centre of the map at a small unmarked island that sits in the exact centre of Mir. 'This is us here, the red pins must be where they are contacting.' She quietly states to Hono with her eyes unmoved from the glowing unusual map.

'Hmm.' Hono vocalises as she turns her attention over to some loose papers that sit on a smooth flat square table between two more shelves. 'I will go and check those papers... I might find something...' She mumbles, hoping she will find nothing negative. She looks back over at Toakase who is in a hyperfocus on the map. 'Toa... Let me know if you can link anything.'

She picks up one of the many letters on the unorganised table and goes to read it. It reads:

Asi malaji ila Salagab, nakhorria ilana ila jak woshiwoshinga im ila naninan non jak alionogura KARTIM anuh.

The island of Salagab has considered the conditions of the negotiation to an alliance with the KARTIM.

Unsure of what to make of the message, she picks up another letter to read that one as well.

Pline malaji ill mo jamalah umella mo na KARTIM. Asi mo lamban ila renu talla non kamaman non perigona. To mo imma talla na gerasuluk samouh ila na malaji.

Pline island will gladly join the alliance of kartim in return for resources of food and supplies to reduce the rot that plagues the island.

More unsure of how to feel about the next letter. She as a woman is never allowed to be involved in any political affairs. She wondered to herself if her father or brother knew about Pline's poison. If it was the same black stuff she found in the forest weeks earlier when she searched for her brother. The black slimy mould or fungus that covered some plants and the side of a tree. Could that be what Pline is talking about? She asked herself. But most of all. What is KARTIM? She puts the note down and reaches for the next.

Wham kinamalan raviga len tak denka domonan hakisah ilana. Tam ital nam mo nakish non miltanyan mo ritam ro na mukdisat. Harkra ila lo mo tempak raviga imanoku tak. Asi na mizu to imu paolake wotush natish ill mo na gamukas a hakkiea na imanoku mo lorakishah

'Woah!' Alefosio shouted from across the room, interrupting her reading and thought process as she barely got through the first paragraph.

'What did you find?' She shouts back.

'I think I found something about Tohroshatan.' He holds onto a scroll which he takes back over to the round table.

'Let me read.' Toakase demands. She glances back at Hono, noticing that her emotions are beginning to flood in. 'Hono keep looking at those letters. Look for a different dialect or something.'

Hono looks at Toakase, she takes a deep breath as she attempts to let go of the anxiety surrounding the scroll. She takes herself back over to the square table to read more letters. But to her own dissatisfaction, most were incomprehensible for her as they are all in dialects that are practically different languages.

She grabs the letters she had either already read or got partway through and takes herself back over to the map table. Only to see Toakase standing with the scroll in her face, her eyes wide while darting left to right and her mouth gaping.

'These two are in a different dialect confirming an alliance.' Hono interrupts as she takes herself back over to the map.

'But we are already allies. All the islands kinda are. This does not make any sense.' Koloa interjects, pointing at Hono with another scroll.

'It does if it is a rebel or terrorist alliance.' Toakase states, putting the scroll onto the map table which makes a loud zap noise, startling her. She quickly takes the scroll off the table and keeps hold of it. 'Do not touch the table.'

'I really hope this is something very small.' Alefosio says.

'We can hope that, but… It does not seem to be the case.' Hono hands him the three letters she found.

Toakase snatches a letter from Alefosio and hands him back the scroll so she can read. He hands the scroll to Hono so he can read the other two letters himself. Instead of watching their reaction, Hono decides to open the scroll and read it for herself. She needs to know what happened to her brother, if the authorities have been deliberately avoiding their job or what's going on.

She begins to read:

Asi na kinamalan raviga lentak Kaji Tohroshatan mukdisat im mas mo to cumant matshi a mo ramijish ila zachadin. Natish wotush na rapanantala kilaeen natish nan zulakh ilana er tramanalisah anuh KARTIM.

Asi na raviga imanaku tak ilana ital nam mo nakish na malaji tamaya ill mo dwaligab ko natish na ila, rem mo anuh mos yuba na dragalit mo matashu ko Tohroshatan. Gillatam ila samouh mo foildah na malaji noulhab trachi ko na pakarigala ko Mir.

Kamji mo na raviga imanoku tak che mo ko trakamo uzaeat ila mana. Echallam non mos killap ila hekokomelov ko ill mo mos whakabailla non na shuri ko malaji. Gaui ko mo kanji ila, beshi-yushu tiaba anuh.

His Imperial Royal Highness Kaji Tohroshatan cannot be found and is presumed to be dead, potentially by suicide. This gives us the upper hand and we can move forward with the KARTIM. The Imperial family has requested that the other islands shall be contacted and that is what we shall do, just not regarding the death of Tohroshatan.

Plagues are sweeping over the islands and gangs are forming on the outskirts, it is time the imperial family step away and reveal the power they are

*hiding, especially as they will not help with the problems of the surrounding
islands of Mir.*
It's time we start anew, down with the monarchy.

'Power my family is holding? What?' She quietly questions.

'It says you have a secret power that you have had for generations.'
Alefosio gently states.

'Ale... I do not get to see a lot of the things my father does. The
family have traditions that are mens only... No women allowed.' She states in
a soft tone, now unsure what to think or believe about her family.

'What if you are two spirited?' He questioned out of pure curiosity.
But he couldn't find himself understanding why a family would have a male
only tradition.

'I do not know.'

'Hono.' Koloa interjects under a deep breath. 'Are you ready to hear
the hard news of this scroll?'

'It's about my brother isn't it?' Her anxiety begins to spike as she
feels her heart and stomach sink simultaneously, making her feel queasy. She
needs to know, but she doesn't want to know. She didn't want to bear facing
more devastation among the threat of violent conflict.

'About half of it is yes.' He says.

She takes a deep breath, forcing herself to calm down. 'Okay... Tell
me.' She forced out.

He takes a deep breath himself, also forcing himself to remain calm
as he goes to read out the scroll. 'Okay... The investigation for your brother
ceased as it was deemed a suicide... Which I think you probably learned
earlier today. But this scroll is suggesting they never really searched... A lot of
the authorities did but they were ordered by this group to stop.'

'Whoever this group are, they are high ranking.' Alefosio interrupts.

'They call themselves the KARTIM, I've never heard of them before
tonight so I don't think they can be high ranking.' Hono states, unsure and
unable to process her emotions.

'This is not good, but they are using Tohro's death as a means to start
something or overthrow? Are you aware of the power your father is
supposedly protecting?' Koloa questions as he rolls the scroll back up.

'There is no power my father is protecting. He looks after a stone
every morning, but that's men's only which I mentioned. It's just a dumb rock,
as Tohro has said many times.' She states, now unsure whether it really is a

dumb rock like her brother said and these terrorists are lying or whether there really is some power her family holds.

'They do not know what it is but. It looks like they want that stone. They think that's why your father is emperor and because there is no heir or Tohro, only now you, a daughter. They want to take over. Hono... You are in danger... You and your family are in serious danger.' Toakase says, realising the stakes of this and what she saw and heard the other night was a lot worse than she thought.

'What do we do?' Alefosio asks.

'I think we need to train and plan... Maybe get my father to somehow listen.'

'Grab these scrolls, we need to take them to Sanmos.' Toakase instructs the others.

Alefosio carefully picks up the letters and tucks them into a satchel under his cloak and the scroll into a large pocket in his loose pants.

'We need to go.' Koloa interjects.

Soft voices chatter outside the cave door, talking about their masks, uniforms and possibly being followed. The four of them freeze and not one of them knows how to possibly escape the situation.

'Put your masks and hoods on. We need to get out of here.' Koloa instructs.

The four of them rush to put their masks back on. They then put their hoods back on before surveying the cave for somewhere to hide as quickly as possible. Alefosio briskly gets behind two lime covered shelves with Hono following quickly behind giving herself enough room to watch the entrance.

Toakase and Koloa cram themselves behind some thick spiky lime rock with enough room to peer through to watch the meeting.

'Shut off your lanterns.' Hono whispers to everyone.

The four of them turned off the flame of their lanterns, just in time for the door to open. Five people walk inside, each of them suspicious as they survey the room.

'The door was unlocked.' A familiar masculine voice mutters.

'We know, check the papers and the map.'

Chapter 39

Ookonan walks through the long grass in the plain, his mind focused on the small child-like figure which stands motionless, seemingly staring at him. 'Hey!!' He shouted as he got close enough to make out the figure was a child, but the closer he got the more he could hear a muddy chime, like a bell in thick liquid.

'Hey! What are you doing alone out here?' He shouted, loud enough for his voice to push past the wind. 'It is not safe! Where is your village?' He hoped for a response from her or even a motion, but the girl remained still, almost statuesque as the breeze moved her hair. She's a tanned little girl with thick long wavy black hair and she stands no taller than Ookonan's hip, half of his height.

'What are you doing out here?' He questioned more gently once he reached a few metres from her. He takes a few steps closer and squats down to reach her level realising this was just a little girl.

He attempts to ignore her strange gleaming stares, it's almost as though she is staring right through him. 'It is okay... You are safe with me, where would your parents be?' He questioned in a soft tone. All he wanted to do was comfort her, ensure she's safe and get her home. However the glassy eyed stares become more unsettling as she tilts her head to the side, the once blank face grows a wide smile.

'He he he… Eeeehhh hahahahahahaha.' The child giggled.

He stands back up, feeling chills rush down his spine as the hairs on the back of his neck stood up. He didn't know what she was and he couldn't understand how she looks so fresh if she is a demonic or maybe she is another kind of demonic he has never seen before.'What are you?' He steps away from the small girl, almost nothing frightens him but she was an exemption. Her wide child-like grin directed at him was chilling and she looked to be no older than six years old, but her glowing black eyes suggested otherwise.

'I do not think you are human anymore…'

He feels his stomach and his blood pressure rise as he takes another step away from her. Every step he took away from her she would take two or more steps towards him, her wide grin never fading and the giggling never stopping.

'What are you?' He questions yet again. Besides the fear inside himself increasing, he somehow felt fragile or wrong in a way to feel uncomfortable and afraid of a little girl.

'Hehehehe hahahahahahahahahaha… The last thing you will see today.' She straightened herself as she took several more quick steps towards him, gliding effortlessly through the knee high thick grass. 'Hihihihi I will kill you.' She giggles.

As Ookonan takes several more steps away from her, she brings her knee to her chest then slams her foot onto the ground. The earth ripples in a circular wave around her, vibrating the land and disorienting him.

He looks down at her feet, seeing the foot she slammed into the earth is now buried. Believing he has some time to get away, she twists her foot and before he has time to process what is to happen she launches herself at a sonic speed towards him, striking him in the abdomen. He was thrown backwards parallel to the ground for a few short moments, but was able to roll backwards off his shoulder to land back on his feet.

'What was that?' Shocked and winded, the last thing he expected was something so small to be unfathomably strong. He rubs his stomach as he quickly scans the grassy plain for her to see her running towards him. Every step she took affected the ground like a shockwave, forcing her forward with an unfathomable amount of speed.

He swiftly jumps out of the way of the child who launches herself at him. She flies right past him, however she almost effortlessly comes to a stop. She skids along the ground, ripping up grass and turning over the hard soil. 'Hehehe.' The child giggles as though it is going to be a fun game of hunting prey.

†

The royal bathroom is an incredible sight which Kaji did not expect to ever enter let alone bathe in. Once the steam mostly settled he was able to see the size of the bath. It was like an indoor lake or pond he could find on his home island in Mir, except it's filled with foamy soapy bubbles and the aroma is like floral detergent or like the oil from trees.

He steps down the colourful tiled steps and into the hot soapy water. It's so large he decided to see if he could swim in it, however, the thick foamy bubbles made it unpleasant to do so. He floats on his back with the thick foam moving over him as he stares at the ceiling and even that was an incredible well crafted sight of a colourful mosaic pattern and pictures of romantic people around a large tree. As his body turns in the water he is able to see the stained glass window. Colourful pieces of glass cut into shapes and held together with metal.

The window picture was of a man and a woman hugging and kissing while being surrounded by lush country greenery, colourful flowers, fruits and vegetables. As the sun hits the window, the stained glass colours the rays which dance around the bathroom like a kaleidoscope. He closes his eyes and feels his aching body float in the soothing water.

He hasn't felt this relaxed since he was home in Mir, he feels relief rush over his body as it's been weeks since he was able to properly relax. Opening his eyes after some moments, he swims around the bath, checking out the colours of the bubbles, and the colours of silver, copper, purple and blue on the tiles. He adores the copper plumbing that snugly structured around the room for the bath to fill.

He takes a deep breath before submerging himself under the warm water. Running his fingers through his thick curly hair, he let his mind wonder how he would like the moment to last for hours. He's missed the water, the weightlessness, he feels like he is back home in Mir again only with the added temperature.

His mind wanders over to the warm waves, the coral reefs and swimming with the marine life. But he cannot stay here forever. He rubs his body, cleaning behind his knees, his toes, fingers and under his arms, all while thinking how much he missed being clean and safe in Mir and most of all, his family.

Finally resurfacing with his face and hair covered almost entirely with bubbles, he quickly wipes it all off before surveying the room again. He

271

gazes over at the sink where the towel and clean clothes lay before taking a deep breath and lifting himself out of the bath.

He briskly dries himself off and slips on the new clothes he was given. They feel different, strange almost. The old worn and burnt pants he took from Mir lay on the ground. As glad as he was to wear something covering and clean he felt almost a grief looking down at the filthy remains, the last thing he would see from his home in Mir.

He rubs his hair dry with the towel just to watch it fluff up in the mirror before he picks up the Mirish remains and heads to the exit. As he opens the door, he feels the cool dry air hit him, seemingly refreshing but the humidity felt a lot better.

'Enjoy your bath?' A guard asked.

Startled, Kaji swiftly turns around to face them. 'Nice it was... These where I put?' He shows the guard the burned filthy clothing and the wet towel. He couldn't help but feel the guard standing by the door to be off putting, while he bathed, no one at home ever did that.

The guard points to a square tiled hole next to the bathroom door.'Through that hole.'

Kaji slips the filthy remains and wet towel into the tiled hole in the wall, watching it fall into the black abyss before turning his attention back to the guard. 'Aagneya... Where?' He questioned. Hoping his Euro Hondonian was clear and unbroken.

'I will escort you to her.'

The guard leads Kaji through the long private hallway, they both exit it through a large wooden door through some long winded corridors until they reach a small arched passage leading to a tall spiral staircase. He follows the guard all the way up until they are met with a door that somewhat mismatched the rest of the palace. It was dark wooden with iron bolts and it smelled like a forest floor.

The guard opens the door revealing the last thing Kaji expected. A dying brown garden with a strange tall water fountain of filthy water in the centre.

He slowly takes himself through the depressing sight, surveying the tower. It's open and the streams from the fountain run through the so-called garden and off the edge of the tower. Although murky water was present, plants were dry and crusty or they were damp, moist but decayed.

'Kaji, come and have a seat.'

Startled, he swiftly turns around to see Aagneya sitting on a stone bench. He gives her a quick nod and sits down next to her. He can see in her hands the same horn he and Ookonan retrieved from the grey forest. Forcing him to reflect on how dangerous Hondon really is. Incomprehensible for a Mirish person.

'Why horn you have?' He questions, fearing about what the horn would do.

'That is what I wanted to show you...' She softly replied. 'How was your bath? Do you feel refreshed?'

'Relieving it was. Good to clean clothes have also. Why dead plants?' He asks, wondering why they bothered to keep the graveyard garden.

'It is very difficult to keep things alive and well in Hondon. That is what the horn is for. It should clean the land.' She finally said. She gets up and walks over to the filthy tall fountain.

'Come along with me.' He gets up on his feet and makes his way over to her. The fountain smelled like sewage, there was no wonder nothing was alive. He couldn't help but wonder why no one has bothered to do anything about it. But the last thing he expected was to watch her take a deep breath, clutching the horn in both hands and stepping into the pool of filthy water, he felt himself gag.

'I really hope this works.' She mutters as she scoops some of the filthy water into the horn. A profound shock mixed with amazement, happiness and relief crossed both their faces as the water that exited the horn as she poured it out was pure and clean. She gets on her tiptoes and reaches for the tallest peak of the fountain to rest the horn where water can enter and exit almost simultaneously. Once there, they both waited and much to their disappointment, nothing happened.

'Why is this not working?' She loudly asked herself as she adjusts the horn in the fountain.

'Small water maybe?'

She takes the horn from the fountain groaning as she steps away, groaning at the possibility of her efforts being a failure. She examines the horn, the patterned markings and gold engravings. She scoops up more of the murky water and pours it out. Purified and clean.

'I have an idea.' She muttered in a somewhat hopeful tone.

'What?'

She sighs as she looks between the horn and the fountain. 'I did not really want to do this.' She grips the horn and approaches the fountain a second time.

'Idea what? You not want to do why?' He asked curiously, sceptic about what she could possibly mean.

'We are all champions of gods so you will see.'

She puts the horn back up on the top of the fountain and while keeping a hold of the horn she takes some deep breaths. Her mind wanders elsewhere as though she concentrates on her senses and purpose. Before long, her eyes glow a bright forest green and glowing swirls and patterns appear on her exposed arms and legs.

After some long moments in deep concentration the water finally runs clear out of the fountain. She maintains her grip on the artefact as she silently watches the water run down the fountain edges and into the shallow pool and she waits patiently for the water to clear.

Kaji intensely and silently watches it all unfold. He finds it satisfying as the murk flows away and he finds it admirable that this was one of her many goals, to cleanse the water of a garden. But deep down he hoped this would be for more. As the streams of water clear, he watches Aagneya's next move and to his surprise her focus never changes.

She releases the horn in the fountain and makes her way down the stream, every plant she touched revived and every step she took awoke moss and grass. She steps back onto the dry soil, letting the water follow her and travel through the pavements and dirt, reviving the mosses and small little bits of grass and weeds that grew in the shade or cracks.

She takes a stand and concentrates her energy into her feet, grasping the roots of the garden. Within seconds the plants closest to her started to change colour and move almost like lungs. Within minutes the energy reaches the raised beds and the plants act the same and within a couple more the plants that were corpses in Kaji's eyes have returned entirely back to life while new life trailed like snakes around the gardens. Before long the place was green and lush with colourful flowers, butterflies, bees and crawling insects. An incredible sight to witness.

The glowing patterns on Aagneya's skin fade and her eyes return to normal. She pulls her feet from the soil and shakes the roots off as she walks over to the crystal clear stream. 'Does all water look like this in Mir?' She asks him.

'I think. Mir water not all I seen.'

'Have you seen water like before?'

'Not I suppose.' He admitted.

'I did not know this place could look so beautiful. Do you know what this means?' She asked him as she looked around the garden.

'No.'

'Look out at the city.' She said as she walked over to the edge.

He follows her and looks down at Brogan. So far nothing happened, but slowly something spread. The brown streams next to the buildings slowly disappear as a sporadic green spreads outwards, transforming the city.

'The land can be fixed, this proves it.' She remarks.

'The monsters?' He asks.

'I do not know. But this is a start.'

Chapter 40

As Ookonan ran faster and further the pyramids grew denser around him. Behind him stood a girl whose sole purpose appeared to be playing a twisted game of tag where she was it. Keeping a keen eye on the corrupted child, Ookonan made a relentless effort to maintain a safe distance ahead of her.

Each stride the girl took managed to leave footprints in the dense soil and cracks along the decrepit and obsolescent rocks. She watches him run towards the dense pyramids as if hoping to get lost amongst the ancient graveyard.

'You can not escape!' She giggled.

Fighting his stomach's urge to sink from the demonic child's remark, he was now convinced that what he was dealing with was in fact a Vassel. Briefly turning to look at the aberrant child, he aimlessly projects a gust of wind towards her before picking up his pace in a drastic effort to defy her words and escape.

'Hahahaha what will a small breeze do?' She sneered, ridiculing him with a laugh as she ran through the breeze unscathed and unbothered.

'Aaahhhhhhh.' He howled in distress, grinding his teeth as he forced himself to run faster and further into the pyramids.

Wind brews around him and distorts any form of resistance, he empowers himself to soar faster through the dense landscape. He turns tight corners with haste in a miserably unsuccessful attempt to lose the child.

She watches him turn a sharp corner into yet another pyramid and as he does she jumps high into the air and lands on the edge of the same pyramid, smashing it and leaving an opening in the structure. Surveying her surroundings, she briefly halts her movements but is met with rage when she can't find the noticeably large man anywhere in sight.

As Ookonan runs through the tall pyramids, he takes note of each structure having their own distinguishable pattern and unique texture. So densely packed together are the structures that there appears to be no definitive pathway or ground area. Slowing down to catch his breath, he eradicates his self-made storm before quickly scanning the area, looking between the pyramid structures in search of the vassel. Finding nothing, he brings himself to the realisation that he must have outran the child. Either that or the vassel was simply hiding and waiting for the best time to strike.

'Where are you?.. I WILL FIND YOU!' She screeched, her voice similar to that of nails clawing against a chalkboard. Following en suite, the sounds of smashing bricks, rolling rocks and falling debris radiates through the intimate atmosphere.

Ookonan takes a deep breath and swallows it, thinking hard on what his next directives should be. He moves between the pyramids as silently as possible, keeping his eyes peeled for any sign of the girl.

'IF I DO NOT KILL YOU THE DEAD WILL!' The vassel shouts, echoing throughout the pyramids.

He takes another deep breath and releases it slowly as he makes his way across two tall pyramids. Taking another step forwards without heeding what is beneath him, his heart skips a beat. Echoing through the pyramids is the sharp and sudden sound of a twig cracking beneath his boots. Silence ensues, deafening and palpitating. Ookonan had almost forgotten that silence could be this loud.

The vassel twists her head towards the sound of the breaking stick. She takes off and starts to run towards the noise faster than anyone should be able to run. She jumps on and over pyramids and runs past the demonics crawling out from the holes beneath.

'THE DEMONS ARE AWAKING!! Better run hahaha.' She laughed as she stomped on a crawling demonic, putting her foot through its chest and creating a hole in its abdomen.

Ookonan feels painfully lost on what to do, he always knew how to deal with demonics and he thought he understood Hondon and everything in it.

'I will fiiind you... Hei-ahh.' Her laugh radiates throughout the pyramids followed by the disquieting sound of pyramid walls and edges smashing.

His breath grew heavy as he tried to remain calm. His lungs felt tight and he felt his body become hostage to an erratic shaking, starting from his hand and slithering its way throughout the rest of his body. He peers around the corner to scan for the Vassel, still being met with nothing despite being able to clearly hear the smashing of pyramids, the growling of demonics and her screams of frustration. Beneath her screams it seemed like she was also enjoying herself, finding some twisted fun out of tormenting and toying with Ookonan.

He places his back against the wall of the pyramid and closes his eyes. Taking a moment in an attempt to calm down, he thinks about who this girl might be and if there is a chance of winning or getting away. He felt doomed as he took another deep breath. He knew that he had to accept his increasingly possible demise.

'REVEAL YOURSELF!' She screamed louder. 'I will smash everything here until I find you!'

Disregarding the noise of smashing rock and flesh, he opens his eyes and slowly breathes out, letting all the air out of his lungs. Gripping the handle of his sword, he takes a step away from the pyramid. His stomach sinks when he sees the Vassel standing there, smiling at him.

The pyramids and ground around her are cracked and partially smashed with a few of them having chunks taken from them. Slime slowly oozes out of the pyramid's openings but Ookonan's attention is held by the twisted child whose eyes are black as night and somehow old yet youthful all at once.

'There you are hehehe hahahahaha.' she laughed, straining her neck. Black veins crawled across her face, arms, legs and neck.

'If this is my last day... I will make sure it is yours too.'

Starting to redirect the wind around himself, he charges small amounts of electricity around his body. The gentle wind manages to move the dust and any other dry dirt around him as he tries to analyse what could be done to stop the demonised child.

The girl grits her teeth through her strained smile as she smacks the wall of the pyramid with her open palm, cracking the surface all the way through. Launching herself at Ookonan, she charges her right arm ready to strike. Relying upon his reflexes, Ookonan lifts his sword above his head and swings it down with great force.

Looking up at the large man swinging his battered sword at her almost pitifully, she quickly readjusts herself and strikes upwards, punching the blade and shattering it. She lands back down on her feet and quickly rolls away.

Ookonan looks down at her as she stands back up. She is smiling at him as though she is amused by his now broken weapon. He looks down at the handle of his sword, the blade is gone and the hilt is bent.

He had possessed that same sword for years and no demonic had ever managed to break it, but now shattered pieces of his blade lay scattered around his feet. His stomach sunk as he listened to the girl laugh at him, he couldn't wrap his head around her strength.

'HAHAHAHAha, why use a weak weapon on me?'

She takes a few steps back from him, her smile fading and turning into a frown. She watches him stand there, shaking with anxiety for a few moments before running towards him. She jumps into the air and strikes him in the abdomen.

He is thrown backwards through a pyramid, smashing a large hole into the structure. Landing on his back against another pyramid, he leaves behind a crater. Sliding down the pyramid to his knees, he examines the Ookonan shaped hole that he created.

The slime slowly started to ooze out of the opening and the hibernating demonics started to open their eyes and crawl towards the new exit.

He drops the handle of his sword and quickly gets to his feet as the vassal jumps through the hole, ignoring the slime and the demonics filling the structure. He blasts air at the vassal but the attack is ineffective and ignored as she continues to step out of the hole, hitting demonics out of the way. He continues to blast air at her as he moves to the side of the pyramid until he is in the clear.

He uses the air to make an escape as the vassal slides down the pyramid and starts to run after him. He zooms past every demonic and bit of slime that has crawled out of the pyramids while the vassal smashes through it all with complete carelessness and brute force.

He speeds through the pyramids with the vassal following closely behind, until he comes to a dead end. The pyramids are tall, jagged and stacked on top of each other, not allowing anything through.

He turns around and ceases his storm as he sees the vassel smiling at him as she walks slowly towards him. She is covered in demonic blood and the black viscous slime.

He surveys his surroundings and takes note of the pyramids behind him being covered in the thick black slime. Demonics are crawling out of any hole in the pyramids they possibly can before trudging slowly behind the child.

They are different from the demonics he is used to. Their eyes glow red, their teeth are short, sharp and clear, their skin is pale yet covered in black slime and each of their physiques are bony and frail.

Taking a deep breath and closing his eyes, he stands still and lets his arms hang beside him. He listens to his breathing and tunes out the laughs of the vassel and the growls of the demonics.

'I have had a good run… I guess we all must come to an end…The land is doomed.'

✝

Kaji strolls alongside Aagneya through a wide, well lit hall of the Brogan palace. There are windows letting in natural light on one side of the hallway with doors on the other side leading to one of the many of the palace's rooms and dorms.

He looks down at his bare feet and the carpet as they walk, getting lost in his own thoughts. He feels guilty that Ookonan couldn't see the horn in use and even more guilty about letting Aagneya speak to him that way all due to a prophecy he doesn't understand. He looks back up at her, still wondering where she is leading him.

'Ookonan, do you know where he go?' He finally asked.

'Why does that matter?' She snaps back under her breath.

'A little worried I am.'

'Well. Try not to worry. You are the most important and your destiny is to heal this land…' She says trailing off as she starts counting the doors along the hall.

'Yes…' He responds with barely a whisper, beginning to feel hopeless about ever seeing Ookonan again. All the visions he had of him, he knew they are connected not himself and Aagneya.

She turns to face a door down a very short hallway before approaching it, gesturing for Kaji to follow her. She opens the door, revealing a large and almost bare room. Towards the back of the room is a large glass window speckled with splotches of colour in the glass. Against the right hand side of the room sits a large puffy bed on a wooden platform and on the left hand side sits a set of drawers, a wooden privacy barrier and a large wooden table.

The floors are all made of dark hardwood boards and the walls are decorated with carved hardwood, marble and copper to form intricate patterns of dragons, Hondonian beasts, warriors and magic.

'This is your room while you stay here.'

He offers a quick smile as he walks into the room. She walks in and stands beside him, seemingly excited to show him his new room in the palace.

'How do you like it?'

'It is beautiful.' He exclaims, walking around the room, his eyes are drawn towards the thick blue curtains hanging from above the windows and around the bed before taking note of the floor mats with the floral, electronic and ancient designs. He smiles, never having seen anything similar.

'I am glad you like it.'

Suddenly, a series of knocks are heard radiating from the other side of the bedroom door, ruining their moment. They both turn to look at the tall guard standing in the doorway.

'Princess Aagneya.' The guard says, saluting.

'Yes. What is the issue?'

'You have been called into a meeting. By your fathers orders.'

She hesitantly nods at the guard and starts to walk towards the door. 'I will be right back, make yourself at home with your new room.' She says to Kaji as she follows the guard out of the room.

Kaji remains standing, staring at the door, feeling unsure what he should do next. He walks over to the door and walks down its short walkway.

He sees Aagneya and the guard walking down the hall composedly, yet Aagneya seemed to have some agitation brewing beneath her otherwise calm demeanour. He walks back into the room and takes a deep breath.

'Hmm. I was hoping to see Brogan city and beyond the gate.' He mumbles to himself, walking towards the window and leaning against it as he looks out.

His eyes were drawn towards a courtyard in the centre of the palace grounds. The courtyard is surrounded by palace buildings engulfed by vines that are slowly turning the walls and windows green.

The courtyard in of itself is small in size and composed of statues and various pathways. Trees, grass and small plants are present that are starting to flower, slowly livening up the dense brown of the courtyard with a concoction of vibrant colours.

He walks away from the window and towards the bed. Slumping himself onto it, he puts his head in his hands, feeling lost and homesick. He had been told about a prophecy but he had no idea what it meant or how to fulfil it. He had no idea why he was chosen or what he was destined to do. He wasn't even sure what to do now or how to get back to Ookonan.

In the centre of the room a ball of flame appears, illuminating the room in a bright flicker of orange and red. Heeding no attention to it, Kaji instead finds himself even more lost in the battlefield of his own thoughts.

'Kaji… You seem troubled.' A soft yet deep womanly voice says.

Surprised to hear a vaguely familiar voice, he quickly looks up and sees a bright fiery woman. 'Hestia… I did not expect to see you.'

He felt shocked by her unexpected visit. Standing up and walking over to the door, he doesn't take his eyes off of her for a second. 'Let me close the door.' He says closing it.

'What are you feeling right at this moment, Kaji?' She asks, watching him walk back to the centre of the room.

'Uhh.' He vocalised, scratching the back of his head, unsure of what to say. He didn't want to offend her but he still didn't want to be in Hondon either.

'I believe you may be feeling guilty…' She says, watching him closely as he stood motionless yet filled with emotions he didn't know what to do with.

'Come and take a seat.' She said, gesturing towards the bed.

He takes a deep breath before walking back over to the bed and stepping up onto the step in order to take a seat in front of Hestia. He hopes that he can say what he wants to say in a way that makes sense.

'I do not know where Ookonan has gone… I am worried, he should not have been treated that way.' He rambled.

'And what else? There is a fair bit bothering you.'

'I worry for my family. I hurt my sister badly. I worry for my mum and my father… Father has issues but he isn't a bad person. I worry for my friends. Before I left no one really noticed me when I was studying in trees or parks. I would just be reading a book. The authorities and the guards were talking about a civil war… I worry for my family if it is real.' He said, throwing words out and hoping that they would string together to make sense to Hestia.

'Kaji. Calm yourself, it is okay. You are filling with emotion which is very human.' She says in a soothing tone.

'Mmmhhmm.' He vocalised, holding back tears that so eagerly wanted to escape his eyes.

'Do you know why I chose you?' She asked softly.

'No I do not. Aagneya thinks it's because I am royal.'

She looks at him as her earnest expression turns joyous. She giggles before taking a moment to adjust herself. She takes a breath and explains to him that the choice for the chosen two has nothing to do with royalty or family background.

'I had already chosen a champion initially. He named you Kaji and chose you as he had started to age, while the second half had not been born when he was in his prime. He and I discussed that yes you have access to the great rune stone and you are royal. But your care for your family and your friends was like no other. You would do anything for them.'

'Yes but I do not understand, is the prophecy bound by royalty?' He asks, being careful as to not cut her off.

'No it is not, but if the world depends on you being here, and you being here will save your family from the catastrophe that is to come... Would you remain in Hondon?'

He raises his eyebrows, trying to think: about his family, about his friends, and about his home island in Mir, its food and its people. He does feel worried about Ookonan and he does want to find him as well.

'I do not know.'

'For the prophecy to be fulfilled, you need to go to Ookonan. Fulfilling the prophecy will save your family and any future generation.'

She narrowly looks at him with each palm placed out. To either side of her she opens two tall oval portals. One leads to Ookonan in the pyramids faltering as he makes an effort to fight the demonised child, while contrarily, the second portal leads to Hono, Alefosio, Koloa and Toakase in the cave hideout, being beaten by the traitors.

'You will need to choose one.'

He remains seated as he tentatively looks at both of the portals. Each portal had a fiery ring surrounding a depiction of present time events. It was all too real, Kaji could hear the screams of his loved ones and the noises surrounding their environments. He knew they were far away but by some miracle they were right in front of him at this moment. He stands up and walks closer to Hestia before turning his attention towards the portal containing Ookonan.

Feeling lost and terrified, Ookonan has been cornered by the demonised child and surrounded by the black slime and some ancient pale demonics. Kaji wasn't aware that fear was an emotion Ookonan possessed.

'You thought you had a chance… that is cute.' The demonised child says behind a giggle.

Kaji cringed at the bittersweet voice of the child. He takes a fractured breath and turns to the portal holding his sister and friends. It appears that three authorities and two palace guards are in the room.

Two of the authorities are bashing Koloa while the third authority has Toakase in a painful arm bar with their palm firmly on the back of her elbow. One of the guards is fighting Alefosio and trying to corner him while the last guard has grabbed Hono who appears to be the only one wearing a mask and hood.

The guard holding onto Hono slams her against the ground before removing her mask and hood, revealing to Kaji his sister.

Kaji leans closer to the portal. He starts to panic as he sees the side of his sister's face being pushed onto the cold cave ground and his friends being physically harmed by the authorities of the island.

'Hono! Hono!! What is going on!! Hono!' He shouts through the portal.

Swearing she heard her brother's voice, she looked around the room to see if her friends could hear it too or if she was going insane. Koloa is too preoccupied trying to get two people twice his size off himself, while Alefosio is preoccupied trying to get the authorities and guards away from himself and his friends.

'Tohro…' She says, searching for Kaji in the increasingly limited areas where she can move her eyes.

'Shut up!' An authority shouts from across the cave.

'Tohro!! You're alive!!' She screams, defying the command of the so-called authority. She knows deep down that he is in another location. She cannot locate where his voice is coming from but she is aware that there is a potential device he is speaking into. 'I'm so happy you're alive but stay where you are, don't come here. DON'T DO IT!'

Kaji takes a step back away from the portal, he feels conflicted. He couldn't believe they thought he was dead and they are being badly harmed by people who are meant to protect them. He looks over at Ookonan's portal, it seems as if he has accepted his doom, he has no weapon in hand and he isn't using his powers.

'They thought I was dead…'

'They did. The choice is up to you.'

He looks back over at the portal towards Mir. His sister Hono has been seated upright and tied up, one side of her face is now bruised and swollen. Toakase's arm has been broken at the elbow by the guard who was restraining her, Koloa is passed out on the ground and is covered with bruises and blood, while Alefosio is desperately trying to keep the traitors off the badly injured girls.

'Tohro don't come back, you will be killed.' Hono called out through the cave.

'Tohro if that is you... Do what you need to do.' Toakase called out with a firm and strong voice although pain could be heard behind it.

'Do what you need to do. We love you.' Hono's voice radiates through the cave once more.

Kaji takes a step away from the portals. He looks away from Hestia and thinks about his sister. He misses her more than he realised and she is in danger but he knows that death would be waiting for him if he returned.

His eyes wander towards Ookonan where he watches him give up from the sidelines. Giving up was something Kaji had never expected him to do. The black slime is pouring down the pyramids, demonics are crawling towards him and the twisted child is smashing demonics and structures in her way as she makes her way slowly towards Ookonan.

'You win. I have lost.' Ookonan muttered softly.

'Hahaha... Look at you. It is more fun when they kick and scream but you... Hahahaha you just accept it!' The demonised child ridiculed him as she walked closer.

Kaji weighs his choices as he stares at the portals in front of him. If he doesn't go to Ookonan, he will die. Contrarily, if he doesn't go to Hono, she will live despite her injuries.

'Do what you need to do.' He says to himself in barely a whisper.

He looks over at Hestia and nods before looking back over at Ookonan. Closing his eyes, he takes a deep breath. Holding his breath and opening his eyes, he jumps through the portal.

Chapter 41

Ookonan stands still as hopelessness claws its way through his mind. He takes a deep breath and closes his eyes, accepting his fate as the slime etches closer towards his boots. The vassel is walking through the slime towards him, now standing only an arms length away when Kaji appears next to Ookonan in a blast of fire, throwing the slime, demonics and the vassel away in a shockwave of flame. He looks up at Ookonan whose head is still bowed down and whose eyes are still shut. He was completely untouched and clearly unaware of Kaji's fiery entrance.

'Glad I am you alive...' Kaji says in a somewhat placid tone.

The Vassel had been thrown through the edge of a pyramid head first. She hits the pyramid adjacent from the pyramid she went through, as the surface belts her head and her shoulders, jarring her.

She slides down the pyramid while keeping an eye on the ball of fire, seeing another man appear out of it, unharmed, as though he created it.

'You will not win with your TRICKERY!' She screams back at them both.

Ookonan opens his eyes, feeling somewhat shocked. When did Kaji get here? He asked himself. He lifts his head and surveys his surroundings.

He couldn't believe that the slime and demonics had been blasted away. How did Kaji get here and how did his blast not touch me? He thought to himself before turning his gaze towards Kaji.

'I apologise for my behaviour but now is not the time.' He says, feeling somewhat relieved. He takes a small hitched breath and looks at the demonised child who has been seemingly almost effortlessly thrown through the edge of a pyramid.

Kaji looks around, noting the charred demonics and slime around them. He can see how close Ookonan was to becoming one. If he were to have been even a few seconds too late he would have been gone, no longer himself but instead one of the many unhuman beasts. What he couldn't quite understand though was how a small child was beating up a giant like Ookonan with any amount of success.

'What is she?' He asked, pointing at the demonised child.

'That is a Vassel.'

'Vassel what?'

'She is a vessel of another god that is controlling her. She is very powerful. No more questions, we do not have time.' Ookonan explained.

The Vassel gets back up onto her feet, she looks at the two of them from a distance through her eyebrows. She smiles at them both with a fierce and angry visage, almost as if she is hungry.

'You want me to do what?' Kaji asked, turning his gaze from the Vassel to Ookonan.

'I need you to set the place on fire.' He says candidly with conviction. 'Aim at the slime and demonics.' He continues as he keeps a close eye on the Vassel who is storming her way towards the both of them, leaving cracks and dented footprints in the solid ground beneath her.

'How deal with her will you?' Kaji asks, as his concern bubbles to the surface, fighting and frankly beating his urge to bury it deep within himself.

'I do not know. I do know though that setting everything else on fire will help.'

They both watch the Vassel stomp closer to them, giggling with a bloodthirsty look behind her eye. She punches a demonic in the leg, snapping it clean in half without any difficulty.

'How will fire help?' Kaji asked skeptically.

'Blast the demonics and the black stuff. Now! Do not let them touch you!'

Kaji turns to the demonics who are crawling feebly across the ground. He breathes in as deep as he can before steadily releasing his breath with purpose, letting the flames escape his hands. He blasts the demonics crawling along the roads, burning them to an unrecognisable charcoal, then turns to the slime coming out of the holes in the pyramids and redirects his inferno, lighting the pyramid on fire.

Ookonan's eyes meet those of the Vassel's as he walks towards her. He tenses his forearms, forcing his hands to electrify. Throwing streams of strong wind at her, he hits her in the chest and abdomen.

Plainly unaffected and unfazed, she continued treading towards him. He looks at her as fear and uncertainty intensifies within him, fear of her power and uncertainty on how he could possibly defeat her.

Relying on what he knew best, he starts to run towards her, throwing more streams of strong wind. Unsurprisingly, she continues to ignore the gusts, thoroughly untouched and as composed as the devil could be. Instead she strides further and further towards him. Reaching no more than four metres in distance away from the child, he jumps high in the air, manipulating a storm around himself as he projects himself towards the Vassel beneath him.

The Vassel watches Ookonan unimpressed as he launches towards the hard ground. She waits for the perfect moment to extend her arms and snatch him from the embrace of the air only to feel the satisfaction of causing him pain herself, throwing him against the rough surface of a pyramid.

He flies through the air and smashes back first through the pyramid. He rubs his temple, feeling hurt, frustrated and even more baffled by the sheer strength of someone so small. As he passed through the pyramid, he could see the hibernating demonics, all as white as bone. His eyes took note of the surfaces of the pyramid, all of them covered with the revolting black slime.

The world seemingly slowed down as seconds started to feel like minutes and minutes started to feel like hours. He felt horrified that each of these structures were harbouring not only all of these demonics but so much of this slime. Looking down the pyramid, it seemingly went on forever with no ground in sight.

Finally smashing through the other side of the pyramid, Ookonan's lungs were sent into shock as he crashed into the pyramid behind him, cracking and denting it on impact.

His world turns black as he falls unconscious. His senses fail him as he sees and feels nothing except the pain surging through his lungs, ribs and spine. 'Today is not your day to die Ookonan...' The voice of Susanoo gently whispers to him.

'Clear your mind and breathe, all power comes from the breath. Clear your mind and release the storm.'

Regaining consciousness, colour slowly returns to the world around him. His eyes start to glow around the irises, sparking electricity within the glow. He pushes himself off the pyramid and launches himself forward.

He brews the storm around himself, creating strong winds and rain which swirls around him like a small cyclone, sparking much like his eyes with electricity. The storm carries him with great force towards the Vassel while rocks, debris and demonics are thrown around the pyramid.

Heeding no attention to Ookonan, confident in the fact that she has dealt with him, the Vassel turns her focus towards Kaji. Stomping her way towards him, she leaves well formed footprints in the firm ground below.

Noticing that Kaji is unaware of her presence walking towards him, she bursts out into a wave of condescending giggles. 'Hehehe hahaha. Pay more attention little man.' Startled by the vassel's voice, he almost jumps out of his skin as he turns his attention away from the pyramids he had been setting ablaze and the slime and demonics he had been cooking to face the demonised child.

As he redirects his eyes, he also redirects his arm and the flame expelling from it, blasting the child with a wave of fire.

'Little?' He asked, feeling insulted by her comment, especially when she is tiny as compared to him.

Treating the blaze as if it were just a gentle breeze, she determinedly treads towards him, smiling and giggling as she prepared to pounce. Meeting neither of their expectations, Ookonan comes charging towards them from the top of a pyramid.

His eyes were glowing with blue light, the same colour as the electricity crackling in the storm smiling around him. Electricity seemed to steep through his skin and travel through his body as his mouth and nostrils twitched and sparked. He smashes his cyclone onto the Vassel before picking her up from the ankle and throwing her just as she had thrown him.

'Focus on the demonics.' He yells to Kaji with a sense of urgency and directness. 'I have the Vassel.'

'Vassel?' He asked, forgetting what the word meant.

'We have already discussed this. Focus on the demonics and the slime! Watch out for the kumdria!' He ordered before launching himself in the direction he threw the Vassel.

Reaching the top of one of the larger pyramids, he spots the child who has gracelessly crashed against one of the pyramids. She slides down the structure and lands on her feet, looking slightly hurt and dishevelled but otherwise unbothered by the impact.

Ookonan comes crashing downwards on the Vassel as his storm grows stronger corresponding with his increasingly insatiable anger. He barrels towards her engrossed by and immersed entirely into his building storm. Purposefully crashing into her, his strength and size paired with his speed and the raging storm surrounding him forced the girl towards the bottom of the pyramid with a painful amount of gusto.

'I am the target. Not him.' He states as she lays on the ground bloodied and bruised but not ready to cave in. 'You have to defeat me first. You are mine.'

'As you wish.' She says, smiling at him, a certain flickering madness behind her eyes.

Chapter 42

The guards of Brogan linger idly by the watchtowers, surveilling the lands in front of the city. They have a crystal clear view of the almost empty sky, the grassy cliffs and crevices and most of all, the bewitching sky islands and pyramids.

One guard is leaning almost carelessly against the edge of the tower, their weapon propped up against the barrier next to them.

Turning their gaze towards the pyramids, they strain their eyes as they meticulously inspect the environment, noticing what looks like explosions erupting in the ancient mass of structures.

They couldn't bring themself to believing what they were seeing was real, explosions followed by strong winds and shockwaves of electricity rushing over the pyramids. The guard takes a steady breath as they watch another eruption of fire and electricity which ripples over the pyramids in the direction of the city.

The guard approaches the horn on the corner of the tower with a certain haste before inhaling deeply and blowing into the instrument. The horns' sound is long, loud and booming in a midrange pitch that waves through the city and echoes throughout the grassy cliff plain.

'WHAT DO YOU THINK YOU ARE DOING?' A loud, authoritative and eternally stubborn voice shouts from below the tower.

Letting go of the horn, the guard leans over the edge of the tower in order to inspect the entrance gate of the city. Their eyes are greeted by an angry guard who is standing at the lower level, by the drawbridge gate.

'There is something happening in the distance! Brogan is in danger!' The guard towards the upper level said with a great deal of urgency.

'Oh?' The stiff-necked guard countered skeptically.

'Why else would I blow the horn?!' The guard in the tower snapped.

Leaving their post, the drawbridge guard approaches the small window slits either side of the gate. Their eyes widened as they were greeted rather bitterly with a large lightning encrusted inferno of orangish red fire radiating from the pyramids only a few kilometres away from the heart of Brogan.

Slowly stepping away from the window slits the guard tries to register what they had just seen. 'Go and alert the princess!' They shout with a rising severity as they approach the patrol guard. 'Now!'

'For what?' The patrolling guard asks, Not understanding the urgency of the situation and instead bringing themself to the conclusion that the gate guard is an idiot, the patrolling guard rolls their eyes. 'For what?' They ask, unimpressed.

'Brogan is in danger! Go and get her! NOW.'

Deciding to play along, the patrolling guard offers a salute and briskly jogs towards the palace before being stopped in their tracks by an armed palace guard.

'Holt!' The palace guard shouts in demand while aiming a weapon at the patrolling guard. 'Name your Business.'

'We have an emergency... Get Princess Aagneya.' The patrol guard expressed while making an ill effort to catch their breath.

'What emergency?' The guard demanded without lowering their weapon.

'There is no time! Get Princess Aagneya!' The patrol guard pressed, still unaware of the situation at hand.

Lowering their weapon, the palace guard sighs.

'As you wish.' They say, stepping aside.

Two of the countless other palace guards run into the palace, up the tight spiral staircase and towards the connected door. Forcing it open, they swiftly move through the gradually colour changing garden on the peak of the water tower before approaching Aagneya.

She sits alone on the stone bench in the garden admiring the new leaf growth, the little blades of grass and the small flowers starting to bloom and bud. She takes a deep breath and leans back to look at the roof of the tower, covered in vines, mosses and creeping ferns that are slowly reviving, colouring the roof in a rich velvety green.

'Princess Aagneya.' A guard says, breaking the otherwise tranquil silence as he fully approaches. The guard bows out of courtesy as the princess looks down at them.

In reaction to seeing the two guards standing before her, she sighs softly thinking that her father just wants her for yet another one of his tireless meetings about a future raid.

'This better be good... What does my father need?' She asks, trying hard not to pin her annoyance on the otherwise blameless guards.

'You did not hear this from myself or any of us. Your father is untrustworthy. We need you and commander Zelius at the front gate. Brogan may be under attack.'

'Go and get commander Zelius by my order.' She instructed, quickly getting to her feet. 'I will have a quick visit to Greybeard and meet me at the gate.'

Composing themselves, the guards salute her before turning to leave the tower as briskly as their feet would take them. She watches them exit through the connected door before longingly bringing her attention back to the reviving garden. I hope it is nothing so you can provide for Brogan.' She whispered wistfully to the garden and the streaming water, feeling saddened that she may have put so much effort into the tower just for it to be destroyed.

†

Greybeard feels satisfied, accomplished and at ease as she lifts up the completed saddle for Yuma. She looks over at him laying in a warm and sunny spot in the shop. He is relaxed with his head resting on his front paws.

She walks over to Yuma and directs him over to the workbench in order to best measure and fit the saddle on him. Finding leverage on top of the bench, Greybeard attentively lifts the saddle onto him and fastens it into place with the many straps.

'Beautiful. I might need to make more pockets and things.' She voiced, admiring her own work.

Without warning, a viscously thunderous bang resonates from the front door, so loud Yuma's eardrums felt like they were seconds from bursting. Feeling startled and irked by the disruption, Greybeard was glad she wasn't holding anything hot, sharp or even worse a mixture of the two.

'CAREFUL!' She shouted at the figure behind the door.

Almost instantaneously, the door bursts open causing another thunderous sound to reverberate through the shop. On the other side of the door, rushing into the workshop is a flustered and rattled Aagneya. Despite not appearing breathless or entirely anxious, she was clearly on edge, dressed in her cloak and plated armour which she typically wore on her quests outside of the city.

'Emergency! We are under attack.' She said with a rising intensity behind her voice.

'What do you mean we are under attack?' Greybeard asked abruptly and somewhat confused. Who could attack or would even want to attack a heavily guarded city surrounded on all sides by a great wall? She thought to herself.

'We have a threat outside the walls… I need you to have your spare weapons ready and taken to the gate. Is Yuma ready?' She said in a hurry, hoping everything in Greybeard's shop was aligned and in order, ready to go.

'Yes, I will get that sorted and placed into a trailer and over immediately. Yuma is mostly ready. But the pockets can wait if you intend to use him.'

'Use Yuma to haul the weapons over then I will take him into the plains.' Aagneya instructed as she made her way back towards the door she only moments prior came rushing through. 'I will meet you there Greybeard. I need to lead the forces.'

†

An army of Brogan soldiers stand at the entrance of the city gates, waiting on their next directive. Some are weighed down by their heavy armour consisting of a thick layer of a demonic-proof metallic material mottled with patches of lightly coloured leather in order to better see any blood or markings. Some soldiers have instead opted for a lighter armour lacking in any form of metal, instead being composed of a thick woven fabric that allows for easy, quick and agile movements.

'This is not something I have seen before.' Commander Zelius, a muscular elf, tall and large in stature with thick black hair, tanned yellowish skin, a thick yet short black beard and a strong jawline that makes him out to be a rough figure says to the tower guard who blew the horn. He wears thick woven clothing paired with shoulder pads and accompanied with leather. In certain sections of his colourful armour, filled with reds, purples and blues are small but thick plates of iron.

'What do you think it might be?' The tower guard looks into the large and dark blue eyes of Commander Zelius warily, he looks like he has lived through many wars and has trained many people in his lifetime.

'I am not sure but I hope that it is not an army of Demonics with new abilities.' He confirms. Commander Zelius turns away from the guard and examines the army at the city entrance.

'SOLDIERS! Do not expect to go home to your loved ones. What is out there is nothing I have ever seen before. We might be fighting an army of demonics with entirely new abilities. Remember your training!' He takes a breath and allows the weight of his words to settle amongst the crowd. 'As for the guards of the city; instruct the citizens to where they should be if needed for evacuation. Continue to patrol the grounds and focus on the safety of the people of Brogan. We are waiting for Princess Agneya to arrive. I have been informed that she is getting weapons already crafted by the blacksmith Greybeard.'

As he finishes his speech, Aagneya arrives at the entrance, pushing her way past some of the soldiers in order to get within an ears distance from Commander Zelius. 'Commander!' She shouts, moving closer to the tower stairs.

'Greybeard will be here shortly. I need a quick look.' She instructs.

She walks through the tower door and up the stairs. Reaching the top of the tower, she surveys the grasslands and pyramids, immediately taking note of the electric storm and the blasts of fire.

Recognising the powers of Kaji and Ookonan, she states what's on her mind. 'I believe I know what the fire is but I am unsure about the electricity.'

'What is the fire?' Commander Zelius asked her quietly.

'It is Kaji. A human. He needs to be protected but my guess is that this storm is Ookonan.'

The thunderous roar of a large animal is heard from behind the army. Aagneya and Commander Zelius turn their attention away from the grasslands and the pyramids to find that Greybeard has arrived, riding Yuma on his new saddle. They are towing a sizable trailer of stored weapons for the army to grab.

Aagneya treads back down the stairs of the tower with Commander Zelius following closely behind her. She walks past the army and towards Greybeard who is disembarking Yuma.

'Thank you Greybeard, please head to the palace and get shelter with your husband.'

'I will do so Princess Aagneya.' She promised, smiling warmly and assuredly. She walks with two guards on either side of her away from the army and the entrance of the city.

Untying the trailer from Yuma, Aagneya loosely examines the weapons. She grabs a sharp and sturdy spear-blade before getting onto the back of Yuma and directing him to the drawbridge gate, past the army.

'All grab a weapon. Now!' Commander Zelius instructs the army as he walks over to the gate and stands next to Aagneya.

They watch the soldiers all walk in a somewhat orderly fashion to each grab a weapon before lining up where they were: at the entrance, to await their next directive.

Aagneya manages to turn herself around on Yuma in order to look out into the sea of soldiers. 'We knew this day was coming. It is time to stop hiding behind these walls. We are here to protect not be protected. It's now our chance to finally change the history of this land. To stop living in fear.' Roars start erupting from the army, eager to prove their worth and be granted the chance to protect their beloved homeland.

'It is time to finally stand up and push back. Yes it is hard and doing nothing may seem easier. But it is not. We pick ourselves up and keep going. Out there are people not even from this place but are risking it all to save us. It is our turn now. We March. We fight. We WIN!!'

She continued valiantly, holding genuine belief in each word she was saying.

Marching into the grassy craggy highlands, Commander Zelius leads the Brogan army towards the Pyramids. The soldiers all grip their weapons tightly as they prepare themselves for the fight of their lifetime, ready to run towards the blasts and demonics in the distance.

'ALL PREPARE YOURSELVES!!' Commander Zelius instructs clamorously. 'THE DEMONICS ARE COMING THROUGH THE STORM!! SEPARATE INTO GROUPS OF TEN!!'

As instructed, the army separated into ten groups of ten, each marching in their own sections as they awaited Commander Zelius's next order. He draws his sword and holds it in the air, it's made of steel, tungsten and it appears to be attached to a small heating generator, pulsating heat through the blade itself.

Aagneya rides back on Yuma towards Commander Zelius after expeditiously scouting the highlands and cliff sides. 'I will go off ahead, I need to get into the fire. Be prepared, the Pyramids are holding an infestation of Demonics.'

'Do what you need to do Princess, we will be right behind you.' He says saluting her while still holding his sword up.

As she rode off with Yuma towards the blasts of fire in the thickest part of the pyramids, Commander Zelius gave his next command. 'ARCHERS! MOVE TO HIGHER GROUND!'

Proceeding the command, the archers move off in sections of ten towards certain cliffs surrounding the pyramids. After commanding the sword-bearing army to move to the front of the army, closer to him, he takes a composed and collected breath.

'THE REST OF US... CHARGE ON MY COMMAND TO THE PYRAMIDS!!' The groups spread out in a line ready for the demonics to run out and away from the fire.

'IN THREE, TWO... ONE... CHARGE!!' He shouted as loud as his voice would allow while gesturing towards the pyramid grassland with his red hot sword.

✝

'Come on Yuma. Find Kaji and Ookonan.' Aagneya says as she scans the area in search of them both, transitioning from the open space of the pyramids to the more dense area of the ancient structures.

She spots Ookonan hovering in the air, engrossed in a strong electrical cyclone which swirled effortlessly around his body. She slows Yuma down as she thinks of how to get closer to him.

'There is Ookonan... And what is that!?' She asked herself, seeing the demonised child. She whips the ropes attached to Yuma and races towards Ookonan.

'OOKONAN!!' She shouts, however, to her misfortune, he does not hear her and instead continues to move towards the demonised child and the black smoky deity attached to her. He throws streams of strong wind filled with lightning towards the vassel to no avail. She whips the ropes again to get Yuma to move increasingly faster towards Ookonan, jumping off any pyramid in the way.

'OOKONAN!' She shouted again, as loud as she could fathom.

Ookonan turns his head to the sound of his name, searching for the source until his eyes land upon Aagneya on Yuma. He felt slightly surprised to see the saddle already made, but he was in no state to dedicate any level of thought towards it.

'Go and find Kaji.' He urges, his voice sounding deeper and more god-like as his body filled with electricity allowing his eyes, mouth, nostrils and ears to spark and glow a vibrant blue.

'Yes!' She says as she hurries off to the thicker part of the pyramids, towards the inferno of fire.

†

Aagneya directs Yuma through the pyramids, avoiding fire while jumping from surface to surface in search of Kaji. The flames start to consume the ancient structural mass, giving very little area for Yuma and Aagneya to move.

'Come on Yuma, where is Kaji?' She pries, scanning the pyramids for him.

Yuma growls as a large ball of fire lands and explodes just in front of them. She quickly steers Yuma away as they take a different route, running up the pyramid and simultaneously following the fire while making their best effort to avoid contact with the scorching flames.

'Do not worry Kaji, we are coming.' She whispers as Yuma jumps around the pyramids and along the sides of the structures.

She continues to desperately scan the pyramids, until she sees him. Kaji. He is surrounded by burning slime and a small pile of ashen corpses.

'Kaji!' She shouts. 'Quit your fire and jump on.'

Kaji, surprised to hear such a familiar voice, scans the skies above him. His eyes meet those of Aagneya who is sitting on Yuma towards the edge of the Pyramid. He notices the new saddle and is impressed with Greybeard's craftsmanship.

He jumps around the slime, making sure to step in the areas that are untouched as he reaches for her hand which is held out and ready for him. He runs up the pyramid and jumps to grab it.

She pulls him up and helps him onto the saddle before whipping the ropes attached to Yuma and steering them all out of the pyramids as fast as she can, guiding Yuma to jump on each of the surfaces while avoiding the now slime covered ground.

Chapter 43

A carriage filled with crates, wooden boxes and sacks is pulled across the highlands, passing the pyramids and straight towards. But no ordinary creature is pulling the carriage, a Hondinian creature adapted to the lands, a cross between a buffalo and an elephant pulls it.

A masked man sits at the front of the carriage, seemingly unbothered by the islands in the sky hovering above him. 'How are you feeling girl?' The man asked the bufflant while redirecting her rains away from the battle.

'Do not worry, I will make sure to keep some of the carrots and potatoes aside for you. But we do need to sell or trade them, for the good of our village.'

He sees the blasts by Ookonan and Kaji at the pyramids, he quickly looks over at the direction of Brogan and sees their army marching through the grasslands towards the blasts. He looks back at the pyramids and squints his eyes, allowing him to see a tall figure surrounded by a cyclone of storm, fighting a small spec.

He watches the pyramids catch fire, one by one, making him wonder what truly is going on. He looks back over at the marching army, he sees a purple haired woman, in her shining green armour riding a bisonbear. He watches the bisonbear closely as it seems familiar to him somehow.

'I believe we have come at a bad time.' He says to the Buffalent.

†

Ookonan floats slightly above ground as his storm rushes around him. He watches the vassel get back to her feet after sliding down a pyramid. She slowly makes her way to him, walking like a pantomime mocking the size difference and his struggle to overpower a supposed small child.

'Hahahahaha. You are so angry.' She giggles. Old filthy dull chimes click within her, getting louder as the fight goes on.

He tries to ignore the dull chime coming from her, it's like it's trying to derail him. But this isn't going to stop his focus on her. He tenses his right arm, focusing electricity through it into his hand. Throwing the giant bolt, more to his frustration, she quickly evades and dashes towards him. She hits him hard in the thigh knocking him to the ground.

Swiftly regrounding himself he digs his fingers into the rocky ground as the vassel calculates her next move. Pumping electricity and moisture from the air into the ground, he electrifies it and once her foot touches the hard soil near him she is quickly stunned.

Now given the chance he launches himself off the ground and at her, smashing her little body through a tetrahedron and once on the other side he throws them both into the air as his concentrated cyclone carries them. However, much to his dismay, she still has more control as she flips the switch and throws him across the pyramids and over to the sparser grassy land.

He flies almost parallel to the grass until he skids along it and bounces and tumbles before officially coming to a stop. Taking a quick breather after the shock of his lungs, he jumps back to his feet and sprints to the vassel who is sprinting back at him.

Once they both reach each other, Ookonan blasts her with another bolt of lightning which barely does anything to her as she maintains her pace. She jumps into the air and grabs his lapel and holds herself up to put her face into his.

'Hahahahahahahaha… How is your friend doing?' She giggled. Her breath reeked of death and demonic corruption, but also the dull clogged metal chime became loud with every word she spoke.

'WHAT ARE YOU?!'

'Maybe I will show you as you take your last breath.' She said grimly under another giggle.

He throws her off him and blasts her with another bolt of lightning, knocking her to the ground. Sparks of electricity formed around his body as his cyclone also grew more intense. He is lifted above the ground by the strong wind, blasts her with streams and walls of electricity with the goal to overwhelm.

The giggling and smiling fades as her body becomes electrified and she begins to cook within. She stops within her tracks, seeming like she has surrendered. She closes her eyes and breathes out a thick cloud of black oozy, sticky smoke. It transforms like an unraveling, revealing a tall skeletal deity covered in thick black slime.

The deity has exposed bones of limbs and ribs, its torso is bloated and the black slime that covers it drips down the ribs and runs down the bones. Its face is that of an owl but diseased, scarred and badly decaying, its eyes are massive but full of maggots. Its head are covered in wet feathers, coloured black by the ooze. The failing chimes are loud and Ookonan can finally see where it was, the ribs of the deity hangs bells, now covered in the thick corruption.

'EEeaaaaahhahahahahahahaha.' It screamed. 'You have now learned what we are. Time for your eternal doom.'.

Without giving the words of the deity much thought, he zooms towards them with tense charged limbs throwing blasts of lightning at the corrupt god. But the deity is quick and calculated as he moves the girl like a puppet allowing them to avoid his attacks while preparing for a more close combat.

Once Ookonan gets within arms reach, the smiley deity pulls him in close to get into his face.'Hehehe. A pathetic squishy mortal. Do you believe you can beat Ah-Puch? Death?' The deity laughed in a gruelling deep rumbling voice. Its face smelled indescribably putrid, bad enough to make Ookonan's eye water.

It punches Ookonan hard in the chest, throwing him backwards through the air. Once he fell to the ground again, he bounced and flopped before sliding along, tearing up the hard soil from his storm that won't die away. Ah-Puch follows him while dragging the vassel along the ground under it like a lifeless, doll-like body.

Ookonan lays on the ground seemingly unconscious as his storm still continues. Ah-Puch now believing he has the upper hand against him goes to strike down on Ookonan. But to its dismay, no bells chimed. Ookonan's eyes burst open, glowing and sparking brighter than ever. He kicks Ah-Puch in the chest, sending shockwaves of wind, water and electricity into his chest cavity.

'Aaaaaahhhhhhh…. NO!' Ah-Puch screams, moving away and reawakening the vassel to take his place.

The vassel sprints over to Ookonan, ready to strike whichever way she could, however the supercharged Ookonan swiftly did a sweeping kick knocking her onto her back along with Ah-Puch. He swings his leg high into the air then striking down with an axe kick. Blasting the surrounding area with powerful waves of electricity. In turn, badly wounding them both.

She rolls over, coughing in agony as the human starts to regain some ownership. She gets to her feet and coughs uncontrollably until white smoke pours out of her. It all falls onto the ground and travels a short distance before regaining form.

A beautiful woman uncurls, she wears a thick falcon feathered cloak, her clothing is colourful and woven and she wears leather and metal armour which almost seems invisible unless attention is noted. She stares down Ah-Puch, an undeniable anger twinkles in her eyes, yet it's not hatred.

She salutes Ookonan with a nod. He could see one of the most beautiful women he's ever seen, braided blond hair, pale flawless skin and ocean blue eyes. However she did not stick around, she flew off towards the swarm of demonics and the Brogan army.

†

Dusk is starting to fall as the army strategically organises themselves to prepare for the demonics charging at them at large numbers. The demonics are twitching, screaming, growling and smiling their large sharp smiles as they run towards the army.

The army's archers move to a safe distance from the demonics while the other members in their groups all move to different positions around the demonic army. A spearman runs up to one of the stray demonics and throws their spear through the demonics skull while a broad swordsman runs up to it and smashes it in the chest and legs.

The spearman removes the spear while stomping on the demonics head. The army then follows, running in groups towards the demonic army, the swordsmen hit the demonics multiple times, slashing their heads and bodies giving them multiple fatal wounds. The broad swordsman slash off the heads of the demonics while the spearmen give the demonics multiple stab wounds.

Commander Zelius uses both his swords, the heated metal one and a normal damascus steel blade. He moves through the crowd of demonics, hitting each of them he brushes past multiple times in the head, face and limbs, inevitably cutting off each limb he slashes at.

†

Hovering above the vassel and Ah-Puch he waits for their next move, calculating their every subtle movement. Ah-Puch lifts himself, increasing his bodily size as he struggles to maintain control. He zooms over to Ookonan, dragging the child behind him preparing for a pungent necrotic attack.

Emotionless and without flinching, Ookonan grabs him by the neck. He forces high arching levels of electrical power through Ah-Puch's cloud, body and into the girl. He throws him across the grassy lands towards the sparse pyramids and flies after them.

As Ah-Puch flies through the air from Ookonan's force, the girl is dragged along the ground with him. He smashes into a pyramid feet first with the vassel also landing feet first just below him. He felt weak, the energy that was once him depleting further, but before he knew it Ookonan smashed into him, forcing them both into the hollow cavity of the tetrahedron.

The tetrahedron is deep, it's a full ancient structure underground with old trinkets, demonics sleep on old furniture next to skeletons and the slime covers everything. However, Ookonan's focus is Ah-Puch. He forces them both out of the pyramid back into the open atmosphere and when he goes to strike, Ah-Puch grips Ookonan's chest.

He felt the death creeping in, like twisting daggers filled with liquid acid. It burned, it made it almost impossible to breathe. But Ah-Puch was desperate, to take rather than be gifted. 'You are strong, but I am stronger.' He said in his grueling rumbling voice.

'AAAAAhhhhhhhhhhh.' Ookonan screamed, forcing air back into his lungs and turning his storm into a category five as he forced the clouds into rain. The wind around him became saturated, sparking the wind with electrical power. He maintains a hold of Ah-Puch letting the girl dangle below them. He flies them high into the sky. He reaches for the vassel and rips the tether between her and Ah-Puch, severing them both. In full belief that the original owner of the body died long ago, he drops her and lets her fall back onto earth.

'No. No!! No!! AAAAAHHHHHH' Ah-Puch screamed in agony.

'And you called me weak.' Ookonan sneered through gritted teeth. He pumps Ah-Puch with more electricity before nose diving back to the earth.An electrical explosion erupts on the middle of the battlefield followed by the thick black smoke. It threw demonics and soldiers back from the intense force while also throwing dirt rock, grass and demonic body parts into the air. Destroying Ah-Puch and releasing the vassel.

Once released, she gasps for air and begins to cry. Clear bells start to ring like the corruption or filth has been cleaned. Ookonan looks around the frozen dark battlefield to see the vassel, the real girl standing and sobbing with large wet tears. But as the smoke and debris started to settle and time started again, she began to fall as Ah-Puch is no more. He swiftly makes his way over to her, catching her as she fell. She was light, but just a child, yet somehow aged in an ancient way.

'Thank you for releasing me.' She softly utters.

'I- I do not understand.' He stumbled, having never seen this in his life, her ancient eyes tell a story but she's still profoundly human.

'I will take you through.' Her voice is soft, gentle and calm. She holds his face with one hand, an ancient comfort of old, calming him enough to subside his storm before using her other hand to press between his eyes.

The lightning and rain wraps them into a confined bubble. His eyes glow and hers copy, pausing the tears and everything in their small world.

†

Ookonan is transported into an isolating plain, where the air is thick and the atmosphere is foggy. He scans his full surroundings, the ground is that of the grassy plain but nothing else exists, only a cloudy grey. A small hand grips onto his, he snaps his gaze downwards to see it's the Vassel. Non hostile seemingly content and ready for something.

She guides him with her as she decides on a direction to walk. As he follows, the fog shifts around them as shapes of structures and beings appear, but not well enough for him to make out what they might be.

'I lived many years ago. So long its all foggy, but I remember the day it happened, the day the earth changed.' She said as the structures and figures became clear.

A colourful city is revealed, each building is distinctive and the previously shadowy figures are people who walk past them. She takes him through her neighbourhood from when life seemed peaceful. He surveyed the neighbourhood and every individual was human yet they all looked unique, tanned and untraumatised to him.

They both approach a small young family of three, everything about them seemed normal until upon closer inspection he noticed the child was the vassel. Unscarred, a lack of trauma, extraordinarily young in a way he could not explain and entirely innocent. She's being held by a young gentleman who she somewhat resembles and a young lady lovingly and playfully shows her affection as the three of them enter a building he finds unusual.

It's beautiful, built like a clay or brick or stone Brogan palace with a headless legless stick man on the high front. 'Pórtate bien Isabella.' The woman gently says as the three of them enter the building.

'I am not sure how I lost my name until now, but it was Isabella.' She leads Ookonan into the distorting building as the memory isn't sharp.

Inside the building there are rows of distorting bench like seats and the people shifted and changed as both Ookonan and the vassel walk through and find themselves a seat. The memory is scattered but as a human stands behind a pedestal and mumbles gibberish the people say the only clear word once he was finished speaking 'Amen.'

'I do not remember much, but what happened after stayed with me forever.' She explained.

The sound of jingly bells could be faintly heard, then suddenly the building began to shake and distort and people tried to scatter. But before Ookonan could process the people and what was happening, the building collapsed. The atmosphere instantly changed into the foggy darkness as Ookonan and the vassel remain seated on the bench.

'It started with an earthquake… The true beginning of the end.' She explained, she stands up and directs him forward, forcing the world to shift yet again.

They both walk up to heavy rubble, complete destruction of a structure. There were blurry figures of humans removing debris until much to his own horror a terrified little girl was removed. Isabella or the vassel.

'I was the only survivor, I was alone, I now had nothing.'

She guided him past herself and the wreckage forcing the world to quickly mould and change. In no time the both of them were walking into a small settlement. It seemed to be going well, people working together, building new structures out of scrap and gardens everywhere full of food. The place was self-sufficient.

But as they wander through they eventually find Isabella. Worn, scared and vulnerable working in the gardens. A large man approaches her, he scolds and hits her before roughly handling her away from the garden and into a badly built building. Ookonan witnessed his gut sink and he felt sick, especially feeling powerless to do anything.

She directs Ookonan towards the cabin as the large man shoves her onto a seat. He kneels down, caressing her thighs. 'I tried to forget, I thought I did. I should never have gone in there.'

The vassel tugs Ookonan away. She closes her eyes as large tears form. But he was too stunned and mortified to move as the memory imploded into mist. 'I can not look, I beg you to look away.' He swiftly turns his gaze to her. Her cries and tears are of pain, a memory that cuts deeper than any blade.

He squats down to meet her eyes, kneeling into a hug. 'You do not have to show me anything.' He assured.

'No. I must share, I have to.' She grips his hand and he gets back to his feet, ready to follow her lead.

He follows her through the black void back out into the settlement. But this time when he saw Isabella, she was older. She looked the same age as now but properly the right age, not somehow aged by centuries. She still works in the garden, planting plants, removing weeds and pruning whatever needed it. She was filthy, calloused and scared.

'I was forced to do a lot of work, I can not remember how the wounds got there. But this was the new end.'

He surveyed the evolved settlement she took him through. Tall walls wrap around them keeping their community safe. The walls have walkways for armed security to patrol, the gardens were thriving and everything seemed to function. But the undeniable scream caught him off guard, he knew what she was about to show.

The sound of bells could be faintly heard until security started to fire their guns, people ran for cover, all except Isabella. However, security was compromised as a guard was knocked back. A grotesque monster with large red glowing eyes got over the fence and into the settlement.

Before long many more got over the fence into the settlement. Forcing people to grab weapons and fight back. They were bitten, knocked over and mutilated. Isabella ran up the steps of the wall walkway and jumped to the other side.

The Vassel grips Ookonan's hand tighter before pulling him along to follow Isabella into the forest. The vision distorts and the area disappears leaving them to follow her through the foggy empty void. But the piercingly loud mix of screams echo painfully into the bone like the reverberation of hammers hitting metal. 'I did what I could to escape, but I cared not about my own death, I thought I already was. I just did not want more pain.'

Once the noise muffles until it fades, the forest returns around them. Her footsteps light but her breath is heavy. She eventually slows down until a mid paced walk, constantly looking around herself. However, she was not alone. The jingly bells ring again, but this time louder.

Ookonan felt the cold breeze of something running past himself and the vassel. It was chasing her. It launched itself at her once her guard seemed down. But to his and Isabella's startling surprise a figure tackles it.

She falls flat, letting out a blood curdling scream as it decimates the demonic before turning its attention to her. The vassel directs Ookonan to a new angle so he could see it in its true form. Ah-Puch.

He looked different, still a skeleton and still bloating. He wears bells on his exposed ribs and his headwear is feathered. The bells chime but the main difference besides the bloated appearance of his head is that of an owl. The uncorrupt version still reeks of death but now has the difference of care for the young.

He crouches low to her eye level, curious about the terrified little girl. He brushes her cheek with the back of his hand leaving no marks. He wiped away her tears but let her weep. He did not know how to comfort someone who kept trying to crawl away, but he remained calm until the terrified little girl calmed down.

She eventually grabs her knees for comfort, to hide her face from the scary deity. She could not bear to witness more pain yet. But unbeknownst to her, he wrapped an arm around her and assured he was no threat.

'Yo soy Ah-Puch. Dios de la Muerte. Pero no llores, hija mío. La muerte llegará, pero solo para quienes han vivido. Aún te queda una vida por vivir, pues la tuya apenas comienza. Soy la muerte, pero también la del comienzo.' (*I am Ah-Puch, deity of death. But, do not weep my child. Death will come, but only for those who have lived. You have yet to live a life as yours has still only begun. I am that of death, but I am also that of beginning*). He very gently explained contrary to his own appearance. 'Te daré mi fuerza nos convertiremos en uno.' (*I will give you my strength and we will become one*).

She lifts her head up, her eyes sore and red from the weeping. She looks at him in his large eyes, she feels the feathers on his large owl head. It was strange but no longer frightening for her. He caresses her forehead and hair with his fleshless hand, a comfort she had not felt since her mother was alive.

'Here I became the champion of Ah-Puch.' The vassel explained as she directed Ookonan back into the foggy void.

The fog became thicker, covering the ground they walked on, the tension rises as she aimlessly searched for the next memory. Until Ookonan kicked an old piece of concrete. The sounds of children playing fill the air until the fog dissipates. Nothing looked like her life prior. The buildings are wrecks, crumbled and unrecognisable, the land is a grey and green mess.

But in front of both of them appeared Isabella and Ah-Puch once again, but this time playing in the ruins. She got to be a kid, climbing and exploring, playing with rocks and broken toys, feeling the air and chasing other children. Nothing compared to before, she seemed safe without adults.

The dreaded bells rang, she and Ah-Puch knew what was coming. They ran through the ruins as his bells got louder until they could hear the screams of the demonics and worse of all the screams of children.

Ah-Puch disappears into a thick cloud of black putrid smoke, giving her his power. She sprints into the courtyard to be thankful of there only being one demonic. However this one is reasonably fresh, young. There is still some human in its form even through the sharp rocklike teeth and the slimy black patchy skin.

She sprints full force at it, punching it in the stomach. It was knocked to its knees, granting her access to smash its head to the ground. It laid there motionless, gone. It was effortless for her now. She clicked her fingers, transporting it away in thick black smoke to keep the corruption away from the innocents.

The children all run back into the courtyard cheering. Ah-Puch makes himself present again and they all play. 'Ah-Puch and I did everything we could to help every innocent and let everyone whose time is far from the end to continue.' She said directing herself and Ookonan through, letting the world change and fade another time as she travels along her memory path that is becoming more and more difficult for her to navigate.

This next walk became more different as it transformed into a hallway filled with symbols Ookonan could not identify. *1, 10, 25, 250.* She approaches the two fifty on a dark oak door. 'People and races changed at this time, two hundred and fifty years into my future.'

She opens the door which leads them both into an old deep building, like an underground concrete fortress. It was painfully dark, yet Isabella seemed to have no issue seeing. But there was one thing that was unnerving. The loud and constant noise of the bells.

He sees the early gnome people, small, thin, patchy hair and pale. Each of them have large eyes so they can see in their dark world. All of them were a similar size to Isabella. The gnome keeping guard of their underground city pushes her back, refusing her entrance.

'STOP! What are you doing trespassing? This is no place for human ch-' He attempted to say before being gripped and ripped limb from limb by Issabella herself.

'Ah-Puch led me into a fortress of gnomes. I trusted him, but the real him was fading, like something was poisoning him.' She said as the mortifying slaughter her past self did to the gnomes. 'I hate this memory so much.' She weeped.

She let it play out, as painful as it was. She could not forgive herself, the cries of mercy from the gnomes was nauseating for both herself and Ookonan. But once Isabella's eyes turned a deep black, she pulled Ookonan away. Immediately taking them back into the symboled hallway.

She led him down far into the hall, searching for a door with a handle. Her memories are dying, evident as some handles were simply disappearing. Until she eventually caught the handle of an iron door *500*. She turns the handle and leads them through, taking her to Isabella letting herself through an iron gate in the middle of the night.

The building she approached was labeled šhînchônâ (*Orphanage*). He recognised the language. They are in eastern Hondon but from the density of buildings, they are in the protected city of Chéndosi.

They witness Isabella pry open the front door effortlessly, then letting herself inside. However the most bothersome thing for him is how loud the bells are becoming and how distorted they now sound. Like they are filled with gunk, filth or corruption.

He and the vassel follow her up the stairs into a bedroom of peaceful young elves sleeping. But Issabella stands motionless, barely human as she preys. Her eyes glow blackish red as she stepped in.

'He took me to an orphanage, it was like he was now trying to hurt me. I-I thought we were going to go back to the way things were, play games and appreciate new beginnings. But this was the breaking point.' She sobbed. 'It was… The worst… The end of me.'

The room fills with thick black fog, eliminating all that were to come as the vassel could not bear to relive the moment. The only thing left is the drooling, huffing little girl about to lose her humanity. Until the memory forces itself back in, revealing the aftermath, lifeless, bloody children lay scattered. Blood pools on the floor and is splattered on every surface, a horrifying sight, one where Ookonan struggled to remain composed.

'I tried to resist. I really tried to resist. He was so unnaturally powerful and filled with corruption. He was not the Ah-Puch who saved me… He was gone. Then I was too.'

Chapter 44

The dense grey atmosphere fades away as a horrified and shaken Ookonan is awoken with Isabella the Vassel laying in his arms. She was so young yet so old all at once, he thought to himself.

His electric storm starts to fade as he brings himself back into reality. He tries to comfort Isabella the Vassel as she takes her final breaths.

'I tried to stop him… I could not stop him.' She sobbed in a raspy whispered tone as tears escaped her eyes and rolled down her cheeks.

His own eyes looked up and straight ahead as she said she tried to stop the corruption of Ah-Puch. He could see the people and gods swirling around him, yet he found great difficulty focusing on a single person.

'It is okay… I have got you Isabella.' He reassures her as he looks back down at her while supporting her head as she takes her final breaths.

'I have not heard that name in one thousand years.' She said, her voice fractured as her world slowly started to fade.

'Do not feel bad. You lived a strong life until the point you were gone. It is okay to let go.'

A pale hand draped in black fabrics touches Ookonan on the shoulder, soft yet lacking in temperature. He turns his head and looks at the hand for a brief moment before his eyes are drawn towards the being touching him.

She has fair white skin with a scarred yet flawless face. Draped in black fabrics and armour, she resembled a former warrior of the distant past. She looked somewhat disturbing yet Ookonan knew she wasn't a threat.

He lays Isabella down gently against the grassy ground before standing up and taking a few steps away. He looks around and sees countless dead demonics sprawled across the fields. He sees Brogan soldiers standing over the sea of lifeless comrades and demonics, taking in their losses and triumphs.

He sees Aagneya standing by Yuma, patting his neck while Kaji stands alone, half naked and surrounded by charred demonics. Commander Zelius appears to be standing by a pile of rubble and some damaged pyramids.

He looks back at the mystifying woman who put her hand on his shoulder. She has large raven wings on her back that are open and spread as she has leaned over Isabella. She wrapped her midnight black wings around her and kissed her on the forehead.

Time appeared to enter a standstill as the world became motionless and the woman wrapped one of her shadowy wings around the transparent spirit of Isabella to lift her up. Isabella looks around the battlefield one last time as she lets go of the material world around her.

The Valkyrie holds onto Isabella's hand as she spreads her wings and lifts them both into the sky. Slowly they fade away into the clouds, disappearing from the material world entirely.

As Isabella's spirit fades away Ookonan feels a sharp pain in his shoulder where the Valkyrie touched him and he is quickly surrounded by a thick blanket of inky black smoke. He takes a deep breath in and absorbs the essence of Ah-Puch. His shoulder and lungs both felt like they were on fire and as heavy as iron.

'Aahhhh…' He screamed although barely any sound escaped his throat as his lungs felt too heavy to make any noise.

He rushes to take off his backpack which is falling to pieces from the battle. He then proceeds to take off his thick leather jacket to find that his shirt has burned off on his chest, back and shoulder.

As the pain begins to slowly subside, he pats down his chest and shoulder while closely investigating them. A new black marking has appeared. The skull of an owl, decorated with bones, feathers and bells.

After investigating it, he rushes to the remains of his backpack, pushing things aside without much care. He pulled out a couple of leather sacks but more importantly, his teapot and cup. He let out a sigh of relief seeing it had survived, but unfortunately there was a crack on the side of the metal pot.

'Ookonan, that was astonishing…' Aagneya says, walking over to him. 'Your power was like no other…'

Startled, he quickly gets to his feet, teapot still in hand. 'Thank you I suppose.' He says with hesitancy

'I hate to admit it but I was wrong, you are not who I thought you were. You are not the dumb brute, you are powerful, so powerful and… Important.' She mumbled in the end. 'I will do everything in my power to support you as I can. I hope we can start again without conflict between us.'

'I would like that.' He confirms.

Aagneya relaxes her racing mind and smiles at him, feeling relieved that he holds no grudge against her and her overzealous endeavour to be a part of the prophecy. She takes a step back and looks at Ookonan and Kaji, she truly did not believe that those two of all people would be spiritually connected.

'What is that on your arm?' Kaji blurted out, his eyes widened as he looked at the incan mark of Ah-Puch on Ookonan's shoulder.

'I do not know.' Ookonan admitted, rubbing his shoulder.

'I believe I can answer that.' An unfamiliar yet powerful feminine voice resonates.

The three of them all look over at the beautiful goddess, each of them seeing something contrastingly different. Kaji sees a bright fiery woman with dark skin resembling a muscular yet feminine Mirish woman. While Aagneya sees a dark skinned woman dressed in green with long flowing green hair adorned with flowers, in her eyes she almost looks like mother nature. Lastly, Ookonan sees a light skinned woman with neat braided blond hair and blue eyes, she has a muscular yet feminine build and she is wearing weaves and amour.

'You came out of that Girl Isabella. Who are you?' Ookonan asked confoundedly.

'I am Freyja, you may have heard of me. Vassels have the ability to absorb other gods, gaining their powers in the process. Doing so leaves a mark on them, much like the new mark on your shoulder. My champion was destroyed by Isabella and Ah-Puch leaving me to be absorbed by her. But destroying the champion or vassal which you have done can release those gods.'

'So you can have more than one god power?' Ookonan inquired.

'Yes, and you are now much stronger.' She says as she starts to pulse in and out of reality. 'I must thank you for freeing me but my time here on midgard is dwindling. I must leave before I am destroyed.'

Ookonan, Kaji and Aagneya speechlessly watch as Freyja disappears in a glowing cloud of white smoke that quickly falls to the earth.

'Kaji…' Ookonan mutters, turning his attention to him. 'I owe you an apology.'

'Ookonan fine it is…' Kaji starts to counter, taking a deep breath.

'As annoying as you are,' Ookonan continues, cutting Kaji short, 'You are not from here so I should have been more patient and I should not have made comments on your language.'

Understanding Ookonan's stress, Kaji makes his way over towards him with his arms open, 'honestly, it's fine. I am a fast learner anyway, but culture will be something to still get used to.'

'I think you need new clothes again. Maybe something fire resistant.' Ookonan says, pushing him away.

'Let us head back to Brogan, we will need supplies.' Aagneya buts in, she felt it was time they all left the battlefield and moved on.

She looks over at Commander Zelius and gives them a nod to instruct the survivors of the Brogan army to move back to the city. She picks up Ookonan's backpack and places it on Yuma's saddle before turning her attention back to Ookonan and Kaji, guiding them back to the city of Brogan.

†

A woman with thick braided red hair and green woven clothing is walking to the side of Brogan, unseen from the army and from the guards of the city. She watched the battle unfold from afar as she reached the great moat and walls of the city.

'Ah-Puch is dead…' She whispered to herself as she watched Ah-Puch leave Isabella's body in a cloud of inky black smoke. 'I never really liked the bastard.'

Her eyes are drawn towards the great stone walls of Brogan, she can see the lichen growing on the stone as she thought of a way inside from the great cliffs of the mote around the city walls.

'But this will bring more blood to my red river.' She says grinning.